PASSPORT IN
SUSPENSE

JAMES LEASOR

James Leasor Publishing

For Joan. Again

THE YANG MERIDIAN

'There are great variations in the electrical potentials of the skin certain areas show a much lessened resistance than the areas surrounding them. These areas follow certain well-defined longitudinal lines, and along them, at certain points of the skin, electrical resistance reaches zero. The lines joining these points, of which there are approximately eight hundred, are called the meridians....

'In the human body there are twelve meridians on each side ... ten are connected to a main organ by means of branches from the sympathetic nervous system. Each of these meridians contains the "vital energy" which varies in strength and is governed by the "vital force" or nerve impulses arising from the organs. Each meridian is directly linked to its particular organ by means of a communication branch which joins a specific area of the skin to its specific organ.

'Chinese traditional medicine does not run parallel with Western conventional ideas of life. It believes that we are an integral part of the "cosmos", and as such we obey the "polarity" of the Universe and follow its rhythm....

'There is thus an active phase (day-time, summer) and a passive phase (night-time, winter). These two phases are contrary and opposite to each other - the negative and the positive. The positive phase is called Yang and the negative phase is called Yin ...'

Acupuncture and You, by Dr Louis Moss. (Elek Books Ltd)

*   *   *

'If Yin and Yang both have an excess of energy and do not communicate with each other, losing their liaison, there is death.'

Ancient Chinese Treatise on Acupuncture

PROLOGUE

*North Sea; NATO Naval manoeuvres; aboard West German
submarine Seehund, of Green Force*

Like a giant finger thrusting soundlessly out from the darkened, rain-pocked sea, the submarine cautiously began to raise its thin slatted bows and shake itself clear of the waves. Water sluiced away; the weeping sky pressed down on it, a weight of darkness as heavy as the night.

In the control room, lit by the red lights used after nightfall to accustom eyes to night conditions, the Captain moved his hands upwards, away from his body, fanning his fingers. At this signal, the engineering mechanic watching the hands rather than the man, raised the levers of the periscope hoist controls. The periscope and the radar aerial slid up in their oiled glands.

'Two all round sweeps, medium range,' ordered the Captain. The radar operator had a sallow, spotty face with a yellow-tipped boil behind his left ear. One hand went up nervously as though to reassure himself it was still there. It was.

'Contact bearing 240 degrees, sir,' he reported. 'Four thousand two hundred metres.'

The Captain nodded. That must be the ship he had been so unexpectedly ordered to meet. Good. He was in position. He was young enough, and still new enough to command, to feel pleasure at the accuracy of his calculations.

'Stand by to surface,' he said briefly. 'Open the lower lid.'

The Officer of the Watch repeated the orders into the microphone of the ship's intercom. His voice boomed back metallically from the hollow steel shell. Then he reported to the Captain:

'Ready to surface, sir.'

'Surface,' the Captain told him.

In the control room, a rating spun the valves, releasing a rush of compressed air into the long cylindrical ballast tanks to lighten the vessel. Slowly the submarine rose while the rating on the forward hydroplane intoned the depths from the vessel's keel to the surface of the sea.

'Fifty... forty-five... forty... thirty-five...'

At 'thirty', the Captain raised his left hand. They were well up out of the water. The counting stopped. The Captain climbed the brass ladder up into the conning tower, threw open the top lid, went out and on to the bridge.

Fog floated in over the rim of the dark, wet metal. It was so dark that he could scarcely see the special superstructure only feet away that carried the new experimental Telefunken gear they were testing on their manoeuvres.

The Officer of the Watch climbed on to the bridge by his side. There were no riding lights to see, no stars, nothing. The Captain went down again into the control room. Faces searched his own for any reason why they should have surfaced.

The First Lieutenant had turned out when the submarine came up to periscope depth. He was a stocky cheerful man; his father ran a bierhaus behind Hamburg railway station. He wished he was there now with that girl he'd met on the night before these manoeuvres started: Why did he always have to meet girls like that on the eve of going to sea? Or did they just seem so much more attractive because it was his last night?

'All right, sir?' he asked the Captain.

'Of course,' the Captain replied with a confidence he did not entirely feel. He supposed that they were; he had followed the orders, but why the hell had they received these new orders? As he steadied himself against the slow roll of the vessel, his hands in his jacket pockets, looking at the dials before him, at the depth and pressure gauges, the valves with their four cross-spokes, as though their familiarity might somehow provide an answer, he cast back in his mind over the events of the last ninety-five minutes.

At midnight, he had come up to seventy feet, as he did regularly every three hours so that the radio aerial in the top of the fin would be just beneath the surface of the sea, where he could pick up the Very Low Frequency signals. They were keeping transmission silence on these NATO manoeuvres, but his orders were to read the VLF broadcast at least every twelve hours for important signals.

He had been in the wireless office when the petty officer tele-graphist started to decrypt the only signal to come in on his midnight routine. It was a limited access message, for the Captain's eyes only. It wasn't often that they had to deal with one of those. The radio supervisor looked at him questioningly.

'I'll be back in a minute,' the Captain told him. Taking care not to appear to hurry, he walked through to his safe, unlocked it with its two keys, took out the key card on which were printed the directions how to set up the drums on the KL-7 decrypting machine to transcribe this secret signal.

He sat down in the swivel chair, under the red-hooded light, facing the machine, and began to type. The white worm of tape spewed out jerkily to one side. When he reached the end, he folded it up carefully; carried it back to the ward room. He sat on his bunk, drew the curtains, put on the dim reading light and read it.

FROM COMMODORE GREEN FORCE TO SEEHUND. RENDEZ-VOUS ON THE SURFACE POSITION 53 DEGREES 50 MINUTES NORTH 03 DEGREES 45 MINUTES EAST AT 0135 TO RECEIVE FURTHER ORDERS.

Well, that was clear enough. No snags there. Presumably the vessel he was to meet must be the one the radar showed to be

4,200 metres away. This might be quite a distance on land, but not at sea. From the moment an ocean liner was ordered to stop from full speed ahead, it could still go on for another ten miles. Cheered by the accuracy of his navigation, he climbed ' up into the conning tower once more.

Down in the control room, which from his height glowed red as the heart of a furnace because of the lighting, he heard the radar operator reporting the approach of this ship.

'Three thousand five hundred metres, sir ... Three thousand metres... Two thousand metres...'

The Captain raised his night glasses but still could see nothing but darkness, and, as he removed them, the diminished, dim reflection of his own tired eyes. The Seehund was rocking more rapidly now and waves were slapping against the hull. He thought obliquely that they sounded like dead men's hands beating for admittance: drowned men from all the old sea battles, all the shipwrecks. He thought of his father, who had sailed with Lieutenant Gunther Prien on his daring voyage into the Scapa Flow a few weeks after war broke out in 1939, to sink the Royal Oak. They had been so close to a blockship that they had actually scraped an anchor - cable. He wondered whether Prien had felt as he felt now: very conscious of the loneliness of command, and the fact he was only twenty-five. He shivered. It was damn cold up there at that hour.

'Are we picking someone up, sir?' the Officer of the Watch asked him.

'No,' said the Captain briefly, and then took him slightly into his confidence. He was glad of any company, although he did not care to admit it. 'Just waiting. The message just said we would rendezvous. It didn't say with whom or what. Only where and when. Which is here and now. I'll stay up here for a while. You go on down below.'

'Very good, sir.'

The officer's rubber-soled boots squeaked on the rungs of the ladder as he went below.

The radar operator's voice came up again, like a hidden priest intoning a chant.

'Fifteen hundred metres, sir... One thousand...'

That must be the ship. It could be nothing else, yet in all the manoeuvres in which he had ever taken part he had never been ordered to keep a rendezvous like this with so few directions and instructions. The Captain made up his mind, suddenly.

'Port thirty,' he ordered. 'Group up, half ahead together.'

'Port thirty, group up, half ahead together, sir,' repeated the Helmsman up the voice pipe from the control room twenty feet below him.

The Seehund turned in a fury of foam. This ship was coming altogether too close. There could easily be a collision in the darkness and the fog. Why the hell didn't he signal?

'Report radar contact,' ordered the Captain.

'She's altering course, sir. She's coming round in a circle. She's heading straight for us!'

It took a second for the significance of the news to sink into the Captain's mind. His hands were numb with cold, holding the rail, and the wind and the rain seized his breath as he bent beneath the screen and shouted :'Full astern together!' But it was too late. The crunch of the collision threw him off his feet. He fell against the front of the screen, the blow knocking the breath out of his body. He clung to the rail for reassurance, gasping for air, mouthing orders no one could hear.

'Emergency stations! Close all watertight doors!' The Officer of the Watch shouted into the intercom below. The general alarm bell rang through the metal cocoon.

'We're making water for'ard, sir,' he reported.

The Captain straightened up. As he did so he saw something move to one side, so faintly that he thought he must have imagined it in his worry and pain. What the hell was happening? Then in the dim red glow at the edge of darkness, he saw three men holding the rail on the other side of the tower. They must have somehow landed from the ship he should have met, that had apparently crashed into his submarine.

But these were like no sailors he had ever seen. They had no faces, no flesh, no human countenance. Instead of eyes, two round lenses, each three inches across, watched him above snouts like elephants' trunks, streaming with spray. Fear chilled his heart and caught his throat. Were they human at all? Was he imagining this?

'Who are you?' he shouted, his voice thin with fear and horror.

The man in the middle raised his right arm. Spray glistened like glass on his rubber frogman's suit. He was holding a wheel spanner a yard long. The red light from the conning tower touched this, turning it to blood. Then the spanner came down.

The steel crushed the Captain's skull, cracking the bone like an eggshell. His body sagged for a second and then slowly folded over the edge of the screen. The other two men pulled it across towards them and tossed it into the sea. The splash was lost in the angry drumming of the waves on the hull.

The middle man nodded, swung his spanner again to flex his muscles, climbed over the rail, down the ladder. His' companions came after him. One carried a Schmeisser automatic rifle strapped to his back. It was wrapped in a cellophane bag to protect the mechanism from the salt water. The third, a small man, unclipped a gas grenade from his plastic belt as he climbed. They jumped down into the control room, and stood, feet apart, braced against the swaying of the floor. The alarm bell still clanged like a madman with a gong.

'Who the hell are you?' shouted the Officer of the Watch, taking a step towards them, his face blank with disbelief, amazement. The alarm bell suddenly stopped and only the humming hydraulic pumps and the whirr of the ventilation fans punctured the silence.

The man with the spanner raised it once more and deliberately smashed it across the side of the officer's head. The blow splintered the whole of the left side of his face, laying bare the bone, jagged and raw. He sagged, his knees collapsed, and then he fell like, a rubber man. A thin stream of blood seeped over the plastic floor tiles.

Only about a dozen men were awake, and they came into the control room half dressed and yawning, rubbing sleep from their eyes with their knuckles. The rest of the crew were still fumbling in their bunks for trousers, socks, rubber shoes, sweaters.

The Coxswain held a tommy bar in his hand. 'You bastard!' he shouted, and threw it at the three men. The metal bar fell short, the man with the Schmeisser swung his gun from his shoulder, squeezed the trigger through the cellophane. It chattered half a dozen times. Hot shell cases spurted out, burning through the thin plastic cover, and rattled uselessly to the floor. The Coxswain took half a step forward, opened his mouth as though to speak, and then folded up.

'Who are you?' asked the radar operator hoarsely. 'What do you want?' His boil was throbbing painfully.

The man with .the spanner, reddened now with two men's blood, ignored him, and nodded to his companions. The small man pulled out the ring and lobbed the grenade gently among the crew.

They drew back, flattening themselves/against the wall, against the expected explosion, but the grenade only hissed like a damp firework. The room slowly filled with swirling smoke that spread, a heavy, yellow fog, throughout the submarine. As the fumes swam higher, they wiped away the looks of bewilderment and incredulity from the faces of the crew; one by one they fell where they stood.

With the easy precision of many rehearsals, the three men hauled the bodies up through the conning tower and threw them out into the sea. Then the leader, taking a rubber torch from its spring clip on the bulkhead, went down the steps to the engine room, dragged out a five-gallon drum of OMD-110 marine lubricating oil.

He carried this up the conning tower ladder, smashed through the bung with his spanner and poured the thick green phosphorescent oil over the side into the sea. Then he dropped the empty tin back into the control room. His two companions were handing up odd pieces of wood, books, magazines, a uniform jacket, a cap, an empty Schloer bottle - any junk that would float.

He climbed down the ladder again, locked the steering amidships, and waited. He would have liked a cigarette but it was impossible with this mask, and he dared not remove it. His companions had melted away above him into the fog and the darkness of the sea. He heard the rattle of chains; the rough rasp of a rusty hawser; a boom that reverberated through the submarine as though he were in the centre of a giant metal drum. Then the Seehund shuddered slightly and began to move slowly through the water.

When the sun came up three hours later and burned its way through the mist, the pool of oil glowed like a fallen, broken rainbow on the sullen, heaving sea. Here and there bobbed pieces of wood, a page of sodden newsprint, an empty bottle; then a peaked naval cap, floating like a tiny boat, and the humped body of a man.

But when the searchers arrived, first in the Shackletons that circled around the scene, and then in the high-speed Vosper air-sea rescue launches, they could see no sign whatever of the submarine.

It had disappeared completely.

CHAPTER ONE: NASSAU, BAHAMAS

A man on water skis was carefully carving up the blue, sun-soaked sea into long, white, curved slices. Then the speedboat swept him away in a wide crescent of foam, and was gone. The waves closed together so that it seemed to Jason Love, watching from the shore, that no one had been there at all. Nothing had ever happened, would ever happen: it was all done by mirrors. The quickness of the hand deceives the eye, etc.

Love stretched at ease on the cane rocking chair, feet up on the patio wall. He was wondering how, as a doctor, he would calculate the forces operating on the skier's back muscles: let X equal the unknown stress, then, for a start, there would be the static resistance of the sea against the hull of the boat, multiplied by the height of the man's hands from the water, a coefficient that would increase as he pulled upright ... He gave up; it was too hot for such intellectual activity. The sun beat down fiercely through, the filter of the raffia screen, so that, even through half-closed eyes, the varnished expanse of ocean, a shimmering picture framed between two pillars supporting the verandah roof, seemed almost too bright to watch.

He pulled his straw hat down over his face against the glare. The hat had cost him two dollars in the Straw Market when he arrived a couple of days earlier, but was hideously and incongruously embroidered 'A present from Nassau'. But then nothing was free here, or anywhere else for that matter. He reached out lazily for his-beaker of Bacardi rum and fresh lime juice; ice cubes clinked coolly like links in a chain; the mist on the glass chilled his fingers as he lifted it. This was his first visit to Nassau, and to be honest - and he tried to be honest with himself, because, otherwise, who was fooling who? – he felt faintly and irrationally disappointed.

The house where he was staying, out on Cable Beach, beyond the pink, sugar-icing walls of the Sheraton British Colonial, and the squat block of the Mayfair with its rooftop swimming pool, was as magnificent and impersonal as he imagined any rich man's winter retreat would be.

It was reached from the road by a short drive under royal palms, with flower beds ablaze with bougainvillaea and hihiscus, red as blood spilled in the sun, past a fountain that tinkled like falling jewels. A Bahamian gardener chewed a cheroot as he watered the verbena lawn. Yet, perhaps because Love was on his own, it all seemed a little flat; one-dimensional and unreal, a stage-set about to be lit still waiting for the action. Act One, Scene One. Nassau, the Bahamas, out of season-time: the present.

So much of the island contributed to this impression. Government Housed surrounded by its' pink wall, and topped by a copper dome greened by centuries of weather, with cannons pointing open-mouthed and empty towards the sea, could be used in the following scene.

The pillared Post Office building with its green shutters, actually copied from the colonial capital of North Carolina, with Queen Victoria enthroned in stone between two cannon, represented an exile's dream of an England that had never really, existed; except in some ad-man's mind; this could be the setting for scene three. That, or maybe the tourists risking heart attacks as they toiled diligently and needlessly up the Queen's Stairway carved by slaves in a canyon long ago, one step for each year of the old Queen's reign.

But perhaps he was being too hard to please? After all, the sun switched itself on every morning and lasted through each day. The sapphire sea was far warmer than the Mediterranean, and the broiled native lobsters were the best he had ever eaten. So why look on the gloomy side? He was lucky to be here at all - the more so since the visit was costing him nothing.

One of Love's patients in Hishop's Combe in Somerset, Tom Newborough, a leathery old man of uncertain age but certain wealth, owned the house. He had asked Love's opinion of a course of acupuncture, the ancient Chinese treatment of rheumatism and arthritis, and much else, in which fine gold needles are pricked into nerve centres or 'pressure points', and for which some practitioners have claimed remarkable results. Newborough explained that he had tried every orthodox treatment for a rheumatic hip, but without success, so now he was willing to try some unorthodox ideas, and what did Love know about this, eh?

What Love knew about this he had learned from a study of the theories behind acupuncture, and, divorced from unlikely Chinese names, such as the Yin and Yang Meridians, Tch'i, the old conception of an inherent factor of energy, and dressed in more modern language, the theories were feasible; there was no doubt that some totally unexpected cures had been recorded.

Newborough wanted an appointment with one of the few specialists in acupuncture, but when it came to arranging a date, Love explained that he was on the point of leaving for a holiday in Mexico. This was something he had promised himself for years, and the prospect of attending a vintage car rally in Mexico City, allied to remarkably cheap terms for the trip (arranged by another patient who ran a travel agency) had made him decide to go.

From Mexico he planned to fly up to New York, and visit an East Coast meet of the Auburn-Cord-Duesenberg Car Club in Macungie, Pennsylvania. He owned one of the few Cords left in Britain, almost certainly the last supercharged 812 roadster, and to attend one of the A-C-D functions, to meet face to face the American enthusiasts with whom he had corresponded for years, was too great a temptation to turn up. And why should he? He was unmarried, he had no dependants, therefore, surely, every good thing he wanted to do he should attempt; he would not pass this way again, etc.

'In that case,' Newborough had suggested, 'spend a few days in

Nassau on your way. You'll find it quite an experience, doctor,- and it needn't cost you a cent. I've owned a house there for the last six years, and this is the first winter I've not been over.

'Some of the jets to New York come down at Nassau to refuel. Why not break your journey there and stay at my place? Be my guest. Then it's an easy flight on to Miami and Mexico City. And nothing more to pay.

'Also, you'd be doing me a favour, casting an eye on everything. See my houseboy, Ebenezer, isn't swindling me too-much.'

So Love had agreed, but in Nassau the mosquitoes seemed unusually prevalent, and the wind raised dust from the road- side and rubbed it in his eyes. This must be the carefully un- advertised off-season; now Love understood why it was so - carefully .unadvertised. And it had been a mistake to come on his own; even the magic fingers of Blind Blake on the banjo, Fred- die Munnings on the clarinet, the wild jungle beat of the Limbo and the Goombay seemed tame when you heard and saw them on your own. Nassau was a place to be young and in love; and Love had to admit he was neither.

Ebenezer padded out on to the patio in his split canvas shoes and scattered his thoughts like snowflakes in a child's kaleido- scope.

'You got enough to drink, sah?' he asked solicitously. Love nod- ded.

'Plenty,' he assured him. A speedboat was. coming back into the bay; not the one towing the skier, but a smaller, faster craft with a red hull, a white glass-fibre deck. He picked up a pair of binocu- lars from the table near his chair, and, with nothing better to focus them on, focused them on the boat.

The bobbing, burnished waves burst into the room; he saw the silver fin of a flying fish before he caught the speedboat. Behind an angled screen, raked back as sharply as the windscreen of his own Cord 812 roadster, sat a girl. The wind took her dark hair and blew it out behind her; Love thought she looked like a figure on a Grecian frieze or a Mogul horsewoman in one of the Persian miniatures he had seen in Teheran. She swung the cream steering wheel to left, to right, and the slim craft dipped and bucked in a frenzy of power, its wake trailing a pathway of foam behind the big black outboard.

She was travelling fast and yet, watching her, Love had the feeling she was not used to the speed of the engine. Her turns were too sharp; they lacked the grace of the expert. As he looked she turned towards the shore, the bows straining half out of the water, the harsh roar of the exhaust booming over the sea. And then the bow-wave suddenly subsided, the foam melted away, the growl of the engine died in mid-beat. Love focused his glasses on the girl's face. What was she about?

He saw bewilderment, annoyance, perhaps a flash of fear cross her tanned skin, lacquered by spray and sun oil. She tightened her lips, leaned back across the red plastic seat to grip the T-shaped handle of the coiled starter rope, and pulled awkwardly. He was right; she must know very little about small boats, or she would never have pulled from that angle.

The boat rocked dangerously in its dying wash, but the motor did not start. She pulled again, crouched low in the stern over the engine, her hair falling about her like a dark fan. The bows began to turn contemptuously out to sea; the boat drifted in aimlessly on the current. Magnified in his, glasses, the girl's face, brown, with wide-set eyes, looked attractive enough to, merit a closer view; so did her figure, moulded inside an op-art black and white costume. Its crazy zig-zag pattern reminded him of a picture of camouflaged ships in the First World War, which he had seen as a boy in The Wonder Book of Why and What. Was that annual still published, or did too many children know too much about Why and What? There were so few questions left now looking for answers. Too few.

He lowered his glasses. If the tide was changing, the girl could be in trouble. And yet the engine had sounded so healthy, it was unlikely there could be very much the matter. He might as well swim out, and see for himself. He'd nothing better to do, anyway. He could, conceivably, do something worse. He might even discover a partner for a night on the Town, or 'over the Hill', on the other side of the spine of land that divided the island, where, in little native dives, the rhythm blew hot as a blast furnace.

He was wearing swimming shorts under his sail-cloth trousers. He rose, unzipped his trousers, tossed his hat into a corner, walked down the stone steps on to Newborough's private strip of beach. Once more unto the breach, dear friend.

The water felt warm to his feet, colder to his thighs. He dived, swam out resolutely opening his eyes under water to see shoals of multi-coloured fish flickering away from him, like frightened dagger blades, and, beneath them, clean white sand streaked by strands of seaweed, long and dark and lank, the hair of a drowned mermaid.

He reached the boat; gripped its side with both hands. The hull felt warm under his fingers.

'Can I help you?' he asked the girl. The question seemed absurdly stilted; but what else could he ask? She was hunched in the stern, over the Mercury engine, one hand trying to open its cover.

'Who are you?' she asked. Then, not waiting for an answer; 'My motor's stopped.' Her voice faded; she glanced nervously towards the shore where palm trees waved their green feathery leaves at her.

'I know a bit about engines,' said Love modestly. 'It's probably not very serious. Can I come aboard?'

The girl looked down dubiously at the engine and, then at Love, as though she couldn't make up her mind. Then she nodded, moved to the other side of the boat to keep the balance, while Love heaved himself aboard.

He sat down, on a red Turkish towel, in a scent of warm, young flesh and Ambre Solaire. Pools of water formed at his feet, tears for lost years, lost chances, love in a small letter that might not come again.

His eyes followed the black Bowden cable that controlled throttle and reverse, the transparent plastic tube clipped to the mouth of a red drum of petrol. He lifted the lid from the engine, removed the nearest plug lead, tested the spark against the frame; it leapt bluely across, as though eager to be away. He replaced the lead - no strain there. He felt for the .petrol tap, turned it over to R for reserve, gave a couple of pushes on the pressure pump handle, and pulled the starting rope.

The engine spluttered once and died. The girl moved up front to hold the steering wheel. She pushed forward the throttle lever nervously, wanting to.do something to help, but not quite sure what to do. Love pulled the starter again. This time, on full throttle, the engine caught, trembled and began to race with a roar of exhaust. The screw whisked the cobalt sea into foam. Out of the blue comes the whitest wash, etc. The boat dipped sharply to the left and swept around in a wide, frantic curve, banking up a solid wall of green water.

'It's easy when you know how!' Love shouted over his shoulder above the noise, glad he had known how. Then his eyes narrowed. Hell, they were going far too fast.

'Slow!' he shouted, clipping back the cover above the exposed cylinders. But the boat raced on in its mad circle, a faint blue haze of exhaust and steam hanging over the sea behind them. He'd been right; the girl knew damn-all about boats. He turned around towards her, but the steering wheel trembled uselessly under the full thrust of the engine. The girl was lying face down on the horizontal varnished slats in the bottom of the boat.

Love leaned over her, cut back the throttle. The engine choked and died, and the boat rocked uselessly, water glug-glugging under its double-finned hull. He bent down over the girl, automatically felt for her pulse. Nothing.

He rolled her on her back. Under her costume her breasts were still firm. But he wasn't looking at them or at her eyes that stared blankly up at the sky, not seeing him, not seeing anything. He was looking at a tiny round hole that could have been a dot made by a ball-point pen right between these eyes, but wasn't.

She had been shot dead.

He let her hand drop, looked back at the shore. He could see the waving palms, the backs of the big houses, a white Ford Mustang driving out along the coast road towards Emerald Beach Hotel, past the ancient black cannon that opened red horrified mouths to him from their iron ramps at Fort Charlotte. But no one with a gun.

He reached out, turned off the petrol as a precaution against fire, felt the girl's pulse again on the chance that she might still be alive. The back of her head was damp with blood; she had run out of chances. Waves clucked and chuckled against die hull, like unseen old men at a secret joke they didn't mean to share. Water in the bilge slapped to and fro, a moving mirror that hurt his eyes.

The bullet must have come from the shore, perhaps from one of the houses with their blue and white scallop-edged awnings, their fancy iron balustrades and sweet pink-washed patios? Or could it have been fired by someone hidden in the rocks? But why? Why - and who?

As a doctor, he knew better than any of his patients that death always wins the last battle, but she was very young to fight. And death like this seemed so out of place, so unlikely in a speedboat in the sun. Death should be something that happened only to the old and the tired and the grey, in quiet rooms behind drawn curtains, when they had used up their lives and their years. Not here.

Love turned on the petrol, pulled the starter, steered towards shore, tied up at Newborough's jetty. Under the seat, he found a white plastic cockpit cover. He buttoned this down on its Dot fasteners to conceal the body, went thoughtfully up the stairs.

Ebenezer was waiting on the patio for him, his face a mask of oiled ebony. He might have been the model for the Haiti carvings sold in Rawson Square; maybe he had been.

'You got company, sah?' he asked. So he had seen the girl, too? But alive, presumably.

Love shook his head; the dead were no company.

'There's been an accident,' he explained briefly. Might as well tell the man now; he'd find out soon enough. And best to call it that, too. Though how the hell anyone could be accidentally shot fifty yards out in an empty bay took some believing. 'I'd better ring the police.'

'You'll want Inspector McGregor,' Ebenezer told him.

'Who's he?'

'Special Department. Very nice gentleman. Friend of my master.'

'Then you must know his number,' said Love. 'Please get him on the phone.'

He followed Ebenezer into the room. After the heat of the sun, harsh against the baking walls, it felt like entering a cool, dim tunnel. The telephone bell tinkled discreetly as a distant cash machine. The rich, Love knew, dislike sudden harsh sounds. One of the most important things money can buy is silence and the need never to be disturbed. Other men are disturbed for them. Sometimes, others die for them. He picked up the instrument. Ebenezer spoke on the extension.

'Your call, sah.'

Love heard the click as Ebenezer put down the receiver.

'I'm a doctor,' Love began. 'Over from England. Dr Jason Love. I would like to speak to Inspector McGregor on a serious matter.'

A lilting voice with the Welsh Bahamian accent said: 'One moment, please.'

Love imagined someone plugging in the line, the brown reels of tape beginning to turn as they recorded his conversation. Or maybe they didn't do that sort of thing here? But didn't policemen everywhere? Oh, well, what the hell.

A Scottish voice came brusquely on the line, jagged as a Grampian skyline.

'Can I help you, Doctor?'

'Yes. There's been an accident. A shooting.'

'Where?'

The voice was instantly taut. Shootings were sometimes more accurately described by a harsher word.

'I'm at Beechwood, Tom Newborough's house. I'm his doctor in England.'

'I see. What's happened? Is it - fatal?'

How discreet one had to be; this was like the old-fashioned local newspapers that Love remembered from boyhood, where people never died, were shot, or murdered; they passed on, beyond the veil, they were called to higher service. But sometimes, even then, a little before their anticipated time of departure.

'I'd rather tell you when I see you,' Love said carefully. 'Can you come over or send someone else over?'

'I'll be with you in ten minutes,' said McGregor.

The phone went dead; Ebenezer was standing at the door.

'Another rum, sah?' he asked.

Love nodded.

'Make it two,' he said. 'We've got visitors.'

He walked out into the porch, looking over the white chipped gravel on the drive; it reminded him slightly of marble chips on a grave. He was thinking of some words his favourite author, Sir Thomas Browne, the seventeenth-century Norwich physician, had written about the inevitability of death: 'Circles and right lines limit and close all bodies, and the mortal right-lined circle must conclude and shut up all.'

That was all very well, he thought, so long as the mortal right-lined circle wasn't concluding your own life; aphorisms were only of interest when they applied to somebody else. Clichés held no comfort for the dead.

McGregor arrived in a black police Humber, a thin radio-telephone aerial sprouting from the boot His driver wore a Webley .45 at his belt. Maybe violence was not such a stranger in Nassau after all?

McGregor was a slightly built man in khaki drill trousers and bush jacket, faded from many washings, with three rows of medals over his breast pocket. His face was pale, streaked unhealthily in pink; fine blue veins over-ran his nose like minor rivers in a schoolboy's map of India. His eyes were watery blue, the colour of a once-good Persian carpet ruined by the sun. They flitted like flies across the room, noting the arrangement of the windows, hanging price tags on the furniture, even as Love shook hands with him. Love poured out two glasses of Bacardi and lime from the silver beaker, anodized with ice, on the silver tray. Tom Newborough believed in the best, and could afford the expense of his belief. Cheers to Tom Newborough.

'Now what's all this?' asked McGregor breezily, throwing his peaked cap, his leather-covered cane on to a chair. 'Shouldn't drink on duty, y'khow.'

'Then make it a social call,' suggested Love. 'I was on the patio and saw a girl in a speedboat fifty yards out in the bay. Her engine stopped and she couldn't start it. I swam out, got it started - she'd forgotten to go over to reserve petrol – and when I looked round she'd been shot.'

McGregor raised his eyebrows slowly as though they were a heavy weight and took some moving. 'How is she?' he asked, leaving them up on his forehead.

'Dead,' said Love.

McGregor put down his glass; his eyebrows drooped with it; the social side of the call seemed over.

'Where's the body?' he asked curtly.

They walked down the steps, where the little boat nudged the jetty. Love unclipped the cover; the girl's flesh was still warm. A few flies had come in from the sunshine to stroke their legs and stamp their feet on her face.

'So,' said McGregor. 'Cause of death, a bullet through the brain. Did you see anybody on the shore fooling around?'

'No one. Do you know the girl?'

McGregor shook his head.

'No idea who she is. Sorry - was.'

He glanced at a plate bolted to the stern of the boat: Better Boat Products, Miami, Florida. Underneath, a serial number was stencilled on the white paint.

'Have you touched the body?' asked McGregor. Odd, mused Love, how death instantly transforms a person to a body, the present tense is suddenly the past.

'Only to feel her pulse,' he said.

'Well, let's have a look round the boat, now we're here.'

McGregor pulled a pair of white nylon gloves from his pocket, slipped them on, looked into the bow locker, under the seat. There was nothing with a name; not even a handbag.

'Could be a tourist,' he suggested. 'Could be anyone.'

McGregor buttoned back the coyer, straightened up. The bending and the rum had pumped too much blood into his face; his cheeks were purple. Love wouldn't give him an A rating as an insurance prospect.

'How long do you intend to stay here?' McGregor asked.

'I'm leaving tomorrow afternoon for Mexico City,' said Love. 'I'll be staying there at the Bamer Hotel for a few days.'

'You know Tom Newborough well?' McGregor asked, making the question seem a statement. Like a crafty fisherman, he was throwing his net wide, hopeful of any crust he could call a clue.'

'He's been a patient of mine in Somerset for the past ten years.'

'A good fellow,' said McGregor, as though this settled an argument. 'One of the best. And a pretty wealthy man.'

'I suppose so. He's certainly got a fine house in England. But I'd rather have this climate.'

'Hm.' McGregor seemed unconvinced. 'But there are disadvantages here y'know.'

'Such as getting shot in the forehead?'

'Such as that,' agreed McGregor, with a grin. 'Also, when Castro took over Cuba he kicked out a lot of gangsters. America wouldn't let them in at any price, but the Bahamas did. And since we've become self-governing, we've acquired casinos. So there's a lot of hot money around. Too much. That means protection rackets, just as it does in London. And other things you'd never associate with our public image.'

'When you've been a doctor as long as I have,' said Love, 'nothing surprises you. Either about public images or private ones. Mostly private.'

They walked back up the steps, through the living-room, stood in the doorway.

'Even so, I think some things that happen in these islands might surprise you. It's always been a tough place, you know. The privateers started it. Then the pirates. Morgan, "Black-beard" Teach. They've still got his well in the garden of the Sheraton British Colonial up the road. And only a hundred years ago 300 wreckers worked here in Nassau, employing ten times as many men to salvage the ships they lured ashore.

'When that folded, there was gun-running for the Confederates during the American Civil War. Then rum-running during prohibition. Now it's property and gambling. There are still a lot of pirates around, Dr Love. I could ring up half a dozen men now, each of whom could write a cheque for twenty or thirty million dollars ... if he wanted to. Which he wouldn't - for me. Yet all of them, only a few years back, hadn't a cent. Germans, Poles, Latvians. All kinds of men, with all kinds of backgrounds, but one thing in common. Money.'

'Meaning?'

McGregor shrugged.

'Nothing special, I suppose. But if that poor girl did have a rich enemy, he'd have no great trouble in buying a marksman. Ah, well, back to the looms. I'll need a statement from you, too, before you leave. I'll ring you later about that.'

He picked up his cane, his hat, took a step towards his car. The driver, in starched white jacket, peaked cap with deep red band, dark blue trousers, saluted and opened the rear door. McGregor shook hands with Love.

'The only person I've met in your line of business was, oddly enough, another Mac,' volunteered Love, for no reason at all. 'A Colonel MacGillivray. Douglas MacGillivray. And he talks just like you. A cynic'

McGregor was half into the car. He turned around, his face a mask; only his eyes were wary. Had he said too little - or too much?

'You know MacGillivray?' he asked cautiously, as though the question admitted that he did himself.

'Surely. Did a little job for him once in the war, and I've run into him a couple of times since.'

On one of those occasions, MacGillivray, the deputy head of DI6, the British Intelligence Service, had persuaded Love to fly to Teheran, ostensibly as a delegate to a medical conference, but, in fact, to try and discover a missing agent - and he had ended up in a Russian plane thousands of miles away, up near the Arctic Circle. On the second occasion, MacGillivray's knowledge had been useful to Love when he was out in the Himalayas, treating the son of a local prince who was being blackmailed to raise funds to operate a spy ring for Communist China.

But at the moment, with the hihiscus aflame on either side of the drive, with the cobalt sky resting contentedly on the tops of the palm trees, MacGillivray and his web of agents controlled from the cover office of Sensoby & Ransom, a fruit importing firm in Covent Garden, was not only thousands of miles away in space, but nearly as distant in time. .

McGregor paused as though he meant to ask Love something else, then thought better of it, shut the door behind him. Love watched the black car turn out into the road, went back into his room, changed into a pair of dacron trousers, a dark blue shirt. Ebenezer had prepared a lunch of conch salad, and some fresh pineapple in kirsch. The conch was served chopped up and raw with lemon juice and hot peppers. As Love ate it he remembered a Bahamian saying: 'It makes the old man throw away his crutches.' So what should it do for him? he thought.

He had lit his second Gitane after a cup of black coffee when the dark blue police launch arrived; hooked up the boat discreetly and towed it away. To anyone on the beach it would simply appear to be another engine failure, a broken-down boat on the way back to the shipyard for repairs.

What a shock these good visitors from Buffalo and Birmingham would have if they knew it was a floating coffin. But then, Love reasoned, even if they were told, they would still not believe; the human mind conservatively rejects anything beyond the narrow spectrum of its own experience, and the more inexperienced people are, the less will they accept. Hence the widespread scepticism about the fearful facts of Nazi concentration camps, or Soviet forced labour schemes. They had nothing like that in Penge or Des Moines, so why should things be any different in Dachau or Vorkuta?

He was thinking about the strange, uncharted deserts of the human mind when the telephone rang. He picked it up. There was a pause, a brief intake of breath, and a woman's voice asked: 'Are you Dr Love?'

'Who wants him?' countered Love. Surely this couldn't be one of his patients here on the island? There must be some escape from the ills and aches of his Somerset practice. He felt a slight downturn of his spirits as he visualized an emergency call.

'You don't know me,' the voice went on. 'My name is Alcantara, Senora Juanita Alcantara. I've a house on the other side of the island. I'm a friend of Tom Newborough.'

'Oh, yes,' said Love, without great enthusiasm. 'I am Dr Love.'

Out at sea, a motorboat was pulling a skier across the horizon, maybe the man he had seen that morning. The skier held up one hand, like a drowning man, released the rope, sank down. The boat slowed, banked to a turn. The sound of a girl's laughter floated in from the bay. He wondered when the dead girl had last laughed; at what; with whom.

'How did you know my name, or that I was here?' asked Love.

'I read the Tribune,' explained the woman. 'That's the local paper. It usually has a couple of columns about visitors. I'll read you what they say about you.'

She cleared her throat.

' "Dr Jason Love, of Hishop's Combe, Somerset, England, is currently vacationing at Beechwood, ocean-side residence of Mr Thomas J. Newborough, MBE, JP.

' "Dr Love, who owns one of the last supercharged Cord roadsters in England, is on his way to Mexico for a Vintage Car Rally, and then plans to fly to New York for an East Coast Meet, of the Auburn-Cord-Duesenberg Car Club, of which he is a member. Dr Love, who arrived on Friday, is an expert on the works of Sir Thomas Browne, the seventeenth-century Norwich physician-philosopher."'

She paused, 'That is you, isn't it?'

'Guilty,' admitted Love. Hell, how he hated reading things about himself. He didn't quarrel with any of the facts, it was just the naked way in which they were put, entirely unrelated, entirely unimportant.

'Well, I wasn't ringing just about that. It was about the business in the boat this morning.'

'Yes?'

'Yes. The police checked the number of the boat. It's ours. I've just returned from identifying the body.'

What did one say now? Love said, 'Oh.' It didn't carry anything any farther.

'That's why I'm ringing you, doctor. I wonder if I could see you for a few minutes?'

'I suppose so,' agreed Love. He had become involved; he could not very well back out now. 'When?'

'Would now suit you?' Senora Alcantara suggested. 'I'm only about six miles away. I could come over - or would you care to come here? You have a car?'

'Yes. Tom Newborough said I could use his Herald.'

'Good. You come here then. It's quieter. My house is Quendon. White, with green shutters. You drive along Bay Street from where you are, turn right just before the Mayfair, and head towards the centre of the island.

'Six miles on your mileometer, and start to go slowly. Then you'll see our gates on the right. Shall I expect you in, say, half an hour?'

'You do that,' said Love, although he had planned a different way of spending the afternoon. But now he didn't fancy either the sea or the sun; both would remind him of death. This drive would at least give him something to do.

Love noticed a slight movement behind him. Ebenezer was standing in the doorway.

'You're going out, sah?' he asked.

Love nodded. Was that just guess-work, or had he been listening? And did it matter either way? Probably these houseboys knew all of their masters' business.

'I'll be away about an hour and a half,' Love told him.

He walked out to the car-port, climbed into Tom New-borough's Triumph Herald. The ignition key was in the lock. He turned back the trip mileometer to zero, drove off.

Senora Alcantara's directions led him past impressive houses with porticos, beyond front gardens where automatic sprinklers sprayed the lawns. Then the houses grew gradually shabbier and smaller until they were built of grey clapboard, powdered by too many hot days and pushed up too close to the road, with shabby cars nestling thankfully against them for shade.

The sun had yellowed the grass; at the edge of the road palm trees laid black, spongy leaves wearily against stone walls. Waves of heat beat back from the tarmac, every rise shimmered in a liquid mirage. Now the houses were little better than wooden shacks with washing lines strung between two palm trees; lusty bearded goats tethered to stakes watched him out of expressionless, amber eyes, and little children played timeless games in the dirt with unpainted wooden toys.

At a cross-road a grizzled, toothless Bahamian dozed on a stone in the sun, head down on his chest; a little saliva drooled from his mouth. He was dreaming of girls he had never made, journeys he would never make; all the unanswerable injustice of being old and poor in a world beamed at the rich and young.

Love was near Grant's Town, where, a century before, freed slaves had been let loose to start new lives. When the car's trip on the mileometer showed six he slowed down, looking for the gates. High walls lined either side of the road jealously now, and yellow strips were painted on the tarmac to simulate pavements for walkers. He was approaching the Blue Hills; over them lay South Beach and the sea. He slowed for a corner and saw a slice of wood, a cross-section of a tree trunk, all varnish and bark, with one word carved on it: Quendon.

Purple, orange, red and mauve flowers with names Love did not know poured fountains of colour over the wall. Another notice, 'Beware Guard Dogs', hung from a white chain suspended across the drive. Damn Senora Alcantara he thought. She might at least have opened this if she's so anxious to see me.

He stopped, climbed out to unclip one end and was back in his seat when he heard the rustle of a dress behind him. A coloured woman in a print frock was standing at his open window, with a tray of pink paper flowers suspended from a halter around her neck.

'For the Children's Home,' she explained. 'Will you take one?'

Love groaned inwardly. He hated organized charities.

Surely such things should be controlled by the State or left to the genuine spontaneity of people who wished to help? He found one of the new half dollar pieces, slipped it into the tin she held out. It made a hollow ring.

'The first?' he asked.

She nodded.

'We have to start somewhere.'

She took a small pink flower, the size of a Poppy Day flag, pushed it into his lapel. It had a round black centre surrounded by five cloth petals.

'Thank you so much,' she said.

Love let in the clutch.

Senora Alcantara's house was white, hung with creeper. Slatted blue shutters drooped discreet eyelids across the windows. He stopped his car; the scent of bougainvillaea swept over him, overpowering as the sweetness of funeral flowers.

He pulled a wrought-iron handle that looked like a refugee from a lavatory chain. Somewhere, deep in the recesses of the house, a bell tinkled, and a thin voice began to call, 'They're here! Over the top! Up and at'em!'

A fat Bahamian woman in a white overall, steel-rimmed spectacles, opened the door, stood beaming at him. A hole had been cut in her right plimsoll to ease a bunion. She smelled cheerfully of sweat.

'Yoh Dr Love?' she asked.

'The same.'

'Please come in. Ma'am's expecting you.'

The voice kept calling hoarsely in the background: 'They're here! Over the top!'

She saw Love's perplexity in his eyes.

'It's the mynah bird. He likes a drop of rum, that one. He can sing, talk. Almost human.'

'Probably more so than many people,' said Love.

She giggled, quivering with fat.

'Yoh funny man, Doctor. I kin tell yoh funny man.'

He followed her across the tessellated floor, cool as a tomb and twice as expensive, through an archway, into a white-walled room where modern paintings threw daubs of colour on the far wall, splashes of ochre and blood. The white aubusson carpet let his feet take a liberty in their deep pile; it felt like walking through a fallen fog.

He sat down gratefully on a settee. Through the windows, blue sea joined blue sky without any dividing line. Overlooking the beach, white as bleached bone, was a walled patio with a cluster of striped canvas chairs, a beach umbrella, a white iron table from which the drinks had not been cleared away. From the beach a private landing stage pushed a wooden finger out into the sea. This must be where the speedboat was kept. Love sat, trying to think of nothing, almost succeeding. When the woman came into the room, he did not hear her until she spoke!

She was probably in her mid-fifties, with a dark, expressive face, oiled against the sun, hair drawn into a tight bun behind.-her head, black and close as a raven's folded wings. She wore blue canvas trousers, a flowered blouse. A bracelet of gold charms tinkled as she shook hands.

'I am Senora Alcantara,' she said. Her hand was cold and dry, rather like a bird's claw. Hard black eyes flicked up and down him, hanging a Squire's label on his suit, one from Harvie and Hudson on his shirt. They lingered briefly on the buttonhole.

'So you were actually in the boat when the poor girl was killed, Doctor?' she said, making the question sound a fact, almost an accusation.

Love nodded.

'Actually in the boat,' he agreed.

She picked up a jade box of cigarettes that played a few reluctant bars of 'The Skater's Waltz' as she offered it to him.

'A terrible business,' the Senora said carefully. Love noticed she had avoided the word 'accident'. 'Will you have a drink?'

'Bacardi and lime, please,' said Love unoriginally, but why break new ground when the old tasted so good?

She crossed to a black marble table, measured the amber rum into an electrical cocktail shaker, added fresh lime juice, crushed ice, pressed the button. The machine began to whirr. She poured two glasses.

'To a more pleasant stay in the island,' she said. The shaker motor still hummed on like a swarm of honeyless bees. What the hell, thought Love. She's mixed the drink. Why doesn't she turn it off?

She was looking again at the pink flower in his lapel.

'What's that?' she asked. 'Alexandra Day?'

Love shrugged.

'The woman said it was for a children's home.'

'Please let me look. I collect these flag-day things. Rosettes, paper"lifeboats, poppies. The lot.'

She reached out her hand with long silvered nails, removed the buttonhole, glanced at it.

'Could I keep it?' she asked.

Love nodded. Why not?

'You take the flower, Senora,' he said. 'I'll keep the pin. I'm half Scots. It might come in useful.'

'As you wish, Doctor.'

She smiled, twisted off the pin, handed it back gravely to him. He pushed it into the top edge of his left lapel. Senora Alcantara smoothed the five petals, put the flower down by the shaker. The motor droned on.

'Won't you turn that off?' Love asked.

'No, it's new. I want to let it run for a bit to loosen up. Now, come out into the sunshine, Doctor. You're from England, where if it's not wet, it's foggy. No?'

'No. At least, not always. Sometimes it freezes.'

She laughed. Love followed her through the french doors on to the patio. They sat down on the white wrought-iron chairs. She took a small photograph from her blouse pocket and pushed it across the table top, between the glasses towards him.

'Was that the girl?'

Love nodded. The young dead face looked up appealing from the sepia print of a summer's day. She was holding a small dachshund, with flowers behind her; part of a cottage wall.

'She was Carmen, my maid. Or, rather, my daughter's maid,' explained the Senora. 'Apparently, she'd borrowed our motorboat without letting us know. More unfortunately, she wore my daughter's costume, one of these new op-art things.'

'Why was that unfortunate?' asked Love, remembering the black and white zig-zag stripes. The mynah bird called encouragingly : 'Over the top!'

'Because that costume was the only one in Nassau. It was photographed last week for the Tribune - and almost everyone here would recognize Shamara, my daughter. So whoever was shooting didn't mean to hit her maid. They thought they were killing her.'

'So you mean it wasn't an accident at all, but deliberate murder?'

Of course she meant that, just as Love already knew it, but he had tried to conceal the uncomfortable knowledge, to bury it beneath the comfortable fiction of accident, as an oyster covers an irritating grain of grit with pearl.

Murder. The word had a cold echo. Despite the heat, Love felt chips of ice touch his heart, the chill of a new-made grave. He imagined the dead face of the girl on the marble slab of the mortuary, the smell of formaldehyde and ether. Sir Thomas Browne had once described how 'Christians have handsomely glossed the deformity of death, by careful consideration of the body, and civil rites which take off brut all terminations'. But a corpse was a corpse was a corpse. The dead had no beauty, no matter what the poets said. They hadn't seen as many as he had.

'Yes,' said the. Senora, sipping her drink, watching his reaction! 'Deliberate.'

'But why?' asked Love, for something to say, not that it concerned him. His business was with the living, not the dead.

Senora Alcantara shrugged.

'There have been attempts before,' she said casually, as though she was discussing the inadequacies of a new hairdresser, the fact that the little woman around the corner wasn't quite as good at running up a dress as she had thought.

'What sort of attempts?'

She drew on her cigarette.

'We're Cubans,' she said, as though this was sufficient explanation. 'We have enemies in a way you English, in your cold, remote, little island; don't understand, because you've never had to try.

'Let me explain, Doctor. Before Castro came to power, my husband and I controlled one of the largest cosmetic firms in Havana. There was every kind of corruption to fight, and Castro played on this. He was going to lead a middle-class revolution. We actually helped him - so did lots like us - because we genuinely believed he'd stop the corruption. And he did. Only then he started new corruptions, new confiscations instead:

'Ours was one of the first firms he seized. But one thing we managed to hide - the formula for our biggest seller, a face cream.

'I don't know if you know much about the science of cosmetics, doctor, but most creams contain one special individual ingredient or combination of ingredients that gives them the edge on the competition.

'Helena Rubinstein, for instance, went out to Australia from Poland as a young girl. She found that the Australian climate dried out the complexions of quite young women, and made them look old. She remembered some cream her mother used to make to use on her own face back in Europe, so she sent home for the formula. Within months she found she could sell as much as she could make in Australia - and she was in business.

'Our firm was very much smaller, of course, but we were still big in South America. Castro compelled us to make over - our trade marks, our plant, everything, in return for getting out with our lives. The only thing we managed to smuggle out was that formula.'

'How did you get away with that?'

'My husband has dual nationality. His mother was Mexican. He's in Mexico now, trying to set up a new factory. The customs at Havana airport stripped both of us, but they found nothing. There was nothing to find. My husband had memorized the formula.'

'And your daughter?'

'Shamara was in England then. At London University. We rented this house, for it seemed on neutral ground, between Mexico and England. And the tax advantages are considerable, if we register the company in Nassau.'

'So I understand. But who would try to kill your daughter because of all this?'

'Castro's men. That's who.

'There were attempts only, at first. Just to frighten us, to make us surrender the formula. After each one we'd have a phone call warning us that next time it could be fatal.'

'Have you told the police?'

'Of course. But what can they do? Be realistic, doctor.'

Love thought, that was the trouble with him, he wasn't real-istic. Life could seem so peaceful in Somerset, cushioned from violence, remote from change, that all this took some believ-ing. But life was rarely peaceful, not when the stakes were high. He looked out at the shimmering sea. It was hard to believe that just beneath that smooth sunburst surface it teemed with fish, struggling for survival: marlin, giant tuna, bonefish, the great groupers, the white-bellied sharks, all ready to kill so that they could live. But few signs of these myriad tragedies appeared above the smiling waves. The political refugees, the people who had supported the wrong leader, who ended on the losing side after the wrong revolution, also presented serene faces to an un-caring world. What else could they do?

He only found the Senora's story hard to believe because of his own sheltered life. He had heard that even the Bacardi family, who had opened a magnificent new rum distillery in Nassau, had been forced to abandon their enormous concern in Cuba, worth millions of dollars, and fly with only a suitcase each.

Conversation sagged between them like a slack wire. Love's drink seemed suddenly tasteless. He stood up.

'Was there anything special you wanted to see me about?' he asked.

'Yes. I was going to ask if you could possibly help me, Doctor.'

'Ah.'

Here it came then. Why was it that, as a doctor, someone always seemed to seek his help? Invariably, their problems were ini-tially small; it was only when you became personally involved that they suddenly grew in importance.

'The paper said you were going to Mexico.' A pause for him to confirm or deny this; Love did neither.

'If you are, I wondered if you could take my husband a book?'

'A book?'

'Yes. He was a collector of old books in Cuba, and we managed to bring some of them here before things got too tight. This is one he's asked for several times, but I think it's too valuable to risk sending through the post. It's Burton's Anatomy of Melancholy. A copy of the 1621 edition.'

'Then it's very valuable. My own favourite reading is Sir Thomas Browne.'

'Ah, yes,' said the Senora. 'I think the newspaper mentioned that. Didn't they live about the same time?'

'Indeed they did. And they had something else-in common. While Browne was a doctor, Burton would have liked to be one. He used to say he was "by profession a divine, by inclination a physician".'

'Well, that's what I wanted to ask you, doctor. My husband's in Mexico City. Where are you staying, by the way?'

'The Bamer.'

'How extraordinary. So is he.'

'Then that's not very much to ask,' said Love thankfully: he had expected some far more complicated request. 'No strain at all.'

'I'm so glad you think so,' said the Senora, equally relieved. 'Shamara was going. But, after this - she gave a twist of her hand that made the bracelet jangle like tiny temple bells - this shooting, I think she'd better stay here for a bit, and keep out of sight.'

'Of course. But who would have done the shooting? Any theories about that?'

'There are Cuban, thugs here in Nassau who'd do it. They are professional killers from the Baptista regime whom Castro has run out because he doesn't need them. He has his own. For a safe return to Havana, they'd do a lot.'

'I see,' said Love, as though he really could see a way through the dark, inner labyrinths of international politics, the terrors behind a dictator's assurance, the treble-talk of peace means war means death.

'Here's the book, then, doctor.'

She handed him a thick volume bound in faded fawn leather, the tide imprinted in gold leaf, blackened and faint after three centuries. He opened it, felt with pleasure the rough texture of the pages, crudely cut at the edges, thinking of all the people who had owned it, handled it, enjoyed it.

'What about something to carry this in? It's too valuable to carry raw like this.'

'Ah, yes,' she said brightly.

Her eyes darted around the room as though there should be all manner of suitable covers in view. Then she picked up Christopher Hibbert's classic, Garibaldi and His Enemies., removed the dust-jacket, folded this around the leather book.

'There,' she said. 'Are you quite sure you don't mind doing this?'

'Positive,' said Love, and meant it.

She walked with him to his car, watched the little white Herald out of sight, and then walked slowly back up the steps and into the house. The bird chirped from its perch, 'I can see you! I can see you!'

She snapped her fingers at it, crossed the room, switched off the electric cocktail shaker. Then she picked up the pink flower, and holding it carefully in her open palm, sat down at her desk. She opened a drawer, screwed a jeweller's magnifying glass into her left eye, examined the petals and the centre closely under a reading lamp, turning the flower over and over.

Then she took a pair of sewing scissors from the drawer and deliberately cut into the bright black button.

Its hard, shellac surface cracked suddenly into dust, and tiny dark chips. With a pair of nail tweezers she picked out the minute blue blob of a transistor. From it grew a wire, thin as a hair, that had connected it to the metal pin. She turned the transistor over, examining it expertly. The apparatus consisted of a super-sensitive Continental buttonhole microphone with a midget transmitter, no larger than a match-head, behind it. The pin would act as an aerial and give it a range of two or three miles. So that would mean someone else within that range with a receiver to pick up the signals.

What would they try, next? She crushed the transmitter between the jaws of a pair of pliers. Carefully she shook the pieces into an envelope, sealed it, wrote the date on the back, locked it away in the drawer.

She wondered about the doctor. He appeared to be a pleasant enough fellow, not the sort of man who would be easily suspicious, and, anyhow, what could go wrong? It was unlikely he knew anything about this, although when she'd heard he had actually been in the boat when the girl was shot, she had wondered. Now she had met him she was sure he was what he appeared to be - a country doctor on holiday - and nothing more.

She picked up the telephone and asked for international directory inquiries. When the operator came on the line she said she wanted the number of the Hotel Bamer in Mexico City. The operator told her it was 21.90.60. She replaced the receiver, then dialled the long-distance operator, asked for this number.

While she waited for the call to come through, Senora Alcantara walked across the tiles to the patio and stood looking out to sea. She was smiling now; the sun heliographed happily back to her from the waves.

Then the telephone began to ring, and she walked back into the room to take her call.

*   *   *

Four miles up the road, just past where it forked, a grey clapboard house crumbled resentfully in the sun. A few hens pecked dispiritedly among empty beer cans and thistles around the back door. The blinds over the front windows were down, eyelids closed in an exhausted face.

Upstairs, in the main bedroom, behind these faded, threadbare, cotton blinds, four men crouched on the floor, around a Grundig tape recorder and a Decca VHF set. A hasty aerial had been strung from hooks on the picture rail; a mezzotint of Holman Hunt's painting of Christ, a lantern in His hand, 'The Light of the World', hung from a nail in the peeling wallpaper.

Two of the men were small, with dark, Spanish faces,-dancer's hips and squeezed-in features, like men in miniature. They wore faded blue jeans and pointed plastic shoes pricked - with ventilating holes. The others were Bahamians, big-boned, very black, with oddly pale gums.

They squatted on their haunches, watching the turning reels of tape, the flickering green electronic eye on the recorder. The air felt sour with sweat; a few bluebottles buzzed half-heartedly against the dirty window panes as though even they wished to be elsewhere.

One of the small men had a lightweight pair of US Army surplus earphones clipped over his oiled hair. The name 'Garcia' was embroidered in red over the left breast pocket of — his shirt. The bridge of his nose had sunk in; horizontal ridges scored his carious splintered teeth, a legacy from the syphilis that had finally killed his mother. She had been a whore in Havana, until she had died, two years previously, in a poor-house outside the city, a festering, lingering, stinking death, that he still sometimes dreamed about and woke up choking with horror, because he had watched her die.

She claimed she had first caught the disease from a British sailor in one of the old coaling vessels that used to ply along the coast. There was some doubt about this, of course, for her clients came from many countries. But, ever since, Garcia hated the British, possibly without quite realizing the real reason for his hatred. Now, since Castro's police had closed down the more ostentatious call-houses in Havana, including La Pompadour, where he had ponced since puberty, he hated the Cubans as well - and the British even more because he had been forced to ask their aid.

The American immigration officers in Miami knew all about Garcia and refused to let him land; the officials in Nassau were more lenient; they had allowed him to stay for a maximum of three months.

Garcia's time was almost up, his request for an extension had been refused - maybe the Bahamas immigration people had not been so ill-informed, after all - and he was in the . unhappy position of having no country he could call his own, when the other small man in the room had approached him in a bar down by the harbour, off Bay Street. He explained that he was also a Cuban, but somehow he had a British passport - he had been able to produce a Maltese birth certificate. His name was Luis, he knew all about Garcia's troubles, and he had a proposition to make. Garcia listened; he always listened to propositions. In his time, he had heard many; some had been interesting.

What Luis had to say made sense. He explained that if Garcia would agree to do certain things, he would be allowed -to return to Havana, and would not have to face charges of any kind; the past would automatically be erased. He showed Garcia a document to prove this; it looked official enough, although Garcia could not read very well and was too proud to admit this disability. But from what he could make out, someone else must have thought he would agree, for there was his name all spelled out with lots of twirls and flourishes. So Garcia had agreed. In all the circumstances, he really had no alternative. Then Luis had explained what would be asked of him.

Now Garcia crouched on the rough boards of the floor, foul with squashed cockroaches, sharp with cat's urine, listening to the tapes. A voice from far away poured its news into his ears.

'He's just left Quendon now. He's driving the same .white Triumph Herald, number NP5757801. She saw him to the door. He's carrying a book which I managed to get a close on. Garibaldi and His Enemies. Watched him get in the car. Couldn't see a bulge of any weapons. Seems to be unarmed. He's going out of my sight now. Back on the Nassau Road. Going. Gone. Now. Out.'

The voice stopped. Luis turned the dials on the receiver. Another voice came in, nervous, lilting.

'He's driving towards me. He's turned into Beechwood. Alone. He's stopped the engine, taken out the keys. He's carrying a book under his arm. I can't see what it is from here. These glasses aren't good enough. He's going into the house. The front door's shutting! Over and out.'

Garcia threw the switches, pushed the earphones up over his forehead, waved his hand in a wiping-out motion to Luis, who also removed his earphones. The thin brown tape went on turning.

'He's gone. He's back in Beechwood.'

'I heard. Play over those tapes and see how much that flower gadget picked up.'

Garcia pushed over the switch to fast rewind, began to play the tape. It crackled at first, then they heard the sound of a car engine. A car accelerated, gears changed, tyres crunched on gravel, the engine stopped. A bell rang, a faint voice called,

'They're here! Over the top! Up and at 'em!'

The men in the room looked questioningly at each other.

A woman's voice asked: 'You Dr Love?'

A man's voice replied, 'The same.'

Garcia put over the switch to Stop.

'Do you want any more?' he asked.

'Wind it on a bit,' said Luis. 'That's all chat. Let's get what the Alcantara woman asked him.'

Garcia spun the reels forward for twenty feet of tape, and then threw the switch for play-back. The noise of a fast running electric motor filled the room.

'What the hell's that?' asked Luis sharply. Garcia shrugged. He wound the tape on again for a further ten feet, played it back for the second time. The buzz returned like a flight of wasps.

'That bloody transistor must have gone, man,' he suggested.

Luis shook his head.

'No, not it. We were rumbled, man. That Alcantara woman saw the doctor fellow. Then one of them got on to the flower. That noise is from an electric motor. A coffee grinder, something like that. It's been turned on to drown our microphone.'

'What do we do, then?'

'One of them must be on to us. We'll leave the Alcantara woman because she might be useful. At least she's a lead. But we'll report this doctor. He could be dangerous if he's left. And we haven't time to take chances. My bet is, we'll be told to deal with him.'

Luis looked at the two big Bahamians, his black eyes bright as chips of coal. They stood up awkwardly, flexing their long, cramped legs in their creased jeans. Garcia switched off the Grundig, unplugged the radio, began winding in the aerial wire. He knew what Luis meant and did not want to meet his eyes. He had been a Catholic once; he still wore a thin gold-plated crucifix on a fine gilt chain around his neck. He slipped the coil of wire into a cardboard box, lit a cigarette nervously. No one said anything; there was no need for words.

Christ looked down at them from the wall.

CHAPTER TWO: NASSAU, BAHAMAS; ABOARD S.Y. ENDYMION III

Love had bathed, changed into a dark blue Airey and Wheeler lightweight tropical suit and was sitting in a chair overlooking the sea with a Bacardi arid lime at his elbow. The heat had deserted the day, and the wind sucked half-heartedly at the canvas awning and then let it go again; it would have more strength tomorrow. Love turned over the title page of the book:

The Anatomy of Melancholy. What it is. With all Kindes, Causes, Symptomes, Prognosticks, and Severall Cures of it. .In Three Maine Partitions with their Severall Sections, Members and Subsections. Philosophically, Medicinally, Historically, Opened and Cut Up. By Democritus Junior.

He understood how Burton felt, especially the Opened and Cut Up bit.

Ebenezer came out on to the patio and stood by his chair, the genie with the dark black hair.

'I was out, sah, when you came back,' he announced. 'There was a telephone message. From Inspector McGregor. He wonders if you could see him tonight?'

'When?'

'Eight o'clock, sah.'

'I see. Where?'

'Down by the water. In Deveux Street. Just off Bay Street, through the town.'

'Why there?' asked Love. 'Surely it would be more convenient to meet in his office?'

'He didn't say, sah. He just said it was urgent. Maybe he has a launch to take you to his home. I think he lives out Paradise Island way.'

'Thank you,' said Love.

Ebenezer waited for a second longer, and Love looked up at him sharply.

'Anything else?'

Ebenezer bowed, shook his head.

'Nothing, sah. Just, what time will you have dinner?'

'When I come back,' said Love.

Ebenezer padded away into the kitchen. Love closed the book under its new wrapper, put it between Richard Hough's Dreadnought and Roy Meyers' The Dolphin Boy on the shelf, stood up. He wondered why McGregor wanted to see him. Maybe he simply wanted to take a statement.

He glanced at his watch; seven thirty-five. There wasn't a lot of time to spare. He took off his jacket, pulled a loose cashmere sweater over his shirt. With the sun going down it could be chilly on a launch. Then, hands in pockets, he walked down the small drive, out into the street.

Although the sun had lost its heat, the buildings and the tarmac road had stored it up, and threw it back at Love, as though the earth were smouldering just beneath his feet. An air of tension hung over the island; even the wind, hot and dry, seemed stained with violence. He thought that if he struck a match the whole street could explode.

On the small public beach opposite the Mayfair, a handful of coloured boys wrestled happily in the scruffy sand. A crowd of American students with tight blue Bermuda shorts, crew cuts and sun glasses, drank Coca-cola through straws. Outside the Sheraton British Colonial, a Bahamian doorman wore top hat and tails, and blew his whistle for a taxi.

Love went up the crescent-shaped drive, through the swing doors, into the babble of arrival and departures within. He found a telephone booth, looked up a number, dialled it, spoke to the man who answered, made him repeat what he had said to make certain he had the right message, walked back into Bay Street.

At the corner, by the Cathedral of the Bahamas, the self-drive American tourists, unused to tiny cars, squealed round the right-angle bend in hired Triumphs. The back of the British Colonial, with a clock and columns copied from the Parthenon, faced down the road. Behind an equally impressive building thundered the big dynamos of the Bahamas Electricity Corporation, built on the site where, only a few generations back, slaves had been bought and sold and bartered.

The sunshades were still out on Bay Street; at Rawson Square a traffic policeman stood, on a round dais the size of half a barrel of beer. Beyond the palm trees, Love could see the red funnels of a tourist liner from Miami. Passengers in sunburst shirts and sandals bought straw hats like his own from fat old women in the market. There was a brisk trade in rubbish to clutter up the sitting-room of many a North American home; a pink conch-shell, strangely vaginal, a dried crab without legs, a carved ebony face on the ebony stand.

Love walked on, past the strange mixture of ancient and modern architecture, like a stage set for a film that would never be made; the Nassau Art Gallery, Charlie's Pic and Pay, Stop-n-Shop. Tired horses in straw hats broke wind dispiritedly between the shafts of purple surreys. The evidence of Nassau's past - Blackbeard's Tavern, the Blockade-Runners' Bar - was as proudly in evidence as the discreet black and gold lettered boards listing company registrations outside the .offices that specialized in such things. There were so many tax advantages in registering a company in Nassau; too bad the Cuban girl wasn't alive to enjoy any of them.

He reached the pink wall of the Paradise Island Club, where, on his left, Deveux Street turned off towards the sea. It was about sixty yards long. On one corner stood the Bank of Nova Scotia, dignified as any bank should be, with pillared porch, fanlight over the front door, neat white window frames;

On the opposite corner was the Harbour Moon Restaurant, then, farther down, a three-storey block of flats. Two Chinese children played in the gutter with a candy-striped ball. Outside the beaded curtain of a Bahamian restaurant, a man dozed in a cane chair, barefooted, straw hat down over his face; flies buzzed unheeded around his horny feet. Otherwise, the road was empty.

The sky blushed with brief purple twilight. Soon, it would be dark; the crickets were already winding up their rusty ratchets.

This was the time, this must be the place, but where was McGregor? Love glanced at his watch; it was exactly eight o'clock. He hated unpunctuality, but he'd better give the man at least fifteen minutes.

He walked slowly, up Deveux Street; at the far end, the sea glinted like black oil, and the road petered out into a jetty marked by three red and white oil drums. Huge tree trunks banded together by metal strips had been driven into the bed of the sea, to make a mooring for power-boats.

To the left, the Paradise Island Club jetty pointed its pink finger, pretty with white slatted shutters, into the channel between the mainland and the island a few hundred yards away. Before the millionaire Huntington Hartford had bought and transformed Paradise Island into one of the world's most splendid resorts, its eight hundred acres had been known by a humbler name: Hog Island. What's in a name? thought Love. Answer: about thirty million dollars, if you wanted to do the kind of job Huntington Hartford had done.

He strolled on. To the right stretched a rough beach with some small boats drawn up on the mud, the rusting body of an Austin

Healey sports car. From a concrete building, a circular saw complained at being worked so late.

A slight wind carried the smell of fish; the time was eight minutes past eight, and growing dark quickly. Moths spread wide wings against the silence of the sea; a bat fluttered from the eaves of a house.

In the block of flats, a radio blared suddenly, then the music dissolved into a squall of static. A news announcer began to read of earth tremors in Peru, a political coup in Nicaragua. High up on the spine that divided the island, the water tower exploded unexpectedly into the shape of an illuminated crown, a reminder of a visit by Queen Elizabeth.

What had happened to McGregor? Maybe he was waiting for him at the other end of the street? Ebenezer had not said which end. Or perhaps there was another Deveux Street? Love began to walk back slowly towards Bay Street. He had taken about six paces when a bead curtain rattled like loose teeth in a skull. ;

Half a dozen Bahamians, wearing short-sleeved shirts and oil-stained faded blue slacks, were coming out of the cafe. They were big, heavy men with broad shoulders, and belts with buckles. One wore a straw hat without a crown; another, a leather band with two metal clasps around his left wrist. A third carried a wooden stave peeled of all bark, white and smooth as bone.

They stood on the steps, lit by the light behind them, watching Love with the grace and insolence of dangerous animals. They knew they looked frightening, and they enjoyed their knowledge; it rinsed away some of their resentment at being born black and raised poor in a white man's, rich man's world.

They crossed the road, walking slowly, in step, so that they were between Love and Bay Street. Then they stopped. The man carrying the stick stood, feet apart, swinging it gently from his left hand, so that it seemed to be a part of him, an extension of his arm.

Love moved to, pass them, but the man suddenly flicked up the stick to bar his way. The rest shook their heads, watching him dispassionately, without interest. Love was suddenly reminded of his days as a medical student, examining some biological specimen beneath a microscope slide. Now he knew how the specimen must have felt. But the knowledge was useless; it came too late, and he would rather be without it. The small hairs on the back of his neck began to crawl. This looked like trouble. And where the hell was McGregor?

'Are you Dr Love, sah?' the man in the straw hat asked him. He was chewing gum. He spat it out with a green gobbet of phlegm at Love's feet. He didn't sound as though he greatly cared how Love answered his question: his own mind was already made up. His teeth were yellow and chipped like a mouthful of broken bones. His nose had been smashed years ago and reset badly in a different shape; it lay along his face as though it liked being close to his cheek, all the way. Love didn't like that nose, or the man who was wearing it. However, this was not the time to voice such opinions.

He said quietly, 'I am Dr Love. What do you want? Who are you?'

'Just friends of enemies of yours,' replied the man, and suddenly raised his stick and whipped it down at Love's head.

It would have stunned, had Love allowed his head to meet it. But he had seen the almost imperceptible narrowing of the man's eyes that preceded the blow, and ducked. Years of practising Judo, and almost as many teaching it in his spare time to British Legion classes at Hishop's Combe, made his reaction an automatic reflex. Love half turned on his left foot and kicked out backwards with the side of his right boot at the other man's knee-cap. Powered by his thigh .muscles, the strongest muscles in the human body, the tremendous blow smashed the bone. The man crumpled in a whimper of pain, and writhed in the dust, a huge black beast trying to burrow away from the agony that engulfed him.

For a second, the others hung back, and then they attacked. Love struck back with atemi blows, using the edge of his left hand as a hammer, gouging eyes with the knuckles of his right, ducking, flexing his knee; but the numbers were too many and the men too strong; Three went down but the three on their feet also fought without regard to the Queensberry Rules.

Like a man moving in a dream, a weightless, phantasmagoric figure, Love's whole body one burning focus of pain, he sagged under their blows. Then, through the red mists of exhaustion, he saw other men running, men with staves in their hands. Down on his knees in the dust, they seemed merely phantom figures, fighting in silence, expertly, viciously, above him.

Mercifully no one was hitting him now. He raised his head cautiously. Feet in black boots, feet in scabby, rotting canvas plimsolls, thrust about him in complicated steps of violence, attack and defence.

Love shook his head to try and clear away the fog of pain and reaction. Six men, big-built, in khaki shorts and shirts, with black berets, polished black belts, wooden staves secured to their right wrists by leather thongs, had overpowered his attackers. But who were they? All effort of thought and reason seemed beyond him. It was enough that he could see what he saw, without attempting to understand. Now they were running with the men who had attacked him, holding their arms twisted up behind their backs, dragging through the dust those who could not walk. From nowhere a crowd had gathered to watch. A man in dark blue yachting trousers, a silk scarf at his neck, was kneeling in the dust by Love's side. It was McGregor.

'You're bloody late,' said Love slowly. He didn't feel able to speak quickly; if he did, he was sure all his teeth would fall out. Even the effort of slow, whispered speech hurt as though each word was being wrenched out of his throat with pliers.

'Better late than never, to coin a phrase,' said McGregor, helping him to his feet. 'Are you all right?'

'Ask a crazy question, you'll get a crazy answer. I'll live the, night.'

'That's something. Sorry I was out when you rang from the British Colonial. Luckily, I had to call the office about something else, and my clerk told me you were here. We came right on over. Another few minutes and it might have been a different story.'

'Correction,' said Love. 'For "might" read "would".' He leaned back wearily against the wall of the Paradise Island Club. Open windows framed faces at the block of flats opposite; neither hostile nor friendly, simply aware. Love could feel the warm roughness of the pink cement beneath his fingers. He wondered whether he was going to be sick.

'Let's get out of here,' said McGregor, watching him closely. 'I've a car at the end of the road.'

'Lead me to it,' said Love. He began to walk shakily towards Bay Street. 'Who were those characters?'

'Hired toughs,' said McGregor. 'I told you, you can always buy strong arms here. If your money is the right colour.'

'But why should they attack me? Do I look that rich?'

'You tell me,' invited McGregor, glancing at Love quizzically. He held open his car door for him.

'What can I tell you?' asked Love, climbing in.

'Did anything happen after I left you this morning?'

'Nothing much. I had a phone call from some Cuban woman, a Senora Alcantara. She asked if I'd go over and see her. Something about the shooting in the boat. So I went along and she told me the girl in that boat had been her maid. Or rather, her daughter's maid. Is that so?'

McGregor nodded.

'The Senora has been having a rough time herself. She told you about her husband and his factory?'

'Yes. And since I was going to Mexico she asked, me if I'd take along a book for him.'

'What sort of book?'

'A seventeenth-century thing.'

'Worth a lot of money?'

'Not enough to be beaten up for. And, anyway, I wasn't carrying it.'

They drove up to Beechwood. Love opened the front door. Ebenezer had gone, but a meal was ready on the table; cold turtle pie, Royal salad, a Thermos flask of black coffee.

'Have you had dinner?' asked Love.

'Yes. I'll watch you eat.'

'I don't feel like eating.'

He poured out two Bacardis instead.

'I feel like getting out of here. Why should those bastards be after me? Do you think it's anything to do with that book?'

'As you say, you weren't carrying it. How were they to know how valuable it was? Let's have a look at it.'

Love handed him the Anatomy of Melancholy. McGregor held it up by the spine, shook the pages free like a fan. Nothing fell out.

'So,' he said, handing it back. 'That seems harmless. Maybe they knew you'd been to see her and thought you might have something to do with her. No doubt it was just another warning to her.'

Love flexed his neck; the muscles were bruised. He poured out another drink.

'Next time, maybe, they'll warn her direct.'

'Maybe they will,' said McGregor flatly. 'What time does your plane leave?'

'Noon tomorrow. I change at Miami.'

'I've a good friend in the ticket office. I'll see if I can get you on an earlier one.'

'That would give your good friend another good friend,' said Love. 'Me.'

They walked out on to the patio. The sea stretched away to join the sky in darkness. Farther up the coast, rows of distant lights flashed messages of enjoyment. A guitar scattered music from its strings. The distant beat of Goombay drums hammered like the hooves of hurrying horses.

McGregor half turned to Love, still looking out to sea.

'You mentioned Douglas MacGillivray today,' he said casually. 'Not working for him now by any chance?'

'Good God, no.'

'Just wondered,' said McGregor. 'I was trying to find a reason - any reason - for that little involvement in Deveux Street tonight.'

'That's not it.'

'Seemingly not. Well, doctor, if you do get a sudden rush of brains to the head about anything, please get in touch with me. OK?'   _

'OK,' agreed Love without enthusiasm. If he had no clues now, how would he find any elsewhere?

'Right, then. I'll put a policeman on the house for the night, just in case anyone has any ideas of continuing the action. But I don't think they will. They didn't act on their own, you know. Only under orders. And I must find out whose. If you're down at the airfield tomorrow at 8.30 am I'll guarantee you a seat on that early plane. Feel better?'

'No worse.'

They drank another Bacardi and lime each, and then another; the drum beats grew louder, and suddenly stopped. Under the moon, the sea lay white as a sheet of snow.

*   *   *

Well out beyond the islands, beyond the three-mile limit, the big yacht was riding the channel cross-currents. The davits that had swung up the speedboat still hung their crooked fingers over the side. The little boat rocked beneath them like a toy, its white hull glistening.

In the stateroom, Garcia waited behind the glass door, near to it as possible, as though he felt it would be easier for a getaway should things turn against him. He had not expected to make this trip, but Luis was busy with the recorder; or maybe he had only said he was, because he was afraid to come himself this time. Luis only liked to report success; messengers who brought bad news often had an unhappy knack of being blamed for it. Some of the sourness of failure inevitably brushed on to them; they became tainted by other men's mistakes. Luis, he thought, was too clever for this.

The luxury of the furnishings; the rich, white carpet, the red drapes that covered the walls, thick enough to soak up un-wanted sounds and throw back silence, the silk-shaded lamps that swung gently from brass brackets, accentuated Garcia's thin, nervous face, his narrow shoulders, the cheapness of his clothes. His eyes flickered nervously like pale little flames in a high wind. Now and then he licked lips that fear had dried.

He stood at the position of attention, clenching and unclench-ing his moist hands at the seams down the sides of his trousers.

Across the room, behind the centre table with its solid circular glass top four inches thick on a single central aluminium leg, another man sat in a dark green leather chair. It had wings at each side and a border of round-headed brass nails that winked in the light, but his face remained in the shadow.

He was a fat man, but not too fat. His pale grey mohair suit hung cunningly from his shoulders disguising his bulk. A Siamese Bluepoint purred on his lap, turned its blue eyes towards Garcia, and then looked away. As a thoroughbred, it had no time to waste on the shoddy.

The man's hands, pudgy, pale and well manicured, were folded one across the other, over the curved head of an Indian warrior on top of a tapering ebony stick. He had waited until the steward had left them alone, until he knew from the speed of this stranger's breathing how nervous he felt, and then he spoke.

His voice was deep, like an echo in a well. He had been a powerful orator years before. He had been in great demand as speaker in the early years of the Party. Some shrewd observers had said he was as good a public speaker as Roehm, but, of course, he knew he was much better. He was also far more clever.

Roehm's homosexuality had provided a convenient lever for his downfall early on, while he had survived a war, a defeat, the accusations of former colleagues and of enemies alike. What had happened to the others? They were dead. How right Schiller had been when he wrote: 'Mit der Dummheit kampfen Gotter selbst vergebens' - with stupidity the gods themselves struggle in vain.

Yes, all the great of those days were dead or forgotten, while he was alive with a new name, even a new and growing reputation for philanthropy. And after his treatment by the Rumanian professor, Oeriu, whose life study was the chemistry of old age, after his regular injections with Oeriu's therapeutic discovery folcisteina, which was said to have rejuvenated the ageing Chinese leader Mao Tse-Tung, plus his equally regular doses of royal jelly, flown each week in refrigerated containers from his personal physician in Lucerne, he did not feel his age.

He sighed, swung his mind back like a compass to consider this idiot, sweating with terror behind the door. How sour and rancid was the smell of fear and dread. Something had gone wrong; this sweat always gave failure away. He had learned that under Heydrich in Czechoslovakia. People can lie as much as they like, but they can't stop the truth sweating out of them. How true that had proved! But again, what was truth? Pilate had not known, so how could he be sure? He sighed. The floor creaked gently as the currents changed, almost the only sign they were at sea.

'So you found this yacht easily enough?' he asked in his deep, booming voice.

'Yes, sir. I had your bearings.'

'Of course. And what did you discover? Who is this English doctor? Is he involved at all?'

Garcia shuffled his weight uneasily from one foot to the other as though his body, like his forebodings, had become almost too heavy for one man to bear.

'He's only a tourist, sir,' he said desperately. 'A harmless person.'

'Most of the trouble in the world is caused by harmless people,' the other man pointed out. 'I've heard the transcript of his interview with Senora Alcantara. Either she knew the room was bugged, or he did. And, more important, one or other of them knew just what to do about it.'

'I don't think that the Senora is entirely harmless. So there is no reason to suppose that this Dr Love person is, either. Tell me, was he ever in the British Army?'

'Yes, sir. The Register of Medical Practitioners says he was.'

A pause.

'Did he fight against my - against Germany?'

'No, sir. He was in the East. India. Burma.'

'Ah.'

He was sorry about this; it would have helped if he could have some tangible fact of direct enmity on which to focus his animus, as mild sunshine can be focused through a burning glass to a pin-point of white heat.

'You have him outside?'

This was the moment Garcia had dreaded, had fought to avoid. No wonder Luis had ducked this interview; he was too smart to be involved. , 'He - he's not actually here, sir.'

'Not actually here?' So this was the reason for the man's fear. 'What do you mean? You reported to me you were having him brought aboard as I ordered. Where is he? Dead?'

'No, sir. I had six men to pick him up. They got him down to his knees, but the police arrived unexpectedly.'

'And?'

'They rescued him, sir, and seized the men I'd hired. I was watching from across the road.'

'Were you seen?'

'No, sir. I was pretending to be asleep.'

'You do not need to pretend to take that role. So your harmless English doctor must have suspected something - and told the police of his suspicions. I cannot understand how you consider him to be so innocent. Unless, perhaps, he has come to some arrangement with you? Something more beneficial than the one we have together?'

'No, sir. Most certainly not, I do assure you.'

'I believe you, Garcia. You would surely not be so foolish. Originally, I intended to meet this doctor just to find out what he was trying to do, who he was working for, how he became involved at all. Now there's no time left for such a gentlemanly approach. You will use the more direct, continental way. Get rid of him.'

'You mean—?'

Garcia knew exactly what he meant, but the thought of being so deeply involved horrified him. He was doing what he did for a promised return to Havana. To eavesdrop, to organize a beating-up, an attempted kidnapping, was routine enough. Such assignments ranked in his mind with photographing a cheat in a whore's bed, because the man would pay more for the negative than for the girl. They were business deals, no more, no less.

But murder was altogether different; a finite act. Also it was the unforgiveable sin: 'Thou shalt not kill.' And he well remembered the old priest of his boyhood and his teachings; the sweet smoke of incense, the cool spaciousness of the church after the sour heat of his mother's cramped room; all those strange men on the stairs, the scent of powder and the sweat of lust.

He had already killed one person, a girl in a boat, a girl he had never seen before. Was he to kill a second time within twelve hours? They had told him that the girl was an enemy of his country, that if this were war he would be a hero in removing such a one; and, fuddled with rum and pot, he had agreed because he wanted to agree, because he needed to ingratiate himself with these people.

But he had no quarrel with the man in the boat, although he was a hated Englishman, and yet now he was being told to kill him. But why? Was there no way out - or no one else who could do this? How many more such demands would be made?

He wanted no part of this, but, dear God, how could he avoid it?

The other man was talking, his voice now soft as Tia Maria and cream on a summer evening.

'You did not tell the police here about the business of the drugs and that English society kid who killed herself two months ago? Remember? The police might not be willing to let you go, if they knew. And they could know. As they could so easily learn more about the girl you shot today. They will know the calibre of the bullet that killed her. What if the line that fired that bullet were to be found in your room, Garcia? I could so easily tell that inspector man, McGregor.

'Now, you do this one last job for me, Garcia, and I will keep my silence. You will be back in Havana by the end of the month. But try to back out and you will not leave Nassau. Do you understand me?'

'I understand you, sir.' Garcia mouthed the words, but spoke them with another man's voice, a voice he did not recognize.

'That is good. Now, I do not wish to hear from you until afterwards. Then radio me. You know the wavelengths and the times for transmitting.'

'But if I can't manage to - to deal with the doctor, sir. What shall I send then?'

The other man smiled; the light reflected gold in his teeth.

'You will send nothing, Garcia. Nothing at all. In that situation, we will send for you.'

He took one hand off his stick and began to stroke the cat with his palm. The cat purred, its claws stretched briefly against his light suit, then, with a lithe leap, it jumped up on his shoulder and sat washing its paws.

Garcia could imagine its curved claws, sharp as fish-hooks, at his jugular. His throat choked with his imaginings; he wanted to be away, anywhere but in this scented stateroom that rolled so slightly with the sea. It might be day or night inside, because the curtains were never opened. He did not know how long he had been standing there, what time it was; he had lost all sense of measuring the passage of the hours. He dreaded the journey back to Nassau in the motorboat on the choppy waves, with the spray soaking his hair, straining his eyes for the marker lights, but even that would be a relief after this evil place. His fingers went up to the small crucifix he wore on its chain around his neck. How far he had come since the day he had bought it, years before; if there was a heaven it was farther off than when he was a boy.

'Is that all, sir?' he asked.

The other man nodded.

Garcia bowed, opened the glass door, shut it silently behind him and stood for a moment in the creaking corridor with its polished plastic floor that reflected the bulbs in the ceiling as round pools of light. He wiped his sweaty face with his handkerchief and began to walk up the companion way towards the deck. Then he paused. The ship seemed deserted, creaking in that secretive, lonely way of all ships, speaking to itself, answering the whisper of the waves. He tiptoed back to the door and stood flattened against the wall, listening. Maybe he held no cards at all; but he could never better his position unless he tried; and nothing could make it worse.

The fat man was speaking, probably on the radio telephone, because Garcia could hear no answer. Garcia did not speak German, but some words he understood; his mother used to have many German visitors, especially during the war. Also, some German words had a phonetic affinity with Spanish. But what nonsense was the man talking? He was going to turn the tide and so turn the tables? He seemed to find it amusing, because he laughed; he had never heard him laugh before, so perhaps it was a riddle, or else he had heard it all wrongly;

Suddenly the man stopped speaking; the faint tinkle of the telephone being replaced gave him its plain warning. He had better go before he was discovered. Garcia held his breath and tiptoed away towards the companion way and the open deck.

Inside the room, the fat man pushed away the receiver, reached out with his right hand into an open box of soft-centred chocolates. Like blind white serpents, his thick, pale fingers fluttered through the crinkly brown paper. They closed over a chocolate in the shape of a strawberry. He raised it to his lips, bit into its soft red liqueur centre, wiped his fingers afterwards on a silk handkerchief. Then he settled back hi his chair. The cat purred as though it had swallowed a dynamo.

In moving, the man's elbow had touched a shaded desk light on a side table. It shook for a moment, lighting up the face he preferred to keep in darkness. The skin was fearfully burned and twisted, foul as a dead foetus, rashed with purple scars and thick, fleshy incrustations that ran, raised and reddish, crisscrossed with the marks of stitching.

It was like the rough model for a human face, something not finished, that would never be finished, a crude oudine begun and uncompleted.

And behind his dark glasses, where his eyes had been, two empty sockets were open, sightless windows into a living skull.

CHAPTER THREE: COVENT GARDEN AND WHITEHALL, LONDON; NASSAU, BAHAMAS

It was nine o'clock on Sunday morning in the office with the double-glazed windows and aluminium-lined curtains that could screen the most sensitive listening device, two floors above the fruit firm of Sensoby & Ransom in Covent Garden.

The streets lay bare as bone under a May wind that lifted newspapers, sweet wrappers, empty cigarette cartons from stacked fruit crates and the gutters, and made them turn handsprings on the pavements. A cat arched its back in boredom at the green horizontal slats of a roll-up door; a stray dog rooted hopefully in a discarded package of sandwiches. An abandoned Morris Minor wore a yellow parking ticket under its windscreen wiper. A coloured man, a square of cellophane wrapped round his head like a scarf, picked his nose near the coffee stall. MacGillivray wondered whether he felt the cold of an English spring and, in wondering, wished he were elsewhere himself, somewhere warm, where that man belonged; Jamaica, Barbados, Nassau.

He looked out across the cobbles towards the main market building with its columns and clock and elaborate wire netting to defeat the pigeons, and found no pleasure in anything he saw. He rubbed the back of his head with the palm of his right hand, as he always did when he was tired or puzzled or bored, and now he was all three.

MacGillivray had been in the office since six that morning, which was early for any day and murder for Sunday, expecting a Top Secret from Rangoon. But there had been an inexplicable delay. Some vital groups of cyphers had been missed somewhere in the transcription, or lost in the air between one radio station and another.

The decoding officers with their decrypting machines were still at work in their underground air-conditioned office far beneath the Cenotaph, but no permutation of numbers or codes could produce the missing groups. He would have another half an hour to wait, probably longer, before he could know what had happened.

He hated waiting. Too much of his life had been spent passively, waiting for a suspect to crack, an agent to report, for the last elusive piece of the mosaic to drop into place. And when you had completed that puzzle, you were handed another and none of those pieces fitted at all.

MacGillivray was a tall man with red hair growing grey at the edges, hard eyes and a face that cynicism had nipped with calipers on either side of his mouth. He had seen too many cruel deaths, sent too many brave men on impossible missions to provide information that successive governments refused to believe, ever to be surprised or disillusioned. Surprise was a luxury, and on his pay he could not afford luxuries.

Sometimes he felt tired of his life, of his job, of himself; this was one of those times. Even so, he maintained a certain subdued raffishness in his dress; his green check shirt, the tweed tie, the Harris tweed suit with the two vents in the jacket. His Tricker brogues were as well polished as when he had been a colonel in the Gunners, his back as straight as when he would stand to propose the loyal toast in the Mess at Woolwich.

As second in command of DI6, the overseas branch of Her Britannic Majesty's Secret Service, with a bank overdraft he could never pull for long below £1,800, a flat he could not really afford off the Brompton Road, and a wife who, believing his job simply involved importing and exporting fruit, could never understand the extraordinary hours he (of all fruit importers and exporters) seemed forced to keep, MacGillivray felt he needed no other worries. Now these missing groups had given him one.

How could so many be missing and inevitably the most important groups at that? He turned back irritably from the window, lit one of his thin Pwe Burmese cheroots, that Weingott, the tobacconist in Fleet Street, still imported, pushed his hands deeper into the pockets of his jacket.

It was imperative that he had the whole telegram deciphered by noon, for the Prime Minister was holding a Cabinet at Chequers, and MacGillivray's chief, Sir Robert L, had assured the PM personally that the message would be there. On its arrival hung a serious political issue; should part of the Strategic Reserve be transferred from Aden farther up the Persian Gulf, or moved out altogether?

The message had originated in Aden, but to avoid direct interception it had been routed, as such secret messages often are, by way of other, seemingly unconnected cities. First, it had gone to Durban as a request for leave facilities for sixteen oil-drillers; then to Calcutta as congratulations upon the silver wedding of a tea planter leaving Assam for England; on to Rangoon as a delivery advice note regarding some second-hand AEC buses to be exported to Burma, and finally to Sensoby & Ransom as a quotation for mangoes and cans of paw-paw slices. All of which was interesting, but none of which helped him at all.

A discreet knock sounded outside his door.

'Come in,' he called, not looking over his shoulder.

The loyal Miss Jenkins, his secretary for many years, entered with a Thermos of coffee on a tray. He raised his eyebrows quizzically. She shook her head.

'No, nothing at all. I've been on to the coding room again. Not a peep. But they're rechecking back all through the route.'

MacGillivray nodded, opened a drawer in the desk, took out his round tin of shortbread with the picture of the Stag at Bay in five colours on the top. Not for the first time in his career he sympathized with the stag; he wondered if the stag would also feel sorry for him.

Miss Jenkins poured out his cup of coffee. He offered her a triangle of shortbread in return. She shook her head. This was all part of an established routine; each knew how the other would react, yet they went through it every day as though for the first time. He sipped coffee that tasted black and bitter as his own irritation, but he said nothing. It wasn't Miss Jenkins' fault; she had to get it from the machine; she had done her best.

'There's no need for you to stay,' he told her. She worked such long hours, in any case, and he felt guilty that she should be wasting another Sunday morning on his behalf. He wondered how and where she lived; somewhere with her mother, nearly bedridden, in one of the more out-lying suburbs, Catford or Croxley Green.

Presumably, she must have some private life of her own that had not been investigated by the patient detectives who continually checked on all his staff, even, he guessed, on him. But who checked on them? Quis custodiat custodes? That was an interesting point. He must ask Sir Robert about it some time. He thought how very little one ever really knew about other people, no matter how closely you worked with them, or for how long. He hoped that she knew as little about him. Miss Jenkins scattered his thoughts with a shake of her head.

'No, Colonel,' she said. 'Thank you, but I've a few things to tidy up. Also there's been a call from Sir Robert's office. He would like to see you this morning.'

'I'm sure he would,' agreed MacGillivray, irritation mounting again. 'But there's no point in my seeing him until I've cleared up this blasted telegram. It's not twelve yet, is it?'

'But it's not about the telegram. It's about something else that's just come in.'

'Why do these things always come up on a Sunday? Can't it wait?'

'His adjutant said, no. It was rather important.'

MacGillivray thought that if he were an enemy preparing to attack the West, he would do so on a Sunday morning, when offices were locked and empty, when twenty-four-hour telephones were unaccountably unstaffed, when key people who should be available were out playing golf. But there was nothing new in this: Hitler had always made his moves at the weekend for these very reasons. The Japanese had attacked both Pearl Harbor and Singapore while the defenders slept late on a Sunday morning.

He put down his coffee half-finished; he'd better see Sir Robert; he'd have to in the end.

'Where is Sir Robert now?' he asked resignedly.

'He's in his office, too.'

'That's a change,' said MacGillivray sourly, meaning it was a change from the two hundred acres of Sir Robert's farm in Wiltshire. He wondered whether he had stayed overnight in London. He could imagine his sage green Bentley Continental sighing its way over a deserted Salisbury Plain, on past Sandhurst, winging silently towards London in the early hours.

'Then I'll go round and see him,' he said. 'Ring me if those groups are found, won't you? If not, I should be back by ten-thirty.'

He picked up his tweed hat, with the fisherman's fly in the band, from the clothes horse, pulled it down on his head, went out by the side stairs to the rear of the building, climbed into his black Ford Consul. He took a different one every week from the car pool, or sometimes the same one with a different number, and an extra spotlight or a couple of car club badges. Once or twice, to his horror, he had even been given one with a tiny dangling skeleton in the middle of the rear window, or a panther on the shelf behind the rear seat.

All this was part of the regular procedure, to make identification and pursuit by an unfriendly person more difficult. But sometimes MacGillivray wondered whether it achieved anything more than confusing himself. Once, he had forgotten what colour or make of car he was driving and had to wait, late at night, in Edgware Station car park until only one car was left, and he knew it must be his.

He drove out past Covent Garden Underground Station, closed on Sunday, down an empty St Martin's Lane, across Trafalgar Square where people, even at that hour, were already feeding the pigeons, along Whitehall and into Scotland Place. He stopped, locked the car, showed his pass to the one-armed doorman with the faded First World War medals on the blue serge uniform of the Ministry of Defence, went up to the third floor.

The doors off this corridor had no numbers, but each one was painted a different colour. He knocked at an amber door, went inside. A young man, obviously a Guards officer dressed as an off-duty country landowner (which, in fact, he wasn't; his father had bought his expensive education from cash profits selling used cars off the Harrow Road) stood up respectfully when he saw MacGillivray, pressed an intercom button.

'Colonel MacGillivray to see you, sir,' he said.

'Show him in,' ordered the voice from the plastic speaker.

The green light flickered twice above the door at the far end of the room. MacGillivray went through. The door clicked shut behind him. The light would glow now until the interview was over; the door was held shut automatically by its electric locks.

Inside his office, Sir Robert was also playing the part of a country landowner, which he was. His Hawes and Curtis suit showed a puff of silk handkerchief at his left sleeve, his brogues were tanned as chestnuts after a month in the sun.

There are three of us in the act now, thought MacGillivray rather sourly; and from the looks of the others, I must be the only one without any money.

Sir Robert waved him to a chair without standing up. He was

elegantly dressed to the point of being a dandy; the gold Rolex watch on his wrist, the fine silk cord of a monocle around his neck.

'Sorry to get you round here on a Sunday,' he said, trying, but not too hard, to sound convincing. 'I stayed the night in this town - a regimental dinner. And when I looked in here this morning something struck me as rather odd.'

'Ah, yes,' said MacGillivray politely. Something also struck him as rather odd - the fact that he was sitting on that leather chair in that particular room on a May Sunday when he would infinitely rather be out on the Scottish hills; or even if not there, at least in his own flat, living an outdoor life by proxy through the estate advertisements in Country Life.

'It's not about this message from Rangoon, is it, sir?' he asked. 'We're still missing the groups. But I've organized a complete check back.'

'Oh, no, not about that,' replied Sir Robert, as though he had forgotten completely about that, which, indeed, he had. A good private income made a wonderful cushion for a poor memory. 'It's these three reports, from three different places, that I find, well - odd. What do you make of them?'

He pushed across the desk three pieces of pink flimsy on which were typed several lines by an electric typewriter in clear paragraphs without either indentation, address or signature. MacGillivray glanced through them without much interest.

He knew from the code groups that preceded each message, who had sent it. The first was from a part-time Intelligence agent, a former Lieutenant-Commander on the Reserve named Innes, who owned a hotel in the Scilly Isles. The second, from an agent in Bermuda, whose cover was a travel agency and bookshop. The third sender was a policeman they used in Nassau, McGregor.

He read them through quickly. Nothing odd about them, so far as he could see; or maybe he wasn't seeing far enough that morning?

Each message reported the sight, estimated speed and course of a westward-bound submarine, travelling on the surface by night. In the Scilly Isles, Innes had watched it under a full moon through a pair of Admiralty night-glasses. Turner, in Bermuda, had picked it up on a secret radar set concealed in the tower of a disused lighthouse that could scan the passing silhouettes of all surface and under-surface vessels within a radius of one hundred miles. McGregor reported it sceptically by hearsay from a sub-agent, who ran half-a dozen powerboats he hired out to tourists for tunny fishing.

Each report commented that the submarine carried an unusual kind of trellised mast or tower behind the fin, but no other identification, no number, no flag.

'Well, what do you make of that?' asked Sir Robert triumphantly, seeing from MacGillivray's face he could make nothing of it;

'It's just a submarine with a strange shape, sir. I don't put it very technically. Maybe it's American, or one of ours, or Canadian? They do use rather odd aerials these days with radar and sonar stuff. Perhaps that's what the trellis thing is.'

'Yes, yes,' agreed Sir Robert testily. 'No doubt. But you would agree that it could be the same submarine?'

'It would seem to be so, sir,' agreed MacGillivray cautiously.

'Don't be so bloody canny,' growled Sir Robert. 'I'm not asking you to sign anything. I'm only asking for your opinion. You know damn well that's the same sub. So do I. So I checked with the DNI (Director of Naval Intelligence). He says only one submarine he knows about answers this description. And it's not one of ours. It's in the West German Navy. Nothing revolutionary about it - quite conventional, really - except for that Eiffel Tower thing behind the fin.'

'Then, sir,' prompted MacGillivray, with a patience he did not feel. 'What is so odd?'

He was beginning to fidget about that Top Secret. At this rate, he'd be here all morning; he knew that when Sir Robert got his teeth into something that intrigued him he'd worry it like a terrier.

Sir Robert stood up, ran his thumb and finger of his right hand down to his left wrist, easing the strap of his Rolex. He looked for a moment, through the double-glazed windows, at Whitehall. Across the grey, cold tarmac, beyond two empty No. 11 buses, running in convoy, an early morning handful of rubbernecks stood feeding sugar cubes to the horses of the Horse Guards. Sir Robert turned away in distaste: God, the people who were in London these days. He was always relieved to be back on his farm; a weekend in London was a weekend in the arid wilderness of coach tours and sweet papers and grumbling, dreary families up on day trips from heaven only knew where; or cared.

'Do you remember, that two weeks ago,' he said slowly, during a NATO naval exercise in the North Sea, there was an accident?'

'Vaguely,' said MacGillivray, which meant he didn't. Two weeks ago he'd been worried about the non-arrival of a Top Secret from Vladivostock. Why the hell should he be expected to be an expert on what had happened in some ridiculous North Sea exercise as well? From the things they expected him to know, they should be paying him treble the money. And if he had treble the money, be knew the sort of life he'd lead, the house he'd buy in Peebles or Sutherland. Acres of .land, with a long, rolling, open view across the purple hills, streams clear as gin, bubbling over rocks. Which reminded him: he hadn't rung about that Kirriemuir place. He'd get on to the estate agents - not the secret agents (to hell with them) - on Monday. The thought cheered him, for even though he might never be able to buy such an estate, it was somehow comforting to know that they still existed. MacGillivray spent one half of his life in the phantasmagorical reality of espionage, the other half seeking an equally phantom dream; the perfect house he would never find, for if he did he could not afford it; and if he could he would pass it by because then he would have nothing left in life to want. But Sir Robert was talking again. Sir Robert was always talking, just when he wanted to think.

'I couldn't quite catch that, sir,' MacGillivray said. 'My ear.'

'Bugger your ear,' retorted Sir Robert inelegantly. He was also more worried than he admitted: he did not usually use such words. He thought their use showed a lack of taste, and surely no one could accuse him of that?

'What's on your mind - that Rangoon business or one of those damned houses of yours? I'll repeat what I said. There was an accident during this exercise. A trawler or some other ship no-one seemed to have noticed before - though why, God only knows, with all the radar and stuff they carry nowadays — collided with a Naval vessel, which sank immediately with all hands.

'This was in the early hours, in a heavy sea mist. And what with the confusion and general shambles, the trawler disappeared. Perhaps it didn't even know it had hit anything. That's happened before. Well, this Naval vessel was never recovered. They found a big oil patch and bits and pieces of junk floating about later in the day, and it was presumed it had gone to the bottom in one of the deepest parts of the North Sea.'

He paused.

'Well?' asked MacGillivray, throwing the word into the silence, knowing how Sir Robert liked a cue to help him reach a dramatic climax.

'Well,' echoed Sir Robert triumphantly. 'That vessel was the German submarine Seehund. The only submarine known to exist with a mast like this - in fact, the only sub in that whole exercise.

'So we have an interesting situation, MacGillivray. A German submarine sunk with all hands. The vessel never recovered. A memorial service held in Bonn for the crew. All the NATO countries expressing their regrets with the bereaved. An official inquiry is ordered, and now, only weeks later, this same submarine - and it can be no other, for no other answers to this very clear description - is seen first in the Scilly Isles, then passing Bermuda, and finally off Nassau. Answer me that if you can, eh?'

MacGillivray shook his head; this just wasn't his day. Perhaps no day was ever going to be his again.

'And that's not all,' Sir Robert went on. 'Half a dozen bodies were washed up; one or two very badly smashed about the head, almost as though they'd been clubbed. I've seen the photographs.

'Then last night the DNI was a guest of honour at the dinner. Sat next to him. He told me another body had surfaced - they take a while to come up usually, you know. This was the coxswain. Apparently, he, appeared to have been shot several times. So maybe this wasn't just a simple accident at sea after all. Maybe it was something else.'

'Like what?' asked MacGillivray.

"That's what we'll have to discover. When we find what that sub is doing.'

To avoid the impossibility of saying something when he didn't have anything to say, MacGillivray pulled the notes towards him, read them through for a second time. Under the one from McGregor was another smaller sheet he had not noticed before. He read this, too.

332/509/125 routine informative stop English physician dr jason love of hishops combe somerset holidaying here in villa beechwood belonging to thomas newborough of same somerset village claims friendship with dr stop subject not known here believed travelling mexico was in boat when cuban girl was shot from shore stop report of incident following stop subsequently subject was attacked by six local strongarms but rescued by police stop strongarms under interrogation claim paid ten dollars each to take him aboard unnamed yacht due nassau stop unable make contact any such vessel stop please advise soonest whether subject bluffing in friendship claim with dm also whether clean or involved endit.

'That must be Dr Love, our friend of Teheran and Shahnagar,' said MacGillivray. 'There can be no other doctor with that name in a place the size of Hishop's Combe.'

Sir Robert pulled the paper to him again and re-read the paragraph. He scowled. He remembered his experiences with Dr Love in Persia and the Himalayas.

'You speak for yourself,' he said shortly. 'He's certainly no friend of mine. So far as I'm concerned he should have stayed in Hishop's bloody Combe. And he's not involved with us.'

He looked up suddenly, an awful thought occurring to him.

'He isn't, is he, Mac?'

MacGillivray shook his head.

'Not so far as I know, sir. All the same, I wonder why anyone in Nassau would want to beat him up - unless they thought he might be. Intriguing, isn't it?'

'Very,' said Sir Robert with heavy sarcasm. 'But you haven't given me your views on this sub. What do you feel about it?'

And so depressed did MacGillivray feel he almost told him.

*   *   *

Shaven priests in a Burmese temple were beating a brass gong with golden hammers, and making a good job of it. Their blows sent splinters of sound through Love's head.

He rolled on his side away from the noise, opened his eyes. The alarm clock near his bed trembled with the fury of its bell. He reached out, switched it off. The priests vanished with their hammers. Seven o'clock. Another day. Every day in every way, I am getting better and better. Emile Coue True or false? False as hell. Every day in every conceivable way he felt worse and worse.

As he sat up, the telephone rang. He picked up the receiver; it only wanted a patient to be on the other end with some rambling tale of vague pains which moved all over his body, and his day would be made. But it was McGregor's voice that spoke into his ear.

'So you lived the night?' he said.

'Only just,' said Love. 'It's the morning that bothers me.'

'Isn't it always? I'm ringing to confirm you're on the nine o'clock plane to Miami. It's a BOAC 707 from Bermuda. Change at Miami to an Aeronaves de Mexico. There's a good connection. Just in case you have any serious enemies, your seat's booked in the name of Clarke. No more on this open line now. If you have any interesting experiences, give me a shout. You know my number. See you on your way back, maybe?'

'Maybe,' said Love. 'And thanks.'

His suitcase was already packed; he had only to bathe and shave, to face Ebenezer's excellently prepared breakfast of coffee, hot rolls and honey, and fried eggs. He found this no hardship. Afterwards, he felt almost human again; not quite, but moving slowly in that direction.

'You'll be wanting a taxi, sah?' Ebenezer asked him.

Love nodded. Never stand when you can sit, never sit when you can lie down; never speak when a nod will do. Good advice for everyone, including doctors.

'I'll ask around for you, sah.'

'Do that thing,' said Love.

Like so many bachelors, he had foibles: one was that he loathed being late at any airport. When the time on a ticket advised him to be there half an hour before the plane left, he liked to make it an hour just in case he had a puncture on the way, or the road was being repaired, or some such thing.

The taxi arrived, a bronze, four head-lamped Ford Galaxy. The driver was equipped for both worlds with an ivory crucifix dangling from his mirror, a transistor radio stuck to the dashboard with Sellotape. He was a slightly built man wearing gold-rimmed sun glasses, a loose alpaca jacket, shoes stamped with ventilating holes.

Love climbed into the back seat, palmed a note to Ebenezer, who accepted it professionally without looking down to check its denomination, and they were off.

'How long does it take to the airport?' asked Love.

They were going to Windsor Field, named after the King who had become a Duke and then Governor of the Bahamas during the war.

'Maybe twenty minutes. There's not much on the road at this time.'

They cut into the centre of the island, and the houses fell away. The road grew high banks, tufted with speary, dusty grass. To the right, they passed Lake Cunningham, then Oakes Field, the former airport, named after Sir Harry Oakes, a millionaire whose murder in 1943 was still unsolved. A few small trucks swung towards them packed with workmen in floppy hats singing cheerful calypsos, and one or two cars; otherwise, the road lay empty as a collection plate.

Suddenly, beyond the long silver of the lake, the driver pulled over to the left of the road. Thick dust shrouded the car like fog, as he bumped over a rutted track into a disused quarry. He switched off the engine; the car rocked thankfully on its springs, dust settling over them like a subsiding sandstorm.

'What's wrong?' asked Love.

'My mistake, sah,' the man explained. 'I told my boss we needed a full tank, but he's forgotten to fill up. I have a tin of petrol in the boot, sah.'

He climbed out. It was nothing serious, then. Love thought it was lucky he wasn't pressed for time, lit a Gitane and watched dust motes dance on the long, bronze bonnet. He heard the boot lid open and clang shut behind him, then the driver was standing by the rear door. Love wound down his window. What was wrong?

'Can you get out and help me, sah? I've a bad hand. I can't undo the cap of the tin.'

'Surely.'

Love opened the back door, swung out his legs, stood up.

'Where is it?'

'Here.'

The driver's voice was tight as a g-string; sweat varnished his forehead. He was standing barely two yards from Love. In his right hand he gripped a .35 Lüger, as though he knew how to use it.

'What's that?' said Love stupidly, looking at the gun. The open muzzle looked back at him. 'Where's the petrol tin?'

'There's no tin,' said the man. 'Put your hands up.'

Love raised them; that Lüger was a good persuader; but he kept his elbows in to his sides.

'What do you want?' he asked. 'Money? My passport?'

The man jerked his head to one side.

'Come away from the car,' he said brusquely.

His voice was flat and dead now, the voice of a man whose mind was made up. So he was going to kill him, Love thought, but, first he needed him away from the car so that he could shoot without the bullet marking the door. But why pick on him? For the same reason as the men had ambushed him last night?

Love glanced briefly around the quarry with its small pyramids of stones, its convenient quilt of dust. This would be a perfect burial place. He felt his skin prickle under his shirt. He'd never imagined travelling to his own funeral in a Ford Galaxy. He didn't like to think of it now.

'Why are you doing this?' he asked, playing for time, because there was just the thinnest chance that some other car might come into the quarry. But the chance was too thin to survive. From where he stood he couldn't even hear the sparse traffic on the highway. They were out of sound as well as sight.

'Do as I say,' said the driver sharply. 'I haven't got all day.'

If I don't get out of this, thought Love bleakly, I'll have all eternity. It seemed altogether too long. He moved slightly to one side and felt the edge of die open rear door against his left thigh.

'Hurry,' said the driver.

'Where do you want me to stand?' asked Love quietly, moving his head to the left and right, to show his willingness to move. The man jerked his revolver slightly towards the left, towards the front of the car.

'There,' he said. 'Over there.'

As the man's eyes left Love's for that fraction of a second, Love brought up his left leg behind him, kicked shut the door. In the confined space of the quarry, the bang seemed an explosion.

Love swung to his right, knocked away the Lüger with his left elbow, twisted it out of his hand, at the same time drove his right knee up into the driver's groin.

The man went down on all fours. To make sure he had no inflated ideas above his station, Love seized him by the collar, dragged him up, gave him a straight left to the jaw. He dropped and did not move. Love massaged his muscles, stood up.

The gunman's sun glasses had come off in the fight. His face blank in unconsciousness as a page without print, meant nothing to Love; he never wanted to see it again. He opened the man's jacket; the pockets were empty, but on the left breast of his shirt a name was embroidered in red cotton: Garcia. Love dusted himself down, dragged Garcia to the back of the car, threw him inside. He picked up the Lüger, checked that it was loaded, slid it into his own jacket pocket. Then he climbed in behind the wheel.

The key was still in the ignition lock. He started the car, drove out on to the wide grey ribbon of road, kept on driving until the airport signs came up. He parked at the side of the airport, near the red and blue and silver private aircraft of the millionaires, took his suitcase out of the boot, threw the Lüger in its place, slammed down the lid. He found an old raincoat in the back of the car, pulled this over Garcia, so that he would be screened from any rubberneck. Then Love went to the men's room, took off his jacket and brushed it, washed himself, smoothed down his hair, and checked in at the airline counter. He still had several minutes in hand, so he used them to ring McGregor.

'Your most regular caller,' he said, when the inspector came on the line. 'People will think we're in love. Look. A man, with the name Garcia sewn on his shirt, picked me up in a Ford Galaxy this morning to bring me out here to the airport. I thought it was an ordinary taxi - like I'd ordered. Seemingly, it wasn't.

'On the way, he drove into a quarry, ordered me out of the car, and wanted to shoot me.'

'And did he?'

'No.'

'Where is he now?'

'Unconscious in the back of the car at the airport here. It might be an idea to send someone out to pick him up. I've only got minutes before my plane leaves or I'd wait.'

'Will do. What's the car number?'

'I didn't get it. But it's die only bronze Galaxy here. You can't miss it. Possibly the only Galaxy with a body in it, for that matter. And the man's gun is in the boot.'

'Thank you, doctor. I hope the rest of your trip is a bit less, ah, turbulent.'

'You can say that again,' said Love, and rang off before McGregor could.

CHAPTER FOUR: MEXICO CITY AND DUR-ANGO, MEXICO

Mexico City stood on its end - a sweep of white concrete cubes, a wider glitter of glass, of lakes, avenues and parks, ringed in by smoke-blue hills - as Love's Aeronaves de Mexico 707 banked to land.

He sat resignedly through the usual wait, while steps were wheeled out, unseen mechanics shouted incomprehensible orders in an unknown tongue, and passengers coagulated impatiently and pointlessly in the gangway. Then a walk through a sloping tunnel into the long, pillared hall of the airport. The sun was shining, but it was light without heat; the air felt chilled, possibly because of the altitude.

An illuminated sign spelled out the time, 13.50 on a rooftop, and beneath this a neon blazed: 'Bien venido a Mexico.' Love hoped the welcome was sincere; after his experiences in Nassau he could use some sweetness and friendship. On a stall of tourists' souvenirs - Mexican copper bracelets, leather belts, ceramic ashtrays - he noticed a track of black beetles, each tied by one leg to a fine gold chain on a brooch. Living ornaments. Buy one now and watch it live, move, grow. And die. Welcome to Mexico.

Love waited for his bags to come up on the conveyor, then hailed a yellow Chrysler taxi with jagged black teeth painted on a central white band around its body, told the driver, the Bamer Hotel.

The main roads were wide and impressive four lanes of traffic each way. At intersections traffic lights flickered from red to green with instructions: 'Alto' and 'Paso'. The Bamer faced a park where jets of water poured endlessly into a circular pool, never filling it, like some arithmetical problem from Love's boyhood involving running taps and a leaky bath.

An old man sat on an upturned box under a palm tree, near the pool. In front of him, on another box, he had spread out slices of pineapple on palm leaves. What he couldn't sell, he ate. He'd got things both ways, thought Love, as the porter carried in his bags. A good example of the double-headed penny technique. If he couldn't have a profit, at least he had a meal.

'Ah, yes, Dr Love,' said the clerk at the reception desk opposite the circular lounge, as he signed the register. 'There is already a letter for you.'

'For me?'

Love was surprised. In a mirrored wall, he saw himself open the thick manilla envelope.

'Dear Senor Love,' he read. 'It is with very great regret that I have to inform you that the vintage car rally has had to be postponed for a few days.

'This has been done at the request of the Police Commissioner since, in view of the imminent elections - unexpected when plans for our rally were first announced - it is felt, quite wrongly in the view of our committee, that some people may use the occasion for political demonstration. Consequently, all processions, and other gatherings likely to attract crowds, have been postponed until after the election. I have telegraphed to your home in England with this news, but I am writing now in case you left home before my cable arrived.

'I regret this postponement when you have come such a long distance, but since the elections will be held on Wednesday, we intend to hold our rally on the following Saturday.

'In the meantime, should you be, as you English say, at a loose end, I will be very happy to offer you hospitality at my house in Mazatlan. I know from our correspondence that you are a Cord enthusiast, and I have here a Cord 812 Phaeton and a Duesenberg

Town Car with a Murphy body which might interest you. If the writer can be of any service to you, he is yours to command. Fraternally, Pietro Gomez.'

'Damn that,' said Love. He hadn't even known an election was being held in Mexico; so much for the news service of the papers he read, or the attention he gave to them. Anyway, now he was here, he could see some of the sights, such as the new University, the National Museum of Anthropology with its 20-ton Aztec calendar or the floating gardens of Xochimilco. Or he might even take up Gomez's invitation, wherever Mazatlan might be. All was not gloom.

'Is it bad news, senor?' the clerk asked solicitously, watching his face. 'Can I help you?'

Love shook his head; then he remembered something.

'Yes. You could. The number of Senor Alcantara's room. I've brought a parcel for him.'

'Senor Alcantara? One moment, if you please.'

The clerk put on a pair of reading glasses," inspected the register at the back of his office, then consulted a sheaf of private messages held in a spring clip.

'Here we are, senor. I'm afraid that Senor Alcantara is not in this hotel.'

'But he must be,' said Love. 'Only a few hours ago I saw his wife. She asked me to bring this parcel.'

'Ah, yes, we are expecting him. But in the meantime he's out of the city.'

'Where out of the city?'

'He's at Durango. A house called the Casa del Sol, Avenida del Sol.'

'Where's Durango ?'

'A city five hundred and seventy miles to the north-west, senor.

Capital of Durango State. A mining centre. It has a solid mountain of iron. El Cerro del Mercade. All metal. Very unusual.'

'Very,' agreed Love; he was learning geography if nothing else.

'How can one get there?'

'By auto-bus. Or you can fly. That is the quickest way, of course. We can book you a ticket with the travel agent's desk here. If you leave in the early morning you will be in Durango by lunchtime. Shall I make you a reservation?'

'I'll think about it,' said Love. 'And while we're on the geography of this country, where's Mazatlan?'

'On the west coast, Senor. About a hundred and thirty miles from Durango. We could book you a round ticket, all the way. No extra charge.'

'I'll think about that, too.'

Love went up to his room, had a bath, changed, looked out of the window and thought about it. He had three days to kill. One of them might as well die in Durango. Then he could go on to the coast, see Pietro Gomez's cars and come back. It would be more pleasant to be out of the capital during an election, in any case. The attractions of Mexico City could await his return.

He rang down and told the clerk to book him on the first plane to Durango, then on to Mazatlan. It was due out, the man told him, at six o'clock on the following morning; and he had booked Love into a very good hotel, the best, senor, in Durango, the Posada Duran.

Love drove to the airport through empty streets washed with morning light. The air felt cold, rinsed by altitude; it was like breathing near a block of ice. On the souvenir counter the same black beetles crawled painfully at the end of their gold chains; they must have had a sleepless night. The lights over most of the airline desks were not lit; Mexico City airport is not busy at that hour.

A small four-engined plane was warming up on the tarmac. He was to fly to Torreon, and then change for Durango. The plane was not full; half a dozen passengers smoked cheroots and chattered to each other excitedly. A plump hostess served black coffee and hiscuits as the desert unfolded beneath them, brown and sandy, striped by straight roads lined with trees.

The sun burned like an Aztec print, a poached egg in the sky. The desert flowed into foothills, a few buildings and walls painted yellow ochre, the colour of the dry earth. Isolated trees and towers threw long shadows on the ground and left them there. Windows in scattered houses caught the sun and winked at Love as though he also knew their secrets.

From the air, Torreon stood at the centre of a desert, seemingly without beginning, without end. From the ground, it looked little more interesting. A few burros stood, heads down, tethered in the car park. He waited for the next plane on the airport's Moorish verandah, behind a screen of privet hedge, while heat made the tarmac tremble, like a mirror of liquid glass.

The plane on to Durango was even smaller; two engines instead of four. If we're going much farther, he thought, I'll be flying myself, going through the motions, intrepid birdman. Only two passengers were with him now; a woman who sat pessimistically with her air-sickness paper bag open on her knee and an adenoidal man in a creased suit, with brown and white crocodile skin shoes, a spare suit on a hanger in a plastic bag. He wore yellow eyes to match his yellow teeth, and whistled as he breathed.

The plane bucked and dipped wearily in unseen eddies. The woman made noisy use of her paper bag, and all the while the door dividing the passenger compartment from the pilot, banged to and fro unceasingly, giving cut-off and unreassuring glimpses of dials and lights and switches. Love was glad when, at last, they were running down into Durango, beyond a rim of hills, rusty brown from iron in their earth.

A cluster of old taxis huddled hopefully at the little airport. A mariachi band, small brown men with black moustaches, playing on unpolished trumpets, saxophones, tubas, in a blare of defiant brass, made Herb Alpert sound as though his men used mutes. The mariachi beat would have made the dead dance. It even cheered up the woman with the paper bag, and took years off Love's age.

He hired a yellow-topped de Soto cab, told the driver, the Posada Duran, and sat back thankfully, glad to be on land again.

Loose gravel chips rattled like gun-fire on the underside of the car as the driver tried to force the throttle pedal through the floor with his foot. Outcrops of rock scarred the landscape, rashes of rust on the hills. Here and there, a distant pool of water, still as a glass sheet, caught the sun and threw it in his eyes. On the highest hill stood a cross, black against the blue sky, fluffed by the clouds of morning. Then they were running into the town along a main road with curved lamp-posts in a central strip of shrubs and cactus plants.

The Posada Duran was a Moorish type of hotel built around a courtyard. In the middle of this yard a man in bare feet was cleaning out a round ornamental pond. Fat carp and bloated goldfish fluttered iridescent sides in inches of water.

Love booked in at the office, was given room No. 12, on the first floor, in a corner near the balcony overlooking the courtyard. The ceiling was unusually high, and, like the rest of the room, of stained wood; it reminded Love vaguely of a church. He hung up his spare suit, went downstairs to lunch on turtle steak, a Blanca Carta beer.

It didn't feel any too easy to digest; or maybe the altitude had some odd effect on the enzymes. He asked the man behind the desk for the whereabouts of the Casa del Sol; the sooner he had delivered his parcel and was in Mazatlan, the better. He'd like to see a Cord again. And a Murphy-bodied Duesenberg town car was something he had yet to see; there wasn't one left in Britain.

'Is it a big house, senor?' the clerk asked him, picking his teeth with a match, examining what he found as though it could be valuable.

'I don't know,' admitted Love. 'I believe that a Senor Alcantara lives there.'

'It's a very common name,' pointed out the clerk unenthusiastically. 'There are several houses called Casa del Sol. But only one of them is rented by foreign people. They take it for a week, two weeks, a month. And you are a foreign person, senor, so perhaps that is the one you seek? You go down the main street outside this hotel for several blocks, maybe a mile, maybe more. Then you will see the Avenida del Sol. It crosses over the main road. You will find the house on that street.'

The afternoon was still sunny, but the wind had turned cold, drying Love's nostrils as he breathed. The dust felt like fine wire in his nose. A middle-aged man pushed an ancient crone along the road in a crude wheelchair; her face wrinkled and dry as a tortoise's neck; only her eyes showed life, bright as black evil beads. His mother? Or his mother-in-law?

He passed open-fronted shops full of spare ribs and red blocks of roast meat; stalls piled high with oranges, candy, pineapples.

The main street was the Avenida 20 Nqvembre, the date of their Revolution, Love knew, but which, and when? Not for the first time, he wished he had paid more attention to history lessons as a boy.

The wind sandpapered Love's face as he walked. Amber-haired dogs turned rusty, distrustful eyes on him and cringed away until he had passed them. It was a feast day of some kind; children in white blouses were marching along behind banners and a crucifix covered with flowers. Soldiers in American style uniforms, with shirts tucked into their belts, watched it under the long yellow wall of the jail. Above their heads, guards with carbines stood in iron-roofed sentry boxes.

Some shops were closed, their grey and green shutters carefully rolled down like the tops of giant bureaux; wires criss-crossed the street against the blue sky. He saw a number of interesting old American cars; an Auburn Phaeton trundled past slowly, then a Hupmobile, even a Pierce Arrow with its strange headlamps sunk into the front wings like the wild, staring eyes of some enormous metal owl. He must see whether he could find any spares for his Cord. He needed a spare set of first and reverse gears; they had been one of the weaker points in the original design. If these other old cars had survived, no doubt a few Cords would also be around. And maybe he could find a few car nameplates to add to his collection of forgotten makes that decorated the hall of his home in Somerset.

He was thinking about this and so nearly missed the Avenida del Sol, a cross-street that ran out into scrubland amid the shells of rusty motor bodies, and cactus plants.

The houses along it were single-storied, ringed in by high garden walls with broken bottles cemented on the top. Every window wore a wrought iron grille. The Casa del Sol was the third house down from the main road, with red Moorish tiles, an arched verandah that framed the glitter of a blue-tiled pool. Its iron gates were closed.

Through their vertical bars Love saw an automatic sprinkler turn back and forth on the lawn like an arm beckoning to him across the yellow, tufted grass. A gardener in ragged khaki trousers and shirt prodded a flower-bed with a hoe as though it had done him an injury. Let into one gatepost was a square ceramic tile with an image of the sun on it, and underneath this the name of the house, then a round metal grille and a bellpush. Love pushed the button.

Through the grille a woman's voice spoke in Spanish to him. Love let her finish her lines, then bent down and spoke into the grille himself.

'I have a parcel for Senor Alcantara,' he said in English.

'Tengo un paquete para el Senor Alcantara,' he repeated. He had worked this out with the aid of a guide book of Spanish phrases and felt rather proud of it.

A pause, a metallic click, and the whine of hidden motors as the gates opened automatically. Love walked up the short path, climbed the marble steps to the front verandah. A middle-aged woman in blue denim overalls, with half a dozen keys on a ring at her belt, stood waiting for him on the top step. She threw a mouthful of Spanish words at him. He shook his head. She obviously thought he knew far more Spanish than he did. So much for vanity. .

'No hablo Espagnol,' he told her regretfully.'

'Uno momento.' She held up one hand. Her bare feet made no sound on the marble floor, but the keys jangled as she walked. She returned with a younger man, brown skinned, eyes bright as polished currants, hair cropped down to his skull.

'Please?' he asked in English.

'Good afternoon,' said Love, feeling absurdly like a door-to-door salesman. 'My name is Love - Dr Jason Love. I've got a parcel here for Senor Alcantara. From his wife in Nassau. It's a book.'

The man slid his eyes down to the direction of the parcel and back again to Love's face.

'A book?' he repeated, as though the word was new to him, and he liked the sound of it. 'For Senor Alcantara? I don't think...' He paused, and added, 'I don't know that he's here just now. Perhaps he is just coming?'

'Well, whether he is or he isn't, I've got this book for him'

'You are English?'

'Yes.'

'Your first visit to Mexico?'

'It is.'

'When I speak to Senor Alcantara, I'll tell him. And thank you. And where are you staying, so that we can contact you if need be?'

'The Posada Duran.' Love handed over the parcel. The man took it reluctantly, examined the address, then held it up slowly to his ear as though he expected to hear something, through the brown paper.

'Goodbye, senor.'

The man bowed, the woman closed the door. As Love walked back down the drive, the gardener did not look up. The gates closed silently behind him and locked themselves. Well, that was that. Now he had the rest of the day to kill. The morning plane could take him on to Mazatlan.

An old Packard eight coupe barrelled along the road past. him, then a model A Ford, and a Hispano, a rarity, still with its fly-ing stork mascot, copied from the badge Georges Guynemer, a French ace of the First World War, had painted on his Hispano-Suiza engined planes. Durango's clear air, dry climate and high altitude must all have helped to preserve woodwork frames that would otherwise have rotted.

Love stood irresolute at a cross-roads, wondering which way to walk. Sometimes, when he was in a strange town, he would just follow his nose, and like hunters after other antiques, he had by this means ferreted out treasures in unlikely places. Once he had discovered an Isotta Fraschini in a shed behind a cafe on the Nice to Cannes road; on another occasion, one of the very rare 1929 Mercedes SSK's, still in its original white paint, in a barn near Wick, in the north of Scotland.

Anyway, whether he found anything now for his Cord or not, to look would be an agreeable way of passing the afternoon. From where he stood, he could only imagine one more pleasant way, and that was impossible.

As he waited for the traffic lights to change, the small man, who had been walking behind him on soundless sorbo rubber soles, touched him tentatively on the left arm.

'Excuse me, senor,' he began deprecatingly, 'Por favor.'

'What do you want?' asked Love, instinctively fearing some hard luck story, a touch.

'You are a stranger here, senor?' The man answered his question with another.

'I am.'

'Then I, José Manuel, am here to help you. There are many pleasant sights in Durango, much to interest the tourist. I can arrange a car trip. Somewhere to eat?' He smiled, man to man. 'Perhaps a friend to pass the afternoon?'

'No,' said Love firmly. 'Thank you very much. But I have all the friends I need.' And the enemies, too, he thought, but didn't add.

The lights flicked to red, and he began to cross the road. The man followed, dropping into step, half a pace behind him.

'Is there any way I can help you, senor? This is my town. I was born here. And my father before me. You are American gentleman?'

'No. English.'

They had reached the other side of the road now. Which way should he go? On the impulse, he turned to the man.

'I'll tell you how you can help me,' he said. 'In England I have an old American car, a Cord. I'm looking for somewhere that might have one of these cars, maybe a wrecker's yard. I need some spares. You don't know such a place, I suppose?'

The man's eyelids fluttered like the wings of frightened moths.

'But of course I do,' he said triumphantly. 'It's only two blocks from here.'

'Then I'd be very grateful if you would show me.'

'It is my pleasure. This way, if you please.'

Again he fell into step. They turned up a side street, dry and crumbling with heat and inertia. Women carried babies wrapped in striped Indian rugs or blankets with flaps to shield their heads. The altitude made Love's heart thump uncomfortably. „

'How much farther?' he asked.

'It is just here, senor.'

They turned down an unmade alley between two high mud walls. To their right, a stone propped open a wooden gate. Beyond this lay a graveyard of ancient cars. Love paused for a moment, gazing incredulously at the treasure trove.

Here was a blown Graham with the forward-facing radiator that had anticipated the Jaguar Mark Ten by thirty years. Next to this, a 110 Talbot, its huge Rotax headlamps like giant eyes too close together, a Marendaz Special with the two outside exhaust pipes; a Sunbeam Dawn, the horse-shoe radiator of a Bugatti, the heel-shapely radiator of a Delahaye; a Horch half under a tarpaulin; an Essex Super Six with wooden spoked wheels. And, lurking at the back, covered by a curved sheet of corrugated iron, the familiar coffin-shaped Cord bonnet, blunt as a bottle-nosed whale.

This was for him. Love walked through the gateway, but José Manuel pulled nervously at the sleeve of his jacket.

'Here it is, senor. But we must meet the owner first. He's a friend of mine. Senor Kernau. He is in his house.'

'You go and see him,' said Love. 'I'll stay here.' They wouldn't believe him back in England if he told them of these machines in this condition. He wouldn't have believed it himself unless he had seen them. 'I'll wait for you.'

'No, no, senor. That is not possible. You must see Senor Kernau in his house. It is the custom.'

'All right,' said Love reluctantly, with a bad grace, 'but let's not horse about.' He had only one day here in Durango, and he wanted to spend it here, not chatting up some senor.

His eyes caught a V.12 Lagonda with an unusual roadster body, nestling by the side of a scarlet Fiat Balilla. What make of car was not represented here?

'It will not take a moment, senor, I assure you. He always likes to meet Englishmen. Originally, he came from Europe himself.'

José Manuel led Love fifty yards past the gate to another in the wall. Behind this was a yard, then a house wearing ornate metal grilles-over its back windows. Their design seemed familiar to Love. Then he remembered; he had seen them on the front windows of the Casa del Sol. This was the back entrance; what a coincidence that the owner of the wrecker's yard should live here!

A Mexican watchman holding a six-foot stave dozed on a rope mattress frame, just inside the doorway. He stood up, made a vague gesture of salute to José. They spoke rapidly in Spanish. The watchman nodded towards the house. As José rang the bell, the watchman closed the gate behind them.

The woman who had opened the front door to Love led them across a black marble floor, past cactus plants that threw up thick green fingers from open-mouthed stone pots. Although they had met only minutes before, she gave no sign of recognition. The house was hollow: Love looked through a glass wall, at a small courtyard where a fountain played and fish moved lazily like plump golden torpedoes. There were some cane chairs, a table, a wicker settee. Senior Kernau must be a most successful car wrecker; or maybe old cars were just his hobby?

The woman knocked on a matt-black door, slid it on silent rollers to one side. The walls of the room within were covered with pale green hessian; four or five black leather chairs were grouped around a Swedish semi-circular table with a swivel chair- behind it. On the table stood two telephones, a small

Mexican flag on a silver stand. Through the parallel slats of the Sunblind over the long window behind it, Love could see the hills tremble in the distance, blue under the afternoon sun.

The door slid closed behind them. Love glanced at José Manuel. His face was twitching. Was he ill, or was he just a nervous little man, anxious to please everyone, the small fellow in a big man's world?

Another door slid open in the left-hand wall. Two men came through, closed it carefully behind them, as though it was important to do so. They were of middle height, middle aged, very broad shouldered, with hair cut close to their skulls, like a faint powdering of grey dust. Their faces were pale and set, like masks in wax; they seemed as cheerful as morticians at a convention. These were not the sort of car wreckers Love knew from his experience of the genus in Somerset. He glanced at José Manuel again; his hands were now trembling visibly. What the devil was the matter with him? Was he going to have a fit?

The first man sat down at the table. His companion stood to his right, hands clasped behind his back, watching Love. His eyes were two grey pebbles in his face.

José Manuel said nothing, so Love introduced himself.

'You must be Senor Kernau?' he said. 'I am Dr Jason Love. From England.'

The man behind the table nodded.

'We know,' he said.

'How?' asked Love.

'You told the houseboy here. That's how.'

Of course, it was obvious; he had forgotten.

'Then maybe you know Senor Alcantara?'

The man shook his head.

'No, but you brought a parcel for him. A book. I was very inter-ested in this. I am interested in Senor Alcantara's welfare, and indeed in everything to do with him. So I asked our friend here' - a tiny nose towards José - 'to bring you here.'

'Really?' said Love nettled. 'He told me I was coming to see the owner of the car breaker's yard.'

The man at the desk allowed himself a brief smile, as though he was rationed to one a year, and this was the once-a-year day; even undertakers must have their little jokes.

'Very possibly,' he allowed. 'And if you had wanted to see Mexican pottery, or some Indian carvings, or even if you had wanted a pretty girl, then my man here' - again the almost im-perceptible nod towards José - 'would have assured you that he could accommodate your wish. He would have brought you here in any case. I must regret disappointing you, Dr Love, but I have nothing to do with the rash of old cars that disfigures this road.'

'Then what's all this in aid of?' asked Love.

'That's what we hope you will be able to tell us,' said Kernau smoothly.

He bent down, opened a drawer, lifted out the parcel Love had brought.

'Shall we open it together, doctor?' he asked gently.

'Do what you like with it,' said Love angrily. What kind of ri-diculous set-up was this? He looked angrily at José Manuel; he did not meet his glance.

Kernau picked up a silver paper-knife, first slit the string, then the manilla envelope. He shook the book out on to the desk. Carefully, he removed the dust cover, held it up to the window behind him as though trying to see through it. Then he picked up the book by its spine, shook the pages. They fanned out; a few grains of paper fell like minute snowflakes on to his blotter. So some bookworms were getting something out of all this. Good luck to them, thought Love. It was more than he had managed.

'Now then, doctor, what is this book?'

'I've told you. A book Senor Alcantara's wife asked me to bring to him. It is quite rare, possibly valuable.'

'Value is relative, doctor.'

'For God's sake, don't give me these aphorisms. We are simply wasting each other's time. And since I have only an afternoon in Durango I don't want to spend it all here.'

'Not so hastily, doctor. We are not quite finished. What else is in that book?'

'I've told you. Nothing,' said Love. 'Why can't you leave it to the man to whom it's addressed?'

Kernau opened the book again, and placing his right hand firmly down on the pages, pulled gently at the leather cover. The binding held. He began to cut through the thread carefully, precisely, like a surgeon, until the spine fell away. Then he lifted the cover, smoothed both the outside and inside with his palms, pressed it face down on the desk so that the five raised ribs on the spine were uppermost.

Then he began to slit the top rib. Inside was a piece of twine used as packing. He picked this out with tweezers, laid it on the table. Love watched him, fascinated. What was he up to - and why?

Kernau picked open the second rib with equal care. This time, his eyes narrowed; he gave a little grunt of triumph. Inside lay a thin wire, an inch long, attached to a green and black capsule, the size of a phenobarbitone tablet.

'So,' he said triumphantly, holding this up between the tweezers. 'So, doctor. Here we have the reason Senor Alcantara wishes to receive a very old book.'

'Which is?'

'But you must know,' said Kernau, looking up at him with his pale blue eyes. 'Wait one moment.'

He opened a silver cigarette box, placed the capsule and wire inside, closed the lid carefully.

'Now,' he said. 'We can talk. That little mechanism, as you must know, is a transmitter. It would have broadcast everything we might have to say to each other, possibly anything anyone said in the whole house for, perhaps, as long as a week.

'The messages would be picked up by a receiver somewhere within a mile or two of here. But in that metal box it will be screened and quite harmless.

'Now, it doesn't altogether surprise me that someone has seen fit to introduce such a very rudimentary listening device into my house. What I'd like to know is why it had to be you, apparently an English country doctor on holiday? With, it seems, a taste for old and useless automobiles?'

He paused.

'I don't know what the hell you're talking about,' said Love. 'I've told you all I know. Senora Alcantara in Nassau asked me to bring this book to her husband. All this talk of listening devices is meaningless to me.'

Then he remembered her interest in the flower in his lapel, the way she had turned on the electric mixer. Perhaps that flower had also contained something like this? Perhaps she had simply used him as a courier to bring this other transmitter. But why?

Kernau saw doubts written on his face.

'You sound very convincing,' he said, 'but I feel you are having second thoughts. We've checked your background, and there certainly is a Dr Jason Love in Somerset. Maybe you are that man. Maybe you're not. It is immaterial. What we want to know is why you are here. And who sent you.'

'I've told you,' began Love, and stopped. He was beginning to feel like a Kafka character, an actor thrown on a stage in the middle of Act II without knowing what had happened in Act I. What use were words except to lead him farther into this meaningless maze?

'I see. So you are obdurate. Well, we will attempt to make you change your mind. Now, who are you working for?'

Love shrugged; it was useless going on.

Kernau nodded to his companion, who moved away from the wall, came round the side of the desk, and stood facing Love, his hands loosely at his sides. He was a short man and wore a small black moustache, neatly cropped. As he stood, he folded his hands in front of him.

Love watched his eyes for that almost imperceptible narrowing that would precede an attack. There was something about the way he stood, the cut of his clothes, the wideness of his trouser turn-ups, that rang a distant bell of memory. Where had he seen a man like that before, in a. suit like this? Then he remembered. It had been years ago, in wartime photographs and newsreels of Hitler and his generals; taking the salute on balconies as thousands goose-stepped beneath through streets already arumble with tanks, addressing a rally of thousands at Nuremberg.

'You are German,' said Love, thinking aloud.

Kernau pressed the tips of his fingers, together, his elbows apart on the desk, and lowered his head slightly.

'Does that carry our knowledge of each other any farther?'

'It's a step in the right direction,' said Love. 'I've told you all I know 'about this book, so I'll bid you good-day. I have more important things to do.'

He was thinking of those cars.

'So far as you are concerned, doctor, there is nothing more important in all the world,' said Kernau, and smoothed down his hair with his left hand. The other man moved suddenly. He hit Love on the left of his neck with the edge of his palm, momentarily paralysing that side of his body. Pain raced like fire through him. He sagged across the desk, his whole' frame taut with agony. Kernau flicked his right hand up casually and caught him across his throat. Love collapsed, and the red tide of oblivion mercifully swept over his head.

'His face isn't marked is it?' asked Kernau.

Manuel shook his head.

'Not a thing, senor.'

'Good. He'll be more tractable when he comes round. So long as his face isn't marked, he could have fallen downstairs, got drunk anything.'

'Like the old days,' said the short man.

'Yes,' agreed Kernau. The old days to him meant a riot outside the Braunhaus, steel-tipped boots crunching against opposing bone, a knee in someone's crotch, the crowd breaking and running in uproar beneath the hooves of the police horses. Ah, München, those were wonderful days!

He stood up, made no offer to help as the other two men carried Love out into the courtyard, put him on the wicker settee, undid his tie, slipped off his jacket and shirt. Manuel bound Love with webbing straps by his ankles, his waist and shoulders to the twisted, smooth spines of cane.

Kernau sat down in a flowered chair by his side, lit a cigar. Manuel brought out a tray of glasses, slices of lemon, a silver salt cellar. Kernau filled one with tequila, the pale Mexican drink distilled from the juice of the maguey plants, picked up the salt cellar, poured a tiny cone of salt on the back of his left hand. He licked this with his tongue, tossed back the glass of tequila, sucked the lemon slice, filled the glass again for the second round, and leaned across, watching Love.

The short man pulled a chair up to the settee, sat down. From his trouser pocket he took a small lens, the size of a spectacle glass, glanced briefly at the sun, then held the lens at about two feet from Love's bare chest, brought it down slowly until the focused sunlight glowed with a fierce blue intensity. He narrowed his eye against the glare.

Love stirred uneasily through the mists of unconsciousness. A little saliva dribbled from the left side of his mouth. He could feel pain scoring into his flesh, hot as the remorseless tip of a tungsten drill. He tried to move his body, but it seemed to be fixed. The message ran to his hands; he could not move them, either.

Wearily, he opened his eyes. The sun was burning him. He raised his head to see what could be causing this spearpoint of pain, and he saw the two men watching his face, and the point of light on his chest; already the flesh was beginning to smoke. He wanted to ask what was happening but he could not mouth the words. His body was one large complicated bruise. His mouth was dry; all his lips would form was one word,

'Why?'

'Because you must talk, Dr Love,' said Kernau, gently. 'That's why.'

The other man moved the lens. The pain receded for a second and then grew under his heart as he concentrated the sunshine for a second time. Where he had focused before, a red weal was already beginning to blister, pink and throbbing like another pulse.

'If you'll talk, you'll make it easier for yourself and for us,' said Kernau, as though he were discussing a perfectly rational situation. 'We extract no pleasure from doing this to you. We simply wish to know who sent you.'

'I told you,' said Love slowly, as though from a great distance of time and space, as though another man was using his voice.

'I brought this book for some woman's husband.' He could no longer remember the man's name. All he could remember was the pain, the long needle of light boring into his body. His flesh began to burn again.

'Move that bloody thing,' he said. 'You can make me a burned offering, but I can't tell you what I don't know.'

'We're not asking you to do that, Dr Love,' said Kernau. 'Only what you do. Who are you working for? Who sent you?'

'Oh, my God,' said Love wearily. 'When will you ever believe anything? I've told you.'

The short man looked questioningly at Kernau; He shook his head. The man moved the lens down to Love's navel. Pain began to grow for the third time, like some fearful tree driving down a cruel curving root through his living flesh.

Love tried to arch his body on the cane settee, but the bands were too tight, and for every inch he managed to move out of focus, the man moved with him. Behind him, the fountain poured out its water; above, the heaped clouds of afternoon drifted slowly towards the hills, castles in the sky.

'I've told you,' he repeated, and then paused. Somewhere a bell was ringing; two long, one short, one long.

'Stop,' said Kernau and stood up. The other man slipped the lens back in his pocket.

'Where shall we put him?' he asked.

'In the cellar. He'll talk later. Now that he sees we mean business. Get him out before I go to the door. The fewer people who see him the better.'

'You will have a little time in which to make up your mind,' he told Love. 'Maybe you will decide to be more helpful. It will be much less painful for you.'

He walked across the courtyard into the corridor. The short one slipped the straps from Love's middle, then paused, holding the straps around his ankles.

'Don't get any ideas, doctor,' he said. 'No judo, either. You might get hurt. Verstehen Sie?'

Love understood. The man threw him his shirt, jacket and tie.

'Take these,' he said. 'And come with me.'

'And if I refuse?'

'Refuse,' echoed the man, grinning.

Love cupped his hands round his mouth.

'Help! Help!' he shouted. The cries echoed back emptily from the walls.

'Shout as much as you like,' advised the short man. 'This is not London. They don't speak English much here. You might as well save your breath. Now start walking.'

Love turned over in his mind the idea of a sudden attack, but his opponent was fit, in command of the situation, while Love felt as though he had been beaten carefully and systematically with a sledge-hammer. Maybe he was growing old, or just growing sensible.

'Walk,' said the short man, and nodded towards the sliding door. Love walked slowly. Every step was painful, and he still hoped there might be a chance of reversing their roles. There wasn't. The corridor ended-in a wall of plastic composition flecked like stone. His companion raised his left hand above his head and pressed on a tile near the ceiling. The wall began to slide to the right on oiled rollers. Beyond the opening a metal staircase, with a steel handrail, led down into the darkness.

'In there,' ordered the man, pointing to the doorway.

Love hesitated. The other man took a step towards him. Love hit him in the stomach with his right fist, hard, the knuckles bunched, all his weight behind the blow. It landed on banked muscle, tough as leather. The man only grinned at him; his teeth were brown with nicotine.

'I'll pay you in full. Later,' he said softly. 'In the meantime - this.'

His right foot flicked out like a snake's tongue, caught Love on his left shin. Love collapsed and fell. In falling, his body folded over as he bumped down the stairs. The man threw his shirt and jacket after him, and the door slid shut.

Love lay for a moment, stunned, at the foot of the stairs, not sure whether he had broken any bones, seeing nothing but blue and golden stars exploding in his head. They faded, and he stood upright cautiously, feeling all his joints. Two arms, two legs, a very sore head and neck, plus some second degree bums, but otherwise he seemed as nature made him. He stooped, felt in the darkness for his shirt, pulled it on, tucked it into his trousers, pulled on his jacket. His tie he could not find. He gave up trying to search; bending down brought on too ferocious a headache.

He sat on the bottom step. He was in complete darkness, in some kind of cellar. He could not see a window, yet the air felt cool and fresh, strong with the smell of new cement and kerosene. The house could not have been long built.

Gripping the stair-rail with his right hand, he stood on one leg and stretched with the other toe out in front of him to feel whether there was a hole in which he might fall if he moved. The floor seemed solid enough. He knelt down rubbed his fingers across it. It felt dry and rough with concrete dust. If only he had a torch or a cigarette lighter, even a match.

He straightened up, and, as he did so, heard a faint rustle in one corner. His hair prickled at the back of his neck, adrenalin poured through his veins.

'Who's there?' he asked, not expecting any answer. His voice sounded flat: the rough concrete walls soaked it up, and kept the echo.

A further rustle, and then, in the darkness, he heard breathing. He was entombed in this cellar with someone else - but, who?

He stood, back pressed against the wall; holding his breath, listening to the footsteps as they drew closer to him.

CHAPTER FIVE: THE REPUBLIC OF DELGUEDA, OFF THE COAST OF BRAZIL

The early morning sun threw the cross of the window frame on the far wall of the adobe room. It hung there like a crucifix, accusing him. Weissmann's bed was in the corner, out of range of the five o'clock sun, for he was a bad sleeper. Even so, he stirred uneasily, pulled the threadbare sheet over his old, grey, used-up face. No one, he sometimes thought, could be as old as he felt, as he looked. This was one of those times; most mornings were.

Although he had been here for years, almost a generation he had recently been experiencing a strange, uneasy, lost feeling just before awakening. Where was he? Why was he in this white-washed room, on his own, with no possessions except those he could carry, when he was really so rich he could underwrite the entire economy of this wretched Republic - if only he could reach his wealth? If only. The two saddest words in any language. He saw the cross on the wall, and for a second it had a vague ecclesiastical connection: a choir singing, the. clear, round voices of the young, air heavy with the sweetness of tiny flames consuming the candles on the altar, lit for the souls of the faithful departed.

He was a choir boy again in Kitzbuhel, and, after the service, there would be sleigh rides, with the bells tinkling on the black polished harnesses of the horses, and the warm smell of their droppings, their breath steamy in the clear morning air, so cold and sharp it hurt to breathe, but to be hurt like that was a pleasure, for he was young.

He opened his eyes, and he was old again, in the room that measured five metres by four. He knew this because, in his careful Teutonic way, he had measured it often enough, pacing it out wall to wall, corner to corner. The window wall was eight centimetres out; this annoyed him with a blind unreasoning fury. It provided an object on which he could focus his hatred, his wide-ranging bitterness at the incredible change in his fortunes. Above his bed hung the Iron Cross, Second Class, that he had been awarded in February 1943, for his work in the Amtsgruppe D, the department of the SS economic organization responsible for the running of the Nazi concentration camps. It was his most worthwhile souvenir.

Across the back of the cheap, unpainted wooden chair (a tin under each leg against the red ants) hung his khaki drill jacket, as near to uniform as he could manage, faded with too many washes, too many summers; then the neat square pile of his clothes on the chair bottom.

He sat up, rubbed the stubble on his face. A lizard flickered into a corner. Even the reptiles had homes, he thought; he had none. The window was too high to see anything except patches of blue sky, squared by the frame, clear without cloud, like some backcloth to the mists of eternity. As a boy, how often had he wished for sunshine instead of snow, and now, for nearly twenty years, he had known only two seasons, the months of sunshine for twelve hours a day, and then the months of rain, when leather turned green overnight, when dampness seeped into his bones, rusted his joints, and the walls of the wretched house streamed with tears of moisture.

Another day, he thought; one day nearer the grave, one day farther away from the years when he had been happy, or when he thought he'd been happy, which was much the same thing, sometimes a far better thing.

He sat up in bed, swung his legs slowly over the side of the rope mattress. He scratched a mosquito bite under his right arm-pit and looked down at the concrete dust that clotted the strands of the Indian-weave rug, making it rough as a rasp. A chameleon turned the colour of the grey walls at the creak of the bed frame. Weissmann felt heavy, as though he had been drinking; it was the climate. He'd never got used to it, and he'd had all those years of trying. Oh, God, he hated himself and this miserable existence, eked out on old memories and what might have beens.

He looked down at his one foot with the toes splayed out, at the wide, horny-ridged nails. He had been so far lost in the dreams of long ago that temporarily he had forgotten his injury. Often he still had nightmares that he was on his hands and knees behind Martin Bormann, the Deputy Fuhrer, and Johannes Rattenhuber, heads of the Reichssicherheitsdienst, Hitler's detective-guards, and Hans Baur, his personal pilot, and others, creeping through the streaming sewers beneath the Chancellory in Berlin while the city rocked above them under the rain of Russian bombs. Behind them, thin spirals of smoke, streaked with the smell of burning flesh, marked the funeral pyres of Hitler and Eva Braun. And ahead of them - what?

The cautious emergence through a cellar window into a street strewn with glass and electric wires, with swollen corpses, faces black and blistered like negroid frescoes in a lost cathedral. Then, still stinking and foul from the slime of the sewers, they had begun to crawl carefully from one cover to another; fifty yards more and they would be in the Ziegel-strasse, and behind the thick high wall of a brewery. The others reached it, and then scattered, some to the Spree Canal, others along the Stadtbahn towards Lehrter Station.

Weissmann held back; the firing was heavier now and the buildings burned so fiercely that the ground felt hot through the soles of his boots. Then, as he made up his mind, he heard the shriek of steel tracks on concrete that still ended each nightmare and made Weissmann wake up sweating and dry-mouthed at the horror of remembrance.

He had looked up and there, watching him through the letterbox slit in the throat of the tank, were the eyes of a Russian soldier; two cold, hard eyes that still reached out over the years, through thousands of nights, looking at him, looking through him.

He had seen it all so closely that every tiny detail was photo-graphed on his mind: the hooded guards around the tank's side lights; the glitter of the bright metal tracks; the copper radio aerial, thin and trembling as a fishing rod. Then the two guns came down slowly, two accusing fingers; the big twenty pounder and the small machine-gun, its barrel-shield drilled with cooling holes.

'Nein! Nein!' Weissmann cried. 'Kamerad!'

The machine-gun chattered and jerked; the black mouth poked out a tiny darting tongue of flame. Weissmann fell screaming in the road, his right leg shattered, blood seeping out through the filth that encased his trousers, his face contorted with pain, mouth open like a gargoyle in his giant agony. Then the tank turned on its tracks and was away.

Rattenhuber and Baur were captured; Bormann got away - though some said he had been wounded; but Weissmann, the keeper of the Archives of all the Concentration Camps, lay where he fell. Some German soldiers had appeared from the ruins and dragged him - bleeding, groaning, clutching their arms with fingers curved into claws by despair - behind the shelter of a wall. Then, as they crouched, they had heard the distant hollow roar of a shell, an express train in the sky.

They crouched, heads down, hands clasped behind their necks, forearms over their ears, waiting for the explosion. The earth shook, rubble poured around them, and in the extremity of his agony, Weissmann voided and pain overwhelmed him, wave on red wave. The rest was darkness and the long fall past rows of cold, uncaring stars.

When he regained consciousness, he was lying on straw in a barn, the salt smell of drying blood in his nostrils. He stirred and knives of pain stabbed his right thigh. He reached out with his fingers and felt the flesh through his trouser leg, and then he felt nothing. His leg had gone: someone had amputated it just above the knee. The blood he smelled was his own.

He turned his head weakly on the straw. He wanted to cry, but he had no tears left. He sobbed dryly and each breath hurt his leg again and he felt pain in the foot that wasn't there. His severed nerves would take years to learn this, but he did not know that then. He did not know a lot of things then.

He knew nothing for instance of the long and complicated escape route out of Germany for wanted men like him. The farmer who had shielded him explained that, when he was well enough, he could .travel through to Austria, then over the mountains into Italy, to Genoa, and board a ship .for the Argentine, But there was a high price for escape: it was the number of his secret numbered account in the 'Credit Suisse' in Geneva; a matter of several million Deutschmarks for a one way ticket in a submarine crewed by Navy deserters. There was also the matter of rewarding those who had risked their lives to bring him to the farm.

Weissmann had paid. The only other alternative was his liberty and possibly his life. Others of his ilk were reaching the same decision. They journeyed to strange ports to keep odd assignments with men whose names they never knew, to sail alien seas in looted lifeboats, in submarines, even on rafts.

They came to the ports by circuitous routes; in dung carts and hay wagons; some dressed in captured American uniforms, with forged or stolen papers; others by way of monasteries on lonely hillsides, where monks, doubtless moved by Christian principles of succouring the needy, would pass them on to brothers in another order, fifty miles nearer the sea.

They travelled as monks, as priests, sometimes even as nuns; a few in coffins piled high with mountain flowers to conceal the air holes. At last they had arrived in South America, this, pale, wounded, ill stripped of their fortunes, except for those clever enough to have acquired more than one hidden bank account.

How long ago had all that been? Twenty odd years - or an eternity? Time could only be measured when you had the instruments to measure it; events, anniversaries, the marriage of a son, the death of a brother. And here he was in the wilderness without these homely milestones, with nothing to look forward to; only regrets and years of exile to look back on.

He swung across the bed and reached up to the wooden peg driven into the wall, from which hung the crude artificial leg they had made for him secretly soon after his arrival in the Argentine in 1947. It was heavy, and its imbalance hurt his back and set up compensatory pains in his good left knee, but at least it meant that he could get about.

He dusted a little talcum powder into the palm of his hand, patted it on to the stump, blew into the cup of the artificial leg in case, with all that accursed abrasive dust from the crumbling walls, some should have settled there overnight. Then he strapped on the leg; the leather belt that went, round his middle had almost worn through where it gripped the buckle. He sat for a moment, his head in his hands, fighting back the waves of self-pity at having no roots, only memories of a world long gone, and radio news of a world he dared not discover.

He pulled on his clothes. Years ago he would never have started a day without a cold bath, a brisk rub down with a warmed towel. He felt again that clean male pleasure of a scrubbed body, a newly laundered uniform shirt, the ringing of the steel tips of his boots on granite pavements. Then he stood up, walked painfully across the room, removed the concrete block he kept behind the door as an additional barrier against entry, slid back the two bolts, threw open the door.

His house was one of a cluster in a semi-circle around the bay; in the distance the grey mountains crouched like the back of some broody, historic monster. He wondered who lived on them, what the view of this enclave was like from that other side of the bay.

He took his crutch from its home behind the door and walked down the hill to the mess. Other men of roughly the same age, the indeterminate fifties and sixties, were leaving their huts at the same time. They nodded a greeting to each other, and then walked on singly or in pairs, to a hut a little larger than the rest. They were like the inmates of an old folks' home, he thought, not for the first time. And yet they were not really old in years or body, only in spirit. They all lived in the past, clinging to forgotten ranks and meaningless distinctions, because they had no part in the present, no belief in the future: they were living on borrowed time, or overdrafts from God.

They had their feuds, their friendships, sometimes even their love affairs; but nothing meant much any more. He remembered a line from the English poet Housman - there had been an anthology of poems in one of the houses where he had stayed on his way to Genoa - and the words seemed cruelly apt: 'Runners whom renown outran, and the name died before the man.'

All their names were dead now, except to the Israelis, who pursued them with detached and scientific ferocity. The Americans, the French, the Russians, the British, no doubt would let the past lie; there had been talk of a Twenty Year Amnesty, but not with the Jews, never with them. They had lost too many, they had suffered too much for talk of that kind. They could not be bribed or squared or bought off. Their vengeance was a living thing; they might grow old but that would never grow old. Heat was coming into the day now and the dust swirled under their feet, but he shivered at his thoughts.

Weissmann stopped at the door of the hut, looked round behind him, shading his eyes against the reflection of the sun oh the sea. He could see the grey hills on which their houses were built, then the double rows of barbed wire perimeter, and the guard dogs, their jaws slavering and open already in the heat, as they padded behind the two layers of wire, sniffing at stones, cocking up their legs against sticks and dead plants. They were there to keep away strangers, so the Government said, for their protection; but they also looked uncomfortably like dogs to keep them in their place, behind the wire.

He sat down at the scrubbed table; the room smelled slightly of disinfectant, as impersonal as everything else in his life. The hand of an orderly, with the round, blunt, thick fingers of the Bavarian peasant, put down a metal plate of scrambled eggs, another hand poured a beaker of black coffee. Some greyish bread was on the plate beside him.

A man wearing a white surplice, with very blond hair, and a pudgy red face, one of the most assiduous homosexuals among them, stood up. He made the sign of the cross.

'For what we are about to receive, O Lord, may we be truly thankful.'

Weissmann looked out of the ends of his eyes at the men around him. Why should they be truly thankful to the Lord for what they had received so far?

True, they were alive, but what was life under these, conditions? It was reduced to a matter of eating and excreting the food; then sleep, punctured by dreams in which the dead rose up and cursed them, thousands of cadavers from Auschwitz and Belsen and Dachau. Surely to die was better than to live like this?

The man sitting next to him seemed to read his thoughts. He nodded to Weissmann.

'Another day,' he said.

'It's always another day.'

'You have decided what you're going to say?'

'What I'm going to say?' repeated Weissmann, not understanding what the man meant; and then he remembered what he had forgotten.

'My God,' he said, aghast. 'The funeral's at nine, isn't it?'

'The grave's already dug.'

'Poor Manfred,' said Weissmann.

He suddenly had no appetite for his breakfast. He pushed away the half-finished plate of congealing egg, sipped the black, bitter coffee that was sour before it reached his stomach.

'That makes only forty-three of us left.'

'Yes. Two deaths last year, one this. Forty-three. Maybe, if we'd stood our ground like the others in forty-five we'd have got away with it. Now we'd have a Mercedes 600 each - and our Swiss money. And what have we got here? A bit of land grudgingly allowed by these South American bastards, who play it both ways.

'We act as advisers to their wretched miniscule Dago army, their corrupt police force, their ludicrous Intelligence service. And so we are grudgingly allowed, on sufferance, to stay in this - this graveyard. They give us some barbed wire, some guard dogs, in case the Israelis try and kidnap us - as they grabbed Eichmann. But if the pressure ever gets too harsh outside, if the Jews ever come too close, or if our usefulness ended, they'd give us up at once.'

'The Jews aren't as clever as all that,' said a man sitting farther up the table. His cheeks carried the high bones of the Prussian, with the parallel duelling scars, like tribal marks, under his eyes. His hair was grey as iron filings, his eyes, pieces of ice that had crept into his skull.

'What makes you think not, Axel?' asked Weissmann, for something to say, not that he really cared for his opinion. They had gone over and over this too many times already. They had discussed everything too much and for too long. Everyone knew everyone, their dreams and their lies; mostly their lies.

'They didn't get Mengclc,' said Axel, and looked about him significantly, as though this proved his point completely. Joseph Mengele had been Chief Medical Officer at Auschwitz during the last two years of the war. In this capacity he had murdered Jews by the thousand in gas chambers, by injecting phenol, air, even petrol, into their veins. Then he had wisely disappeared.

After years, Israeli agents had finally established that he was living in a second rate hotel outside Ita in Paraguay. This news was reported to the West German Government, but the President of Paraguay, General Alfredo Stroessner, a man of German descent, who had thoughtfully staffed his army with former SS officers, threatened to break off diplomatic relations with West Germany when they sought to extradite Mengele.

Thus it was decided to visit his hotel and kidnap him, as Eichmann had been seized in the Argentine. But the manager of the hotel had also been a Party man in the old days, and he warned Mengele, who escaped out of a back window and fled away into the jungle.

So he had got away, but to what future? To a few more years in some remote South American village, too small to be marked on any map, to live in fear of the stranger's knock on the door, the creak of surreptitious feet, the shadow that was deeper than darkness? Was that worth escaping for?

'No, they didn't get him,' agreed Weissmann. 'But perhaps it would have been better if they had. We can't go on running away forever.'

Axel said nothing; this was always the end of any argument: eventually, no matter how long the chase, death or capture would decide the matter. Weissmann remembered lines from another poet, Stephen Hawes, in that anthology: 'For though the days be never so long, At last the bell ringeth to evensong.'

Well, the bell had already rung for many, of their number, and for Manfred only on the previous evening. And now, over his body, decently wrapped in a grey blanket, Weissmann, as the senior officer, would give a short oration, and then his comrades would shuffle the dry corroded earth into the grave. Schrafft, the SS major who had specialised in carving human bones into grotesque figurines and knife handles in Dachau, had carved Manfred's name and a tiny swastika on a piece of dried drift wood to mark his grave.

Weissmann walked to the door, stood looking out at the bay. What should he say? What could he say? The Government of this country allowed them to keep the three old submarines that had brought many of them from Europe. They were harmless enough. Men from Peron's navy had dismantled their guns years before, but they were permitted to keep the electric motors and diesel engines and the batteries. They used the submarines now for fishing, and had rigged up wooden masts to each conning tower to carry home-made sails.

On their plot of land they grew sweet corn, peppers and some wheat. For the rest; they were given small salaries from the departments they advised, just enough to buy meat and clothes, what simple medicines they might need. Whenever they asked for more money, they had been pointedly reminded that they were fortunate in being allowed to remain there at all. Not many countries in the world still gave shelter and. some semblance of safety to ex-Nazis, and especially to men with records like theirs. For this, perhaps, they should be truly thankful.

Life had been much simpler in the Argentine just after the war, for Israel had enough problems of her own in 1948 without attempting to trace old enemies. But when Peron fell from power in 1954, the Nazis had moved on, some to Bolivia, others to Paraguay and Brazil. A few took the risk of going north to Mexico, buying a stolen passport, and then crossing into the States; they'd done quite well there, from what he had heard. If he'd stayed in Germany, of course, he might have done even better. Or he could have gone to Egypt or Syria, where his contemporaries were still welcomed, largely because, like the Egyptians and Syrians, they were fundamentally anti-Jewish.

But what sort of life was that — measuring out your days under an assumed Arabic name in the filthy souks of Damascus and Cairo, knowing that as soon as your usefulness was over, your life could also end? Also, he had never had the chance. The whole question was only academic.

Weissmann turned away from the sameness of the sea, the sameness of this endless mental regurgitation, and walked back to his hut. By the time he reached it, his body was clammy with heat and exhaustion. He sat down on his bed, pulled from an inner pocket a faded photograph of a woman with the plaited hair of the thirties, standing next to a small boy, perhaps nine or ten. They smiled out of the faded sepia print. What was she doing now? And his son? Was he dead or alive? Did they think of him as a dead man? The black-ringed announcement in the local paper: JACOB WEISSMANN, mein lieber Mann, unser guter yater ...in lieber Trauer ... Did they ever think of him at all? And if they met now after all this time, what would they have in common but their language and their name?

It was five to nine; a bell began to peal. The pastor had fitted this to a beam in the hut where he held services which nearly everyone attended, regardless of their original religion or agnosticism. It was as though they were all anxious to invest in eternal life insurance, desperately trying to store up a bonus in heaven.

Weissmann reached for his straw hat, pulled it down over his eyes, went into the little bathroom with its ewer and bowl of water, lifted the square of beaded muslin that kept out the shiny, blue-bodied flies, poured some water over his hands. He wished he could stop them trembling; they had been growing worse these last few weeks.

Then he dried them, walked down the path, and the group already waiting outside the church, two SS Generals, the former deputy chief of the Gestapo in France, the one-time Commandant of the concentration camp at Lublin, an ex-Intelligence chief from Riga - parted to let him go by.

The pastor was the last to enter. They stood up when he came in. He bowed to the altar, made the sign of the cross, and turned to face them. The air in the little room was thick and sweet with the scent of death. In that climate, Manfred was not being buried too soon.

'My friends,' said the pastor, 'before I begin the service for our friend who has departed this life, Brigadefuhrer Weissmann, as the senior officer, would like to say a few words.'

He turned towards Weissmann.

'Gentlemen,' began Weissmann speaking from the heart, for he had no notes, 'this is the third time in almost as many months, that I have been called on for this sad duty.

'There are no words of comfort I can give you, just as there are none you can give me - or, if I may say so, pastor, without offence - that you can give us.

'We were young when we escaped from Germany, and now we are old. A whole generation of change and progress has passed us by. We have lived here on the banks of the river of time, and every year our numbers diminish. If this progression continues, it must come about eventually that there will only be one man left to mourn, and in time he will have none to mourn for him.

'I wish, gentlemen, that I could offer you some comfort, some hope that we will one day be united with those we left behind in the Fatherland. But, you know as well as I do, that such a happening, in the present climate of world opinion, is almost impossible.

'Thus, although we grieve that Wolfgang Manfred, former Brigadefuhrer in the Eastern Territories, is no longer with us, although we will miss his counsel, his personality and his presence at the games of chess at which he excelled, I cannot in all sincerity grieve for him. At least his sentence here is finished.

Perhaps deaths as the pastor would have us believe, is not the end but the beginning.'

He bowed his head in the direction of the grey blanket where the flies already buzzed inquisitively, and limped slowly back to his seat. He had not said what he had wanted to say: but then what had he wanted to say? The pastor went on with the service.

Afterwards, the younger and stronger men carried the body from the tabletop to the newly made grave. As the earth rattled in, loose and" comfortless, the pastor mouthed the words: 'Ashes to ashes ... Dust to dust... The Lord giveth and the Lord taketh away ... Blessed be the name of the Lord.'

His mind was not on the service: he was thinking of the young villager he had seen bathing from the next bay,: his firm thighs, his flat stomach, the hard male bulge in his trunks had excited him; the old fever was running in his blood. He was going to see him this afternoon; he wondered what he should wear, whether this would be the first time. As he intoned the words sonorously, pausing automatically here and there for effect, he was too involved with his own thoughts to notice Axel tiptoeing behind the mourners who murmured Latin responses as the earth was shovelled in. Axel gripped Weissmann's elbow excitedly.

'Look,' he said urgently. 'Out in the bay. Am I imagining it - or is it real?'

Weissmann brought back his scattered thoughts; he had been playing chess with Manfred in Vienna just after the brass band played a Strauss waltz as if they really liked it. The Danube was always blue when you were young.

'What's that you say?' he asked to cover his confusion, but he had already raised his head, and was looking out over the bay.

In the glittering sea, a long dark shape was slowly rising. Water sluiced off its black sides; the black, red and yellow flag of the West German Federal Republic broke at the masthead. There was some superstructure behind the conning tower he had not seen on a submarine before, but that was not surprising; he had not seen any submarines since the end of the war.

'It's German,' he said, his voice louder than he intended, sharp-edged with disbelief. 'It's one of ours!'

The mourners looked towards him, their Latin instantly forgotten, and followed the direction of his eyes to the bay. The two men shovelling earth paused, looked for guidance not towards the pastor but towards Weissmann. Their faces shone with sweat and excitement; they might be seeing a vision.

'Finish the job,' ordered Weissmann, as calmly as he could. 'Then we'll go down to the beach and see what it is.'

They went on shovelling. He turned to Axel.

'You go on ahead of us,' he told him. 'See what's happening.' It was a vague command, but no vaguer than many he had given before, and it had the merits of brevity and decision. Axel set off willingly enough; like many Germans, he preferred to receive orders rather than to give them. This also had the great quality of not being held responsible should they turn out to be the wrong orders.

No one had any more interest in the grave. The pastor gabbled through his last few words, waited for the swift 'Amen', and snapped shut the black cardboard covers of his Bible. He hoped that the arrival of this submarine would not interfere with his own plans for the afternoon.

The submarine had now completely surfaced. Men were moving purposefully about the deck. One, in officer's uniform, was scanning the bleak, grey rock, through binoculars, focusing on the group around the grave.

'We're ready now,' said the pastor.

'Then we'll go,' said Weissmann.

The little group moved slowly down the track, past the cactus plants, the rough outcrops of rock, whitened with the droppings of sea-birds.

'You're sure that's the new German flag?.' asked a stout man nervously. He had been a camp commandant in Poland. 'You're sure it's not the Israeli flag?'

'Certain,' Weissmann replied, but a fearful doubt lingered in his own mind and stomach. Submarines had sailed under false flags before. What a coup this would be for the Israeli agents to take so many wanted ex-Nazis at one swoop! It was the sort of scheme he would like to have planned himself during the war; it had the panache of Skorzeny's rescue of Mussolini, the audacity of their plan to parachute millions of forged banknotes over Britain to disrupt the economy.

Only minutes before, he had felt almost suicidally depressed at the thought of spending the rest of his life in this bleak outpost, but now even this prospect seemed preferable to an arrest, to trial in a hostile land, with the unknown relations of unnumbered dead accusing him.

They reached the beach and stood in a shabby huddle, staring at the submarine with puzzled faces, eyes screwed up against the glare from the water. The sea threw a few waves at them halfheartedly, for it was hot, and they drew back a couple of paces. The officer on the conning tower lowered his binoculars, raised a transistorized megaphone. He directed it towards them. His voice came clearly over the hundred yards of shimmering sea.

'Sind Sie Deutsch?'

They were Germans, but should they admit it? How could they not admit it? The men must know who they were, to have surfaced so near them. The question was only rhetorical.

Weissmann cupped his hands round his mouth and shouted back: 'Ja!'

'Wir haben Neuigkeit fur Sie von Deutschland. Wir wollen

landen. We have news for you from Germany. We wish to come ashore.'

What could they want with them? How could they have found them out? Was it all a trap to seize them and carry them back for trial? Questions poured through Weissmann's mind like a flood through a sluice as he stood, his hands still cupped at his mouth. The submarine was not large enough to take all of them as well as its crew, but maybe there was another vessel somewhere out at sea? Or maybe they did not want all of them, but just the leaders, the men with the longest records?

Also, these men would undoubtedly be armed, and they were in no position to resist any attack if they insisted on landing against their wishes. It would be better only to allow two or three to land in the first instance. Then there could be no attempt of immediately overpowering them or of kidnapping anyone. And, in the last resort, these men might prove useful as hostages.

'Nur drei Personen mogen landen,' he shouted back. 'No more than three of you can come ashore. We will await you at the jetty.'

He pointed towards the ramshackle wooden structure they had made from tree trunks, and the sides of packing cases.

'Ich werde mit zwei anderen kommen,' replied the officer in the submarine. 'I will come with two others.'

He lowered his megaphone, and began to give orders down in the control room. A hatchway opened, a collapsible rubber dinghy was brought on deck. The men on shore watched in silence as two sailors connected a bottle of compressed air, and its grey sides swelled with air. They lowered it over the side, clipped on a small outboard engine.

The officer climbed into the dinghy, steadied it while the two other men followed him. They seemed to be civilians; they wore linen suits against the heat. The sun frantically heliographed an unknown message from their gold-rimmed sunglasses.

The officer turned to the tiny outboard motor, pulled the cord starter. The engine buzzed like an infuriated wasps' nest. A haze of blue smoke billowed out from the exhaust and the dinghy, trembling in the sea, headed slowly towards the shore, pushing, an arrowhead of water in front of it. Behind it, the submarine moved silently out to sea, and submerged. By the time the dinghy had reached the jetty, there was no sign of it whatever. The sea was once more as smooth as a whore's smile: and, thought Weissmann uneasily, just as dangerous, for what else might it not conceal?

The fact that the submarine had not remained on the surface made the landing seem somehow dangerous and hostile. These men spoke German, but that was nothing. There were German Jews still, although they had destroyed more than six million. And in Israel there were Jews, so he had heard, who looked like Frenchmen, Portuguese, English, even Asiatics. And they were clever. What other race had such a capacity for repaying old debts - or such enormous reasons for revenge?

Weissmann's fears were reflected in the furrowed, worried faces of the men around him. In silence he led them towards the jetty. The rubber dinghy nudged one of the tree trunks, and a shoal of silver fish fled away through the clear green water.

The officer stopped his engine, threw up two handling ropes, climbed out. He carried a waterproof pouch, slipped it smartly under his left arm and saluted. Weissmann saluted back. It was the first time he had saluted for more than twenty years, and even now he found difficulty in not giving the Nazi salute of the arm stretched out from the shoulder.

'Are you in charge here, sir?' asked the officer.

His face was very pale. They must have been submerged for a long time, Weissmann thought. The man's mouth was small, the lips thin, a rat-trap in his face. Weissmann didn't take to him, but then this feeling could be mutual.

'I am the senior officer here,' he agreed. 'Who are you and what do you want?'

The officer glanced briefly at the others before he replied.

'I have something very important to discuss with you!'

'Who are you?' asked Weissmann, not moving.

'I've come from the West German Government in Bonn.'

'How did you find we were here?' asked Axel shortly. The scars on his face pulsed with intensity as though they had a life of their own. The officer glanced at him for a moment before he replied.

'I can tell you that, sir, if we could go to a place where we could discuss this matter. I can prove who I am and why I am here by the papers I carry.'

He touched the pouch under his arm.

'Who are these two men?' asked Weissmann. There was something about their appearance, their sallow, dead faces with the high cheek bones, cold eyes, black and dull as olive stones, that he did not like.

'They are colleagues of mine, sir. From the Foreign Office.'

'Why has the submarine submerged?' asked someone else.

'Because we do not wish to draw attention to our presence here. We have no authority to land.'

'Are you armed?' asked Weissmann.

The officer shook his head, opened his uniform jacket. There was no sign of any holster under his arms or around his waist. Weissmann glanced down at his calves; his trousers were too narrow for even the smallest automatic to be concealed there.

'What about your friends?'

'The same goes for them, sir.'

'All right,' said Weissmann, making up his mind. 'We will hear what you have to say in the mess hall.'

They walked up the hill together, silently, in two groups, the older men clustered together instinctively, the newcomers a little way behind them. Weissmann noticed that they soon grew short of breath with the climb. Either they had been submerged for a long time, or they were very much out of condition; or maybe both. He turned to the officer.

'You haven't told me your name,' he said.

'It's Hermann Kinder. Oberleutnant.'

He turned to the two civilians.

'This is Herr Grosschmidt. And Herr Heissner.'

'I see,' said Weissmann. 'My name is Weissmann. Jacob Weissmann.' He paused. 'Formerly Brigadefuhrer.'

'I know,' said the officer casually. 'The Gestapo. You worked with Oswalk Pohl in the WVHA. (*Wirtschaftverwaltung Hauptamt, the HQ of the SS 'economic administration'. This collected from corpses in the gas chambers such items as gold teeth, wedding rings, even the gold rims from spectacles, so that they could be melted down.*) Do you remember that odd banquet the Reichsbank gave you?'

And, with horror and alarm that became almost a physical pain, Weissmann remembered. With Himmler, Heydrich and his successor, Kaltenbrunner, and Pohl, who ran the Konzentrations Lager, the general administration of all the camps, he had been invited to this celebration at the Reichsbank early in 1943.

Before cocktails were served, their hosts took them down to the vaults where they could inspect the triple-locked safes containing thousands of gold ingots. And to prove that these had all been melted down from gold taken from prisoners, they also saw the separate piles of stylos, spectacle rims, drawn teeth still stained with blood, but redeemed by their gold fillings.

After this inspection, they all went upstairs to luncheon: It was an excellent meal for those times; Weissmann remembered that, too. As it should be: the total deposits of the SS at the bank, in that year, were in excess of a hundred million marks.

'And I'll tell you what you drank,' said the officer, watching Weissmann's face. 'A Reisling. Right?'

Weissmann nodded.

'Right,' he said hollowly. 'But how do you know this?-Who are you?'

'I'm coming to that,' said the officer. 'You have Herr Manfred here, too, I believe? He was in Mauthausen camp once. I remember, he ordered two young Dutch Jews to be shot on arrival. He admired their skulls - and wanted them as paperweights on his desk because they had perfect sets of teeth. I'd like to see Herr Manfred.'

'You can't,' said Weissmann dully. 'He died yesterday. There's his grave.'

He pointed towards the mound of rough earth with the cross at one end. His finger trembled in the still air. He had forgotten all these things this man had told him, but others had not, and others never would.

'Ah,' said the officer. 'I'm sorry. I had a message for him from his son.'

'Where is he working?' asked another man, a mean-faced gnome with eyes too close together and a crucifix at his neck. 'My own boy used to be a friend of his. Decker is the name.'

'I know about you, Herr Decker,' replied the officer easily. 'You were on the staff at Auschwitz. A chemist. Your job was to melt down the bones of the dead for fertilisers. You used their fat for soap. And the women's hair was found useful for lining the slippers of railwaymen in bad weather - and for submarine crews. Your son is working in Essen.'

'What does he think about me? Does he know I'm alive?'

The little group had stopped by the mess hut.

'He has a photograph of you in uniform on the mantelpiece in his living-room,' said Kinder. 'He is very proud of his father. And of the work he did so bravely in the late war. He will be pleased to hear you are alive.'

'My God,' said Decker. 'My little Baldur.'

He put up his hands to his face, pressed the palms into his eyes and wept.

'And my wife?'

'She is also well. She is living in Munich, near your old home.'

'How do you know all this?' asked Weissmann.

Kinder patted the pouch under his arm.

'It's all here,' he said.

'What about my wife? My father? My son?' Other voices clamoured around him.

'Please, gentlemen,' Weissmann rebuked them sharply. 'This is not a mind-reading session.'

He led the way into the mess hall, stumping between the tables. As he moved, he could smell his own sweat; it was sharp with fear.

'Be seated,' he said, indicating the bench.

The three men from the submarine sat down at the head table, putting their cases on the scrubbed boards in front of them.

'Now,' said Weissmann brusquely. 'Who are you? Talk.'

'I am an officer in the new German Navy,' said Kinder addressing them all, but looking at Weissmann as he spoke. 'I have been seconded for a special task, which is why I am here.'

He paused, licked his lips as though he were nervous. Weissmann noted with distaste that his tongue was white and furred.

'I am here at the specific request of the Foreign Office in Bonn. I have been given a list of many of you to show that we do know who you are and where you are. Not all, of course, but a fair percentage. And I have brought news of your relations - those, at least, whom we can trace.

'It is because the Government in Bonn knows your feeling for those you love and had to leave behind, and also your feelings for your Fatherland, which is now so sadly divided, that I have made this special trip from Hamburg with these gentlemen with a proposition.'

He paused again. This time Weissmann used the silence to speak.

'Before you go any farther, Kinder,' he said, carefully not addressing him by his rank to show how senior he was. 'Remember that we have been away from our homes for more than twenty years. You seem to know so much about us and our past lives. You say you are an officer in the German Navy. But we have only your word for this. And who are your colleagues? We have lived for too long under the threat of Israeli intervention not to feel suspicious.'

Kinder nodded understandingly.

'Forgive me, sir,' he said soothingly. 'I have run ahead of myself.'

He unbuttoned his oilskin pouch, took out a folder of papers. Some were in old-fashioned German script, but most were typed with an electric typewriter under the seal of the West German Federal Government.

He pushed them across the table to Weissmann, who ran the tops of his fingers over the crest. It seemed genuine enough.

He held up the page to the light, and the watermark of the eagle showed through. That convinced him. He began to read, missing out sentences in their stilted phrascology, covering the gist of the document: 'To whom it may concern ... guarantee ... in return for services to be rendered ... of a nature to be described ... by the bearer Hermann Kinder, Oberleutnant West German Federal Navy ... given his day ... under our seal...' Then came an indecipherable signature for the Foreign Minister, Government of the Federal Republic of West Germany, Bonn.

Kinder was watching him. When Weissmann had finished reading, he handed him his naval card, and two other small identity cards, folded over.

'Here is my personal identification card, and also those of my colleagues Grosschmidt and Heissner, with their Foreign Office passes.'

Weissmann glanced at the photographs on the hard-backed cards, compared them with the faces of the three men at the table. They were obviously the same. It was remarkable, he thought, handing them back, how readily one believed words on a piece of paper when you would not accept the same words spoken. How infinite was the magic of the printed word, the scrawled signature, the official stamp.

'So what brings you here, Kinder?' he asked, his voice more friendly. 'What is the proposition you mention?'

'I will tell you, briefly, sir, and then Herr Heissner will leave his briefcase with you so that you can study the papers fully for yourselves.

'As you probably know, even although you are far from Europe, the name of Germany, of our Fatherland, is regrettably still tainted in many minds, by some of the excesses of the one-time Nazi regime.

'You may believe, as I personally do, that these stories have largely been exaggerated by countries and people for their own gain, but this does not alter the fact that very serious prejudice exists.'

He paused and looked around at the old, lined faces, wrinkled with years and scepticism. He shuffled his papers; he was corning to the difficult part.

'You have been exiles from your homes, from your Fatherland, as Brigadefiihrer Weissmann says, for more than twenty years. On this desolate spit of land you eke out your days, and always - as he has also pointed out - there is the threat that Israeli agents will discover you. After all, if we could, so could they. Or again, the value of your services to your hosts here in South America could diminish, and your presence become an embarrassment to them, with the same result.'

He paused.

'Tell us something we don't know,' Kinder,' said Axel sourly. 'You haven't come all this way to give us a political lecture. What is your proposition?'

'This. I have come here, as I said, on a special mission. I could easily have flown to Rio, and have arrived much more easily than by submarine. But I might have been watched by Israeli agents, possibly before I even left Bonn. They have their spies everywhere. In booking offices, among immigration officials, even, I sometimes fear, in our Government. So I came as discreetly as I could. And no one could follow me.

'Under certain conditions, gentlemen, the Government - as you will see from these papers which I'll leave with you when I return to the submarine - is prepared to offer you what amounts to a safe return home.

'You will be given new names - new faces, if need be - and pensions as of the date you agree with our conditions. All back pay and allowances due to you as from the date they ceased -May the eighth, 1945 - will also be paid.'

'What are the conditions?' asked Weissmann bluntly. This seemed far too good to be real. Yet these men were real enough.

Kinder smoothed the papers with his ringers.

'Our Government is concerned with what advertising men call Germany's image. A chance has unexpectedly presented itself to change this, and they seek your support.'

'Ours?' Weissmann's voice was shrill with disbelief. Who in Germany now could want the help of these old, decrepit men?

'Yes, yours, gentlemen. After years of experiment, our scientists have finally evolved what appears to be a commercially feasible way of extracting plankton from sea water.

'As you probably know, plankton is what the fish feed on and if a blue whale can grow up to 60 feet long and weigh 50 tons on it in two years, it must contain concentrated food values. And it does.

'During the war, one of our professors at Gottingen, Richard Harder, extracted edible fat from plankton.

'Then, in 1943, an American patrol boat picked up three torpedoed sailors in the South Atlantic, two Dutchmen and an American. They'd been adrift for 67 days - living on raw fish and sea water.

'And a few years ago, Dr Alain Bombard, the French scientist, crossed the Atlantic in a dinghy also living entirely on raw fish and plankton from the sea. His voyage took him 65 days and he proved scientifically that plankton can support human life - and that, in fact, a cubic foot of water contains nearly two hundred times as many living organisms as the same amount of earth.

'Obviously, with this knowledge, many countries have tried to extract this food commercially, for plankton tastes very pleasant - rather like shrimp paste - and there's so much of it that the source can never dry up.

'The British set up their Microbiological Research Unit in Trinidad, and they've got their Oceanographic Laboratory in Edinburgh, and various other agencies are working on this problem. The Americans are also heavily involved, but so far we in Germany are beating them both. And that's why I've come to ask your aid.'

'What can we do here?' asked Weissmann.

'I'm coming to that, sir. The best areas for plankton – it comes from a Greek word meaning "that which is drifted" -are in the Polar seas, and along this coast. We can't collect it near the Pole, but we can collect it here - if you will help us -and only if you will.'

'How?' asked Axel, his voice thick with disbelief.

'At present, plankton is collected in a mechanism towed behind a boat. This is like a movie camera with an open hole instead of the lens. And instead of any film inside there's a strip of silk winding on to rollers. The water pours through the front hole and out through one in the back, leaving the plankton on the silk:

'But this is very slow - it takes about five miles of towing to fill two square inches of silk. Now, if we can use the old submarines I understand you have here, we can collect it at a greater depth, and, by the use of controlled and harmless detonators under the water, can actually drive the stuff into far larger nets.'

'And then?' asked Axel sceptically.

'And then, once we've proved we can collect the stuff quickly, floating factories for collecting it, canning it, dehydrating it, deep-freezing it, can be set up.'

'How does this improve the image, as you call it, of West Germany?'

'After the processes are patented around the world, our Government proposes to give thousands of tons of canned plankton to the various countries in the East and Africa that face famine. India, Pakistan, the Congo.

'The world will look up to Germany, not as the most powerful military nation, but because of her positive contribution to save thousands of people who could otherwise have died of hunger.

'But to do these tests secretly, we need submarines in this ocean. If we sent our own, they'd be tracked and watched and the whole operation could be in jeopardy. But who here would give a second thought to your old subs going out to sea one evening? Am I right?'

'I think so,' agreed Weissmann. 'We have permission to use them for fishing. They are quite harmless, of course. They are unarmed.'

'But you have radios?'

'Oh, yes, we've been allowed to keep those. And we can submerge.'

'Good,' said Kinder; this was going better than he had dared to hope. 'So you could dive after dark and sail on unseen?'

'Yes. Unless some listening device picked us up.'

'And what if it did? They'd know something was there, but not who. And by daybreak you could be back in these waters after a good night's fishing. In fact, the best night's fishing you - or anyone else in history - will ever have made.'

'And you seriously suggest that you are offering us a safe conduct home, with all the other benefits you have enumerated, just for this?'

Weissmann's incredulity showed in his voice.

'As I have explained it, extremely briefly, it may sound very little. In fact, it will be a fairly sophisticated piece of navigation. You will have to keep a prescribed distance between you, travelling at different depths in radio silence.

'At a pre-arranged time you will make a signal and the equipment we have brought over from Germany will be set off by a VLF transmitter. It will not be easy for you with the currents and in old submarines, I assure you. But it is the enormous value of the operation to bur country that prompts the offer.

'It is purely fortuitous, gentlemen, that someone in Bonn remembered how a number of SS officers had used submarines to escape after the war. Does that take care of your question, Brigadefuhrer?'

Weissmann nodded slowly; he was not wholly convinced, but he was on the way.

'It is simply a business equation,' added Kinder. 'We need your help, and in return we can help you. However, I suggest we return to our submarine and await on you again when you have had a chance to discuss this - and to see these papers.'

Weissmann nodded.

'You will appreciate that your visit comes as an enormous surprise to us,' he said. 'We would like to study the papers you speak of, and also to see the news you have about our relations.'

'Of course.' Kinder pushed his oilskin pouch towards him. 'And now, gentlemen, when shall we see you for your answer?'

'Let us say the same time tomorrow,' said Weissmann glancing at his watch. 'We have a lot to discuss. The risk for some of us can be supreme. You understand that, of course?'

'Of course.'

'In that case, we will bid you wiedersehen. I don't walk any more than I have to because of my leg, but my colleagues will see you to the shore.'

Axel led the way down to the dinghy. As soon as they were out of hearing, the men in the mess hall shook out the papers from the pouch and began to search them eagerly, frantically, for pages that bore their names.

Weissmann walked to the door of the hut, and stood, one hand on the lintel, warm now in the sun, watching the backs of the visitors. As the dinghy put out to sea, the submarine began to surface. They were certainly well organized; everything seemed to be planned with the Teutonic efficiency that Weissmann remembered with pride. And, ah, how wonderful it would be to return home!

He had a sudden, almost overpowering urge to hear cowbells again, to admire-the big dray horses at the Munich Oktoberfest, to say 'Grüss Gott' to a stranger, to taste a dish of sauerkraut.

He was still thinking of these homely things, tears misting his eyes, as the submarine took the three men aboard, and sank down again like some black whale.

And then there was nothing but the sea, ablaze with lightly shooting splinters of fire at his burning eyes, through his aching, tortured head, through his impossible dreams.

CHAPTER SIX: DURANGO AND MAZAT-LAN, MEXICO

Love flattened himself against the cellar wall and listened. The footsteps stopped. The breathing went on. So what was happening? What was it that walked and didn't breathe, and breathed and didn't walk?

'Who's there?' he called softly. Now the breathing stopped, too. A girl's voice replied in English: 'Who are you?'

It had a slight accent which Love could not place. Not American or English, possibly continental. The question didn't carry human knowledge much farther, but at least it went a little way.

'We haven't been formally introduced, but my name's Love,' he said. 'Dr Jason Love, of Somerset, England. Who are you, and why are you here?'

'That's too long to tell a stranger,' said the girl.

'If we're down here for very long, maybe we won't be strangers,' replied Love.

'That is a possibility,' the girl agreed gravely.

She lit a butane cigarette lighter. An oval face danced in the tiny flame, pale cheeks framed with dark hair, a Burne-Jones portrait in black sweater, dark blue jeans, blue canvas shoes. Love held out his hand.

'You haven't told me your name,' he said.

'Shamara,' she said.

The name sounded familiar. Where had he heard it before? Someone in his practice? Or in Mexico City? In Nassau? Check. Senora Alcantara had told him that her daughter was called Shamara. But wasn't she still with her?

'Do you know a Senora Alcantara?' he asked. 'In Nassau?'

The girl nodded.

'Yes. But don't talk about her here.'

'Why not? What else is there to talk about? She must be the only mutual acquaintance we've got.'

'Possibly. But this cellar may be bugged.'

'With microphones?'

'Yes, what else?'

My God, thought Love. Here I am, back again in this dark labyrinthine world of half-truths and hidden microphones. Was there no way out? Was he doomed to become involved every-where he travelled, like some refugee from a Greek myth pur-sued by the furies, for a reason he did not know and which no one would tell him?

'I take it you're not down here by your own wish?' he said.

'You take it correctly. But don't discuss that now either. We've got to get out.'

'I second that motion,' said Love. Imprisonment with a beauti-ful girl could have its moments, but to be free would offer far more.

'Are you sure there's a microphone?'

'No. But there could be.'

'Well, let's have a bloody look then.'

He started to go round the room, holding up her cigarette lighter. Shadows danced the watusi on the walls.

'You won't find it like that,' she said. 'It'll be a tiny thing, the size of a nailhead.'

'I don't see why there should be one,' said Love confidently, try-ing to convince himself. 'Even if there is, what have we to lose? I lost that years ago.'

She said nothing.

'I came here with a book for Senora Alcantara's husband,' he went on, 'but some character upstairs - name of Kernau -said there was a transistorized transmitter concealed in the binding. I thought he was mad. But he wasn't. He took the book to pieces, and, dammit, something was hidden in it.'

The walls were of breeze blocks, with dollops of cement hanging down between them like grey icing. The house must be very new. He flicked off the lighter, closed his eyes to accustom them to the darkness. A faint glimmer of light came from one. corner. He took a step towards this, and, in the distant darkness, a machine began to whirr like an angry fan. There was a sudden growl and grumble, a boom and the pale light turned amber.

Love walked carefully towards this flickering glow, hands outstretched in front of him, like a blind man. He passed through .a low archway without a door, lined with rough cement and unfinished plaster, which led into an. even smaller cellar. Against the far wall, flame blazed in a small porthole. This must be an oil-fired boiler that probably supplied hot water for the house.

He went on - and fell flat on his face. He scrabbled about in the cement, felt for the lighter, flicked it on. He had tripped over a small pile of paint tins. That's what came of trying to see in the dark.

Next to the scattered tins, three brushes stood in a jam jar of dirty water; then a paper bag of cement, a small pile of pink and black bathroom tiles, and, wrapped in tissue paper, a chromium tap and shower unit for a bath, with a long flexible, chromium hose. This must be where the builders put the bits and pieces they hadn't used. But how did that help him?

The pale light he had seen was coming from a circular hole in the wall at eye level, about two feet across, screened by an ornamental grille, three bars of twisted iron, painted black. He put up both hands and pulled with all his weight on the iron; they held firm. Outside, he could see a courtyard of granite chips. This must be at the side of the house. He took Shamara's arm, brought her up to the boiler. She felt warm to hold; pliable and young. He wished he was holding her differently in different surroundings.

'Even if this place is bugged, it wouldn't pick up our voices above this noise,' he whispered. 'How long have you been here?'

'Two days. They let me up for meals. They even allow me to have a bath.'

'Who?'

'I can't tell you here,' she said. 'They may just pick up our voices.'

'If we do get out, how do we get away?' asked Love, changing the subject.

'Leave that to me,' said Shamara. 'Can you get us out?'

'A good question,' said Love. 'I was coming to that later in my lecture. A whole lot later.'

He handed the lighter back to her; he did not want to exhaust its tiny reservoir of gas. His eyes grew more accustomed to the darkness, and he knelt down among the paint tins, feeling for any length of pipe, anything long enough and strong enough to break the metal grille. He found an adjustable King Dick spanner, with a handle a foot long. He gripped one of the cross bars of the grille in its jaws, tightened them, tried to turn the spanner. All he did was to turn his wrist. The bars were stronger than they seemed.

He heard a metallic click from a thermostat switch on the boiler, the roar of its blower died and the flames went out. He had the same arrangement in his own boiler at home in Hishop's Combe. The boiler would fire up again as soon as the temperature fell below a set degree, and burn until the heat of the water had risen beyond this. Then the whole cycle of events would begin again.

He removed the spanner, examined the grille more closely. Then he glanced at his watch, timing the silence until the boiler lit up.

If he hadn't a lever long enough to bend those bars, how the hell could he move them? He could saw through them. For a moment, he thought with longing of the minute flexible trepanning saw he had carried concealed in a shoe lace on his visit to the Himalayas.

Well, as he hadn't a saw, how else could he cut a metal bar? He could burn it away with a welding torch. Another damned silly idea. But was it? Couldn't it be adapted? The boiler grumbled into life, the redness of the flames inside the porthole trembling on the far wall. He knelt down by the boiler to examine it more closely. There was a large main jet and several subsidiary jets, through which oil vapour was pumped to be ignited by some electrical device. The heat in the main jet might just be strong enough to melt the thin metal bars, but how to move that jet to the grille, at least two yards away?

Then he remembered the flexible chromium pipe on the shower attachment. He knelt down with his spanner, unscrewed the big hexagonal nut that connected an end to the top unit; the pipe itself was about seven feet long. Although the heat of the jet would be terrific, he guessed that the pipe was probably made of chrome steel; it should hold out longer than the window bars. Not much longer, but enough.

Shamara was watching him closely, and raised her eyebrows in an unspoken question. He shook his head, put one finger against his lips. It would never do for them to be disturbed now, and he had no time for explanations.

The thermostat clicked again, and the flame went out. By his watch, it had been out for about two minutes before it relit itself. He could bank on no more than this space of time now.

He knelt in front of the boiler, opened the port-hole, wrapped a handkerchief round his right wrist. A crust of ash glowed red with heat. Shamara knelt beside him, and held her cigarette lighter so that he could see to adjust the jaws of the spanner around the jet unit. The first time he tried to undo it, the spanner slipped and he was thankful for his handkerchief that protected his wrist. He'd been burned enough already.

He tightened the spanner another half turn, and gave a long slow pull, to test, the jaws. When they still held, he tried a quick jerk. The spanner banged against the metal of the boiler. He had loosened the jet.

He wrapped the silk handkerchief from his breast pocket around this, unscrewed it quickly. Then he pushed one end of the flexible tube over the pipe where the jet had been. The screw threads were not quite the same, but he could tighten up the nut some way before they slipped. He bound the handkerchief around the joint to make it more oil-tight, picked up the jet, crammed this into the other end of the pipe. Then he wrapped his other handkerchief around it about six inches down, where it should not grow too hot to hold.

The thermostat clicked again and the blower began to hum. Love jabbed the jet on its pipe into the still-hot mouth of the boiler; for an instant the smell of kerosene filled the room, and he thought his experiment was not going to work. Then there was a loud boom, a flash as the jet caught, and a tongue of fire six inches long blazed from its fish-tail.

He pointed the jet against the bottom bar of the grille. The pungent burning of the paint as it blistered, crackled and smoked made his eyes smart. Heat began to feed back along the pipe through his handkerchief. Finally, the bar grew wrinkled and turn grey and pink. Love picked up the spanner, clamped the jaws on the bar and twisted. The bar - bent and snapped like a stick of toffee. Then the boiler went out.

He removed the paint brushes from the jam jar, soaked his handkerchief in the water: the end of the pipe was growing too hot to hold comfortably. Then he waited until the boiler started, relit the jet and burned away the second bar.

The smell of leaking kerosene was sickening and when the boiler cut out again, Love leaned against the wall, sweating with weariness. There was a growing chance of explosion with so much vapour escaping, but this was a risk he had to take. The only other alternative was certain discovery, and then what?

As the boiler started for the third time, he lit the jet and played it on the third and last bar. If he could cut through this, he would have made a hole wide enough for them to crawl through. As the flame blistered the paint, he heard a faint noise beyond the stairs in the other cellar. Someone was about to open the door.

'Can you stop them,' Love panted to Shamara.

'What with?' asked the girl desperately.

There was no point now in concealment: once that door was open, their only way of escape was gone. Shamara ran back into the cellar, leaned against the sliding door, beat on it frantically, shouting 'Wait a minute, you've trapped my hand. Please!' The intensity of her voice made her shouts seem convincing. The noises stopped on the other side of the door.

'Move away,' called a man's voice. 'We're coming in.'

The third metal bar was smoking now, growing heat wrinkles, turning from black through pink to white. Still holding the jet in his right hand, Love seized the bar at the centre with his spanner and twisted it.

The tortured metal bent, parted. He pushed the bottom stump back and forward until it cracked, and the bar gave way in his hand. He threw it on the floor.

'Now!' he shouted to the girl.

She ran back to join him.

145

'Through there on your hands and knees,' ordered Love. 'Quick!'

Shamara seized the stumps of metal with her hands, pulled herself up and through. Love followed. As he was halfway through, the door opened. He heard shouts of anger and surprise, running feet. He dragged himself free and turned, leaning back into the cellar, still holding the flaming jet in his hand.

It lit up the faces of three men. Jose Manuel, the short man who had hit him, and a stranger. The short man whipped a gun from a shoulder holster. In the second before he could fire, Love tossed the flaming jet back among them, and jumped to one side, pulling Shamara with him.

As the jet hit the floor, it touched off the reeking kerosene vapour. The explosion blew a tongue of flame twenty feet long through the window. The screams of the men incinerated in this tide of heat were lost in the roar of the furnace.

'Run!' shouted Love hoarsely. They were across the courtyard, out through a side gate, down the empty road by the car wrecker's before the fire bells began to ring behind them.

They dodged into a gateway and paused for breath; the sweat was drying on Love's body; he felt almost unbearably weary and cold.

'Where are you going?' she asked him.

'Back to the hotel, where else?'

Ask a crazy question, and what kind of answer can you expect?

'Don't be an idiot,' she said. 'That's the first place they'll look.'

'What do you expect me to do? Sleep in the street? It's the Posada Duran for me. I've booked a room. Can't the police protect me, if no one else can?'

He started to walk; he was beyond any more running. Shamara ran after him, pulling him back by the arm.

'The police,' she repeated contemptuously. 'What kind of protection will they give you? Don't be a fool. They'll have been the first people to be fixed.'

Her face was appealing, even in the unhealthy green glow of the street lights. Also, what she said could be true. Love had a British distrust of foreign policemen, with their fancy uniforms and guns and funny hats.

'You don't believe me, do you?' she went on. 'All right, telephone the hotel then. Prove it, if you must. But for God's sake don't prove it by going there.'

The reasoning made sense.

'Where is there a phone box in this wretched town?' asked Love.

'The Telegraph Office. I know the way. Round the back streets.'

She led him away from the main road, down narrow alleys where cats snuffled in the dust, and mangy dogs started away guiltily at their-approach, backs arched like springs. The air was sour with urine; even the mosquitoes were complaining.

The Telegraph Office had a courtyard with green and white tiles: pink pillars held up the ceilings, from which chains supported fly-blown fluorescent tubes. A beggar woman with a moustache dozed in rags on the stone steps. As they ran past, she opened eyes dark as capuli cherries, and with as much understanding, closed them again contemptuously. Their haste had nothing to do with her; they were only foreigners. To hell with them.

Inside the office a fan was turning somewhere, squeakily, as though it resented not being turned off. Shamara tapped impatiently on a glass window at the counter until a clerk came out from the back. He was eating a tortilla; little flecks of egg clung yellow in his moustache. She spoke to him in Spanish. The man nodded, indicated a grey wooden telephone booth near a Pepsi Cola dispenser. More discussions in Spanish, coins changed hands; the telephone bell in the booth began to ring.

Love picked up the receiver.

'Posada Duran Recepcion,' a voice told him.

Love cleared his throat. The booth was hot and airless. People had written telephone numbers, drawings, messages on the wall in pencil; a few flies were holding a meeting on the naked bulb above his head.

'I would like to speak to Dr Love,' he said. 'I'm a friend of his.' At least he has one friend, he thought; he has me.

'We've already rung his room. It is empty,' the voice told him in English. 'Someone else has also been telephoning for him. And he has two friends who have just arrived, waiting in the lounge. Who shall I tell him rang?'

Love said nothing. So the girl had been right. In the mirror, above the directions for calling police, fire, ambulance, he watched his forehead go damp with the sweat of horror. The voice went on: 'Who is that speaking, please? Who shall I say it is, senor? May I have your name, please?'

Not on your nelly, thought Love, and replaced the receiver, cutting off the questioning voice. He opened the door slowly, heavy with thoughts he didn't want to think. The flies buzzed away as the light went out; they weren't enough to make a quorum.

'Well?' asked Shamara gently. 'Was I right?'

He nodded.

'I'm sorry to say you were.'

'I've got a better plan than yours,' she said, taking his arm.

'What's that?'

In the present state of play, it wouldn't take much to improve on his.

'The airfield. I've a plane there,' she said.

'How far is that?'

'About four miles.'

'We'll never make it on our feet,' said Love. 'Let's get a car.'

'We'll not find a taxi out as late as this.'

The main road out of town lay empty as a poor man's purse. Yellow lamp standards, planted like curved trees among the palms and bushes, poured down their golden light on deserted concrete. Love felt his throat constrict with the beginnings of despair.

'There must be a taxi somewhere, surely,' he said.

An old truck turned out of a side road and chugged towards them. The front part had started life as a Chevrolet car; the back was sawn off to make a platform, stacked with oil drums roped together. Shamara shouted to the man in Spanish, and he shouted back and then he stopped.

'Come on,' she said. 'He says he'll give us a lift there for ten dollars. It's on his way.'

'That's more than the car's worth,' he said, his Scottish blood revolting at waste, even in this extremity.

'It's our money or your life,' retorted Shamara. They climbed aboard, drove slowly past a skyline of saw-toothed factory roofs, a trellis advertising Mexico Courts Motel, a spherical water tank on a tower, a silver roc's egg on stilts. The taste and smell of dry dust, dry herbs, of a dry country, lay in Love's mouth and nostrils. He sat back thankfully on the old plastic seat.

Christ in gold looked across the empty square with the dusty trees and the shuttered shops and the dead neon signs. Christ in verdigris watched from a wayside shrine, and behind them soared the Cathedral. Next to it a huge blue sign flickered above the Posada Duran roof. Under that roof lay a bath, clean sheets, a meal, he thought. But between him and these simple delights were men who sought him for a reason he did not begin to know. He sighed. Somerset was never like this.

The little houses on either side of the road, shuttered and dead, lacked depth and dimension, as though they were only cardboard laths. The feeling of unreality he had noticed in Nassau returned. A man on a bicycle, carrying a girl on-the pillion, pedalled the wrong way down a one-way street. A soldier in a peaked cap, rifle .over his shoulder, rooted under the light of a gas flare on a wheelbarrow; an old woman in black, like a hoody crow, watched him silently.

Then the houses fell away. Black and white cows grazed by the roadside, their dim, surprised eyes lit up like reflectors by the ancient headlamps. White stones marking the edge of the road stretched across a vast plateau, ringed in, under the moonlight, by the rusty hills scattered with cacti and thorn bushes. The trees had no leaves, only grey crackly branches looking in the lights like the bleached bones of huge, unknown animals.

The road dipped and rose and turned past little cones of grey gravel chips where it heeded resurfacing. In the distance, unseen coyotes lifted long snouts to lance the night with calls of loneliness.

The driver slowed unexpectedly, said something in Spanish to Shamara and stopped. He left his engine running.

'We're here,' Shamara told Love. They climbed down.

To the right of the road some huts clustered together for company under the shadow of two hangars. Through a lighted window in one, Love saw odd aeroplane wheels and bent copper pipes hanging on a wall; a radio was tuned to dance music, but nobody was dancing. On the hills behind, folded like a dark cloth, a mass of lights shimmered coldly, a glacier of fallen stars. It was a silver mine, as busy by night as by day.

Love gave the man a ten dollar bill. He examined it closely under the single dashlight, tightened it between his two hands, put it away carefully in an inner pocket of his jacket.

'Adios,' he said.

'Adios,' Love repeated. He hoped it was goodbye.

Shamara took his hand, and they watched the single red tail-light die in the distance.

'Where's your plane?' asked Love.

'In the second hangar,'

'Well, let's get it out quickly,' he said. 'You're a qualified pilot?'

'Of course. As qualified as you are a doctor.'

'Then God help us.'

'Amen to that,' she said.

They grinned at each other, suddenly liking to be together, even in this situation, or maybe because of this situation.

'Where are you going to fly to?' he asked her.

'Mexico City.'

'But what about my luggage at the hotel here?'

'Never mind that, doctor. You can buy another shirt. But not another life.'

'Is it as bad as that, then?'

'Yes. Maybe worse.'

'But why? Who are all these people? What's it all about?'

'I can't tell you here,', she said. 'But I will tell you.'

'Thank you very much,' said Love dryly. 'So long as we know.'

'You'll know. Meanwhile, I need your help in opening that hangar door. It's a sliding door, but we mustn't make too much noise. When they find you're not back at your hotel and that I've gone, this is bound to be the next place they'll look. The train goes every other day. A plane's the only other way out. Any more questions?'

'Not now,' said Love, but he was asking himself one about Shamara, and he hoped he knew the right answer.

Vertical ribs of corrugated iron towered above them; even the horizontal metal beam from which the sliding doors were suspended hung at least thirty feet above their heads. There was a padlock hasp, but no padlock. Love opened the hasp, pushed against the door. For a moment, its weight resisted him, then it began to roll easily.

A warm, unfamiliar smell, an amalgam of fuselage dope, of petrol and oil and still-warm engines hung like musk on the night air. Shamara's plane was in the right of the hangar, a blue and silver Cessna.

Love went inside, pulled the chocks from its wheels, began to manhandle it out clumsily, by the front wing, while Shamara steered it from the tail. Out on the tarmac the aircraft looked absurdly small. Love knew nothing about flying; the sight of the single propeller and the memory of the desert over which he had flown that morning, did little to cheer him.

They pushed it out on to the runway.

'Climb in,' she told him.

Love put one foot on the step in the wing, opened the tiny door on the left of the fuselage. Inside, there were seats for two pilots. He took the left-hand one, strapped himself in carefully. Wasn't there something in his life insurance policy about only being covered for scheduled flights? So what? There was nothing in it either against being beaten up, threatened with revolvers, thrown into a dungeon. He'd better see his broker about all this when he got home.

The cockpit was padded in cream quilted plastic. The dark circular dials of the instruments reflected the stars through the windows like pin-points in the floor of heaven. Shamara climbed in beside him, strapped herself in, ran through the switch and control drill, then turned on the ignition, pressed the starter button. Through the windscreen Love watched the blades of the propeller begin to turn reluctantly, and then more willingly. The engine fired, and blew out a gout of black smoke. She warmed it up against the brakes, looking back towards the road behind the hangars for any sign of pursuing headlights. But there was nothing.

They began to move slowly down the silent runway into the wind, their small tyres bumping over the joints and corrugations in the concrete. Slowly she opened-the throttle, then accelerated more fiercely; the ground raced away from them and they were airborne. She turned above the airport and headed south-east back towards Mexico City.

Below them, toy trucks and trailers crawled along roads, their headlamps throwing fans of light. Rivers lay cold and pale as glass. The cockpit, Love thought; glancing around him, was not all that much warmer. Shamara casually flicked up a toggle switch on the dashboard and then wiggled it up and down sharply. 'What's wrong?' asked Love.

'The fuel. We're only on one tank. That's full. The other's empty.'

'Well?'

'It's not well at all. We can't make Mexico City. It's too far.'

'Show me the map,' said Love resignedly. Why the hell hadn't she checked this before? Women pilots.

She pushed the map across to him; it was clipped to a board, beneath a transparent cover; a pencil hung from a piece of string. There was a scale on the mica. In the green glow of the dashlights, Love measured the distance from various towns marked with the outline of an aircraft to show they had landing grounds. The choice seemed to be between Torreon, where he had changed planes on the way up, or Mazatlan on the West Coast. If they went back to Torreon, they would have to fly over

Durango and could be seen: also, it only had a tiny airfield and refuelling might be difficult without advance notice. Mazatlan, on the other hand, had an international airport. They could buy tickets to Mexico City easily enough, or they could refuel. There was also another reason in the back of his mind, but he could not recall what it was.

'About face,' he said. 'We'll head for Mazatlan.'

Love reset the compass as the plane banked and turned.

'Know anyone there?' he asked, and in asking remembered the subconscious reason why he had selected Mazatlan.

Shamara shook her head.

'Do you?'

'In a way.' He had remembered Pietro Gomez, the secretary of the vintage car rally. He could be a useful friend. Old car buffs might not agree on each other's choice of old cars, but invariably they were friendly to each other. The shared enthusiasm for individualistic automobiles bound together all such individualists.

'Where did you learn to fly?' he asked, watching Shamara.

She pulled a set of earpieces over her dark hair, began to tune the radio.

'Years ago,' she replied noncommittally.

'I said where?'

'With the Israeli Air Force.'

'Ah. You were going to tell me what all this business back in Durango was about?'

She removed the earphones, looked down out of her side window before answering. Love looked with her. Huge pillars of rusty rock sprouted from the brown emptiness like the gateposts of some strange, long-vanished city. Here and there grew groves of trees, a field of unbelievable greenness in the early morning light. It was like passing across a half-finished landscape; all the ingredients were there, but had not been assembled. Or perhaps they had been assembled thousands of years ago, and were now in pieces again. Either way, it was not a good place for a crash-landing.

'I can tell you something, but not all,' Shamara said slowly, breaking into his thoughts. 'What do you want to know first?'

'Who is Senor Alcantara?'

She smiled. Her teeth were very white and even.

'There's no such man,' she said.

'What do you mean, no such man?' protested Love. 'I brought a book to him from his wife in Nassau. Senora Alcantara told me her daughter's name was Shamara. Aren't you her daughter?'

'No,' said Shamara,. looking ahead. 'My mother died in 1943 in an "S" truck.'

'What's that?'

'The letter "S" stands for Saurer, the German firm that made the trucks, and sonder a German word meaning 'special'.

'They were special all right. Each truck took about twenty-five people from our concentration camp to a mass burial, ground. The exhaust gas from the engine was fed into the back, as they drove. It was sealed and killed them within a quarter of an hour. Not a pleasant way to die.'

'I never heard about this,' said Love. 'How many prisoners were killed like this?'

'Three-quarters of a million in Russia alone. My mother among them. Rather more in Poland.'

'That's a lot of journeys at twenty-five a time.'

'Thousands,' said Shamara tonelessly, looking straight ahead.

'Murder by mass production. The Nazis hadn't time to shoot or hang them all, so they did it this way.'

'Was that the only reason?'

She smiled bitterly.

'Not quite. They really began using these trucks because Himmler, the head of the Gestapo, once watched a firing squad in Minsk shooting a batch of women and children. Not all the victims were killed, but they buried them just the same.

'Surprisingly, this made him faint - a great loss of face, as you can imagine - so he announced that he'd spare German soldiers these traumatic experiences. In future, women and children would no longer be shot. They'd be gassed instead in these special trucks.'

'I'm sorry,' said Love inadequately, because he was.

The girl put out her left hand, touched his.

'Thank you. But tell me, how are you involved?'

'I'm not involved at all. I mean, not intentionally. A doctor from Somerset in England, on holiday. Or at least, I was. And I can prove it. My passport.'

He fumbled in his inside pocket. She shook her head.

'I'll take your word for it. Proof like that doesn't mean anything in my business.'

'Your business?' Echoes from the past sounded distantly and dangerously in Love's mind. 'Are you an agent of some sort?'

'Not exactly. I am Jewish. I'm going to marry a professor at Tel-Aviv University.'

'That doesn't mean anything, either. Not in-my business,' countered Love. 'What are you doing over here so far from Israel?'

'A branch of our government asked me to come.'

'I see.'

This sounded ominously like MacGillivray's apparently innocent request to him, when he had flown to Persia and ended up
in Canada. He didn't like the recollection - or the similarity.

'Did it also ask Senora Alcantara and that Cuban woman to come
as well?'

She nodded.

'And something else,' added Love. 'You never owned an op-art
bathing costume, did you?'

She shook her head.

'Why?' she asked.

'I wondered.'

Events were beginning to drop into place in-his mind. A few, but
not all; and maybe not even into the right places. But they were
moving. Someone had shaken the snowstorm in the crystal ball,
but now the snowflakes were settling. Some of them.

'Before you tell me more, I'll tell you something,' he said. 'I was
in Nassau, staying at a friend's house, when I saw a girl shot in a
boat. She wore a black and white op-art swim suit. Then I had a
call from Senora Alcantara. She told me the girl had been your
maid, and had been wearing your costume. Ergo, she had been
shot in mistake for you.

'She also told me that her husband was in Mexico City to restart
a family firm that Castro had taken over in Cuba. She asked me
to take a book to him. We were apparently both in the same
hotel. The Bamer. So I agreed. After all, it wasn't much to do.

'The clerk at the Bamer said this man was in Durango, so I came
there, and then the strong arm stuff started. I don't think that
the girl who was shot was ever a maid, or a Cuban. Any more
than Senora Alcantara is your mother, or a Cuban. Any more
than there ever was a Senor Alcantara - as you admit. That was
all a load of bull to dress up the real request.

'Someone had to carry a concealed radio transmitter. The girl who should have done so was rumbled and shot. So then the Senora went through the local papers to find if any tourist could conceivably be used. Someone who was going to Mexico. She happened to strike me. The newspaper said I was in-interested in Sir Thomas Browne, a seventeenth-century -English doctor turned author. So she comes up with a book by another seventeenth-century English author who wished he'd been a doctor - Robert Burton - and she fits the set into this. Plus a sob story about the family firm that had been seized, and so on. Am I right?'

For a moment, the girl said nothing. Beneath them, the empty landscape, edged now with the early alchemy of morning, slowly turned from dross to gold.

'You may be,' she admitted.

'Don't you know?'

She shook her head.

'No. I only know my own part.'

She looked at him, then, into his eyes. He believed her. He had faced too many people in his surgery, telling him lies, even to be deceived easily.

'What's your part then?'

'I was asked to go to Nassau by our people responsible for capturing Eichmann. We've had what we call a station there for some time - a sort of base - which Mitzi Alcantara runs. It's convenient. Near the States, yet not actually in them. You know?'

Love knew.

'Go on,' he said.

'Well, they'd had a tip about some new tenants in that house in Durango, the Casa del Sol. They were obviously German, they could be worth investigating. We get information like that all the time, mostly from Jews who've suffered. Our contact in Durango runs a decorating business. He was a displaced person who'd lost everything: his wife, his parents, his business. He reckoned he'd know a Nazi anywhere. He'd done some work at the house and he deliberately left a bit of wood, wet with paint, on the floor or somewhere. Someone moved it and this gave him a perfect set of prints. He sent them to us.

'It was only a routine check at first. Then we checked more carefully, for they fitted the designer of the "S" trucks. He worked under Untersturmfuhrer Dr Becker, who was in charge of the project.

'When the victims realized that these trucks were only death wagons, this man had the brilliant idea of disguising, them as caravans. That way, the women and children could believe more easily the rubbish they were told about being transferred to a better camp.'

'Who was he?' asked Love.

'Kernau is the name he uses now. I wanted him for my own. So did several others. We drew lots as to who should come. I drew the winning ticket.

'I was supposed to check on his activities and report back. Then he could be whisked out like Eichmann and tried. I agreed, but so far as I was concerned he was guilty. I meant to kill him as slowly and painfully as I could.

'The deal was for me to fly to Durango and case the house. Then Carmen - she'd come from Riga, her cover was a Cuban maid - would follow with a concealed transmitter. We'd got several - in cigarette cases, in a talcum powder tin, and some spare sets to fit in any special hiding place - like that book. The Casa del Sol was always being let to foreigners for short periods, so this could be concealed in a parcel. The decorator told us there were letters in the hall for half a dozen different people who had moved on, or who hadn't arrived yet. We fixed him up with a receiver to pick up and record everything that the transmitter put out.

'Then things began to go wrong. The other side must have got on to us somehow - I suppose in Nassau. You won't find many Nazi sympathizers in Haifa, where we planned the thing. Carmen was shot. I was already in Durango, so Mitzi had to rush about to find someone who'd bring the transmitter. She found you.'

'And I found you.'

'Yes, but you shouldn't have done. You wouldn't have done if I hadn't loused everything up.'

'How?'

'When I actually saw Kernau in a car in Durango, I forgot all my orders, all my intentions. I just trembled. And when I saw him face to face at the Casa del Sol, I couldn't keep my feelings out of my eyes and my face. They knew I hated them. It was an animal thing. And they feared who I was, who had sent me. After all they've been on the run for a long time - more than twenty years. So they put me into the cellar to try and find out.'

'Why in Mexico, I wonder?' asked Love, looking out of the window. Two trains were rushing towards each other across the plain. They passed and parted, a long worm breaking in two. The lines glittered, two snakes that had died side by side.

'It's always been a useful place between North America and South - like Nassau from our point of view. It's where the Russians killed Trotsky. Where Baptista's overthrow in Cuba was plotted. Where the attempted Communist take-over in Guatemala was worked out.

'You can easily get over the border into the States. And you can melt away just as easily into half a dozen Latin Republics.

'South America is still thick with ex-Nazis. They've moved from the Argentine to Brazil or Paraguay. Some are still in little enclaves along the East Coast. They'd like to get but. But where is there left to run? Nowhere, except back to Germany.'

'But Bonn doesn't want them either, surely?'

'Not officially,' agreed Shamara.

'But there are many ex-Nazis in high places throughout West Germany. If there was some way of getting these men back, maybe doing a bit of plastic surgery on them, giving-them new beginnings, new names, they wouldn't all be turned away. Now. This man you know in Mazatlan. Can he be trusted?'

'How the hell do I know? I've never met him.'

'I thought you knew him?'

'I've a letter from him. He's running the vintage car rally in Mexico City.'

'Oh, my God!' said Shamara. 'What are we going to do in Mazatlan then?'

'See him first. Maybe we could all go back to Mexico City Together. They're looking for two people. They might not think of looking for three.'

Love spoke so confidently that he almost believed himself. The girl looked at him sharply. He smiled. Suddenly, they both burst out laughing.

'You could only be English,' she said. 'You're so absurd. Do you know the risks we're running?'

'I never think about risks,' Love assured her, looking out of the window at the razor edges of the peaks beneath. 'If you're going to cross Niagara on a tight rope, you don't bother about what may happen if you fall. You know damn well what'll happen. So you make up your mind to get to the other side. Safely. You might be running a risk yourself, being in a plane, with a strange man.'

'Meaning?'

'What about that professor in Tel-Aviv? The one you're engaged to?'

Shamara smiled, looking at him: the sun was shining in her eyes. She looked like all the girls Love had ever known, and even better.

'There isn't really such a man,' she said shyly. 'I invented him. As a sort of protection.'

'Against men like me?'

'Against men. Not necessarily like you.'

'Then against men who do this?'

He turned in his seat, pulled her towards him, kissed her. For a second her body stiffened, then relaxed. The plane trembled. They drew apart.

'Against the wrong men doing that,' she said carefully. The sun threw their shadow like a travelling cross on the brown wrinkled mountains. Ahead, in the distance, the hills merged into a misty haze, and then suddenly they fell away, and the sea stretched out beneath them.

Mazatlan airstrip ran parallel to the shore. A handful of ships lay like toys in the port. Love saw a rash of shabby huts, a lake of stagnant green water, the word 'Chevrolet' painted on a corrugated roof. He wondered where Gomez lived; he hoped it was not far away.

Shamara switched on the radio, spoke in Spanish to Control, banked, turned and came down. They taxied up to the airport buildings. She switched off the engine, locked the brakes. They climbed out. The air smelled damp from the sea; after the drumming inside the cabin, Love's ears still rang as though he had been boxed around them.

Near the long, single-story airport building, a miniature Eiffel Tower supported a cluster of wires. Three silver fuel storage tanks were marked: '100 OCTANOS - NO FUME'. Behind the sea, to the left, three small hills rose out of the water. On the centre the name of the presidential candidate, Diaz Ordaz, was painted in enormous white letters. Sea-birds wheeled and dropped lime on it. They hadn't any votes.

'How much money have you got?' asked Shamara.

'Couple of hundred dollars,' said Love. 'That'll surely get us back. I've a Diner's Club card, too, which should take care of the fare.'

A man was leaning against the wall of the building, watching them. He prised himself away, pushed back his cone-shaped sombrero and walked forward to meet them. His face was lined and creased as a wooden carving. A Don Ameche moustache clung to his upper lip as though it liked being there.

'You want a taxi?' he asked in English. His teeth were very white, tipped with gold. His mouth seemed expensive, just to look at.

Love nodded.

'Yes. To the Avenida de los Insurgentes.'

'It is early yet, senor,' the man pointed out. 'They may not be awake. That is a rich part of town. They sleep late. Would you riot like to see Mazatlan first? The hotels, the market, the harbour. No?'

'No,' said Love.

The driver shrugged; he held open the door of the red and white Studebaker. He had not expected any other answer, but he had done his best.

On one side of the airport road a dozen kite hawks, the size of black chickens, clustered around the rotting carcass of a mule, picking its bones. One, feathers reddened, was actually inside the looped ribs of the beast. They stopped pecking to watch the car go by.

The sun was creeping up the sky, as carefully as a lodger before a husband's return.

'You want a drink of water, senor?' the taxi driver asked.

'No, thank you.' Love shook his head. Was the man learning English or something? Why should anyone want a drink of water at this hour? Tea, coffee, rum; anything but water.

The man suddenly swept off his sombrero from his bald head. Fixed by a red rubber sucker to his brown polished pate was a chromium-plated bathroom tap.

'How do you like that, senor?' he said, grinning, turning the top of the tap. 'As you English say, I don't need water. I can make my own! Ha! Ha! Ha!'

He roared with laughter, slapping his fat thighs. The car swerved dangerously.

'Thank you very much,' said Love wearily. 'Very amusing indeed.'

He only needed this, a nut. But, who except a nut would be out at the airport at that ungodly hour?

They drove past the American Consulate, where the flag drooped in the morning mist, as though it had also had a rough night. The sands were deserted. Wooden poles held up thatched umbrellas, shelters against the coming sun. A handful of blue wooden chairs, still damp with dew, waited for the morning trade. Sea-birds, brown and grey, with long thin legs like knitting needles pecked about hopefully under the tables.

They drove inland from the front, and almost instantly the veneer of elegance fell away; they were among settlements of filthy shacks, with straw roofs and mud walls. Barefooted children scratched in the dirt with hungry dogs; cooking fires were already lit.

'You smoke, senora?' asked the taxi driver; glancing back at Shamara.

'Not now, thank you. It's too early.'

'Please. Try one of these.' He handed a silver cigarette case across the red plastic seat.

'But I don't want one now. I've told you.'

'Then keep it for later, senora.'

She sighed, opened the case. Twenty dummy cigarettes flew in all directions under a spring.

'Please,' said Love irritably. 'You're shortening my life span. Just drive. Spare us the jokes.'

'You want to be happy like me, Fernandez. Look. I give you my card.'

He handed Love a photograph of his face, the size of a postcard, with the name, Fernandez Manchele, on it, and underneath: 'The Happiest Driver South of the Border'.

'Keep it,' said Fernandez grandly. 'I have friends everywhere. New York. San Francisco. Madrid. Everywhere you name, everywhere you think. They all know Fernandez. The Happiest Driver.'

I wish I didn't, thought Love; at this hour it was all too much.

They drove up through the market, where stalls were already covered with raw meat, dried devil fish, coloured mosaics; a straw Christ hung on a straw crucifix.

Pietro Gomez lived in a steeply sloped street, considerately lined with palms. The houses stood close together as though conscious of their cost. Their gardens were overgrown in a runaway tropical fashion, with plump cactus plants, and brightly berried bushes.

'Wait in the cab until I see if my friend's at home,' Love told Shamara.

'No,' she said. 'You don't speak Spanish. You may need an interpreter. I'll come with you.'

They walked up the short path, pressed the bell, stood looking at each other as it pealed emptily inside the house. Footsteps shuffled in the hallway; the rattle of a chain being removed, the creak of a board. The door opened half a foot, and a heavy-eyed house-boy regarded them without enthusiasm. Sleep still matted his hair.

'We want to see Senor Gomez,' Shamara told him in Spanish. 'We apologize for calling so early, but it's very important.'

'The Senor is not here,' said the house-boy. 'He has gone to Acapulco unexpectedly, to see his cousin, Senor Diaz. There is sudden trouble in his family.'

And in mine, thought Love, as Shamara translated. More every minute.

'When will he be back?' she asked.

'I don't know. Maybe he does not come here for several days. He's going to Mexico City. There's a rally for old cars. Maybe he'll fly there directly from Acapulco. Yes, maybe he will do that.'

The girl translated all this to Love.

'Then let's get out of here,' he said, turning back towards the gate. He hated inactivity, what he called horsing about: any action could be better than waiting.

'Where can we go?' asked Shamara, more practically.

'We'll discuss it back in the cab.'

'Thank you for your help,' she told the house-boy, held out half a dollar. Fingers, with nails black-edged like mourning cards, folded over it; footsteps flopped away down the corridor.

The morning air felt heavy with the sweet, cloying scent of flowers, almost too heavy to breathe. Love rubbed his hand wearily against his chin. He needed a shave, a bath, a change of clothes. They'd better book into an hotel, and think again.

He clicked the gate shut behind him, his mind miles away. Their taxi had turned and was facing the other way. Fernandez was leaning against the front door, his arms folded. He made no move to open the door. He was smiling. There seemed enough gold in his teeth to stock a bank.

As Love put his hand on the handle, Fernandez unfolded his arms. In his right fist he held a snub-nosed automatic.

'Stay right where you are,' he said softly. 'Not to move at all. Hands up. Reach for Jesus.'

CHAPTER SEVEN: THE REPUBLIC OF DELGUEDA; NASSAU, BAHAMAS; WHITE-HALL, LONDON; ERITH, KENT, ENGLAND

There was no sound in the mess hall but the distant thump of the lighting generator, muted by the thick walls, and the harsh whistling breath of the man next to Weissmann.

He had been in charge of the decompression chambers at Dachau, where prisoners were submerged naked in icy water for hours on end in an attempt to discover why so many Luftwaffe pilots, shot down uninjured over the North Sea, should die after only a few hours in the water.

The Dachau experiments produced no results, but one of the victims, a Russian officer, had suddenly clawed at the windpipe of the Gestapo officer supervising the experiment. The wound had never healed properly, and he still breathed partly through his nose, partly through this extra orifice. Weissmann hated his choking, bubbling breathing; it reminded him of too many slow deaths he wanted to forget. He tried to blot the sound from his mind as he looked at each of the set faces in turn.

'So we are agreed, gentlemen?'

They nodded one by one, catching his eyes.

'No. I don't like it,' said a short, fat man suddenly. He had black, lobster eyes, embedded in a cushion of soft flesh he used for a face. 'It is far too pat. Why didn't they send an ambassador or someone like that instead of a junior submarine captain?'

'He explained why,' said Axel irritably. 'If he'd come in a straight-forward way, he might have been followed.'

'How did he know we'd be here?' persisted the fat man. Weissmann shrugged.

'They have their sources of information - as we all had in the old days.' He hated this plodding, timid man, a former schoolmaster who had amassed a fortune as a purchasing clerk in the Gestapo 'Bureau d'Achat', in the Square du Bois de Boulogne, in Paris.

Here, on behalf of his country, he had bought and bartered such unlikely merchandise as steel, tungsten and rubber by the ton, and had taken his private profit on each deal - for what French merchant in 1944 could refuse a Gestapo officer his due, and live?

With the money he had bought houses, shops, a chateau in Chantilly where he filled the fire extinguishers with jewels, and hoarded bars of gold under the terrace; he did not trust the banks. But after the war, as he lived in style under another name, an old contact had informed the Americans and he had been forced to flee Spain, then on to the Argentine and finally to this wretched place. He was easily the richest man there, but his wealth was useless; it was all beyond his reach.

One part of him desperately wanted to risk returning to reclaim what he had hidden, but years of careful caution rose up against any such folly. He smelt treachery in everything.

'If we could be certain that the offer was genuine, you'd fall in with this?' Weissmann asked him.

'Of course, but how can we?'

'We will test Kinder's sincerity,' said Weissmann. 'I will tell him that, as the only serving officer among us, he must travel with me in case I cannot understand the instructions.

'But we'll not tell him this until we decide to go, in case he comes up with a counter-suggestion. But I think his offer is genuine. As he says, the West German Government needs our help - and is prepared to help us in return. The fact is, gentlemen, we have all lived too long in the shadows. We see twists and turns when the road is really straight. Does this satisfy you?'

The fat man nodded. It was a clever idea, and so simple. Old Weissmann was a cunning fox. He would spend that fortune yet.

'In that case,' said Weissmann thankfully, 'I'll ask Kinder to tell us exactly what we have to do in order to play our part.'

He limped across the floor, opened the door. Kinder, and the two men who had accompanied him before, stood in the porch. The sun was falling behind them into the sea, and, for an instant, the bay seemed full of blood, and Weissmann had a terrible premonition, a fearful unease, that he was about to make a decision more momentously wrong that anything in all his life, with the exception of joining the Party in his teens.

Then the sun set, and the sea was calm and dark and peaceful with no waves and no sign of the submarine. He had made up his mind; there would be no going back. For the first time since Weissmann had crawled out under the ruins of Berlin, he felt he was not drifting at the mercy of events; he was in command again: a man.

'Come in,' he said, and he was smiling. 'We are agreed, gentlemen. We are going to accept. Now, will you tell us what you wish us to do?'

Kinder nodded.

'It is the decision I had hoped for,' he said, holding out his hand. They were both overcome with the emotion, of the moment. Others crowded around them to shake their hands. Some were grinning, some wept openly. It was as though they were already on their way home; at last the end of their exile appeared in view.

Kinder led the way to the table, sat down. He seemed subtly to have taken command; Weissmann stumped along with him, but already he was slightly behind. Kinder held the key to freedom; he was going to say when and how it opened the lock.

He took a German naval chart of the area from a folder,

smoothed it flat on the table with his palms. One or two with naval experience looked over his shoulder and were surprised to see that its mica cover was already marked with blue lines and crosses and circles and numbers, as though Kinder had known in advance what their decision would be. , 'I suggest that we take this stage by stage, gentlemen,' he said.

'I know that some of you are not sailors, so I'll explain everything in the simplest way I can. If there are any queries, please ask them as they arise, for it is essential that all of us know exactly what we have to do.

'This is an operation which must be planned like the great military campaigns in the glorious years of the Third Reich. And it is one, gentlemen, that I prophesy will have infinitely more valuable results than any of those battles.'

He looked around at their faces again; some rapt, cruel, hopeful, suspicious; others scarred by old wounds, or etched with greed, perversion. Faces from the past, from a dusty, tattered, terrible picture of a nightmare that had nearly come true, but all now illumined with the almost unbelievable news that they could be on their way home.

Kinder cleared his throat and began to speak.

*　　　*　　　*

McGregor's black official Humber hummed past the Princess Margaret Hospital on Shirley Street, in Nassau, past the bottle-shaped royal palms with the staff buildings under their shade, past Dog Flea Alley and Lover's Lane, going east. He was on his way to the weekly lunch of the Rotary Club at the Montagu Hotel. It was half past twelve and the rest of the day was his own. So was the following one and the two weeks after that, for he was off on leave, and for the next fortnight, so far as he was concerned, police matters could look after themselves.

He sat back on the black leather, watching the white and pink houses, the Dad and Lad Shoes and Clothing Shop, the Shirley

Street Theatre (showing 'Robinson Crusoe on Mars'), then the trees behind the hotel. He frowned. A whole thatch of empty bottles marred the undergrowth beneath them. He hated untidiness, the unmethodical ways of these people. Anyone picnicking there could cut himself, and bleed to death. Ah well, that wasn't his department, anyway. Let them bleed.

His driver turned left into the hotel driveway, past the white stones that marked the edge of the parking place, where the palms leaned gracefully into the wind. Across the road, on the forefront of the Royal Nassau Sailing Club, the motorboats were drawn up neatly on trailers, each in its own parking space - marked by yellow lines.

As the driver stopped, and bent forward to open the door, the green light over the radio telephone nickered twice. Damn, a call. Another minute and he'd have been out of earshot. He picked up the receiver, pressed the scrambler button. The voice of his Number Two, a Bahamian, came over loud and clear.

'Sorry to disturb you, sir, but something rather unusual has just come up.'

'What?' asked McGregor impatiently, without interest. In the life of a policeman nothing was unusual; only the usual made a change.

'That fellow Garcia.'

After Love's telephone call, Garcia had been picked up at the airport. He had lost a couple of teeth to Love's fist and his face was bruised. His Lüger was in the Galaxie boot, but, almost unbelievably, he held a firearms permit; so there was no reason why it should not be there. He had strenuously denied all accusations that he had held up Love - he said he had been beaten up by a driver, who said he had cut in on him. A small-time crook was McGregor's opinion of Garcia, and the sooner they could be rid of him the better. There were no witnesses either way, so McGregor had released him.

'What's unusual about Garcia?' McGregor asked now.

'He's been taken ill.'

'Well, what's that to do with me?'

'I don't think I can handle it myself, sir,' said his Number Two.

'Handle what?'

Why the hell did these people talk.in such riddles? He looked at his watch irritably; he'd be late. He was looking forward to his pre-lunch gin and lime. Why must complications invariably arise when he was technically off duty?

'It's like this, sir. Father Flaherty has been in to see me. Garcia's had some kind of seizure. They think he's going to die. And there's something he wants to tell us. He's had Extreme Unction, but the priest naturally won't say anything. And Garcia wants to tell you personally. Says he won't tell anyone else.'

'Oh.'

What could the confession of such a man amount to? A life of pimping, acting as a ponce, selling drugs; maybe a bit of strong-arm work on well-heeled queers, a turn of blackmail, extortion; it could be any of these things, and probably was all of them. Was it worth missing lunch for such a sordid recital?

'Can't you go?' McGregor asked, waving a greeting through the window at a couple of friends walking up from their car. He made the gesture of raising his right elbow as though he were drinking, and wished he were. To hell with this sod Garcia.

'He asks especially for you, sir. I think it's something quite serious.'

'How long is he likely to last?' asked McGregor practically.

'The doctor isn't sure. He doesn't think it can be very long.'

'Oh, well, I'll come. Where is this bloody man?'

'Up along MacConnell Street. The corner house. Mother Ramsey's.'

'Oh, that place. I know it.'

It was a crude wooden shack, with the upper story partitioned by hardboard into little cubicles, and rented out by the night; sometimes, to couples, on the hotter afternoons, even by the hour.

Mother Ramsey was a mulatto, also a fairly consistent police informer - but only after she had been paid for her silence from those clients involved.

It suited McGregor's department to let Mother Ramsey run her house; it saved them a lot of trouble looking for her clients elsewhere. Most police forces in most cities take a similar view.

'Mother Ramsey's,' he told the driver. 'And quick as you can.'

He sat back, took out his silver snuff box, sniffed deeply, snapped it shut. He'd miss his gin, but, with a bit of luck, he would be back in time for the lunch; it was usually a self-service affair. He could just make it.

A handful of skinny chickens pecked optimistically in the dust of Mother Ramsey's backyard. He went up the wooden front-steps; the third one from the top was split and broken.

He did not trust his weight on it; McGregor was a prudent man.

Father Flaherty, the priest, he didn't know. He had only arrived recently from Canada, so there was no reason why he should. He was waiting for him now on the verandah, a pale man with close-cropped hair and wide spatulate hands.

A lizard on the faded, powdering paint watched them shake hands, and then went to sleep. They seemed to plot no harm for him.

Behind the priest stood the acting police surgeon, a former RAF doctor, thin and sardonic in a lightweight suit. He suffered from poor digestion, which gave him a look of extreme anguish;

sometimes the state of his stomach justified his appearance. This was one of these times.

'What's wrong with him, Jack?' asked McGregor.

The doctor shrugged his shoulders, held his palms uppermost.

'Aneurism.'

'My God,' said McGregor with feeling. 'What's he got then - pox?'

The doctor nodded.

'Tertiary stage. He might have lived a bit longer, but I think the shock of the blow that this Dr Love fellow gave him has accelerated things a bit. Something you can't prove, though. Only a hunch. Anyway, not to worry. He was dying, anyway, and didn't know it.'

McGregor thought that everyone was dying, anyway, from the moment they were born, but he didn't clothe the thought with words.

'How long do you give him?'

'How long do we give anyone?' replied the doctor testily. 'I wouldn't say much after this afternoon.'

'All right. Let's go and see for ourselves.'

The driver handed McGregor his briefcase. He opened it, switched on the midget Philips tape recorder inside, put the case under his arm, followed the doctor and the priest into the room. The walls were greasy and streaked with oily dirt, spattered here and there with round smudges where a bug had died under someone's fingernail. McGregor took care not to touch anything; pox to him was like leprosy. He even breathed as little as he could in case the air was somehow infected.

The room was small, bare-boarded; in the far corner, a brass bedstead wore a round, knob at each corner. From under a pile of grey sheets a greenish, yellow face protruded, sunken in and apathetic, already almost a death-mask.

Garcia's eyes were dull, old olives that had gone bad in his head. McGregor thought of the spirochaetes pouring through his blood, and shuddered. There was a cane chair at the bedside, with a basin in case Garcia wished to vomit, a carafe with a dirty glass inverted over it, a stained towel draped over the back. Flies buzzed hopelessly or hopefully around the window. Someone was playing a calypso record in the room next door; the brisk male beat of the band came through mockingly.

On the dressing table, with one leg gone, and a book jammed under the corner instead, two dollar bills lay beneath a conch shell, next to a cheap Japanese watch, a Commando knife in a sheath. Agreed, there were no pockets in your shroud, and you couldn't, take anything with you, but it still seemed to McGregor a pitifully small amount to be leaving behind.

'Well, what can we do for you?' he asked Garcia, not unkindly; as though he did not know there was nothing anyone could do for Garcia, ever again.

Garcia moved his head slightly to the right, trying to look at him. His eyes would not obey his mind; already they were beginning to film over. He made a grunting, animal noise.

'He wants you to sit down,' translated the doctor.

'I'd rather stand.'

'You'd better sit,' said the priest. 'Otherwise you'll hear nothing. His voice is very faint.'

McGregor moved the chair nearer, lifted the basin and carafe, trying not to hold them more tightly than he had to. Garcia turned his face with its fallen-in nose, its characteristically ridged teeth, towards him. Even from a yard away, his breath smelled sour as an open sewer.

'There's something I want to tell you,' he began slowly, thickly, as though he were speaking against a wall of wool, and had to force each word through with will-power.

'I've already told the priest. I've not been a good Catholic, but to be any Catholic is better than to be nothing.'

McGregor waited. Garcia went on.

'I must tell you this before I die. Because I am dying, and I want you to take notes. I want you to do something. A bad man...'

The voice faded, messages from the brain were becoming confused; the present, the past and the future were streaming together, like water-colour in the rain. A drop of sweat ran down his forehead, down his cheek. A fly settled on it greedily.

McGregor bent down, waved the fly away, dipped his hand into the open briefcase, turned up the volume control.

'Go on,' he said. He would never get to the Montagu in time for lunch now. And somehow, after this, he did not feel hungry. He would go home and have a bath with Dettol in the water, and send his clothes to be dry-cleaned.

'Listen,' said Garcia. 'There's a man in a yacht. A man who is blind. He's going to turn the tide. I know he is. I heard him talking. I shouldn't have been there. Don't tell him I was. He's a bad man... And there's another thing... A girl in a boat at Cable Beach... She was shot... We had a deal... An arrangement. I shot her... He promised I could go back to Havana if I did...'

Garcia's voice tailed away; the effort had lacquered his face with sweat.

McGregor glanced across at the other two men in the room.

'I need hardly tell you, gentlemen,' he said in a pompous whisper, 'that anything you may hear is absolutely confidential.'

'Of course,' said the priest, nettled by this.

The doctor nodded impatiently. He had forgotten more confidences than McGregor had ever heard. Also, he did not like McGregor.

Garcia began to speak again. His voice trailed on more slowly, more painfully.

On the mantelpiece, a clock began to whir and ting, the hands nibbling away remorselessly at the little of his life remaining.

*   *   *

Sir Robert L was puzzled, and because he was puzzled, he was doing his best to appear pleasant to MacGillivray, an effort he did not always make.

'Look, Mac,' he said, in the way a house-master will talk to a dim erring pupil, in a mixture of regret and admonition, 'I know you're busy as hell with this Rangoon business, and the fact that you're pretty sure someone on the route is working for the other side, but we're all dealing with a dozen things at once.

'I'm not asking you to solve this problem. I'm simply asking for your opinion. What the hell do you make of it? Read the message again. It's either bloody serious, or it's bloody mad.'

He pushed a sheet of flimsy across the desk and MacGillivray turned it towards him. It had no prefix, no paragraph indentation, only the sender's number.

He read:

33251022 INFORMATIVE STOP WAS CALLED BY PRIEST TO BEDSIDE OF CURRENTLY STATELESS EX-CUBAN GARCIA JUAREZ STOP HE WAS CHARGED BY POLICE WITH THREATENING ENGLISH DOCTOR JASON LOVE WITH GUN POSING AS TAXI DRIVER STOP DOCTOR LOVE UNMET BY ME AND FLEW MEXICO CITY STOP GARCIA RELEASED OWING LACK OF WITNESSES STOP GARCIA DIED TODAY SYPHILITIC ANEURISM STOP WISHED TO CONFESS FOLLOWING TO POLICE INSPECTOR MCGREGOR.

FIRSTLY HE CLAIMED HE HAD BEEN PROMISED REPATRIATION CUBA AND SAFE REHABILITATION. CASTRO REGIME IF HE COLLABORATED WITH UNNAMED BLIND MAN IN PROJECT WHICH HE CLAIMED INVOLVED QUOTE TURNING TIDE UNQUOTE

STOP UNNAMED BLIND MAN PRESUMABLY OF CONSIDERABLE WEALTH STOP WAS MET ONLY ABOARD UNNAMED WHITE STEAM YACHT EX-NASSAU.

SECONDLY GARCIA ADMITTED SHOOTING CUBAN GIRL AL-LEGEDLY ON INSTRUCTIONS ABOVE BLIND MAN IN RETURN FOR SAFE RETURN HAVANA STOP.

THIRDLY GARCIA DIED BEFORE COULD ELABORATE STOP HAVE MADE DISCREET INQUIRIES NAVAL AIR FORCE COAST GUARD SOCIAL CONTACTS AS TO POSSIBLE WHEREABOUTS THIS YACHT BUT ROUTINE AIR PATROLS REPORT NO VESSEL THIS SIZE DESCRIPTION WITHIN 250 RPT 250 MILES RADIUS ENDIT.

MacGillivray pushed back the paper.

'I make no more of it than you, sir. On the face of it, I wouldn't say this seemed anything for us.'

'You wouldn't, eh? You don't think it's got anything to do with that German sub that seems to be roaming around? No other reports of that, by the way. And our friends over here in the German Embassy haven't heard a peep about it - or so they say.'

Sir Robert grinned, screwed his monocle to his left eye, and looked at the paper again as though, by sheer concentration, he could force an answer from the neatly typed words. The red light flickered on his desk. He pressed the button that released the electric door lock. His adjutant entered with a buff folder tied in pink tape stamped with the single red star for 'Secret'.

'Just arrived, sir,' said the adjutant. 'From Nassau.'

Sir Robert and MacGillivray exchanged glances. Neither gained from the exchange.

'Leave it here,' said Sir Robert.

When the man left the room, the door locked itself. He opened the folder and read aloud:

179

33251023 FURTHER REFERENCE MY 33251021 STOP PER-
FORMED AUTOPSY PURPORTED CUBAN HOUSEMAID SHOT IN
PRESENCE OF DOCTOR LOVE STOP UNDER HAIR FOLLOWING
NUMBER WAS SEEN TO BE TATTOOED 988018 STOP RECALL
FROM PERSONAL WARTIME EXPERIENCE THIS IS GERMAN
JEWESS CONCENTRATION CAMP TATTOO STOP AM NOT MAK-
ING THIS INFORMATION PUBLIC HERE ENDIT.

Sir Robert pushed back his chair, walked round his desk, and
stood, hands in the back of his trouser waistband, looking out
over Whitehall.

'But where does that get us?' he asked.

MacGillivray thought it got them nowhere, but he wasn't paid
for lines like that, so he said: 'He tells us the housemaid who our
man in Nassau thought was a Cuban was actually a European
Jewess. Now was she shot because of that, or because as a Jewess
she knew something about someone else? Or because as a Jewess
she might - it is just conceivable - be working for some Israeli
agency, one of those after Nazi war criminals?'

Sir Robert turned from the window, leaned against the vertical
tubes of the radiator, feeling its comforting warmth through his
ninety-guinea Squires tweeds.

'You may be right, Mac,' he agreed in a tone that said he didn't
think he was. 'And if you are, we're no worse off. I'll find out who
this girl was. We've a good friend in the Israeli Embassy. It won't
take us long. They've got all the numbers filed away. But what do
you make of that yacht thing and turning the tide? That it's just
a lot of old cobblers?'

This was just what MacGillivray did think. But he had his pen-
sion, his overdraft and his pale, complaining wife to consider.
So he shook his head, but not too vehemently in case Sir Robert
was only asking a rhetorical question.

'Not necessarily,' he said. 'When a man is dying he doesn't make
up a story like that. If it isn't true, at least he believed it was, and

why the hell shouldn't it be true? Just because our man asked one or two cronies at the club over pink gins if they've seen a yacht, and they say they haven't, it doesn't mean to say it's not true.'

'If it did exist, it couldn't have covered more than two hundred and fifty miles in the time,' pointed out Sir Robert.

'Not in that area it couldn't. But our man was looking for die bloody thing in the Atlantic. What if it's gone through the Panama Canal, then into the Pacific? What about that then?'

He glanced down at the message for the second time. The first three figures of the prefix were the sender's code number: 332 meant the Bahama's, embracing a vast area of the Out Islands, as well as Nassau. The next three stood for the month and the date - May 10. The seventh figure was the rank of the sender - 1 being the Head of Station, 2 his, deputy, and so on. The last figure gave the number of each particular message. McGregor's rank would be 1 - yet this sender was giving 2 as his organization code; and these were also only his second and third messages that month. The last numbers were the sequence of messages - not a lot for a pro to have sent. So who was he?

'Who's the sender?' he asked, a sudden thought spurring his tired mind. 'It's not that police chap McGregor, is it?'

Sir Robert shook his head.

'No. I've put in another fellow, strictly part-time. Used to be a surgeon in the RAF. Invalided out with stomach trouble. He's acting police doctor there now. Very sound man.'

'You might have let me know, sir,' MacGillivray sounded aggrieved; after all, it was his job to appoint agents, to move them, to vet them, occasionally, to sack them.

'I'm sorry, Mac. I did you a memo. It'll be on your desk somewhere. Only met the man two weeks ago. He'd been vetted by the Air Ministry bods, so there was no need to go through all that business a second time.'

'Anyway, what's wrong with McGregor? We've used him for a year and he's been adequate, hasn't he?'

'Perfectly. Only he's going on leave. We can't have too many, you know. Especially if they're part-timers, and we don't have to pay them except by results.'

MacGillivray was unconvinced by this reasoning: experience had taught him that agents hired on this basis, so dear to Treasury minds, not infrequently raised false alarms simply so that they could be paid for investigating them.

'Why didn't McGregor send the message?' he asked. Sir Robert offered him a cheroot, lit one himself.

'I've no idea,' he said. 'From the contents, he was there. Maybe he thought it wasn't worth sending.'

'Does he know about this ex-RAF character?'

'No. I never believe in letting my left hand know what my right hand is doing. It's always interesting to have two accounts of events.'

'But here we've only got one.'

'Exactly,' agreed Sir Robert urbanely; drawing so hard on his cheroot that the ash at its end glowed like a red light. 'And that in itself is interesting, too, in its way. Well, Mac, there it is. Think it over and let me have your views.' And he reached out and pressed the button to open the door.

MacGillivray walked along the silent corridor with its coloured doors, down the two flights of stairs, out into Scotland Place. A thin, rain was blowing off the Thames, and he turned up the collar of his coat, walking along Whitehall against the drifting crowds of tourists, aimless as autumn leaves.

His mind was far away from London. He was thinking about that potentially interesting Scottish property he'd seen advertised in Country Life, two acres of formal gardens, fifty acres of rough land, a half-mile stretch on a salmon river, the usual out-buildings, staff flat, stable block, even an old motor house with a generator plant for the whole property. Where the devil was it again? Then he remembered; two miles out of Kirriemuir. He must put in another call to the estate agent for fuller details, when he got back to his office.

It was years since he'd been in Kirriemuir and stood in the darkness of the camera obscura and looked down in the white concave screen large as an enormous bowl, while the periscope turned round on the roof, and they could see what was happening outside in the sunshine for a distance of miles.

It had seemed like magic then. The attendant had turned the periscope, and they had watched a young couple from a coach tour kissing in a field. They had thought they were safe from discovery, but they had not known about this curious device. And now, with microphones able to pick up a whisper from half a mile away, with minute transistors no bigger than an aspirin they could be embedded into the concrete foundations of a building, to transmit all the conversations held in that building for years ahead, who could be ever safe now?

Kirriemuir. The Window in Thrums. Sir James Barrie. The Ball of Kirriemuir. He began humming the song as he waited to cross Northumberland Avenue. As he walked up past Charing Cross station towards his office in Covent Garden, he remembered singing the words in half a dozen different messes, before and during the war, and since. Wheels of memory began to mesh his mind. MacGillivray and McGregor. One Mac, one Mc. He'd met him during the two months' course McGregor had under-gone at the Secret Service training school outside Cambridge, in the house apparently owned by the Coal Board and run for the technical instruction of potential provincial managers. But he didn't know him well. He'd been vouched for by other members of 'Six'; there was no reason why he should know him well. Better not to, really, in case anything happened. Anything like this? No, just anything.

When he reached his office he pressed the buzzer for Miss Jenkins.'

'I'd like two files,' he told her. 'Give me anything we have on underwater and tidal experiments - if we have much, which I doubt! I'd also like to see McGregor's file. He's our man in Nassau. Things seem to be happening there.'

As he thought, there was very little in the tidal files. A predecessor with a droll sense of humour had marked the first Miss Jenkins turned up, 'Sea: Waves, movement of. This led to 'Tides, turning of, and this to 'Moon, anticipating pull of, oceans on', which led to a file containing one piece of paper on which was typed: 'Was it worth it?'

The file she finally produced was very thin. It had resumes of reports of Russian experiments north of Japan, of scientific proposals to dam the Bering Strait. This could be done by controlled atomic explosions under the sea and would result in the movement of three powerful ocean currents - The Gulf Stream, and the Labrador and East Greenland Streams -giving the benefit of their warmth to parts of Siberia.

Farming could then be undertaken in a completely new climate and on an enormous scale in areas that now lie buried by snow for much of each year. A side result would be that Alaska would enjoy a better climate, but farther south, much of the United States would suffer, and become virtually a desert.

Another Soviet scheme, listed with names and dates of pilot experiments, was to dam the Tatar Strait. This would also result in Siberia having a warm climate, but could transfer the present cold Siberian climate to northern Japan. The ocean currents, the report added, were the main means of giving climates to land masses. Russia already maintained more than one hundred ships on research work throughout the oceans of the world, more than twice as many controlled by the US. And about one hundred times the number disposed by Britain, thought MacGillivray sourly, as he picked up another report on the Gulf Stream.

He wasn't too sure what the Gulf Stream was, although it was often enough either praised or blamed for the British climate. In brief, the Stream appeared to be a kind of warm river flowing through the seas. He read on. Its temperature was 75 degrees Fahrenheit at first, and it moved at the rate of 25,000,000 tons volume of water a second, travelling at about 72 miles a day in a clockwise circle up the East Coast of South America and the States, then across the Atlantic, north of Bermuda. It was about 2,000 feet deep and varied in width from 40 to 50 miles.

Off the west coast of the British Isles the current divided; one stream went north and west of Ireland, the rest flowed south, past Spain and Portugal, down off the west coast of Africa and then across to South America again. It was largely driven by prevailing winds all this time.

Britain, pointed out one report, lay roughly in the same latitude as Kamchatka in East Siberia. But for the warming effects of the Gulf Stream the British climate would be that of this land of Arctic tundra, bleak and chill, too cold to support either crops or population.

There were other reports of plans and proposals to regulate the flow of ice from the Eastern Arctic into the North Atlantic; to build jetties 200 miles long off the East Coast of Newfoundland to break up the icy currents from Labrador; to alter the flow of the Gulf Stream, by changing the flow of the winds, or by introducing completely cross currents by undersea atomic explosions.

The file also contained a quotation from the Russian scientist, Professor G. V. Petrovich, which MacGillivray, thought an obvious aphorism, but which he read because there was so little else: 'The nation which first learns to understand the seas will con-

185

trol them, and the nation which controls the seas will control the world.'

There was also a quotation from the late President Kennedy in 1962: 'Knowledge of the oceans is more than a matter of curiosity. Our very survival may depend on it.'

So. None of this took him very much further. He put this sheet on one side, read the one underneath it:

RUM: Remote Underwater Manipulator, designed 1962/3 by Dr Victor Anderson, of the Scripps Institution of Oceanography, University of California, USA. Basically, this is an ex-US Marine Corps tank, with all leaks caulked and all openings made waterproof. It is pumped full of heavy-grade oil to avoid buckling of plates at abnormal underwater pressures, then set in action.

Tank is remote-controlled from the shore through a multi-core cable which unwinds behind it as it goes forward into - the sea from the shore. RUM is equipped with a mechanical arm and grab, TV cameras and lighting equipment. It can -be directed to any point on the sea bed. Can retrieve objects, specimens of oil, rock minerals, etc.

SEALAB: Fifty-seven feet long, 12 feet in diameter, it contains cooking galley, bunks, laboratory, chemical WC, has housed teams of ten men for periods of 15 days at a' depth of 205 feet.

These teams breathe a composite artificial mixture of 85 % helium, 11% nitrogen, 4% oxygen. Tasks successfully carried out include salvage of crashed aircraft from the sea bed, construction of an undersea static station to measure sea currents, temperatures, etc.

Difficulties encountered in above:

1. Because they breathe helium, with its unusual heat conductive properties, crews have lost normal body heat at between five to six times the rate on land. As a result, if they stopped working, they became too cold to continue.

2. Helium also soaked through their suits, and destroyed the powers of insulation in their clothes. It also affected their vocal chords, to the extent of giving them high-pitched voices.

MOBOT: Designed by the American company, Hughes Aircraft Inc., is a small robot intended originally for under-sea research for oil companies. Contains four rooms, inbuilt television, controlled, as with RUM, by cable to the shore.

FLIP: Floating Instrument Platform. Also developed by Scripps Institution, in collaboration with the US Government. Basically, a platform 355 feet tall, displacing 600 tons.

Ingeniously constructed so that it can be towed on its side, like a huge boat, to its operating position, where valves are opened, ballast tanks filled with water. It then flips from horizontal to vertical to study currents, temperatures, plant and animal life.

PURISM A: Built under authority of Ocean Systems Inc. (an American Co.) in association with Union Carbide and General Precision.

Simulated descent by two US divers to 650 feet. They lived for 48 hours under pressure of 304.4 lbs per square inch, more than twenty times sea level pressure of 15 lbs per square inch. Afterwards, a six day decompression period was necessary. They breathed helium mixture with 2% oxygen, also a mixture of oxygen and neon. Experiments proved that men can work and live at the depth of 650 feet below surface as efficiently as they could at sea level.

None of this told MacGillivray much, but then he hadn't expected it to. ML he could be certain about was that the lovers who had been observed by the primitive camera obscura at Kirriemuir years ago would soon be no safer if they were cavorting half a mile beneath the deepest sea. What a thought!

He sighed. He must be growing old. Soon there would be no place left in all the world, in the air, in outer space, under the ground, even beneath the surface of the sea, where someone would not be able to watch and listen, and report on the doings of his fellow men. Thou seest me, etc. And it wouldn't be so bad if God were the only viewer.

He threw the file to one side, feeling out of sorts for the day. All this seemed pretty remote from his own problems, or, rather, the ones Sir Robert seemed intent to thrust upon him. A submarine sunk with all hands and now sighted thousands of miles away. A Cuban maid, who turned out to be a Jewess with a concentration camp record, shot dead in a boat with - of all people - Dr Love. A dying refugee confessing to her murder, and then gibbering about a blind man's intention to turn the tide.

He picked up the file on McGregor, skimmed through its main headings:

Born: Norwich, 16 June 1909. Second son of Seymour Bertram McGregor (See file 531 (a) Personnel, particulars of etc.)

Educated: Wellington, Sandhurst.

Commissioned: E. Surreys 1931.

Served: NW Frontier, 1932-33. Southern Command, India, 1933-35. Staff appointment in Malaya (GSO 3 in Singapore) 1936, Seconded/Cyprus: King's Own West African Rifles, 1938.

Wartime Service in Italy, Burma.

Mentioned in Despatches, 1944, Buthidaung.

With the British Army of Occupation in Germany, 1946-49.

Staff appointment (GSO 1) Southern Command 1950.

Attached Governor of Cyprus: Special Staff, 1955-58.

(Brigadier)

War Office: 1958-61.

Retired: 1961.

Became part-time director West Country Broiler Fowls

(1961) Ltd. Resigned over policy disagreement, 1963.

Approached by GSO (1) War Office (Intelligence) through mutual friend Brigadier A. S. Shagworthy (see relevant file) 15/4/63). Subject interested in proposition, but asked permission to delay final acceptance until birth of daughter's ;first child (see below).

Contacted GSO (1) MO (I) 23/7/63.

Agreed to proposition.

Joined as trainee 31/7/63. Posted to Initial Training Establishment, passed grade 'A' 29/9/63. Posted as No. 3, Istanbul, Turkey. 1/12/63 with cover of tourist considering buying house for possible retirement. Admitted his service background.

To Cairo, Egypt, with cover of oil-valve salesman, for Belevedere Trading Co., 3/6/64.

Asked to be repatriated 11/8/64 as he had recognized wartime colleague as hotel manager, thought this might endanger his cover. Repatriation carried out 16/8/64. Without appointment until 31/12/64. Posted Lisbon, Portugal, as No. 2. Repatriated 31/10/65.

Home leave. Posted Nassau, Special Department, under special authority Colonial Office, 2/2/66. (See file BAH/3219/OH24.)

Wife, daughter of the Rev. Albert Nash - Guildford, Surrey, died 1948, survived by one daughter, Sybil Anne, married to the Rev. Richard Little, St Matthew's Rectory, Erith, Kent. Daughter attended St Paul's Girls' School, London; Somerville College, Oxford. One child, Kenneth Seymour, born 12/6/63, Erith Cottage Hospital. Daughter: No known political affiliations. All reports NIL.

MacGillivray remembered how McGregor had told him he had no ties in England apart from his daughter, how he found it difficult to settle in a cold climate, in a social and political atmosphere so different from the England he remembered thirty years ago. He wasn't alone in that, thought MacGillivray, as he closed the folder, retied the pink tape. He pressed the buzzer for Miss Jenkins.

'Nothing?' he asked.

She shook her head.

'No sir. We're six hours late on the routine call from 1.4 in Teheran, in Ahwaz, but that is probably nothing serious. We've had delays there before. Otherwise, situation normal.'

MacGillivray nodded. He remembered the little oil town in the middle of the baking Persian desert, where, according to the Old Testament, Daniel had been flung to the lions in their den, spent the night with them, and survived. The cable routings from it were notoriously slack. He would give his man another six hours before he sent out the cautious, questioning cable about the non-arrival of his promised consignment of stoned dates, ex-Basra, which was the ostensible reason for his being there at all.

'I'm taking the afternoon off,' he told Miss Jenkins. 'Well not exactly off. I'm going to see someone in Erith, the daughter of our man in the Bahamas. Or, rather, one of our men.'

He wished again that Sir Robert wouldn't put in secondary agents without telling him. Sometimes it was better if the right hand did not know what the left hand was doing. Sometimes, if not often.

He took a quick stand-up lunch at the snack bar counter of the Nag's Head, read the lunch-time edition of the Evening Standard, caught the 2.30 pm on the North Kent Line from Charing Cross to Erith.

He counted the stations on the map in the compartment, discovered that Erith was the tenth, dozed for the journey, as he had taught himself to do, woke up as the train pulled into the station. The rain had stopped, but the wind was still coming off the Thames, colder than in London, because the river was much wider here. Between factory buildings he could see grey water flecked with white. He wondered what colour the sea was in Nassau; he really must pull a trip there before he died.

It was early-closing day, and the riverside town seemed nearly deserted. Somewhere, in a workshop, machinery was clanging like a giant hammer; maybe it was a giant hammer.

He walked on up the hill from the station into the town, asked an old man on a bench where St Matthew's Rectory was. The man said he was a stranger. Another was deaf, so MacGillivray turned about, paid a visit to the Public Library in Walnut Tree Road, and looked up a street map.

The rectory turned out to be a Victorian house in lavatory brick, stained by eighty years of sooty rain. Erith had once been a country watering place - one of the roads, Queens Road, commemorated days when Queen Victoria had actually walked along it, when the Thames was clean and boats had landed fish. But the Boer War and two subsequent world wars had resulted in an enormous growth of munitions factories, a rash of housing estates, the devouring of fields and woods.

St Matthew's Rectory must once have been one of the finest houses in the town. Now it presented a sad aspect, like an old lady who has come down in the world and abandoned all attempts to keep up appearances.

A hut of some kind had been built on the tennis lawn; the grass was long and tufted with dandelions. MacGillivray walked up the front drive, virtually two ruts clear of weeds, musing on past glories, present decay. These paralleled in his mind the decline and decay of so much else of value in his country. Yes, he must be growing old.

Through a faded wooden trellis he saw a child's tricyle in the backyard, and towels stretched like flags of defeat from the clothes line. He pressed the front-door bell. A dog barked half-heartedly from an outhouse. The door opened. A little boy stood framed in it, watching him. He carried a Teddy Bear by its leg.

'Who do you want?' he asked seriously, as though there was a choice.

'Is your mother in?' said MacGillivray kindly. He had no children himself; he always felt at a loss under their wide, candid eyes.

'Yes, I'm here,' called a voice from the kitchen. 'Who is it?'

A woman came across the hall. She wore a blue skirt, a loosely knitted jumper. She carried an air of rush about her, a resigned inability to cope with life in a house designed to be run by six servants, and now being run without any. She had been pretty only a few years before, but she would not be pretty for very much longer.

'Can I help you?'

Who was this man? Someone to report a death, an illness, a request for aid? Someone who didn't know, who never came to church, but who wanted all the comfort the church could give at a time when it suited him? She felt irritation rise like a tide in her throat. She wanted to scream, to run away, anything rather than having to stand and ask, as she asked strangers too many times a day already, 'Can I help you?'

'I'm not a parishioner,' explained MacGillivray, 'and you have probably never heard of me. But years ago I was friendly with your father, Brigadier McGregor.'

'Oh, yes?'

At least it wasn't a request for help.

'In the Army, I expect?' she said. How could it be anywhere else? This man had military stamped all over him.

'That's right.' MacGillivray sometimes found it easier to pretend a lie than to tell a truth that would never be believed.

'I was passing through Erith, and I thought I'd pop in. I've not met you before. You must be his daughter?'

They shook hands. Her hand felt cold and bloodless, like the scales of a fish, the fingers reddened and coarse. She had been catching up on some washing that should have been done on the previous day. The little boy looked questioningly from one to the other.

'My Teddy's only got one eye,' he explained to MacGillivray conversationally.

'You run along and play,' his mother told him, and then, turning to MacGillivray: 'Will you come in for a cup of tea?'

'Thank you,' said MacGillivray, 'I'll come in. But you're so busy, I won't stay.'

She took him into the study. A framed photograph of a young man standing upright, arms folded, in gown and mortar board, looked down at- them forbiddingly from the wall. The paint along the skirting board was kicked and scuffed, the air in the room felt fusty and used-up, as though too many people had breathed it too many times. She cleared some copies of the Church Times from a chair. MacGillivray sat down on the edge.

'What can I help you with about Daddy?' she asked.

What could she help him with? He didn't know. He made a vaguely expressive gesture.

'I was just wondering when he was coming back to this country. If there was any chance of my seeing him then?'

She looked at him for a moment as though she could not believe what he was saying, and suddenly her face puckered and creased and grew, old like a wax mask too near a flame. She began to cry softly, and fumbled for a handkerchief in the waistband of her skirt.

'Then you don't know about him?' she said. 'You haven't heard?'

'No,' said MacGillivray gently, handing her his own hand-kerchief. 'But please do tell me.'

CHAPTER EIGHT: MAZATLAN, MEXICO

Like a frame in a moving picture that stops suddenly, the moment stepped out of time and stayed there, frozen.

Love looked from the round blue muzzle of the gun to Fernandez Manchele's eyes, and then the action restarted, the film went on. Fernandez roared with laughter, threw both -hands up into the air at the success of his joke, caught them again.

'Did I not tell you I was a joker? You saw through my first jokes, but you didn't see through that, eh, senor?'

His elephantine body quivered with mirth, as he crammed the toy revolver into his pocket.

'My God,' said Love feelingly. 'Don't do that ever again when I'm around. It could prove fatal.' He didn't say for whom, but from the way his heart was hammering, he didn't need to.

He looked at Shamara. She said nothing.

'I didn't offend you, I hope, senor?' said Fernandez, suddenly contrite, the thought piercing his conscience.

'Of course not,' Love assured him. 'We loved every minute of it. Especially on empty stomachs. Now do me a small favour. Just drive.'

'Ah, I'm sorry, senor. You English, you see, do not understand the jokes of Fernandez Manchele. Now, to business, to which hotel will I drive you?'

'We're not booked anywhere.'

'Then one of the best to try is the De Cima. I will take you there.'

The De Cima overlooked the beach between eleven flagpoles, each draped with a different flag, showing the nationalities of their guests. Half a dozen taxis waited at right angles to the front door. Little boys hawked trays of Chiclet chewing gum to the drivers.

'We've one double room left,' the receptionist told Love.

Love nodded, not meeting Shamara's eyes.

'We'll have that.'

'And your luggage, senor?'

'It's coming,' said Love blandly. 'There's been a bit of a mix-up at the airport.'

In view of what had happened, this seemed an understatement.

'Ah, yes. Shall I telephone the airline?'

'It's not necessary,' said Love. 'We came by private plane.'

'Very well, senor, just sign here. And your passports?'

Love handed his across the glass counter.

'My wife has hers in her baggage,' he said.

'Of course,' replied the clerk, not believing a word of it. He pressed a bell for a page.

'You have room 207. On the second floor. The page will show you.'

They went up in the lift. The room was on the right, all ceramics and white paint, overlooking a yard; a Coca-Cola lorry and a 1930 Ford coupe beautifully restored in white with a red hood, stood under the palm trees. In the bathroom the lavatory seat wore a white strip of paper across it, with a red cross and the information, 'Sterilized for your protection'. Two small polythene bags covered the tooth glasses like hats, but the carafe was empty. The tap water tasted of chlorine.

Love gave the page half a dollar, locked the door behind him, threw himself on the bed, lay with his hands clasped under his head. Shamara sat demurely in a chair.

'Now what?' she said.

'A bath,' said Love. 'A shave. They're sure to have a razor they can lend me in the hotel. Breakfast in the room. Then whatever the night or day may offer. A sleep at least. Then have our clothes pressed, and book two tickets to Mexico City on the plane. All without leaving this suite. The wonders of the credit card system and the electric telephone will both be demonstrated.'

'That's your programme?' Shamara asked levelly.

What's wrong with it?'

Love looked at her closely. She stood up, crossed the room, sat down on the bed beside him.

'Listen, Jason,' she said gently. 'You don't seem to realize what we're up against. You can't go back to your old car rallies as though nothing had ever happened.'-

'Why not?' asked Love. 'That's all I want to do.' That, and one other thing, he thought, but did not say; anyway, he'd have a bath first.

'But they won't let you. Don't you see?'

'Who are they?'

'The people who think you know too much.'

'But I know nothing,' said Love. 'I've told them.'

Shamara stood up. He pulled her down again.

'I'll have to change my plan then,' he said. 'I've given you plan A. Now you can have plan B a little earlier than I had anticipated, but perhaps no worse for that.'

'What's plan B?' she asked.

'This,' he said.

He pulled her towards him on the bed. She rolled over and looked up at him. Her face was completely blank, the face of a lovely stranger; he could see his own face mirrored minutely in her eyes, two men in miniature, and he was both of them.

He kissed her. She was so unresponsive that he drew back and looked at her again, as though seeing her for the first time. Her body was there beside his, but her mind was miles away. Silence fell between them like a shroud.

I'm sorry,' she said, not looking at him.

'Don't apologize,' Love told her. 'Never excuse, never explain.'

'But I want - you know. It's just that - I can't explain it. You wouldn't understand if I tried. You can't begin to imagine what it's like to grow up in a concentration camp, like a frightened dog, everyone, against you. We used to lie, twenty or thirty to a cell, waiting for the steps to stop outside. If they stopped outside the door, it was our turn for the "S" truck.

'I can remember now, waking up, sweating, hearing the scrape of the key in the lock. The gas used to hiss through grilles just behind the driver's cab. I heard it outside, like a great snake, and then the people inside would start shouting and beating on the walls. They were padded inside but you could still hear them. Then the sounds would grow softer and the beating feebler. Only the hiss of gas would go on.'

Love reached out and put his arm round her protectively. She snuggled against him, more at ease now, relaxed.

They lay in silence, feeling the warmth of each other through the clothes, feeling the want grow slowly. Then she said, running one finger down his stubbly chin dreamily, 'Tell me about your life? Tell me about - England. What is Somerset like?' .

'Very quiet. Green. Peaceful. Everything I miss here. Not a lot has changed for a long time. There's been a doctor living in my house for a hundred and fifty years.'

'But you've not been there all that time surely?' she smiled.

'No. I only feel that old. I've a housekeeper, Mrs Hunter. Her husband looks after the garden. It's quite big by English standards - about four acres. And I've some out-buildings, old stables, where I keep my Cord.'

'Really, you men are like children aren't you, with your cars. Perhaps that's because you've never had to grow up quickly.'

'Perhaps,' he agreed. 'But sometimes it's quite nice to stay young.'

'Such as when?'

'Such as now.' He kissed her again.

This time, her mouth opened under his. For a moment they lay like this, and then her tongue found his, her arms came up behind his back and drew him down against her long body. He moved one hand, pulled up her shirt; the brassiere had a front hook. He slipped it, cupped her left breast in his hand, feeling the nipple grow under his palm. She took her mouth away from his.

'Wait,' she said. She undid the belt of her jeans, slid down the zip. Love pulled the quilt on top of them, found her mouth again, and all her body, young and firm and willing, straining against him. He felt his tiredness drain away, her fingers at the buttons of his shirt, so that where there had been two people impeded by clothes, now there were two, flesh on flesh, heart beating against heart; and then there were two no longer but one, and her cry, when it came, was not an end, not a beginning, but the voice of love, the sound of unity. They slept then, as they lay, the quilt light on their tired bodies as the feathers inside it.

The telephone bell jarred the silence. Love struggled up through layers of sleep, scooped up the instrument. The desk clerk spoke in his ear.

'There was a man downstairs to see you, senor. I tried to ring you before, but there was no reply.'

'I was - asleep,' said Love. 'Who was he?'

'He would not give his name, he said he would come back, senor.'

Love replaced the receiver on its cradle, turned to Shamara.

'Who was that?' she asked dreamily, her face still soft with sleep.

'Someone for me. But he wouldn't leave his name. Said he'd come back.'

She sat up, wide awake now.

'Do you know anyone here? Could it be your old-car man?'

Love shook his head.

'He doesn't know I'm here. Anyway, he's out of town.'

'Then they're on to us.'

'But how could they have found us so soon? We've only just arrived here ourselves. You've got me talking like this now, about them and they.'

'They'll guess we took a plane, simply because there wasn't any other means of getting out. So what do they do? They ring the airports at Torreon, Mexico City and here and ask Control whether such a plane landed. We must have flown to one of those places. There's nowhere else for a plane like mine.'

'I see.'

Love reached our, lit two Gitanes, gave one to Shamara. If they could sneak away, they might be able to book on a plane, or hire a Hertz car and drive out of this nightmare. But what about his luggage at the Posada Duran - and his bill there which he hadn't paid? How would the insurance company react to his story that he was unable to return to his hotel because he felt his life was in danger? Probably by a letter, asking him whether he intended taking out a policy against future risks on his life.

Also, why should they flee before their pursuers in this craven fashion? Shades of his Scottish covenanting ancestors rebuked him. Although he who fights and runs away may live to fight another day, as the old Scots proverb put it, he still had to fight on that other day. He was only delaying the moment of encounter, he was not solving anything. But the man who stayed his ground and fought, he either won or lost; in either case, he had no further fighting to do. The matter was decided, finished, over. QED. Love stubbed out his cigarette, turned back to Shamara, his mind made up.

'To hell with running away,' he said bluntly. 'I'm going downstairs to meet whoever wants to see me. We'll take it from there.'

She came up to him and lay closely against him; he could feel the warmth of her body against his. For a second, he half turned, wanting her again, and then she reached out and put her hand on his bare shoulder.

'You don't know what you're saying,' she said. He could see her eyes misty with tears, worry, reaction.

'But I do,' he told her gently. 'You can't run away for ever. Some time, some day, you've got to stop and face whatever it is you're running away from - people, events, maybe even life itself. And the sooner you do, the easier it is. I know. I've lived longer than you. I've proved it.'

'But you don't know these men,' she persisted. 'They're not humans. They're animals. You don't know what they're like. I do. I was in the camp, as a child. You weren't. I've told you about the "S" truck. Let me tell you some more. When the time came for us to go in one, my mother found my sister, but she couldn't find me.

'I was hiding behind a hut in a pile of rubbish. Finally, the guards wouldn't let her spend any more time looking. She was delaying the convoy, they said. I could hear it all. She was weeping. She couldn't bear to leave me. I think now that she felt if we were all together, it somehow wouldn't seem so bad.

'We had all lived together so happily until they took my father away. I suppose, if we had to die, she wanted us to die together so that, if there is any other life beyond this, we could begin it together.

'And the men who drove these trucks, who turned on the valves to murder their passengers, they were only the small fry. They had children of their own, they seemed ordinary people - except to us. If they could murder twenty-five women and children on every drive without any qualms what about the men who gave the orders? Who melted down gold teeth from the corpses, who stole their belongings, the deeds to their lands, their bank certificates, everything - and even used their bones for fertilizer? Do you think they were ordinary people?

'They arranged millions of deaths methodically, filing the details away, working office hours, nine to five, half day Saturday and Church Parade on Sunday. I know. I've read the reports. They hid them in a salt mine at the end of the war, but we found them. These are the men we're up against now.

'I don't know what they're planning, but whatever it is do you think they'll worry about another murder? What's one more against six million? Don't you see? Can't you see?'

She was crying now, silently, despairingly. Love put his arms around her. Outside, beyond the window, where the sun fell hard on the sand, he could hear a woman calling to a child. Years ago, another mother had called to another little girl who had not replied. He could imagine the big engines of the Saurer trucks grumbling away under their khaki bonnets, the drivers irritable at being kept waiting. Oh, let the kid go, they'd pick her up on the next run. But they hadn't. Not that kid.

'If they're as bad as that, all the more reason not to run away,' he said. 'Are you coming down with me or staying here?'

Shamara bit her lip, glanced around the room as though searching for a weapon, a way of escape.

'I can't let you go alone. But I think you're being very foolish. Maybe fatally so.'

'Then why not stay in the room?'

'And be here on my own if they come to fetch me? I'll stay with you.'

'That's my girl,' said Love. 'But first I'm having a bath. If we have to die, let's die with our ears clean.'

Afterwards, they dressed quickly. As Love brushed his hair in the bathroom, in front of the huge illuminated mirror, he wondered when and where he would next see his own face, if he would. His shirt and suit looked tatty, but his appearance was improved by his bath and shave. He opened the door of their room, locked it behind Shamara, pocketed the key.

They took the lift down to the main hall, left the key on the hall porter's desk, walked across to the restaurant. In one corner, a chef was grilling lobsters over a blue flame. Beyond a wide window, the sea blazed in the sunshine. A waiter guided them hopefully to a table near this window. Love shook his head; no need to offer a sitting target. He settled for a table against a wall a few rows back. The waiter handed them a menu. It was no larger than a daily paper, but printed on vellum. Love thought it also made more interesting reading.

They settled for melon, grilled lobster, tossed salad, and Roquefort, which the waiter assured them had been flown all the way from France, and which tasted none the worse for that. After coffee, they sat back in their chairs. No one had asked for them, so it seemed time to ask for someone. If Mahomet wouldn't come to the mountain, etc. Love stood up.

'I'll see the desk clerk,' he said. 'Be back in two minutes/

The clerk was reading a letter, checking it for punctuation, pursing his lips every time he saw a mistake, crossing it out with a ball-point pen. He had hired a new typist that morning and meant to start as he was to continue. He glanced up as Love's shadow fell across the page.

'Senor?'

'I am Dr Love. An hour ago you rang me in my room. Someone was asking for me. Has he come back?'

The clerk glanced around the lobby as though he might see the man, then shook his head.

'But no, senor. He has not come back.'

'What sort of man was he?'

'Oh, ordinary sort. About your height.'

'What nationality? Mexican?'

'Oh no, senor. British.'

'British?'

Love's surprise showed in his voice.

'And he left no name?'

'No, senor. He just went out.'

The clerk's eyes went down to the letter again. Really, that girl had even spelled mariana wrongly.

Love walked back to the restaurant, sat down with Shamara, shook his head. Nothing to report. More traffic was on the road now. Thirty yards away, along the sea front, a blue car had stopped; the bonnet was open, like the mouth of a crocodile. Love watched it idly, wondering what was wrong. Someone was sitting in the front passenger seat, no doubt waiting for the driver. His face was partially obscured by a pillar. Love bent forward to light Shamara's cigarette, and saw the man looking at him. He was Alfred Kernau.

For a second Love froze, then he blew out the match.

'What's the matter?' asked Shamara, watching his face.

'Don't look across now, but there's a car parked up the road. A breakdown. Kernau is in the front seat. Watching us.'

'My God! I told you.'

'Be quiet. The next move is up to them.'

'But they'll kill us.'

'So you keep saying. But, why?'

'Because they've not been able to find out what we know.'

'So far as I'm concerned, that would have been impossible. I don't know a damn thing. I've told them so once. I'll tell them so again.'

Shamara shook her head impatiently.

'Oh, don't be so dumb. They'll never believe that.'

'It happens to be the truth.'

'Truth? What is truth? If Pilate didn't know, how can they?'

The argument seemed unanswerable.

At that moment, a page came into the restaurant, looked around it, as though searching for someone he didn't know, then came across hesitantly to Love's table.

'Are you the English Dr Love, senor?' he asked.

'The same,' admitted Love.

'A man is just now asking for you, senor. At the desk.'

'Who is he? Did he give his name?'

'No, senor. But the clerk said to tell you he is the same gentleman who was here before.'

Love looked at Shamara, bit his lip. Either she was right, or he was. Soon they would know. If she was right, there would probably be the polite request to come outside, perhaps to that blue car, one hand in a jacket pocket. He had seen it all so often on the screen that he could play that part easily enough.

But could he play the part for which he had cast himself? He'd have to find out by trying. He'd certainly come a long way off course from his daily round of visiting patients. Somerset was never like this. And thank God it wasn't.

'Don't come out with me,' he told Shamara. 'But count six and then follow me. Hold a handkerchief in front of your face in case you're recognized. Just by being there you may throw him, if he's turning nasty. OK? '

'OK. And - Jason?'

'Yes?'

'Take care.'

'I always do. My mother was Scots. Canny is my middle name. I'm going to live for ever. That's not a threat. It's a promise.'

The page led him across the restaurant, threading his way between the tables; a sudden, cut-off glance at someone else's entrecote, artichoke, half a cold salmon surrounded by moons' of cucumber, snatches of conversation in Spanish that meant nothing at all. How infinitely desirable the safety of the room appeared now, how lonely the walk to the hall!

The page held open the door for him. Love braced the muscles of his stomach as though by this alone he could hold back a bullet. The clerk looked up from his desk; he was reading another letter now, and it seemed no better typed than the first.

'Ah, Dr. Love,' he said. 'Your caller has returned.' He swept an arm round expansively.

This is it, thought Love. He was ready to duck if there was gunplay, but there was none. A woman sat in a leather chair reading an airline timetable, suitcases piled up to one side, waiting for the airport bus. Two couples stood talking by a black settee. Beyond them, cars flicked to and fro along the promenade.

If the worst happens, I can drop to the floor, Love thought frantically. But surely they'll not try anything here. Not in so public a place. Please God, not here. Or anywhere, come to that.

'Over there, senor.'

The clerk was smiling now. Really, this idiotic Englishman did not seem able to understand his own dreadful language. He pointed to the front of the lobby. A man stood, back towards him, looking out through the glass doors at the sea. He wore a light grey tropical suit. His hands were clasped in front of him. He rocked slightly on his heels.

'Ah, senor,' the clerk called to him. 'Dr Love. He is here.'

The man turned slowly. He was smiling.

For a moment, Love saw him and his face did not register in his mind. Then relief flooded over him with recognition. He was Inspector McGregor.

'Dr Love, I presume?' said McGregor, coming towards him, his face creased in a grin. 'You seem a remarkably elusive physician. When I rang up from the front hall earlier this morning, apparently you weren't taking any calls. Now you look at me as though you've seen a ghost. What's wrong?'

'Nothing,' said Love, smiling hugely with relief. 'Nothing at all: Very much the reverse, in fact. Everything's wonderful. Now. It's just that of all the people I imagined might be waiting for me, I never thought of you. How come you're so far away from your beat, or manor or whatever you policemen call it?'

'Leave,' explained McGregor briefly. 'Two weeks. And a rich friend is taking me sailing. He puts in here tonight. Rather like you in Tom Newborough's house in Nassau.

'I looked in here for a drink, happened to see the visitors' book on the desk, so I had a gander. Old policeman's habit, that; always read any visitors' book, just to see who's where.

'And, dammit, there was a Dr Love, as ever is. Up from Somerset, too, where the cider apples grow. Can't be two with that name there, so I rang you - and here we are. Lucky you're not on a dirty weekend, eh? Be sure your sins will find you out and all that.'

'Well,' began Love cautiously. 'I think there is someone you should meet. And one or two things you should know.'

McGregor raised his eyebrows.

'Aha, the good doctor is not alone, eh?'

'Not entirely. Come in and see for yourself.'

Love led him back through the restaurant. Shamara met them in the doorway, handkerchief at her face. In his relief, Love had forgotten he had asked her to follow him.

'It's all right,' he told her. 'This is a friend of mine. Police Inspector McGregor of Nassau. He's on holiday here.'

'Oh.' Her voice sounded faint with relief.

'This is Shamara,' Love said, and then realized he had no surname for her, so he added, 'Alcantara.' It might not be her real name, but it was better than nothing. McGregor raised his eyebrows half an inch and then lowered them slowly as though they needed the exercise.

'Any relation of the Senora?'

Shamara glanced quickly at Love. Had he told the inspector anything? Love picked up his cue like a relay runner seizing the baton.

'Yes,' he said, quickly. 'Daughter.'

'Pleased to meet you,' said McGregor, shaking hands.

'Now, what brings you both here? Vacation?'

'I'd call it other things,' said Love grimly. He led McGregor into the restaurant. They sat down at his table.

The car with Kernau had gone, but maybe they'd be coming back. He could imagine it turning, someone winding down the window, the car slowing as it passed the hotel. Then the sudden rip of hot lead, the whine of tyres as it accelerated away. Surely not? Not here. But why not here? He tried to think of any good reason and couldn't.

'You asked me to contact you if anything odd happened,' he began. 'Well, so much has happened and, offhand, I can't think of anything that's not odd.'

He told McGregor of his experiences at the Casa del Sol, of their escape, of Kernau in the car outside. As he listened, McGregor's face closed like an oyster when someone squeezes a lemon on it.'

'Unfortunately,' he said sadly, 'simply as a policeman from Nassau, it really has nothing to do with me. Of course, I can pass it on to the proper authorities.'

'And who are they?' asked Love sarcastically. 'MacGillivray?'

'Possibly. And others, nearer here.'

'But that's all Civil Service chat. In reply to your valued memo of the first inst. to hand in re the matter of, etc. That gets no one anywhere. Can't we do something positive?'

'Such as what?' asked McGregor.

'How the hell do I know?' retorted Love. 'But at least we know where some of these Nazis are hiding. I mean, half the world's been looking for these men for twenty odd years and yet all we can do now apparently is to pass the buck to someone else, put a note in someone else's tray. And hope he'll do something about it, which he won't.'

'How do you know they are Nazis? How can you be sure?' asked McGregor, leaning forward in his chair.

'I can prove it,' said Shamara. 'Dr Love hasn't told you my part in it. I work for the Israeli Government. I have checked the prints of this man Kernau, for instance.'

'You are positive?'

McGregor's face was tense with concentration.

'Absolutely certain. There is no doubt at all. None.'

'Well, that does make the case a bit stronger.' He lit a cigarette, blew out a smoke ring, then a second to follow it to show that the first was no fluke.

'What you are suggesting, doctor, is that, in lieu of anything else, we mount some kind of punitive expedition against these men? Or at least, the only one you know for certain is here, this man Kernau?'

'That's putting it a bit stiltedly, but, in a word, Yes. Couldn't we also inform the Mexican police? Don't you have any contacts there? Anything?'

McGregor shook his head.

'The fewer who are involved the better,' he said. 'These people must have access to a lot of money to have survived so long. They'll have bought themselves the best protection they can, that's for sure.' He paused as though considering something, then continued.

'Look,' he said, my friend is due at Mazatlan port early this evening. He's very rich. He'll know more important people in Mexico than policemen.

'Also, there's an election on there, and one side or the other might just be interested in unearthing some scandal. He'll know who to see. Anyhow, it's an idea, and if you think it's worth following up, I'd be very pleased to introduce you.'

'You say where and when,' said Love. 'You've got a deal.'

'I'll pick you both up here at six,' said McGregor briskly. 'It's probably best if we're not seen together till then, if what you say is happening. We can take a cab to the port. OK?'

'OK.'

McGregor stood up, bowed to Shamara, shook Love's hand.

'I only wish to God this was happening in my own manor,'

he said. 'We'd have a net around these characters in no time. Wouldn't do me any harm, either. Even civil servants like to be successful. Well, see you.'

They watched him walk out of the restaurant; he did not look back.

At five to six they were waiting in the front hall. A page approached them.

'Senor,' he said. 'The Englishman is in the backyard. In a taxi.'

Love wondered what McGregor would say at being described as an Englishman. He was sitting in the back of an Oldsmobile, the rear door open.

'I've had a word with my friend on the radiophone,' he said. 'He's not putting in after all. He's gone on to Ensenada, up near Tijuana, where the brass comes from. But he's laid on a plane for us. That all right by you?'

'Surely.'

They drove to the airport. Shamara's Cessna stood where she had left it. A Fokker Friendship was waiting for them. They were airborne within minutes. At Ensenada, a taxi took them to the quay, where iron rings rusted in the stones, and nets lay draped over wooden stakes. The air smelled sharp with the salt of drying fish.

Down a flight of slippery steps, a white motorboat bobbed on the scummy water. A seaman in white uniform held it close to the quay with a boathook until they were aboard. Then the big black Johnson outboard growled and they headed out through the harbour mouth, towards the open sea.

The swell beyond the jaws of the harbour bit them unexpectedly, like a blow, beating the breath from their bodies. Spray blew about them, then they were over the bar, and riding the long, slow Pacific rollers. Love and Shamara sat behind the vee-shaped windscreen, already misted with spray. McGregor was behind them with the seaman. Once, he tried to speak, but the wind caught his words and blew them away. He shrugged, sat in silence, eyes narrowed against the wind.

Behind their white wash, the beach hotels dwindled to the size of sugar cubes and then fell away beneath the darkening rim of the horizon, and they were alone on the wide, empty sea. Love watched the sailor steering by compass, glanced down at his own watch. They had been travelling for thirty-five minutes; the yacht must be some way off shore. The sailor began to veer to port, watching his course carefully, correcting the swell. Ahead of them lay a toy yacht that grew larger as they approached. Love did not know quite what he had anticipated, but it was certainly not as large as this.

She had a squat yellow funnel, two masts; a radar aerial that turned slowly, sweeping the seas. The davits were already swung out to receive their boat. A companion way was lowered for them. Love noted with admiration and approval that all the paint was bright; the brasswork winked at the dying sun. This was no weekend sailor's apology for a sailing boat; this was the sort of yacht he'd often seen at St Tropez, too large/to enter the harbour, riding out in the bay where tourists would come and gaze at them respectfully and from a distance. For the first time since Love had been in Mexico, he began to feel more cheerful. Against the power, the wealth, the influence that this yacht represented, how could a few old ex-Nazis hope to stand? Why, with a bit of luck, he might even get his luggage back from the Posada Duran in Durango.

A seaman waited for them on the small wooden platform at the base of the companion way. He fended off the motorboat expertly as it came round gently. Hooks locked into slots, and their engine stopped.

A steward in dark blue trousers waited for them on deck, led them along a corridor, all varnished wood, with portholes screwed open; even the threads of their screws had been polished. He knocked softly on a double door, paused, pushed it open.

The room was furnished like an executive office, very dimly lit. Rich dark drapes screened square frames around the portholes. Brass lamps on pivots, weighted against too rough a sea, bobbed gently with the slight roll of the yacht. It took Love a second to accustom his eyes to the darkness after the brightness of the sun on the sea.

A man was coming towards them, hand outstretched. He was of medium height, plump, with dark glasses in fashionable square frames.

'My name is Steyr. Paul Steyr,' he said. 'You are the English Dr Love? I am McGregor told me about you on the phone.'

'I'd like you to meet Shamara Alcantara,' said Love. 'From Israel.'

But what was her real second name? He must discover this before he introduced her to anyone else. Steyr's voice warmed; he turned to her.

'All the way from Israel?' he said. 'In the old days, I used to do a lot of business with your compatriots, Miss Alcantara. No doubt we will have many names in common. Many, many names.'

At that moment, the door opened and McGregor came in behind them. The opening door let in a white wedge of light that lit up deep green leather chairs, the white carpet, side-tables with holes cut to hold bottles and glasses in a heavy sea.

It also lit up the man who faced them. As he stood, a Siamese cat leapt from a curtain and perched on his shoulders, as Siamese cats were trained to do centuries ago, when their owners went into battle, ready to leap at the eyes and throats of their master's enemies.

The cat's fur bristled at the sudden light, its eyes flared red as fire in anger at this crude intrusion. Love saw that Steyr's face was lacerated with scars, cunningly powdered over; that behind his dark glasses he had no eyes at all, only empty sockets in his head.

And, looking across at Shamara, he saw horror and blank terror on her face.

CHAPTER NINE: COVENT GARDEN, LONDON; THE REPUBLIC OF DELGUEDA; OFF THE WEST COAST OF THE USA

MacGillivray sat at his desk in his office, looking out over Covent Garden Market. He had two letters on his desk. Neither gave him much pleasure. The way he felt today, nothing would.

The first was from the estate agent about that property in Kirriemuir. His accustomed eyes picked out isolated words and phrases that revealed its worthlessness. .'Secluded', meant miles from anywhere, without water, drainage or electricity. 'Old World' was a euphemism for being rotten with age and decrepitude, unpainted for years. 'Character and charm', meant, in his experience, that some amateur had had a clumsy hand in the architecture. No, that wasn't for him, even if he had the money. He screwed the paper up into a ball, picked up the other letter.

This was from his brother, a dentist in Nottingham, whose second son, having failed his finals in theology at Cambridge, was casting about for a job. Any job. Was there anything MacGillivray could suggest for him in what he vaguely called 'Security'? That term, thought MacGillivray sourly, covered a multitude of operations, from nightwatchmen on a building site to masterspy. No, there was nothing at all he could offer, he thought. Not even that cheapest of all gifts, advice.

He lit a, cheroot, brooded over this, over other things, thoughts flying through his mind as swiftly as the pigeons through the great, glassed-roof market building across the cobbled street.

In most jobs, there were hints and tips you could pass on, even if there was no direct training, no need of specific qualification.

But, in Intelligence, everyone started from scratch, and although not all began at the same level, all built each house up from the foundations. You gathered so much apparently unrelated information, and, like a bundle of twigs collected in a forest, it was all useless until you set flame to them. And, in so many cases, luck supplied the match. You called it the results of contacts, spade work, intuition, coordination; but never by its true name, that four-letter word: luck.

He thought of Richard Sorge, the German journalist in Japan who was also a Russian spy and who sent the message that had possibly saved the Soviet from annihilation by the Nazis - the news that Japan would not attack Russia in 1941 but, instead, was striking south and east towards Singapore and Pearl Harbor.

Against the fear of a Japanese invasion, Stalin had kept two million troops in Eastern Siberia. Sorge's news meant he could withdraw them in time to join Marshal Zhukov's armies outside Moscow. With their help the Russians stopped the German advance on the capital. Good luck for Stalin, bad luck for Hitler; bad luck for Sorge, too.

A girl friend of the moment, who discovered he was a spy, was herself a Japanese counter-agent. When Sorge proposed spending the night unexpectedly with her, she said she must telephone her parents to explain she was not coming home. Instead, she rang her chief. Sorge was arrested in bed with the girl. Now that was bad luck, thought MacGillivray. Lucky for some. Unlucky for others.

He thought of Rudolf Roessler, who had run a Swiss spy network in Switzerland during the war - feeding back information to the British. After the war, Roessler decided to work for the Czechs instead and under the name of 'Hermann Schwarz', of Zurich, he sent messages concealed in food parcels to his new employers in Prague.

One day, the postman could not find anyone at the cover address to accept the parcel; it was put on one side, forgotten about, and eventually returned to Zurich. There, the postal authorities opened it to see whether any other more specific address was inside. There wasn't, but something else was: a pot of honey containing a roll of micro-film on which were reports on American air force strengths, plans for British bases, RAF developments, and much else. Lucky for some, unlucky for others.

The classic remark about luck, thought MacGillivray, came from Colonel Abel, the Russian spy-master in the United States, who for seven years, under the alias of a Brooklyn photographer, Emil R. Goldfus, controlled a vast Soviet espionage organization in Northern America and Canada.

Fuchs, Alan Nunn May, the Rosenbergs, the Cohens who under the name of Kroger were sentenced on the British Naval Secrets case of the early nineteen-sixties - all these and many more came under his care.

And every night during these years of command Abel had broadcast and received messages direct to and from Moscow from his home in New York. Good luck. He was never suspected until an assistant defected to the US Embassy in Paris. Bad luck.

'After all, gentlemen,' said Abel when he was arrested, 'we are all professionals. I merely happen to be here because I have been unlucky.'

But where was the spark of luck he needed in this odd business? Was it that Sir Robert signed up this police surgeon fellow without telling him? In view of what McGregor's daughter had told him, it had certainly been lucky. But was it lucky enough?

The intercom buzzed like a wasp on his desk. He flicked over the switch, pressed down the green scrambler, button. Sir Robert's voice came over clearly, quick with suppressed excitement. Talk of the devil, he thought; even think of him, and he's here.

'Just had a Top in from our Nassau man - the man *I* put in, that surgeon chappy, in reply to a query I sent him. He confirms that McGregor went on leave the day after Garcia died.'

'Well?' asked MacGillivray, watching a male pigeon pursue a female on the crumbling, lime-whitened window ledge.

'We knew that already, sir, didn't we?'

The birds were nearer now, but not that near.

'Yes. Just that fact, agreed, we did. But there's something new, too. Not much, but something.'

He paused for MacGillivray to say, How interesting, really, sir? But MacGillivray said nothing; his cheroot had gone out and he was trying to persuade his lighter to work.

Sir Robert sighed and continued.

'McGregor had told people he was going to one of the Out Islands. But the day he left, our surgeon character was in the police office when the phone rang. Someone at the airport wanted to speak to McGregor. He took the call. Apparently McGregor was booked on a plane to Miami, with a connection to Mexico City and Mazatlan, on the west coast, but there'd been a balls-up. The booking clerk had looked up an old schedule. He'd-have four hours' wait in Miami instead of half an hour. They were ringing to tell him.'

'So maybe he changed his plans?' suggested MacGillivray. Was this the piece of luck they needed? If so, he didn't recognize it.

'Maybe he was on to something?' he said hopefully.

This damn cheroot tasted as sour as smoking camel dung, he thought. They didn't taste like they used to. Nothing did. Weren't made like they used to be, either. Nothing was. Not now. Outside, the female pigeon suddenly grew tired of this tedious stalking and flew away. You never could be sure: there was a time for patience and a time to act. Maybe that was the message for him, too?

'So maybe he was, maybe he will,' agreed Sir Robert smoothly. 'Time alone will tell.'

Not like him to be so acquiescent, thought MacGillivray, tossing the remnants of his cheroot, now simply a dank, damp mass of twisted weed, into the metal waste basket. It would be incinerated with the rest of the once secret rubhish. But at least it would burn then, which was more than he could make it do, now.

'That yacht our man - my man - mentioned,' went on Sir Robert briskly. 'Our stringer in Panama confirms that a white yacht that could be the one went through on the 5th - that's five days ago. It's the Endymion III. I've looked it up in Lloyd's Register. Registered in Panama - of course. A thousand tons. Three eighty feet long. Four steam turbines. Built by Abeking and Rasmussen in Bremen. Sounds like a wonderful yacht,- Mac. Just a little bit smaller than the Britannia. Owner is down as Paul Vincent Steyr, of Limoges, France. Retired industrialist.'

'What sort of industry did he retire from?' asked MacGillivray. He was always interested to learn how men, possibly no older than himself, could make fortunes that allowed them to own a boat only a few tons lighter than the Royal yacht, while all he could make was a hard living.

'Bit vague on that. I've been on to Paris, and they've nothing black on him. But they're starting to dig. Seems to be one of those characters who's made all his money since the war. Maybe he's in property. If he'd only owned a few acres on the Riviera ten years ago he'd be a millionaire now.'

'But there's no evidence he owned anything then, is there?'

'None. That's what I thought you'd find interesting.'

'I do. Any physical description?'

'Owner didn't come on deck all through the Canal. But our man met someone in the Health Department who went aboard. And someone - a steward or ship's officer, I suppose - told him that the owner never did go ashore. Hardly ever even came up on deck. He'd got a whole suite and he stayed there, curtains drawn and just enough lights on for the stewards to see their way round.'

'Why?'

MacGillivray had long ago ceased to be concerned by the foibles of the wealthy. What in a poor man was abominable and ill-bred rudeness was transmuted by wealth into an amusing and en-dearing eccentricity. Even so, this seemed odd.

'He's blind,' said Sir Robert. 'That's why.'

So. Maybe he wasn't to be envied after all.

Limoges. What did the name mean? A city in the centre of France. Limoges china. He flicked over the pages of the Michelin on his desk. Principales curio.: Cath. St-Etienne ... Musee muni-cipal ... autres curio.: Musee national Adrien Dubouche.

No, it could be none of these things. He glanced at the red street map: R. du Clocher ... Bd. V. Hugo. Nothing there either. Av. de la Liberation. That was it. To be liberated you had first of all to be in bonds. The regional Gestapo HQ had been in Limoges; the house of the torturers, in the Impasse Tivoli. Now this could be interesting; this could be getting somewhere. Maybe not fast, but at least they were moving, and to move was always better than to stand still. Say something, even if it's only goodbye.

'The Gestapo,' he said, thinking aloud. 'What about that dead girl in Nassau? The one with the camp number tattooed on her head? Was she dealt with by the Gestapo in Limoges before she was moved to a camp?'

'Check,' said Sir Robert. MacGillivray could almost hear him grin across the miles of wire.

'Our historical section says she was there from the first week of June 1942, until the end of the month. She was about seventeen then. They gave her the treatment. Apparently she'd been ac-cused of writing something rude on a proclamation of General Thomas. Remember him?'

'Indeed, yes.'

Thomas was a name from the past he would have been content to leave there. Thomas, a gross, swollen man, had been SS Brigadefuhrer in charge of the Gestapo throughout France. He'd owed this appointment largely to die fact that his. daughter had been Heydrich's mistress, and had borne him a child. Yes, MacGillivray remembered him.

'Well, she got the treatment. An example was to be made, and all that. Fingernails pulled out, cotton wool burned between her toes, nipples nipped with pliers. The lot. But she was young and strong. She survived.

'She wasn't French at all, incidentally, but had been deported as a slave girl from Riga. A sort of unpaid au pair for a Nazi officer's family in Limoges.

'It's all in the files. Masses of dates, figures, all the facts. The Nazis were very thorough in these matters of routine.'

'Very,' agreed MacGillivray. He was thinking of a memorandum he had seen when Auschwitz had been liberated. It dealt with the uses for hair, shorn from victims' heads before they were murdered. It ended with a phrase that still stuck in his mind like a thorn: 'The hair can only be used if it has attained a length of at least twenty millimetres. Reports on the quantity of hair collected, under separate subheadings for men and women, are to be sent in on the 5th of each month.'

They had been too thorough in their documentation, for, in the end, like true bureaucrats, they could not bear to destroy all their files, but had buried them in salt mines and quarries, and they had been discovered.

Of course, it was unfashionable to recall such things; there were no Nazis now. Hardly anyone even remembered them. But some still did, apparently. Especially those who had survived the torturers, the filing of the teeth, the electric impulses through their genitals. Those who had even survived the attentions of

Dr Hallervorden, who ran the Kaiser Wilhelm Institute's branch in Dillenburg, from which office he asked specifically for the brains of all prisoners killed by carbon monoxide gas (because then they died physically undamaged) and soon had more than even his institute could store.

Those who had narrowly escaped the interest of Sturmbann-fuhrer Dr Hirt, who boasted of his unique collection of Jewish skulls at the Strasberg Faculty of Medicine - and when he tired of skulls, began to collect skeletons. He insisted on making certain measurements before death, so prisoners were dispatched alive to.him from Auschwitz and then considerably gassed so that their bodies were still warm for dissection.

But although the dead had buried the dead, the living remembered. One presumably had been the girl in Nassau. But maybe someone there knew she knew too much; and they had also remembered, and had silenced her.

But Sir Robert was speaking again, and he had missed what he was saying.

'So I'll leave it to you then, Mac?'

'I didn't quite get the last bit, sir. I was checking up on Limoges as you spoke.'

'Looking at some bloody auctioneer's catalogue, more likely,' growled Sir Robert, but not angrily, because he felt he was on the winning side now; and everyone likes that, because, like falling in love, it comes so seldom.

'Now I think this Steyr character had something to do with Limoges in those days. That's why he still gives it as his address. Sort of death-wish, a dare to be discovered. The psychiatrists would call it a Freudian slip. That's my theory, anyway. And in lieu of anything better - and because of what McGregor's daughter says - what I mean to do is this...'

He spoke clearly, a commander giving orders: MacGillivray

pushed over the recording switch. He wanted a note of all this. There could be trouble if things went wrong, bad, expensive, terrible trouble. And even if things went the way Sir Robert planned, there could be no public acknowledgement. Perhaps there would be an odd, rather vague story in one of the Sunday papers, a diary paragraph in a weekly news magazine. But nothing to link the proposed sequence of events with anyone in Britain; and certainly not to a man who looked like a landowner (and was) with an office in Whitehall; and another who also looked like a landowner (and wasn't) sitting in a dusty room with curious, metal-lined curtains above a fruit wholesalers' in Covent Garden.

And it was only right that this should be so, thought MacGillivray. After all, if there was a Secret Service, it should be secret, even if the public did sometimes wonder whether there was and whether it was. Then he remembered something else.

'Dr Love, sir,' he said tentatively.

'Dr Love? What about him?' Even at two miles distance, Sir Robert's voice stiffened like a sail in the wind.

'Do you think we can use him at all? I mean, he's somewhere out there. Or he was when we last heard.'

'Certainly not. No use for amateurs at all. Half the trouble in our business is caused by these damned amateurs messing about, playing at things. This is strictly for pros only.

'What could this doctor man do, anyway - even if you could get hold of him, which I very much doubt? So if you are in touch with him - and you assured me you weren't, and I hope to God you aren't - drop him. Have nothing to do with him at all. Understood?'

'If you say so, sir,' said MacGillivray obediently, and pressed up the switch.

*　　*　　*

Kinder was smoking a cigarette and watching the early morning sun struggle slowly out of the sea. The bay lay about him, calm as glass.

The first old submarine had sailed at five o'clock on the previous evening; the second, at midnight; his own, at three o'clock that morning. It was odd to imagine them all somewhere beneath that smooth and shining surface. He wondered what other strange vessels might be down there, too. It was not a comfortable thought; he tried not to think it.

Weissmann, Axel and twenty-two others waited on the quayside with Kinder. The engines of the third old submarine were turning over. They would be away within the hour. He would see them go and then travel on into the interior. His work was done here. He carried in his pocket an air ticket on to Mexico City, where he would collect his orders.

He had stayed behind against the persuasion of Grosschmidt and Heissner, against even his own feelings, because he wanted to be sure that the last submarine, would leave on time. Weissmann had suddenly shown some reluctance that he had neither expected nor anticipated; he seemed to be unable to understand what he was to do - a sign of his age, no doubt. The only way to be certain he did not hang back was to watch Him go himself. A small rearguard of seven or eight older men, who suffered from claustrophobia and who could thus be a dangerous liability in the cramped control room of a thirty-year-old submarine, would wait with him.

Kinder had not trusted the antique radio sets to receive clearly on the new Very Low Frequency wavelengths over which the signal to detonate would be broadcast, so he had fitted into each submarine the new transistorized sets he had brought with him, with a special electronic switch linkage that would enable the charges in each submarine to be set off from a distance of thousands of miles, if need be, and without 'any over-riding control being possible by the submarine ' crews.

All that they had to do was to be in position at the agreed stations along the coast, at the agreed depths, at the agreed time. As each one reached their destination they would simply radio back one codeword Freiheit - freedom. Then they would wait where they were until control - and Kinder did not even know himself exactly where that was - made their radio signal. The charges would blow instantly, and the greatest scientific experiment since the Nazi medical researches on human guinea-pigs in the concentration camps would have begun.

He would say goodbye to Weissmann now, wait until they had submerged, give them a couple of hours for good measure. Then, after lunch, when the sun was burning a hole in the sky and the wind had dropped and any movement made one stream with sweat, at that hour when old men dozed with their dreams, helped by the capsule he would dissolve in that vile coffee in their mess hut, he would slip away.

And when the sun began to die and the day cooled and they woke and looked about for him, Kinder would be over the frontier in another country, with another identity. A British passport and health papers in the yellow oilskin pouch he wore in the pocket of his canvas body belt under his shirt described him as Thomas Brooks, a lawyer from Basingstoke, Hampshire, England.

He glanced at his watch; it was time for Weissmann to be away. They had only a hundred and ninety sea miles to go, but with their old engines they could not delay their departure any longer. He held out his hand in farewell. Weissmann looked at it and then at him, as though he did not understand the meaning of the gesture.

'Goodbye,' said Kinder pointedly. 'And good luck.'

Really, these stupid old sods. It made you wonder how they could have been so clever in the old days, how they had ever achieved as much as they had, even though the whole lot did fall about their ears in '45.

'Why goodbye, Herr Oberleutnant?' Weissmann said, as though he was surprised. 'We are not leaving you. As I've already told you, I do not think I am competent to carry out our instructions without you.'

'Of course you are,' said Kinder sharply. 'The others have already gone. And my place is here.'

'Why?' Axel's question cracked hard as a whip.

'Because those are my orders. I am under orders, gentlemen.'

'Of course you are, Kinder.'

There was no courtesy now in Weissmann's voice, no friendliness.

'And since you have assured us that our old ranks obtained as from the date of our acceptance of your offer, we out-rank you. And our orders are that you accompany us.'

Kinder felt the blood leave his face. What were these idiots up to? His cigarette tasted dry and sour. He threw it into the water.

'That is impossible, gentlemen,' he said, trying to hold the panic out of his voice. 'Although I appreciate your concern for the success of our operation, this would only jeopardize it.'

He looked from one to the other, on to the next man, trying to will them to believe. They stared back at him, eyes like polished grey stones, just as, years before, when Kinder was only a little boy, they had watched their victims, without pity, interest, belief or concern.

'Why would your presence with us jeopardize it?' asked Weissmann gently.

Kinder bit his lip. He had been a bloody fool to say that. It wasn't true, of course. It would only jeopardize him. But what could he say now?

'I have my orders,' he repeated sulkily. 'I have to make my report.'

'You can write your report with us in the submarine. And we have given you your orders. Come, or you will make us begin to wonder whether there is any other reason why you are so anxious to miss this historic voyage. Now, Kinder. Come!'

Weissmann nodded briefly over Kinder's shoulder to four of the others, younger men, who had quietly moved behind him as he spoke. They took his arms. Kinder broke free of them suddenly and started to run wildly, he did not know where. He tripped over an outcrop of grey rock he had not seen and staggered, and before he could be up again, they were on him, pinning his arms to his sides.

'What shall we do?' asked Axel. He had not expected this..

'Take him to the mess hut.'

Weissmann was also surprised; a tide of panic had begun to rise in his throat, threatening to choke him. Dear God, what if this were a trap after all? But how could it be? How could it possibly be?

'What'll we do with him there?'

'Make him talk.'

'But if you don't go now, you'll ruin the whole experiment,' shouted Kinder, one fear overcoming another. 'It's the timing. The distance you have to sail.'

'To hell with the distance and the timing,' retorted Weissmann. He smelled the sweat of mortal terror, Kinder's and his own. There would be time for their experiment later on, when this mystery had been unravelled. It had waited for more than twenty years; another few days meant nothing.

'You can't mean that,' beseeched Kinder. 'There won't be another chance. As I explained to you, these three charges must be detonated at precisely the right time in the right sequence, at the right depth, or the whole thing's ruined. It's a matter of progressive explosives. Years of experiment and research will be thrown away. And your own chances of freedom. Don't you see? Are you gone mad?'

His face was contorted like a desperate gargoyle. How often,' years before, in long forgotten prisons, in the Villa des Rosiers in Montpellier, in the dark buildings on the Rue des Sausaies in Paris, in the Impasse Tivoli in Limoges, Weissmann had seen other men's faces look like this, twisted with fear, agony, despair.

And he liked the memory; as with the prospect of sex, it aroused deep emotions, the first faint stirrings of anticipated pleasure. By God, if this swine was a traitor, he would have a terrible end. They had twenty years of exile to work out on him.

'No,' said Weissmann softly, his face a bland mask. 'We are not mad. We are just surprised that you will not accompany us on this very short voyage. And we would like to know the reason why. And, in due time, we will. Just how long this time is depends entirely on you, my friend.'

As they began to walk up the hill towards the mess hut, slowly because Weissmann's leg was paining him, it was as though the years began to fall away from them like skins on an onion, veils vanishing: from their minds.

Each man was walking up another hill in the sunshine of some other country, long ago - in Poland, in Russia, in France, in Bulgaria, with some other person about to be tortured. Each man was wondering how the victim would react, when he would break; each felt the same terrible thrill of sadistic expectation, the dry mouths of anticipation.

Behind them, someone stopped the submarine's engine and there was no sound but their breathing, and the dragging of Weissmann's leg on the rocks. Then came a new sound that stained the wind with shame.

Kinder began to cry.

* * *

Steyr turned his blind head slowly from left to right. In the dim light of the room his dark glasses glittered like two green windows in his skull. He said softy: 'Someone's afraid of me here. Which one of you is it? And why?'

'Neither of us,' said Love. 'You are mistaken, Mr Steyr. We've come here especially to meet you.'

This man must be some kind of nut, he thought. Maybe a recluse with a persecution mania. Yet this would not explain Shamara's obvious terror of him.

'I can smell fear,' Steyr continued, ignoring him. 'When you have no sight, all your other senses grow sharper because you use them more, Like knives.'

He moved closer to them, stood between Love and Shamara. The cat purred now, eyes crossed in its pleasure.

'So,' Steyr said finally. 'You are afraid of me, Miss Alcantara.'.

He paused, digesting this. Then he addressed Love as though he could see him.

'My friend here' - he gave an almost imperceptible nod towards McGregor - 'My friend here told me a little about you, as I said, doctor. Did you know that I wanted you to come aboard my yacht when you were in Nassau? But you had other ideas then, apparently. Now, you are here, and I think we shall have much to discuss. And the girl too.

'Why are you frightened of me, Miss Alcantara? Are you related to that other woman of that name in Nassau?'

Shamara opened her mouth to answer, but could find no words. She looked towards Love beseechingly and then put her head in her hands, her shoulders trembling with her sobs.

Love glanced at McGregor in bewilderment. What was all this about, then? McGregor had suggested they should visit his friend because there was the chance that he could help them, had obviously gone to some trouble to arrange it, but now Shamara was terrified of the man, and her terror did not seem to surprise him. Why should a blind stranger terrify her? Or had they met somewhere before? Questions chased answers in his mind, like wooden horses on a fairground swing never catching up.

'Look, McGregor,' he said. 'What's happening? Have you told Mr Steyr why we're here - to ask for his help against these Nazis in Durango?'

'Of course he has,' said Steyr. 'And he couldn't have brought you to a better man.'

He paused, smiling. The gold caps on his teeth threw the light back in Love's 'eyes like a challenge.

'You see, doctor,' Steyr went on, 'a lot of people - possibly your friend, Miss Alcantara, included - think that I'm the most wanted Nazi of all! Well, I don't wish to boast, but I think I could place myself after Bormann, who was Hitler's deputy, and Heinrich Muller, Himmler's deputy in the Gestapo.

'I had charge - as I think Miss Alcantara must know, hence her fear - of all the concentration camp administration in the Third Reich. I ran the Amtsgruppe D, which organized everything - the work the prisoners did, their rations, their transfer to other camps, even their deaths when they had nothing left to offer the Reich.

'I rarely appeared in public, doctor, especially after the accident that cost me my sight. Some so-called resistance-workers had been arrested, and not searched thoroughly enough. One still had an explosive device concealed with sticking plaster under his arm pit. As he was being led away he threw it at a party of us. I was the only one injured.

'Of course, the man was punished. He was a strong fellow. He took a whole week to die. But that did not help me. There were suggestions among some of our medical people that his eyes should be removed and grafted into my body - an operation that is frequently successful nowadays, as you, being a medical man, will know.

'But then life was more primitive, and the operation was not a success. Perhaps Miss Alcantara heard of me - or even saw me? Who knows?'

He chuckled as though he enjoyed considering the possibilities.

Love said, dully, his mind confused, 'If you were in charge, then you have the death of six million Jews on your conscience?'

'Not all on mine, doctor. That was the figure mentioned at Nuremberg, I agree, but there were many others who helped. You do me too much honour altogether. Eichmann was as keen as I was, and just as assiduous, but he has been less fortunate. You see, like too many people in 1945, he ran away. I stayed firm. I became a blind piano-tuner in the Hindelang. Who could possibly look for me? What harm could a poor blind man do?

'But, unlike any other piano-tuners I have met, I also held the deeds of houses, all the patents, the details of industrial processes that scientists and industrialists who were prisoners in our camps made over in the hope of clemency. I was rich even then. And as Germany has prospered - a bulwark-against Communism, as in the old days - the value of all those pieces of paper has naturally grown enormously.

'It was ironic. Here was I, the man who had stayed behind, who had remained loyal to the Fuhrer to the end, rich beyond accounting - and all those who had fled away to - South America to save their own skins had nothing but their skins. This has always amused me.' He began to laugh aloud now at the thought.

He was mad, of course, thought Love professionally, but this realization did nothing to help him. What kind of nightmare had he entered halfway through? And who the hell was McGregor? How was he involved? After all, he had led them here. If they were the fish caught in a net, he had been the fisherman. He spun round on him.

'What's your part in all this?' he asked, a faint hope fluttering in the back of his mind that perhaps he might somehow be on their side. But this hope died as he saw McGregor's face flush with contempt.

'I've known Mr Steyr for a long, long time,' he replied. 'Our association goes back to the war.'

'The war? Then —?' Love could not bring himself to finish the question; the answer seemed incredible. McGregor supplied it for him.

'Then I was working for the Nazis in those days? But of course I was. And why not? My sympathies were always with them. I was born in South Africa. My father was German. From Dortmund. I was brought up to hate the British, and I've found a lot to hate. Hypocrisy. Snobbishness. Slovenliness.'

Steyr interrupted him.

'He is a modest man, doctor, and probably will not tell you of the work he did for our cause, so I will speak for him.

'You will remember the outcry recently when it was admitted that so many French and British agents parachuted over France during the war simply to be arrested as they landed? Our people had taken over the radio network of the resistance. So they said where these men should land - and promptly arrested them. It was all highly amusing. And it was largely due to the remarkable skill of my friend here. He ran the Fahdung Funk, the secret listening service that picked up the radio signals for landings. And then he initiated the Wehrmacht Nachrichten Verbindung Funk Referat III, which pin-pointed the French resistance transmitters in Lyons, Marseilles and Toulon. A remarkable achievement, as I am sure you'll admit, doctor. For, having once found the sets, we then took over the operators and the codes. The rest was easy. It was called Action Donar - Donar is the old god of Thunder, and radio's patron saint in Germany. And he's rather stolen your thunder, eh, doctor?'

Steyr's body shook with laughter again. This fellow's middle name should be Laughing Boy, thought Love, wishing he could see the funny side of his own situation. Sir Thomas Browne might have written charitably in the seventeenth century, 'In venemous Natures, something may be amiable', but he couldn't find it here.

'At least this genius didn't find the transmitter hidden in that book I took to Mexico,' Love pointed out.

'Agreed,' said Steyr, his face clouding momentarily. 'But he organized a very neat device inside a flower for you in Nassau. And, after all, Kernau soon discovered the mechanism in the. book.'

'Maybe. Someone had to. Tell me, was there ever a real Inspector McGregor? Or are you the only one?'

'He had an accident,' said McGregor.

'Where?'

'On the way to Tilbury to join the ship taking him to Nassau. A hit-and-run driver. One of our people. McGregor was carrying his passport, his papers, even his letters of recommendation for the job. It was simply a matter of transferring them to me. I knew his background already. It was a very routine affair. I tell you, Dr Love, this has taken a lot of preparation. We're not amateurs.'

'Maybe not. Didn't anything about McGregor's death appear in the papers?'

'No. A letter was found in his coat pocket, to his only relation, his daughter. The wife of some clergyman in England. It was to the effect that, if he died, he wanted no more notice taken of him - and certainly no more publicity - than if he'd died on active service in any of the hundred-and-one campaigns the silly fool had taken part in. It said he'd been suffering from heart trouble for years, but he'd kept it a secret. Naturally, his daughter respected his wishes.'

'Which were, in fact, yours?'

'Mr Steyr's, to be exact.'

'Well, you did win that move. Now what's the next one?'

He might as well keep the conversation going. Hadn't Churchill said that jaw-jaw was better than war-war?

'That depends on you,' said Steyr. 'We want to find out who sent you. How much you know.'

'Oh, my God,' said Love with feeling. 'Not this again. When will you people ever learn? No one sent me. I'm simply a tourist in Mexico.'

'If you really are only a tourist, then how were you with the Israeli girl agent when, she was shot? How did you agree to carry a concealed transmitter for another agent? And now you arrive here with yet a third! We used to have a saying in the old days, doctor. One coincidence can be believed; two are suspicious; three, impossible. You may be speaking the truth, or you may not. But since you maintain this attitude, I think we'll try the girl first.'

'Like hell you will,' said Love. McGregor pushed him out of the way. Love brought up his right hand in a scything motion, caught McGregor across his Adam's apple. He dropped, writhing on the carpet, his fingers curved like claws in his agony.

Steyr jumped back lightly. His right hand dipped into his inner pocket of his jacket and came out holding a Mauser. Lucky dip, thought Love bitterly. Lucky for some, but not for him.

'Don't move, either of you,' Steyr ordered sharply. 'Don't move an inch.'

He began to walk backwards slowly, his left hand outstretched behind him like an antenna to feel the edge of a desk or chair. He'll have an alarm button somewhere, thought Love, and once the crew come in, it's the end.

'Who are you talking to?' he asked, to delay him.

'You,' said Steyr. He paused, turned towards the sound; stood listening, his body tense, his hand still behind him. His blank green glasses were fixed on the direction from which he had last heard Love's voice.

Shamara hurled her handbag at him. It was all she had, but it was enough. It caught Steyr's shoulder and burst open, scattering lipstick, a powder compact and all the inessentials a girl calls essential.

Love ducked as the bullet from Steyr's gun buried itself in the woodwork behind him.

'Violence won't get you anywhere, Dr Love,' said Steyr reprovingly. 'These sort of actions do you no credit. I thought you had more intelligence.'

Love dived, at the door. His hand was on the key when he felt ten knives gouge the back of his neck. He flung back his head against the spears of pain and felt fur brush his hair. And then, too late, he remembered the Siamese cat. It had jumped at its master's enemy in the way its ancestors had been trained at the court of the ancient kings of Siam centuries before.

The cat's claws were filed talons, tearing at his flesh; its eyes gleamed red with anger as it growled deep in its, throat with the unique ferocity of its kind.

Love put up his right hand; the cat only sank its claws in more deeply. If he pulled it away, he would pull away his own flesh, too. He ducked down behind the back of a chair, in case Steyr started shooting again, seized the cat's front paws, pulled them gently towards him, then jerked them outwards. They came away reddened with his blood. He picked up the cat by the loose scruff of its neck, threw it to the carpet. The beast slunk away; he had hurt its pride, the greatest blow he could inflict on it.

But the cat had succeeded in diverting Love's attention, and this gave Steyr the time he needed. Through the rich thickness of the drapes that muted all sound, Love heard the distant clang of an alarm bell. Two down and none to play.

He took out a handkerchief, dabbed at his bleeding neck, shrugged his shoulders at Shamara.

The unwavering blue barrel of Steyr's Mauser pointed like a steel finger at her stomach.

'Don't move again, either of you,' ordered Steyr. 'Stay right where you are.' He put out one hand, switched off the light.

'When one is blind,' he went on, musingly, 'it makes no difference whether it's darkness or light, day or night. I've lived in darkness for twenty years. It's no inconvenience to me now. But if you move in the dark I will hear you and shoot where you are. I'll shoot you first in the groin, Dr Love, and then in the gut and then in the throat. Those ways it takes longest to die.'

'Those ways it takes longest to die,' repeated Shamara, her voice frosty. 'I remember you saying those words in German years ago at Maidanek. When they were moved, prisoners had the letter "M" for Maidanek or "A" for Auschwitz on their papers. Either way meant the gas-chamber in the end.'

'Of course,' said Steyr. 'I told you I had had many dealings with others of your race. Probably people you knew.'

'My mother, my sister, my father,' said Shamara flatly.

'And yet somehow we missed you. Well, what's one among so many?'

It may be one too many, thought Love. Half crouching in the darkness, holding his breath in case the sound of breathing gave him away, he began to inch his way towards Steyr. But Steyr heard him.

'I can hear the creaking of your shoes, doctor. Stay exactly where you are. I have watched so many people die in so many different ways. I've watched them burn alive, and freeze to death, naked. I've seen them shot through the back of the head, in the testicles, through the kidneys. I've watched them die by degrees with ever increasing electric current.

'I cannot see men die any longer, but I can still feel them die. I can hear them die. As I'll feel and hear both of you die. I'll smell the sweat of your fear, the sweat of your death, and this will give me some pleasure? some recompense for what I have suffered in my own world of the dark.'

'You're bloody well mad,' said Love.

'What is genius but a side of madness?' asked Steyr.

'Suppose I do tell you who sent me,' said Love, suddenly, to humour him, to gain time; for while there was time there was life, and while there was life, hope. Not much, but some.

'Suppose I tell you everything. What will you tell me?'

'What do you want to know?' asked Steyr. This is unexpectedly sudden, doctor. I thought we were going to have a little more resistance from you.'

'Why are you so anxious to know who sent me?'

Steyr ran die fingers of his right hand over the raised Braille numbers of his watch.

'It is now ten-thirty by western standard time,' he said. 'In exactly twenty-four hours from now, I will receive three signals from three old submarines. It will tell me that they are in position, hundreds of miles apart, on the bed of the Atlantic off the east coast of South America.

'When I receive these signals, my radio operator here, acting on my orders, will make a certain signal in reply. He doesn't know what it is yet - I am the only one who knows - but this signal will automatically detonate atomic devices of varying strength in each of these submarines.

'They're all lying in positions calculated first by mathematicians, and then checked by computer. The first device will go off, then the second and the third, and, in so doing they will set off a remarkable chain reaction.'

'Such as "what?' asked Love sceptically. This sounded a madman's scheme.

'Such as this,' replied Steyr. 'You may or may not know, doctor, but the climates of the United States, of Great Britain and parts of Europe are determined by ocean currents, mainly the Gulf Stream, the Newfoundland Stream and others. When these devices explode they will reverse the directions of the Gulf Stream. By reason of their checked positions and their depth, the explosions will force the currents to go, if not exactly the other way, nearly the other way. And, in this case, nearly will be good enough.

'There will be a tremendous tidal wave along the east coast of South America, but this will be put down to the eruption of an undersea volcano or some such thing. It will be a nine days wonder, nothing more. But spring and summer will be late in coming to the United States and to Great Britain. In fact, they won't come at all. And, by next winter, without a summer, without a harvest, people will wonder what's happened.'

'Maybe they will,' agreed Love. 'But they'll know about these explosions.'

'Does that matter? If they don't fall for the volcano cover story a tidal wave could be caused by secret atomic tests being carried out by the Russians, the Chinese, maybe even the French.

'This will be denied, of course, by the country accused, but the more denials, the more likely it will seem that-they are guilty. The newspapers will be full of stories about lost crops, bad weather, ruined harvests, summer holidays spoiled, summer holidays cancelled. And it will be the worst winter on record, for the United States and Britain will now have a climate worse than Greenland, and they are totally unused to such extreme weather. People's breath will freeze in their throats. Pipes will burst, sewers coagulate, rivers freeze from bank to bank.

'And the next spring will be even worse.

'In short, doctor, these devices, on which, incidentally, the Russians have been working for some years, north of Korea, these devices - even if not completely successful,-because of the relatively crude equipment at our disposal, will be sufficiently successful to change the climate of North America, Britain, the eastern coast of France, and parts of Spain, beyond all recognition. And for ever.

'Within a few years they'll be barren lands, if not frozen, at least incapable of ripening fruit and having harvests, of growing wheat. People will emigrate. Towns will become deserted. Villages will fall into decay.'

'Why?' asked Love, mainly to keep him talking. His eyes were growing more accustomed to the darkness; he could distinguish the shape of chairs, a table, the outline of Steyr. 'What's there in this for you?'

'I'll tell you what's in it for me, doctor. A very simple human emotion, and next to sex possibly the greatest and most satisfying of all - revenge.

'I was not always as you see me now, blind and scarred, a husk with only the spirit still alive. I was a man of power and action. My orders affected thousands of people. In the end, possibly millions.

'If the war had lasted even another six months I could have commanded parts of Europe greater than Hannibal or Alexander ever dreamed of conquering. All that was denied to me by the swift advance of the Americans and the British through France and Western Germany. So, although my wealth is of vast importance, it is not all.

'The bomb that blinded me, like the bomb supplied to the men who killed my friend Heydrich in Czechoslovakia, had been made in Britain. And, no doubt, the Americans also had their share in it. So what do I owe them? I hate them all, every one.

'They stopped me when I was at the edge of triumph - and they ruined what was left. I had to take a new name, I could use my money to finance ventures, but only under other names, never my own, which is not Steyr, or anything like it. Always, I had to keep in the background. Always in my own world of darkness. Always acting under an alias in case someone should recognize me.

'I've often anchored off St Tropez or Antibes and nobody has bothered me. But it might be different if I came into Southampton Water or New England Sound. I would not feel safe there - and why the hell should I not feel safe anywhere? So, I decided to teach you ludicrous Anglo-Saxons a lesson you'll remember. I planned this turning of the ocean currents as our military and political campaigns used to be planned. Thoroughly. Nothing left to chance. Everything rehearsed. I contacted old experts long since retired. My charitable foundation financed schemes of study into tides and currents at several universities. And they showed me that I could so easily do what I am doing now.'

As Steyr was speaking, Love's eyes grew accustomed to the gloom and he saw the tell tale flecks of foam, the white milky saliva, gather at die corners of his mouth. Steyr's right hand, came up, fists clenched, to punctuate his remarks. He was speaking again, not in a state room in a yacht off the North American coast, but in a Munich cellar, at a rally at Nuremberg. He was seeing, with the eyes of memory that no scars could obliterate, the serried ranks of listeners,' hearing the drilled shouts of acclaim as he paused, breaking from his text, to greet them as his friends.

There was no doubt about it; he was quite mad. He was also supremely dangerous.

'Who's in these submarines of yours?' asked Love, not knowing whether to humour him or ridicule his plan.

'It's immaterial now whether you know or .whether you don't. They'll be dead within hours, all of them. Like you. They are the men who ran away. The men who were proud and grateful to be allowed to serve in the days of the Third Reich and who, at the end, rather than stand by their Führer, fled away. First to the Argentine. Then to Bolivia. On to Paraguay. Finally, to the little republic where my men found them. 'It struck me as another of life's ironies that these cowards should be lured to their deaths by a promise, just as they deceived so many others by their false promises in the past. But then life is supremely ironic. As the Bible says somewhere, those who save their lives shall lose them!'

'How did you trick them?' asked Shamara in the darkness.

'Ah, yes. You wish to know. Naturally. Well, I appealed to their patriotism. To their honour as Germans. My emissaries arrived - appropriately enough, in a vessel of the West German Navy - with full credentials and letters for them. It was perfectly done.

'We used to forge such documents very well in the Third Reich, you know - as successfully as you people did in Baker Street for the SOE, or the OSS on 42nd Street in New York. Even better, in many instances.

'These papers promised the old men a safe return to families they had not seen for twenty odd years - if they would take part in a complicated scientific experiment designed, of all things, to get food from the sea.

'But I don't want to get food from the sea, doctor. What I will have from the sea is revenge. That is the sweetest food of all.'

'Also, the most impossible,' said Love. 'You'll never succeed with this. You're mad. You ought to be in a home.'

'Please. I do not wish to indulge in a Socratic dialogue with you, Dr Love.'

'Tell me one last thing though, Mr Steyr,' said Love. 'One very small final thing.'

'What is it?'

Steyr's voice was becoming shrill with impatience. The reaction after the emotional orgasm of his speech had turned his face grey; his forehead was damp with sweat. His head was beginning to throb like a huge drum; each beat of his heart hurt him like a blow to the body.

'What is it?' he repeated.

'You're the only person who knows the radio signal?'

'Of course. The secret in every successful enterprise is to keep close command. Tell no one the whole story. Tell each only what concerns them personally. And as little as they need to know for their part in the operation.

'Now, doctor, I have told you my story. You keep your part of the bargain. Who sent you? Who are you working for?'

'No one,' said Love. 'No one at all.'

The room filled with silence; then, faintly in the distance, Love heard the trilling of the alarm bell for the second time.

'So you wish to make fun of me, Dr Love,' said Steyr slowly. 'Well, I think I will have more fun with you.'

Love heard a drawer open and slam shut.

Steyr went on. 'I have here a whip. One of the original rhino whips that Julius Streicher used so often. A very rare item, and a very painful one. Jokes, you will find, doctor, can often cause hurt. Like this.'

The whip cracked like a gunshot. Love felt the flick of cold air near his face, then the burning rawness where the lash had laid bare his cheek. He bit back an exclamation of pain.

'So. I do not hear you laughing now, Dr Love. But we will make you smile yet. Although perhaps on the other side of your face, as you English say.'

Love heard a scuffling sound on the carpet. McGregor was crawling to his feet.

'Now,' said Steyr again. 'Who are you working for?'

'Oh, for God's sake,' replied Love wearily. 'Spare me that again.'

'I'll spare you nothing,' shouted Steyr furiously. He pressed the button by his chair. Double doors swung open, letting in a fan of light from the corridor. Three men came with it; two carried whips; the third, a Mauser automatic. In the brief moment before the doors closed again, Love saw McGregor on the floor barely a yard away, crawling towards him: Shamara drawn back against the far wall; Steyr, with the whip in his hand, standing by his leather chair. Then the doors shut and once more they were in the dark.

'We will have a little game, Dr Love,' said Steyr. 'One we sometimes used to play with some of the younger people in Dachau. I cannot see you, but I can hear you breathe. And my companions are wearing night-glasses. They cannot see very well, but they can see better than you. When I miss, maybe they will hit.'

His whip hissed again, a serpent in his hand. Love heard Shamara's sharp intake of breath as its long oiled tongue licked past her. He held his own breath, took a step forward and kicked hard. The toe of his shoe Smashed against something soft. He heard McGregor's cry of agony. That should keep him in his place for a while, so that he could concentrate on more difficult problems. Then a whip slashed over his shoulders, stinging his left hand like a branding iron. All around him now whips were singing through the air; he felt panic rise in his throat. He was in the middle of a living nightmare. What end could it have but mutilation or death?

A whip stung his neck. He put up his hand instinctively. His left thumb nail caught momentarily in a pinhead, in his lapel. What was that doing there? His tortured mind desperately turned back memories, like pages in a book when you were in too great a hurry to find the place.

Senora Alcantara in her house in Nassau asking him for the little flower. He had given her the petals in the centre, but had kept the pin. What use was that now? He looked towards Steyr, thinking of him now not as his captive, but as a physician summing up a patient. Obviously, the man was a megalomaniac, and about to go into a depressive state. Elation would return later, possibly with a few pills, maybe with the normal switch-back of his twisted mind. But by then he and Shamara could have been whipped to death. Now, if Steyr was the only man who knew the radio signal, if he could be incapacitated, then the moment of tide and time would pass. The submarines would have to re-group, hours later, and in that time anything could happen.

His mind leapt frantically, seeking a link between disconnected names, searching for a way of escape from the sighing of the whips. Beechwood. The name of Tom Newborough's house. The reason he'd seen Newborough at all. Rheumatism. A possible treatment. Acupuncture. His mind stopped searching. If acupuncture - the old Chinese remedy of pricking nerve junctions just beneath the skin, to ease pain - could relieve rheumatism and help to dispel headaches, in the hands of a sufficiently knowledgeable practitioner it could also cause intense, almost unbearable pain.

If he could pierce the Yang Meridian which, according to the ancient Chinese teachings, ran just in front of the superorbital nerve in the left temple, he could bring on a headache so ferocious that the subject would collapse and stay virtually comatose until a needle was pressed elsewhere to relieve the pain.

But could he find the right place in Steyr's temple in the darkness? He would only have one chance and that was slender enough. Even so, it was the only one he had; he'd have to use it.

'I'm waiting,' Steyr's voice cut into his thoughts. 'I can't hear you laughing, Dr Love. Don't you think it funny now? Aren't you enjoying our game?'

His whip rose and fell again, cracking like a split tree. Love winced each time he heard it; but at least the ones he heard were harmless, the ones he wouldn't hear were the ones to hurt him.

Steyr's voice had given away his position. Love inched cautiously towards him, holding the pin, like a tiny dart, between the thumb and forefinger of his left hand. He was thinking of Steyr's life, attuned to the dark, ears alert to the slightest sound of potential danger that sighted people would miss: the sudden hiss of breath, the creak of a loose floorboard.

Another whip cracked and he heard Shamara scream; someone had hit her. Steyr shouted again, his voice thick with exultation.

'You see, we have scored a hit with your friend! Why aren't you laughing, Dr Love? I can't hear you.'

'I'm with you, you bastard,' said Love and seized Steyr's arm. He was at right angles to him; he could gauge where to strike. He pricked the pin into the man's left temple, feeling the short bristles of hair, the dampness of the flesh. As he struck, Love jumped to one side and dropped on all fours, throwing away the pin.

Steyr's scream lanced the darkness.

'Mein Gott! Aaah!'

'The light!' yelled Love. 'Put on the lights! I'm a doctor. He's had a seizure.'

Steyr crashed forward into a table. It capsized beneath his weight with a splintering of glass. Then the wall-lights peered redly through their thin silk shades.

Steyr lay on the white carpet, stained now by red Dubonnet and Campari from smashed bottles on the ruined table. He writhed slowly, squirming in his giant agony. His glasses had come off, and he dug his clenched fists into his empty eye-sockets as though to gouge out the pain from these canyons in his skull.

The guards surrounded him, with worried, pale faces. What had happened? Their whips trailed on the carpet. They looked like children who had broken an expensive ornament at a party. Old and evil children, thought Love. He turned to Shamara.

'Are you hurt?' he asked her.

'It's nothing,' she answered him. 'It only caught my arm.'

McGregor crawled painfully to his hands and knees, stood up shakily, held on to a heavy chair. He had bitten his tongue when Love had hit him, and a thick sliver of dark blood drooled from the right of his mouth. Love seized him by his jacket, hauled him to his feet.

'Listen,' he said. 'Listen, and give your brains a treat. This man's dying.'

'What have you done to him?' asked McGregor hoarsely. His voice sounded thick, blurred, out of focus.

'Nothing,' said Love. 'But he's dying. We all do eventually, I know. But, for him, eventually is now.'

'He can't be.'

'I'm a doctor,' Love reminded him. 'I've seen many, men die. Maybe not so many as you, but you don't have to tell me the symptoms.'

'If you're a doctor, then treat him,' ordered McGregor. 'Cure him.'

He motioned to the guard with the Mauser; the man stuck it into Love's stomach. Love hoped he hadn't an itchy finger. Through a silk shirt that bullet would make no improvements in his alimentary tract.

'Take that away,' he advised gently, as though humouring a child. 'The time's past for persuasion of that kind. If you want Mr Steyr to recover, that is.'

The man glanced at McGregor for instructions. McGregor nodded; he lowered the gun.

'What do you suggest then, doctor?' McGregor laid an emphasis of contempt on the word.

'I suggest nothing,' said Love. 'I'm not hired to make suggestions. It's immaterial to me whether he lives or dies. He's not one of my patients. I'm just giving you a professional opinion for free.'

He put his hands in his pockets, took out a packet of Gitanes, gave one to Shamara, took one himself, lit them both, then tossed the match casually on to the carpet.

'We can make it rough for you,' threatened McGregor.

'Not so rough as it's going to be for you,' retorted Love. 'What price your experiment with the tides now? Canute didn't manage it, so why should you?'

'Don't give me that shit,' said McGregor. 'I want that man cured.'

'And I want eternal life, no less,' replied Love. 'We just can't get all we want - inspector.' It was his turn now to lay the trowel of contempt on the rank.

McGregor swallowed.

'We'll make it pretty hard for you if you don't treat him,' he said hoarsely. 'And for the girl. Get busy, Dr Love.'

'What do you expect me to treat him with? My hands?' asked Love. 'I've got no medicines, no instruments. Not even a thermometer with me. Nothing. I'm not a faith healer. I say he's dying. But it might be possible to save his life, or at least to prolong it a little while if you could get him ashore.'

'That's impossible,' said McGregor quickly. He moved away from the chair, leaned against the table his teeth clenched with the pain the movement caused him. He wiped blood from the edge of his mouth with the back of his hand.

'Well, if it's impossible, he'll die. I'd give him a very short time before he goes to join the millions he's so proud of sending to their deaths. Maybe they'll be waiting for him. Sort of celestial reception committee. If you're so keen to save him, why not get a doctor out here with the equipment he needs?'

'How?'

'You're asking, too many questions,' said Love. 'You've got all the cards. I've got nothing. You've a boat.You persuaded me out here. Why can't you go in and persuade another doctor to come out - with some medical gear?'

'That's risky,' said McGregor. 'Well, then, you make the decision.'

Love smiled as though it was nothing to him now.

McGregor spoke in German to one of the guards. The man nodded, took out a string of keys, unlocked an outer lock on a bureau, then an inner one. He pulled open a small lacquered drawer. Inside lay a black, hard-covered, exercise book. He handed this to McGregor.

McGregor picked up the house telephone and dialled.

'Captain?' he said when a voice answered. 'Where exactly are we? Mr Steyr wishes to know.'

Love heard the voice reply.

'Right now, sir, we're off the California coast. Just north of Los Angeles.'

'Thank you.' He replaced the receiver, opened the book.

'What's in there?' asked Love. 'Visitors' numbers?'

'In a sense,' said McGregor, 'yes. Just, as we knew exactly where to find our old colleagues who had so precipitately removed themselves to South America, so we know where a number of them went when they moved' on from there.

'There are several in San Francisco, some farther up in California, even one or two in Oregon. We'll try one of them, if need be. But not just yet. Well give it another few hours, maybe all tomorrow, if Mr Steyr shows any signs of getting better. No need to do anything hasty, doctor. I don't altogether agree with your diagnosis.'

Love looked at him; so he had failed with his last throw. He was playing outside his league.

'Now,' said McGregor, watching him, 'just in case you get any ideas, we'll put you somewhere with the girl, so that you can both think about what's going to happen to you.'

He turned away from Love and then swung back towards him, hit him with a straight right in the stomach. Love was not expecting the blow; he was too tired, too confused to duck. For a moment he reeled, his body one enormous pain. Then the guard behind him brought down the edge of his hand in a rabbit punch across the back of his neck. Love folded up slowly like a tent with the guy ropes out.

The rest was a raw, red mist of pain and then the long cold fall through darkness to a merciful oblivion.

'Now,' said McGregor, unbundling his muscles. 'We'll deal with the girl...'

CHAPTER TEN: OFF HIGHWAY 101, ORE-GON, USA; WHITEHALL, LONDON; OFF THE COAST OF OREGON; THE REPUBLIC OF DELGUEDA

Kronenbourg was driving slowly because there was much on his mind, and even the throaty growl of the eight-cylinder Shelby-converted engine in his Ford Mustang GT could not cheer him today as it usually did.

He was on the 101 Highway coming in towards Waldport. He reached the bridge over the muddy river, its banks littered with huge logs bleached by wind and weather, and the familiar hills lay ahead of him, covered in pine trees. Many trees had been lopped short, and their leafless stumps stuck out of the sandy earth like solitary hairs in the dandruff of some giant skull.

He had often thought this on other days, and how, with the news he carried in his own mind, .the analogy of death, the similarity to a skull, seemed even more apt. He felt sick inside and turned the wedge of gum over to the other side of his mouth.

Outside the town was a notice: 'Waldport: Population 777 - Drive Carefully.' The last figure was only screwed on so that it would be removed when a new citizen was born, or an old one died.

If what the doctor had told him up in Seattle was right, and he lived here, they would soon be removing that last number. He passed the revolving yellow ball advertising the Ball Realty, the red, white and blue chevron for Chevron petrol, the friendly sign: 'Big-wheel Drive In - Burgers to go'. And not only burgers, he thought; we've all got to go, and I'll be one of the first.

He had often wondered casually how it would feel to be told he had only so long to live: a year, a month, a week, whatever it might be. And now he knew. He didn't feel anything beyond , a vague disbelief. This was all a dream. He would wake up soon and Maria would be there with a cup of coffee for him as she was every morning - only this wasn't morning, nor was it a dream: this was evening and reality.

The sea between the one-storey shacks rolled and glittered in the fading sunshine of the dying afternoon. A mist hung low over the water as though it did not want to let anyone see too much. He passed the pole which carried the names of local organizations: The Lions Club, The American Legion, The Auxiliaries for the Chamber of Commerce, The Veterans of Foreign Wars.

This last always made him smile, despite himself. He caught a glimpse of his face in the driving mirror, wrinkled now, his hair thin as the pines on those desolate hills, his spectacles dusty. Yes, he was a veteran of a foreign war all right, but he had fought on the wrong side.

Advertisements for familiar places and people came and went: Real estate; the city baker; treasure chests, souvenirs; home-town hardware; the bank of Newport; Loyal Order of Moose - Protect our Children. But from whom or from what? He had never discovered, never even bothered to inquire. Anyway, it was all too late now.

A card in a house window caught his eye: 'Nite Crawlers 25c'. He supposed they were some kind of lugworms, but he wasn't a fishing man himself. He had seen the notice for years, and he had never asked just what it meant. Now, according to the doctor, he had only a matter of weeks left in which he could ask; and there seemed so many more important things to do and so little time, so very, very little.

The road lay ahead of him, a grey concrete strip edged with red earth, then a rash of shabby clap-board houses. A new notice in one of their windows: 'Free - 8 Puppies to be given away'; and another, 'We buy junk and sell antiques'. Across the road hung a rash of wires and loops and the amber warning lights that flicker at American cross-roads. Inn signs: 'Choice Seafood, Sizzling Steak; Fine Food, Cocktails'. A bar lit with green and blue lights, an arrow; Vacancies-Motel. Eat at Joe's. The Burger King. A Thousand Pizzas Must Go. And not only pizzas, he thought again, I'm on the way out now, myself.

The mist was beginning to roll over the road sadly, dimming well-remembered landmarks. The trees to his right might have been struck by some disease; they raised empty arms, bare of all leaves, just grey, peeled bark, feathered with ash, as though appealing to the sky. Like mourners, he thought bleakly. God, the night would be full of symbols. Every night would, from now on.

There was an odd luminosity coming off the sea and already, through the swirling mist, he could see the sharp-edged half crescent moon hanging in the sky. The waves had died down, as they usually did at this time of day and year, and the sea itself lay under the mist like a long, glass floor stretching to eternity.

He felt very lonely. The hum of his engine, the green lights on the dashboard, were his only companions. The posts with red reflectors on either side of the road warned him of the soft sand that could take a car, spin it before the driver knew what had happened. He passed rows of holiday cottages ('kitchens, fireplaces, TV'). You brought in your own firewood, driftwood from the beach, and you burned it; just as, twenty years ago, maybe longer, maybe less, he'd brought his own life in from South America, and changed it, and called himself Arthur Kronenbourg, after a label he'd read on a bottle of beer. That was the name on his passport now, but it wasn't his name. No one knew what his real name was: no one here, at least.

The sun had already dropped behind the sea like a giant red tail-lamp of some celestial chariot, misty, opaque, vaguely warning. He drove on until he reached the edge of the redwood country, the tallest trees in the world.

More signs: The House of Burgers. Char-broiled Burgers. Seevue Homes. Homes in a Tree. A Drive on the Dunes. Drive a Train-through a Tree.

He turned off at his own motel, flicked his headlights twice to let Maria know he was home, if she was in, gunned his motor once and stopped it. Silence rushed in on him, then the long, slow sough of the sea, scraping on the endless empty beach, cold as the mist already condensing on his windscreen.

He took the key from the ignition switch, dropped it in his pocket, walked through the swing-door with the clattering bell that rang, smelled at once the composite smell of cotton-seed oil, hot coffee, bacon grilling. He really must do something about that smell, buy an extractor fan, get rid of it. And then he thought, No, that's for someone else to do. I've no time left.

Jackson, the hired help, was sitting, hands supporting his chin, elbows on his knees, watching the box. Kronenbourg glanced at it; he could never understand its attraction. A cowboy was walking down a trail, another man waited behind a tree. Cut to the first cowboy, hand on his gun. Cut to the other man. Cut to an old man with white hair riding on a four-wheeled buggy, the spokes appearing to spin backwards. He'd seen it all before, many, many times. He knew how it would all end. But how would everything end for him?

His mouth felt dry. He wanted a drink and yet he didn't want a drink. He thought of all those cancerous cells in his throat, multiplying themselves amoeba-like, growing, choking them-selves with their own growth, flesh-forming, until the passage in his throat would grow so narrow that no solid food could pass through, and even liquids could barely dribble past. Then he would have to have tubes in him. His voice would fade and, like some husk, still alive, but not living as he understood the word, he would lie in a strange bed, whispering out his last secrets.

He would need a priest or a shot of something in his blood; maybe both. He'd taken all he could take of this world. He had not chosen the moment he entered, and he was not choosing the moment he would leave, but at least in one specific he was different from other men. He knew roughly when that moment would be.

His hands went instinctively to the drawer behind the counter where the cheap photographs for tourists - An Oregon View (felled logs on trucks, men standing inside hollow trees, coloured views of the long, empty coast) were clipped for sale. He needed a cigarette. Christ, he did, but not now. Not ever again. Cigarettes had done enough for him; they were killing him, had all but killed him. He'd better ring old Doc Henderson, with whom he'd played so many games of chess in the back parlour in the winter, when the waves were not just scratching at the shore, but thundering, bellowing, pouring out on the beach all the strength they'd gathered on the way-from Japan, from Russia. Doc Henderson must have suspected what was wrong with him or he would not have sent him to the specialist. Well, he'd be able to tell him that his suspicions were right.

'Have you got to watch that thing?' he asked Jackson sourly. The crash of music, punctuated by drumming hooves, irritated him unreasonably. The man nodded.

'Sure, I like it. Anyway, it ends in five minutes.'

'Mrs Kronenbourg in?'

'Nope. She went to Portland. Said she'd be back around nine.'

'Who's in the motel? Anybody?'

'Nope. Not a booking.'

'The light's not switched on outside. Maybe that's something to do with it.'

Jackson nodded, half raised himself from his seat, eyes still focused on the nickering misty figures who moved like phantoms and shot, and fell, and rode and ran and rode again. He put up his hand, pulled down the big spring switch above the front door, sat down again.

Through the windows frosted with condensing mist Kronenbourg saw the red neon flicker, the green arrow jump and jump
again pointing to 'Vacancies - Robin Hood Motel. Free Coffee.
Free TV. Bathrooms in Every Room'.

Well, that was better than he'd had when he arrived. It was
something to leave his children. They mustn't know what was
wrong with him, not until afterwards. And, if he was a man at
all, he'd be able to hide his sickness and his pain until the last
few days; maybe for even longer. But what about that other life
he'd left, the other wife he'd left, the other sons he'd left, in that
other world long ago?

Perhaps he wasn't a man, after all, not in the true old-fashioned,
European, sense of the word; the sense that you faced up to your
troubles, looked them in the eye, fought them, and either you
won or you lost. But you did not run away, as he'd run away.

He'd had two lives really, one in the old world, then the war as
a sort of intermission, and now this - a world of sham where no
one knew who he really was, what he'd been, where he'd been,
the people he'd known and what he had done to them. Most of
all, what he had done.

As he looked out at the mist, seeing only the face of eternity, he
wondered about that first wife, about his first two sons. Where
were they now? They'd be grown up, of course. No doubt they'd
be married. They'd think he was dead, if they ever thought of
him at all. His old home had been in what was now Western Germany. It would be strange to go back there. He could have gone
back quite easily; lots of others had. He could have moved about
with his new name and, after all, his appearance had changed,
and he'd an American passport, so he should be safe enough. And
all the old photographs of him were nearly a quarter of a century out of date. He had nothing to fear from them.

Perhaps he would still do that; after all, it would be good to see his own country again. But what could he tell Maria? That he was going on a business trip east? No, he'd told too many lies, already; he'd ruined too many lives. There was no room for any more deception in the shrinking horizon of his own. Also, if he went home he might find himself torn between his two families, his two worlds.

So he'd better do nothing at all. He'd sit tight and wait, and death would come to him. It hadn't always been like that, of course. The French, or the Russians, or the British or the Americans had been looking for him, after Auschwitz, but he'd escaped. He'd become a new person, an Austrian peasant, struck dumb so that no one would notice his north-German accent. He'd travelled, paying for his journey with bonds he'd acquired from the cremated prisoners. He'd been stripped of every cent he'd made, on that way down to Genoa to buy a passage on a ship to Rio. And then he'd had years of work in an electrical shop run by a German, saving his money, wondering if the Jews were after him; and if they were, would they ever find him? Then he had made the trip north over the border. Mexico. California. Here.

It had been quite easy to cross, when you were used to crossing borders illegally, as he was; when you knew exactly where the guards were, and what guards felt like at half past two on a winter morning, in the cold. They weren't really concerned with what was happening twenty miles up from their hut. What could they do about it, anyway?

He'd chosen Oregon because it reminded him somehow of the Black Forest. There was so much space and people didn't ask questions; they gave you a greeting, just as they used to say 'grüss Gott' to him in Austria. They were the same sort of people, friendly, simple; like country people everywhere. They weren't curious about who you were or where you came from. You were accepted for what you were, or what you said you were. You might be running a motel, a pizza stand, a gas station. All right, that's what you did, and that was the end of the matter.

And now, just when everything was going well and he was losing his fear of discovery, these pains had begun, this dryness in his throat, his early morning cough that nothing would ease, nothing could cure. Then Doc Henderson's examination, the X-rays, the suggestion to see his friend in Seattle, the sealed letter he'd taken to this man with the grey rubber face, the cold eyes.

He'd sat in his imitation seventeenth-century chair (far more efficient than the original), elbows on the simulated-leather top of his desk, tips of his fingers pressed spatulate together, and looked into his eyes, as Kronenbourg had looked into the eyes of so many other men when he was telling them they were going to die.

The doctor had told him how long he thought he had left. Of course, he said, he. could be wrong. Doctors often were about these things; he admitted that openly. But not this doctor, thought Kronenbourg; not about this thing.

In the old days, he'd been in that position. He'd had the power of life or death, of torture, even release, over everyone in that camp. He hadn't known everyone, of course, and there was no reason why he should, for there were so many; hundreds at first, then thousands, then tens of thousands, arriving packed together, the living dead, in railway wagons.

He'd seen the hopelessness in their faces, just as this doctor with the crew cut, the scented after-shave lotion, must have seen the hopelessness in his. Oh, well. It was full cycle. He couldn't grumble. He wasn't grumbling, either; it was just that on such a night as this, with the cold fog coming in from the sea, with hardly a sound anywhere, not a car on the road, he was wondering what it would be like to die, whether the people he'd sent to premature deaths, people he'd often never even seen, would be waiting for him. They had just been numbers on a sheet to him, code symbols on a profit and loss account. What they would lose had been their lives; the profit to the Third Reich had been the gold fillings from their teeth, their gold wedding rings. And then, afterwards, their bones were melted down for glue, other pans of their viscera were used for manure, for fertilizers.

But what if there was another world and all the religious people had been right?

What if somewhere, beyond that mist of loneliness, beyond that rim of sea and sky and dying blood-red sun, they were waiting for him? It was a horrible thought. He didn't like to think it for it made the flesh creep down his back. He could go mad thinking of things like this. He must watch himself. There would be no other world but this; this was world enough for any man.

Suddenly the bell jingled above the door. Kronenbourg jumped, and his heart raced in his body. He felt sweat break on his brow, on the backs of his hands. He turned.

A man was standing in the .doorway in a raincoat, a man with a soft fishing hat pulled down over his face.

'Are you open?' he asked. He spoke English, but he was not American, any more than Kronenbourg was American.

'Surely,' said Kronenbourg. 'What can we do for you?'

'My friend and I wonder if you can help us.'

'How?' asked Kronenbourg, without enthusiasm. Such a request usually preceded a touch for money, a free bed and a meal, or the use of the lavatory, a telephone call they'd never pay for. He'd had it all before, too many times. This was not going to be another, not the way he felt tonight.

The man turned and jerked his head over his shoulder. Another man came in from the mist. He was taller than the first, also in a raincoat, with a hat pulled down over his eyes. Mist hung like dew on their shoulders. Their faces were wet with spray, but it wasn't raining. Where had they come from to be so wet?

'We've just put in from a yacht out at sea,' explained this second man. 'The boss there has had a seizure. Been out most of last night and all today. We wonder if you've a doctor you can recommend, who could come out to see him? It's urgent. He's in a bad way.'

'Not here there isn't,' said Kronenbourg. He was sorry for this unknown man out at sea in his yacht. But he was sorry for himself, too, and he wanted Doc Henderson himself tonight. He needed him tonight, of all nights.

'There must be a doctor here,' persisted the man.

'There is, but he's away,' said Kronenbourg.

'Is there only one?'

'That's right.'

'Mind if I look at your phone book?'

'Sure.'

He glanced through the yellow pages at the back.

'There seem to be quite a lot of medics around here,' he said.

'Not around here, there aren't. Those fellows are fifty miles up the road. This is a pretty thinly populated area.'

'Here's one. Dr Henderson.'-

'He's out of town,' said Kronenbourg quickly, too quickly. 'I told you.'

The two men glanced briefly at each other.

'We'll ring him,' said the first man. 'Maybe he's got a locum.'

'Maybe he hasn't,' said Kronenbourg. 'I know the man.'

'I tell you, it's a matter of life and death. We've got to find a doctor. Our boss is dying.'

'I'm dying,' said Kronenbourg.

The first man laughed.

'Sure. I know the gag. We're all dying from the day we're born.

Maybe before.'

He rubbed his hands as though to warm them.

'You got a drink here?'

'What do you want?'

'Two rum and Cokes.'

Kronenbourg set them up.

'Anything else?'

'No.'

'Want to eat?'

'No. Just a doctor. Tell me, are you the owner here?'

Kronenbourg nodded.

'This is the Robin Hood Motel ?'

'That's right. Why?'

The two men glanced at each other.

'Could we speak to you in the back room? Privately?'

'Sure. That'll be one fifty for the drinks first, though.'

'Oh, yes.'

The first man unbuttoned his waistcoat, took out a black leather wallet, peeled off two dollars and handed them to Kronenbourg. He pushed them in the cash register drawer without ringing the bell, took out a fifty-cent piece, plonked it on the counter. They let it lie there. He went to the back parlour and stood against the door, motioned them through.

The room was small, over-furnished in the American provincial way; a rubber plant and brass ornaments, easy chairs; a coloured photograph that Maria had clipped from a magazine of President Kennedy in profile, a picture of their two sons when they were seven and eight.

'What is it you want?' he asked.

The first man opened his wallet again, took out a photograph. It showed a young man in black uniform, with peaked cap and swastika badge. He was holding a white cat. He showed the photograph to Kronenbourg.

'Ever seen that before?' he asked easily.

Kronenbourg looked. He saw a picture of himself. He handed it back.'

'Never,' he said, trying to keep his voice straight.

'No? Or this?'

The second photograph was of a woman, big-breasted, with a child on one side, a boy in leather trousers with leather braces. He had a hat with a long feather through it: Magda, and his first son Klaus. Where in God's name had they got these?

'No. I've never seen them before,' he said, but it was hard to keep his voice from trembling.

'Or this?'

The third was a picture of his favourite son Ernst, taken with his own camera. He remembered the picture well, although he hadn't seen it for years. It was the day the boy had started school on his own. This time he could not trust himself to speak.

'You are Berger, aren't you?' said the first man, holding out his hand for the photograph. Kronenbourg bit his lower lip until he felt blood salt on his tongue. Sweat rolled down his cheeks like tears.

'Who are you?' he asked faintly. Was this the moment he had dreaded for years, the moment of discovery, the beginning of revenge?

'Friends of people who knew you years ago,' said the taller man. 'Now will you help us?'

'How can I help you? Where have you come from? Are you police? Who are you?'

'We're not police. We're from that yacht. You can't see it but in the fog there. I said our boss was ill. We must get a doctor to him. Unless you help us pronto maybe we'll drive on into town in your car, and see what the American emigration people have to say about an ex-Nazi with your record living here for twenty years illegally, under a false name, on false papers running a motel. I reckon you'd do a long stretch for this, Berger.'

'I've never seen you before,' said Kronenbourg flatly. 'Why are you doing this to me?'

'For no personal reasons. You just happened to be here. You're the only contact we have. We've a list of all the ex-Nazis on this coast, with their present names and occupations and addresses. It just so happened you were the nearest one. We need that doctor.'

'I've told you - he's not in.'

'Well, find another one who is. We'll give you five minutes to get on that blower and start some action.'

'Five minutes. You don't make it very easy for me.'

'It's not easy for us, either. Now, move.'

'Wait here. I'll do my best.' He started towards the door, then paused. 'How do I know you won't still tell the police?' He could not bear the prospect of all this trouble on top of the secret he carried with him.

'Why should we?' asked the tall man. 'Didn't you always keep your word - in the old days?'

They were grinning at him now, laughing at his discomfiture. Their teeth gleamed white and even under the electric bulb, like teeth in skulls. Oh, God, the death image again. He went out of the room, closed the door carefully behind him, picked up the telephone and dialled Henderson's number. It was engaged.

He put down the receiver, biting his nails in his anguish, then dialled again. This time the doctor answered.

'I wonder if you'd come over here Doc?' said Kronenbourg, cupping his hand around the mouthpiece, keeping his back to the door in case they were listening. 'There's an emergency. It's urgent.'

'Be right with you. I was coming in any case. How did you get on?'

'I'll tell you when I see you.'

'Is that the emergency?'

'No. Something else.'

'Your wife? The kids?'

'No. Someone in the motel. I can't say much here. I'll see you outside and tell you when you come.'

'I'm on my way;'

The instrument went dead in Kronenbourg's hands. He put it down, stood looking through the window, seeing nothing. He'd lived here for twenty years and he'd enjoyed them all, especially the little things; the homely food, the black cap juice, so like blackcurrant juice but so much better; the pancakes, the salmon steaks. He'd enjoyed the people, too, and the air, clear as glass. The sun. The emptiness. The whole clean feeling of the beach, the sea, the sand, of being in a big and new and young country. He thought that his children might grow up here and do something worth while. They were Americans, of course. They knew nothing about the old world and the old hatreds; their allegiance lay here. He liked the way people planted an American flag on a pole in their garden, the golden American eagle with wings in brass over their doors. They were proud of what they'd achieved. Many were immigrants, refugees, people from ghettoes, driven out from far-off countries, who'd been glad to make their lives here, and he had made his with them.

He sat down shakily behind the counter. The last gunman fell on the TV screen, the music swelled to its sugary crescendo, and died. A .young man appeared in a button down shirt, speaking without moving his lips, extolling the virtues of a new cigarette. Jackson switched off the set, stood up, stretching himself.

'Anything for me to do?' he said.

'Just take yourself out,' said Kronenbourg; he'd forgotten he was even there. Well, he hadn't heard much. 'I've got company.'

'OK.' Jackson slouched away into the back premises.

Kronenbourg took out a match, split it, picked his teeth with the sharp end, watching for the lights of Henderson's car. When he saw them, he walked out to meet the doctor. It was colder now, and the sea and the sky had met together; the evening was a Krieghoff painting.

'Hello, there,' said Doc Henderson genially. He was a short, cheery man with lots of teeth. His hair, like bristles on a brush, grew vertically out of his head. Everything about him was clean and dapper and neat as though he had been newly scrubbed and pressed. His handclasp was warm and firm. He was a good guy.

'Listen,' said Kronenbourg. 'That thing in Seattle was pretty rough. I've got six weeks, so that quack thinks.'

'Six weeks? He must be crazy. I'd give you at least...' Henderson paused suddenly.

'Two months, maybe?' queried Kronenbourg dryly 'Anyway, it's not about that I want to see you, Doc, out here. It's something else. I've got two men in the back room.'

'Who are they?' The doctor's voice was wary. 'A hold-up or something?'

'Not quite. I don't know what nationality they are, but they're not American. Maybe they're German. They say they've come from a yacht that's out at sea.' He nodded towards the fog. 'Their boss out there, so they say, the man who owns their yacht, is very ill. They must have a doctor.'

'Uhuh. Is that the emergency?'

'Partly. This is the real bit, though. You've known me for twenty years, haven't you?' said Kronenbourg, looking down at the small man, his eyes already weak with tears at the thought of what he was going to say.

'Sure. Maybe more. Twenty-one, I think. Why, yes, Katy was born the year you came here.'

'I want to tell you something. I'm not Ernest Krohenbourg at all. My real name is Berger. Fritz Berger. I'm German.'

'So what? We're all all kind's of things, if you go back one or two generations - half a generation even. Why, my old man came from Dublin, and my mother from Madrid. How's that for a pair to produce this all-American boy?'

'I know. But I'm talking about me, my own generation. And this is different. I was a Nazi. I was in one of the camps. Not a prisoner. On the staff. Deputy Chief.'

'You? You've gone mad.' Incredulity thinned the doctor's voice. Had what the specialist told him affected his old friend's mind?

'No. I wish I had. I haven't much time out .here, or anywhere else, so listen. After the war, when the Americans were after me, I lay low for a bit and then I went to South America, and finally reached here. I started a new life. God knows, since then I've tried to turn my back on the old one.'

'I don't understand you.'

'I'm not asking you to understand, Doc. I'm just asking you to listen. I thought I could shut that door on the past entirely, but I couldn't.

'These two men from this yacht, they've got pictures of me as I was. Of my first wife over there, with my children. They'll be grown up now. They say they'll take these photographs to the police if I don't get you to visit their yacht. I don't give a damn about the police, not now, for I've only got a few weeks left, at the most.

'But I feel sorry for my boys here, and for Maria. She knows nothing about this, about that other wife, my other sons. I don't want her to know.'

'But...' began the doctor.

Kronenbourg held up his hand.

'Don't interrupt. Please,' he said. 'This is what I think. These men are Nazis, too, or the character out in the yacht is a Nazi, or they'd have brought the boat in. I owe America a lot. It's given me a home, a new start, a new wife. I've given it back nothing but lies. Now here's a chance to change this. I reckon the guy out in that yacht may be a war criminal. They're still turning up. I've lived a lie long enough, I've deceived all you people who've been my friends, not because I wanted to, but because I had to. I couldn't do anything else. Now's my chance to do something else. And whatever you think of me I want you to help me take it, Doc. Now.

'Is there anyone you know in the police or coastguards who could do anything? Intelligence? Security? I don't even know what the names are.'

'I can't promise anything,' said Henderson uneasily, glancing towards the door.

A big Peterbilt lorry, festooned with coloured lights like a travelling Christmas tree, roared down the highway behind them and was gone in a misty glare of headlamps.

'I'll tell the sheriff, naturally. But - I don't understand. What you say doesn't make sense.'

'Most things in heaven and earth don't make sense, not until you know the whole picture. You don't know the whole picture. I'm just telling you a part of it. I'm not asking you to help me. I've lived with this, too long already. No one can help me. I'm asking you to help Maria. The boys. Will you do that? Will you help them? They're innocent.'

The doctor looked at him. Their eyes met and held. He nodded.

'Will these guys hear me if I use the telephone?'

'Not if I turn up the TV.'

'Turn it up,' said Henderson and led the way to the door.

* * *

MacGillivray sat in his office in Covent Garden. His desk was completely bare except for the black blotting pad and the open copy of Country Life where he had already marked three other likely properties. But his thoughts were not on them: his thoughts were miles away, his mind free-wheeling.

He had covered himself as best he could, but that was not perfectly. His contact in the Israeli Embassy had been willing to help, but knew nothing about the yacht or its owner. News would take a couple of days to come from Tel Aviv, he said; maybe three.

MacGillivray's CIA contact had been equally willing to give all assistance he could. He'd send a telex to Washington, and various regional agents along the American west coast had apparently been alerted. But, from necessity, the message had been couched in the broadest terms. A steam yacht, Endymion III displacing 1000 tons, registered in the name of Paul Steyr, country of registration, Panama, might come within territorial waters. If so, this fact should be reported immediately and an attempt made, on any plausible pretext, to board the yacht and search her. But what were they looking for? A man? A plot?

He thought it all seemed a bit nebulous, especially as the original message had come from such a dubious source.

MacGillivray shared his feelings entirely. He picked up his telephone on the impulse to ring Sir Robert, and then replaced it again. Never appear too eager. As Sir Robert had said, never let your left hand know what your right hand was doing. This was easier, of course, when your right hand didn't know what it was doing, either, as was the case now.

He pushed back his chair and stood up, hands in his jacket pockets, in his accustomed position, looking out through the double glazed windows across the market.

The times had seemed numberless that he'd stood like this, looking at the view, not really seeing anything, just waiting for someone to crack, for someone to telephone, for the missing piece of the jig-saw to be miraculously supplied - possibly by someone else, who didn't even know he was supplying it.

Some day, he thought, it just won't arrive, or it'll come too 'late. This could be one of those days. He took out his packet of Pwe Burma cheroots, lit one.

He had inhaled for the second time when the telephone behind him began to ring.

*   *   *

Kinder stood with his back against the rough cement wall of the mess hut. The others faced him, Weissmann in the middle. His leg was paining him again. He held his crutch braced against his body to take the weight off the tortured stump.

'So that's your story, is it?' he said. 'How do we know you're telling the truth now?'

'Because it is the truth,' said Kinder, his voice only a whisper. 'I swear it. You've got to believe me. Anything but that iron again.'

He winced at the memory of the red-hot metal eating its way greedily into his skin; the rash of blisters, black and crisp, the foul sweet smell of smoking flesh, the pain like long knives at his nerves.

'You told us the other story was the truth, too. That business of the free pardons. The new names we would have. The passages back to see our families. You'd got papers to prove that. You've nothing to prove this.'

Kinder shook his head wearily; speech was almost beyond him. He was stripped to the waist. Sweat glistened on his strong, pale body: the burns had swollen to sullen red weals, dark with dried blood.

'Give him the iron again,' said Weissmann.

A way cleared among the old men with their cruel, scarred faces, their dead, evil eyes. One of the cooks came through, holding a poker from the mess fire. It was so hot that he had wrapped a damp sweat rag around the handle, and even the rag was steaming. The tip of the poker glowed white and then amber and finally dull red. He held it within half an inch of Kinder's face.

'Now,' said Weissmann. 'Now. Are you telling the truth?'

'Yes,' said Kinder. His voice was shrill, almost screaming, on the edge of hysteria.

'In the Bible, long ago, so we are told,' said Weissmann, 'Cain was branded. But he had only killed one man. If what you are saying is true, you are deliberately responsible for the murder of more than twenty of your countrymen. Men of my generation who served your country - our country - in peace and war. So you will die whatever happens. But first we will brand you with the mark of Cain. Do you still stick to your story?'

Kinder nodded. He was too far gone to speak. The poker tip came down those last few millimetres in his face and then jarred against the living, sweating flesh. His scream filled the packed, hot room. The red glow of the iron reflected itself in the eyes of his captors.

As though from a distance of miles and years away, filtered by pain and delirium, he heard Weissmann's voice.

'A death for a death. We may not be able to save the lives of our comrades, Kinder, but at least we shall extract some satisfaction in taking yours from you.'

The iron came down on his face for the second time.

*   *   *

Doc Henderson braced himself against the bucking of the little motorboat as the long Pacific rollers buffed against its blunt white bows. Fog threw wraiths around the two men crouched down behind the vee-windscreen, their raincoats streaming with spray.

The cold and the wind seized Henderson's breath. He sat back against the seat, one hand gripping the side of the boat, the other clenching the handle of his black medical bag. He was thinking about Kronenbourg, and who he would meet in the yacht; about the strangeness of life, the many almost incredible stories that patients had told, him, the convoluted sadness of so many seemingly straightforward lives.

The note of the engine changed as the motorboat turned. Ahead of them, like a white wall, the side of the yacht loomed through the fog. The companion way was already down. A seaman in a white, turtle-necked sweater, stood on it, holding a boathook.

'Up this way, doctor,' said the taller of the two men.

Henderson followed them on to the deck. Lights were burning; they looked like haloes in the mist.

'Through this corridor here,' said his guide.

Henderson went down a tunnel of varnished wood, that creaked slightly as the vessel moved against the sea.

A steward was waiting outside a door. He saluted the doctor.

'In here, Doctor,' he said briskly.. He had a sallow European face. He opened the door. Inside, on a single bed, with a shaded green light over the sealed porthole a man lay with a cold compress upon his forehead. He writhed beneath the sheets as though in an extremity of almost unbearable pain.

'This is my patient?' asked Henderson.

'Yes, sir,' said the steward.

'Does he speak English?'

'Yes, sir, but I don't think he's able to speak.'

'What happened? What is the history of his case?' There was a pause. The steward's eyes flicked towards the tall man, back to Doc Henderson.

'As a. matter of fact, sir,' he said, 'we have a doctor aboard.'

'You have? I'll see him then.' Henderson was surprised. What the hell was this? Why had he been brought out with all this fuss if they already had their own doctor, on the yacht? These rich people thought you'd nothing better to do than run after them: he felt irritation rise like bile within him.

'If you will just wait one moment, doctor, I'll fetch him.'

He went out. Henderson waited, looked down at the man, felt his pulse. It was erratic, but fairly strong.

'Are you awake?' he asked.

The man gave a groan of assent.

'Can you speak?'

Another groan, that could be a negative or an affirmative.

He glanced around the small bedroom. It was clinically impersonal, but everything was obviously extremely expensive; the white silk sheets, the washbasin with its marble surround, its silver taps - no mere chromium plate here. He took in the illuminated mirror, the shelves of books, their green and maroon leather bindings tooled with gold. He took one down idly: It was larger than the books to which he was accustomed. He opened it. The little Braille dots stood out in a mass of tiny pimples. So the man was blind. This could present complications.

'What exactly is the trouble?' he asked him, man to man.

The man on the bed gave another groan. The steward hovering in the background, said: 'If you will wait, sir, I think the doctor on board will be able to help you.'

'I hope so,' said Henderson, and meant it.

In the big room, the guards surrounded Dr Love and Shamara. McGregor faced them.

'Now, listen,' he said, voice still hoarse from Love's blow to his windpipe. 'We've got an American doctor here. You can go out and tell him what has happened.'

'All that's happened?' asked Love quizzically.

'Don't start making jokes, doctor. There's nothing funny in your situation, believe me. You'll simply tell him that Mr Steyr fell against the door or collapsed or whatever did happen. You're the doctor. You know what to do. I've waited as long as I could, but there's no improvement in his condition. But don't get any ideas that you're going to tell him something else about your situation.

'We'll keep the girl with us in this room. The yacht is wired for sound, so we'll hear every word you say. If you try and hint at anything else that's happened, or is happening, this girl dies. Here. Now. Understood?'

'Perfectly. You leave no room for misunderstanding. But suppose I write him a message?'

'You won't write him a message, for the steward will be there with you. He'll see to that. If you try and write any message, the steward will at once give the alarm. We'll do the rest. Here.'

'You seem to have thought of everything,' said Love. They had, too, while he'd thought of nothing. Or almost nothing, or maybe just of the wrong things.

'We have,' agreed McGregor. 'Take him away.'

The two men who had brought out Doc Henderson took Love by his arms. They went out, down the corridor. One of the men knocked on the door of Steyr's room.

'Doctor Love,' he announced.

The door shut behind Love. He faced a stocky American in a lightweight suit, with button-down shirt and a crew cut. He had a kindly, quizzical face. Love liked him. The steward stood watching their faces for any lift of an eyebrow, any sign of a signal.

'My name is Henderson,' said the American. 'I hear you're a doctor?'

'I've been called other things. Jason Love, of Somerset, England. Glad to meet you.'

They shook hands.

'Why exactly do you want me out here? What is the trouble? Can't you cope with it?'

'No,' said Love. 'I can't.'

He looked Henderson straight in the eyes, trying to will him into thinking something was wrong. He thought of Shamara, the gun pressed against her spine. If he made a hash of this, she'd be lucky if she died with a bullet.

The steward watched them both, face bland as a bladder of lard, his eyes two black currants that had forgotten how to blink.

'Tell me what happened,' said Henderson. 'I was called out here to an emergency. What's wrong with the patient? He seems to be in great pain, but is unable to speak. Has he fallen? Is it a stroke?'

'I'm sorry. I can't help you much,' said Love. 'The patient here is blind. As you can see, his eyes have been completely removed.' He leaned forward, lifted up the compress. Steyr's twisted, scarred face was like a contour map of hell.

'What was that? A motor accident?' asked Henderson.

'I don't know how it happened. Do you?' Love turned to the steward.

'I don't know, sir,' the steward said carefully. 'Mr Steyr's been blind ever since I've been in his employ.'

'Maybe it's a wartime thing,' suggested Love. 'Anyhow, I'm very glad you came, for I was considering acupuncture on the man as the only means of bringing him round.'

'Acupuncture? You mean this old Chinese deal of gold needles and so on? I've heard about it, but I've never met another doctor who's had practical experience of it.'

'You've met one now,' said Love. 'Since I've no instruments, would you mind if I borrowed the narrowest syringe needle you've got?'

'Sure. Help yourself.'

Doc Henderson opened his bag.

'Matter of fact, I've got something a bit narrower, if it's any help. Ordinary needles for stitching.'

'That would be perfect,' said Love. He lifted one from its white cotton wool base in a box of assorted sizes, sterilized it carefully in a small phial of spirit, turned to the steward.

'I want your help here,' he told him. 'Raise Mr Steyr's right arm and hold it tightly.'

'You want the veins to stand out then?' asked Henderson, surprised. 'I thought you stuck the needle into nerve centres or some such thing?'

'I do,' said Love, and as the steward raised Steyr's arm, eyes fixed on his master's writhing body, Love pricked the needle into the steward's left temple, by the super-orbital nerve.

The man's body doubled up in the extremity of his pain. Love threw away the needle, jammed his right arm under the steward's neck forcing his mouth shut so that he couldn't speak. He held up the index finger of his left hand across his own lips to convey to Henderson the need for silence.

Then, still holding the steward, he said as casually as he could: 'There you are, doctor. An interesting interim reaction. The result of an insertion into what the Chinese called the Yang Meridian. But no talking, please. Silence is absolutely -necessary in the interests of success with this very delicate treatment.'

He leaned over towards Doc Henderson, picked up a flow pen from his breast pocket, and wrote on the mirror: 'Don't talk. Am prisoner here. This room is bugged. Girl is being kept as hostage. Nazis. Vital you get off ship and call police.'

Aloud, he said, 'You see, the situation is extremely serious. I'm most grateful for your opinion.'

'I can imagine,' said Doc Henderson, still bemused by what Kronenbourg had told him. And now this!

'What do you think you can do?' said Love for the benefit of the hidden microphone, the listeners down the corridor. He bent down, picked out a roll of bandage from Henderson's bag and a square of lint, crammed the lint into the steward's mouth, bound it tight with the bandage, then tied his arms behind his back, ran it down his legs, bound his ankles together. Gently, he lowered the steward to the floor and left him there.

'Well,' said Henderson slowly, watching this. 'I'm not quite sure.'

This was quite out of his beat, quite out of his parish. And yet he had always regarded every case in the surgery as a challenge. Looked at like that, this was only a challenge of a different kind.

'It's difficult to say,' he said. 'We'll need a thorough examination, which I can't possibly carry out in a little room like this, without any of my equipment. We'll want a cardiogram. Blood tests. Blood pressure, of course. Possibly a coagulation count. All kinds of things. It's quite impossible even to venture a serious diagnosis here.'

'I see,' said Love, winking and giving him the thumbs-up sign. 'Of course, Mr Steyr is a very rich man. He has a number of business commitments that make it difficult for him to leave the yacht.'

'In that case,' said Henderson, 'I'd better leave myself. I cannot accept the case.'

Love nodded, gave him the thumbs-up sign again. This man was doing fine.

'Come with the steward and we'll discuss this with members of Mr Steyr's staff.'

Love felt inside the steward's jacket, extracted the Mauser he wore in a shoulder holster, opened the door. The corridor was empty.

'This way, after the steward,' he told Henderson, for the benefit of the listeners. He led him down the corridor towards the state room. Outside, he knocked at the door, motioned Henderson to stand on one side while he waited on the other.

'Come in,' called McGregor.

This was going to be the difficult part. Love took a deep breath, opened the door slowly. Through the gap between the door and its post he had a slit-eyed view of the room. Shamara was standing against the far wall, a guard on each side of her, their hands in their jacket pockets. McGregor stood a little to one side, watching the door open. There might not be a chance to fire once he was in the room; he had better take it here. He raised the steward's Mauser, took aim through the crack by the door, squeezed the trigger.

The bullet hit McGregor in his right arm. He screamed with the unexpected pain and then Love kicked open the door, covered the room.

'Drop your guns,' he ordered the two guards. 'Then move along the wall, hands above your heads, backs to me.'

One threw his automatic on to the carpet obediently enough, the other did not move. Love fired again, aiming at the man's right knee-cap. He crumpled like a toppled statue, hands out of his pockets.

'You come here,' Love told Shamara. She picked up the gun from the carpet as she crossed the room. McGregor watched them, his shattered arm hanging loosely by his side, the other raised. His eyes were two hot coals in his head.

'What is this, Dr Love?' asked Henderson. 'I thought it was to be a medical consultation?'

'It was. But it got out of hand,' said Love, grinning. 'I'm damned if I know what it is, but that old bird in there without any eyes is one of the three most wanted Nazis in the world.'

'But...' began Doc Henderson, bewilderedly.

'Never mind the buts,' said Love. 'I must get on shore. There's something worse than this - much worse.'

'Christ,' said Henderson, who was not a religious man. 'What could that possibly be?'

Before Love could answer, the double doors burst open. Framed between them, supporting himself on outstretched arms against the lintels, stood Steyr. Pain had drawn back his lips from his yellow, gold-tipped teeth. His body was contorted with the effort it had taken him to crawl from the bedroom. His eye sockets were deep black bore-holes in his head, open windows in a living skull:

'So, Dr Love,' he said speaking through teeth clenched against the agony. 'So you think you got away with it, don't you? You managed somehow to put me out for hours. But do you seriously imagine I would be unwise enough to memorize a code-word of that importance? Of course not. I put it on tape. It has been broadcast automatically while you've been fooling about in this absurd fashion. You can't stop me! No one can stop me!'

At that moment the moan of foghorns, the ululations of ships' sirens, filled the air.

'You're too late,' said Love. 'It all stops here.'

'What's that noise?' asked Steyr, turning his head in the direction of the sirens.

'Should be the coastguard launches,' said Doc Henderson.

'How could they get here so quickly?' asked Love.

'Because I asked for them,' said Henderson laconically. Hell, this Limey doctor could be a nice guy, but he wasn't going to make the running all the time.

'You mean - it's all over?' asked Shamara..

'I hope,' said Love.

There was a sudden sigh, the sound of someone falling. Shamara collapsed on the carpet. As she dropped, McGregor jumped at Henderson. Love's Mauser cracked like a branch breaking. As McGregor fell, his outstretched arm knocked a bottle of Martini from a side table. The viscous drink streamed on to the carpet like blood.

'Christ,' said Doc Henderson again. Love knew how he felt. He turned to Steyr.

'Do you want to be taken off like that?' he asked. 'In your pyjamas?'

'I'll not be taken off at all,' said Steyr. He began to chew, smiling his terrible madman's smile. It was a second before Love realized what he was doing, and then, although he jumped at him, prising his jaws apart, it was too late. Steyr's teeth locked together, his muscles tightened and puckered in his face. A rope of saliva drooled from the tortured lips. Muscles around his mouth stood out like hard ridges and then he sagged slowly to the carpet.

'Cyanide,' said Love levelly. 'All the top Nazis used to carry a little capsule in a tooth filling. That's how Himmler killed himself, although he was actually captured and brought to Field Marshal Montgomery's headquarters. Goering cheated the hangman the same way. We should have thought.'

'We should all have thought,' said Henderson piously.

And, reaching out, he picked up a glass, held it under the dripping Martini, and drank it gratefully.

*   *   *

Weissmann drew back from Kinder and watched him. Four men held the young man pinned against the wall, his arms outstretched, like Christ on the cross. Now his head drooped forward wearily. His hair was a dank, matted mass. The air in the mess hut was foul with the pungent smell of burning flesh.

'Now, talk,' Weissmann ordered him roughly.

'I've told you everything,' said Kinder, his voice faint and faraway. 'There's nothing else. I swear.'

As he spoke, a sudden chill wind fluttered through the hall. The door rattled on its loose, ill-fitting hinges. The men looked at each other uneasily. Could this be the forerunner of a hurricane? Axel went to the door and threw it open. An immense breeze was blowing in from the sea, cold and urgent and unfamiliar. Sea-birds screamed and wheeled uneasily, their wings spread against it, like parentheses in the sky.

And then, in the distance, he saw the wave.

It came as waves usually only come in nightmares, a green wall of water, concave, reaching up into the sky, as wide as the ocean itself. It curved as it came and on top was a flurry of foam.

But that was not what terrified the watchers. It was the size of the thing. Fifty, sixty, seventy feet high, roaring as it approached, gathering strength, sucking the sea from the sand with the power of all the ocean, the weight of a world of water behind it.

'My God,' said Weissmann hoarsely. 'Look!'

They turned and stared, faces on a frieze, frozen in their terror.

And then the wave broke.

Its thunder filled the mess hut like the anger of the gods. The tottering wall of water cascaded over the crude home-made jetty, upsetting the boats, toppling the ancient submarine like a child's tin toy on a pond. Buildings fell before it like match-boxes. Crosses on the graves leapt under it: roofs and doors lifted like pieces from a doll's house.

The men in the hall stood rigid with fear, unable to believe what they saw, mesmerized by its horror, all strength drained away, leaving their muscles flabby with dismay.

Some dropped down on their hands and knees, or braced themselves against the walls; others threw themselves to the ground and lay along the angle of the wall and the floor, faces buried in their elbows.

As the wave hit the hut, the roof lifted and fell away. Rafters snapped into splinters and were gone. The walls trembled and fell. Tables and benches whirled away on the wash.

'Now do you believe me?' shouted Kinder, as the water streamed down his shining body. 'Now can you see?' And then he was swept away like a puppet.

The water rose, overwhelming the roofless building, moving on remorselessly, sweeping up slopes, over cliffs on to the foothills of the grey mountains.

Then, minutes later, it began to recede. And turning over and over in the flood as it drained back to the sea, brown with soil and sand, thick with branches and roots of upturned trees, were the bodies of the torturers and the tortured, indistinguishable now in the last democracy of the dead.

Rolling back, almost guiltily, the waves fell back to the sea from whence it came.

But no one now was left alive to watch the tide go out.

*   *   *

MacGillivray faced his adjutant as the young man laid the blue folder gravely on his desk.

'Those all the reports so far?' he asked.

'Yes, sir. Sir Robert wants to know what story we're going to put out.'

'Why the hell should we put out any story?' said MacGillivray innocently. 'Nothing to do with us. I think it might be an idea, though if we did put it about casually that the Meteorological Section feels that this tidal wave which has swept parts of the South American coast, must have been caused by a volcano erupting under the sea. Something as vague as that. No more, though.'

'We can't very well say any less, sir, can we?' said the adjutant.

'Exactly,' said MacGillivray looking at him. He must be a naive young man. 'Exactly. Always the less you say in any trouble the better. Remember the saying my old father used to quote, my boy. "Those who excuse, accuse." '

*   *   *

Kronenbourg sat watching the TV set in the front office of the Robin Hood Motel. Endless, ageless cowboys still pursued each other across the tiny screen. They could be the same ones every night, and they probably were. Indians on horseback threw up their hands and fell in a flurry of feathers. Horses rolled over obediently. The bad men were led away. The good men clasped double-breasted girls in demure costumes, against the everlasting sunset.

Suddenly, the screen went blank. A newscaster appeared sitting at a desk, twitching the sheets of flimsy he held in front of him.

'We are interrupting this programme, ladies and gentlemen,' he said, his voice wound up a key by the drama of the moment, to bring you news of a totally unexpected hurricane which has struck along the east coast of South America.

'Widespread devastation is reported in many coastal resorts after a gigantic wave swept ashore, lashing houses, and breaking boats away from their anchors. This follows two unknown explosions which occurred about a hundred miles out to sea, one off Rio de Janeiro, and the other roughly two hundred miles farther south.

'It is believed that these may have been submarine volcanic eruptions. Over now to Jackson McCarthy, our scientific correspondent, for his review in depth ...'

Cut to a man with his hair cropped short, wearing rimless glasses, also holding a bundle of notes, the small-time teacher with the correspondence course degree who, in a world where more and more know less and less, had seen the wider opportunities TV could offer in the field of specialization.

'This wave was entirely unforeseen in any weather forecast, and seems to have been even larger than the freak wave that damaged the Italian liner, Andrea Doria, some time ago.

'It was accompanied by a wind of hurricane force that swept the Atlantic Coast of South America early today. This follows, as you've heard, two undersea explosions, the origins of which are being investigated.

'Well, what could cause them? This is difficult to say as yet, but first reports seem to suggest that underground gas which as you know, is always under pressure beneath the earth's surface, erupted in the sea-bed of the ocean and resulted in this wave and the gale force wind that accompanied it.

'As more news comes in, we'll break into our scheduled programmes to bring it to you. Stay tuned to your friendly coast-side station ... Your station ... Top with the news ... Top with the stars. Top all along the way every day. Back now to the programme we interrupted for this newsflash...'

The Indians began to run obediently across the foggy screen.

Kronenbourg leaned over, switched off the set. The picture shrank to a dot and died. He wondered how Doc Henderson was making out. He wondered who was aboard the yacht, when the fog would lift. He thought about his first wife, about his first children.

But most of all he thought how ironic it was that if they'd simply asked for aid, without any threat, without any lever brought in from the past to bend his will, he might have given it to them. Without thinking, he lit a cheroot, and looked out at the mist that stretched away to the shores of eternity.

He was remembering a quotation of Robert Daley that he had once read, about racing-car drivers: 'Death is like furniture in a familiar room. He knows it is there, but he hasn't noticed it in a long time.' He thought, how true that was.

Then he began to cough.

*   *   *

Doc Henderson said: 'This is the strangest goddam night I've ever spent in all my life. My God, they'll never believe me back in the Elks.'

'Then don't tell them back in the Elks,' advised Love. 'People never believe anything that happens outside the narrow spectrum of their own existence.'

'You may be right there. I mean, do you actually practise medicine? Apart from this sort of - ah - interruption?'

'Of course,' said Love. 'In Somerset. And the sooner I'm back, the better. In the meantime, whatever made you call out the coast-guards?'

'I'll tell you,' said Doc Henderson. 'Something one of my patients said. An odd story. As a doctor yourself, you'll understand how it is...'

Outside, the fog was beginning to lift and the stars shone faintly through wisps of clouds. It would be fine tomorrow.

* * *

Sir Robert took out a cheroot, looked at MacGillivray across the green, waxed leather of his desk above Sensoby and Ransom. He had some newspaper cuttings, and a number of other more detailed and unpublished reports, from Paris, and from the CIA in a folder.

'So, where does it all get us?' he asked, pushing them away from him.

'Us, personally, nowhere at all,' said MacGillivray slowly, measuring each word as if he were paying for it himself by weight. 'But it's not without interest.'

'Quite so. Quite so. But we've used public funds in this.'

'Not many, sir. Not very many, when you consider.'

'But what are we to consider? What am I to tell the PM?'

'I'd begin like this, sir. Our man McGregor was murdered and a pro-Nazi put in his place. And because this man I still think of as McGregor didn't send a signal, you - and I - thought that he should have sent, you, personally, put someone else to work without telling him. Without even telling me.'

'A good start,' said Sir Robert approvingly. 'I rather like that.'

I thought you would, thought MacGillivray. That's why I said it.

'Then go on like this,' he said aloud. 'Tell him that it was part of a mad plan by a wanted Nazi, this man Steyr, who'd amassed his wealth by stealing the share certificates, bonds, deeds, patents and so forth from hundreds of poor devils condemned to death in the Nazi concentration camps.

'Tell him how Steyr was blinded and so he hated the Americans, and the British because he blamed them for this. Lay that on a bit thick, in my view.

'Then tell him, sir, that Steyr had the idea - by no means new, as the Russians have been working on it for years - of changing the tides by controlled atomic explosions at set depths. That, if he'd succeeded, the whole of America would be barren land, as barren and cold and bleak as Iceland. And the British Isles wouldn't be much better, and might even be a lot worse.

'And then tell him, how - ironically - he wanted to use, as the creatures for this plan, those ex-Nazis who'd fled away to South America, and who'd lived there ever since the war, always in fear some Israeli agent would find them.'

'That's a good start to any report,' agreed Sir Robert. 'And what then?'

'Tell him, if you like, that Steyr failed because the Israelis also knew where the old Nazis were, for they'd rented this house in Mexico as a convenient neutral base for the detail work, neither on British or American territory, but near to both. Tell him all the gen that the false McGregor had given us. And by the way, I've just had word from Bonn. They've applied to extradite him. He'll go on trial as soon as they get him back to Germany.

'The first agent the Israelis wanted to send to Mexico was killed in Nassau. And then our friend Dr Love...'

'Your friend,' retorted Sir Robert sharply. 'He's no friend of mine.'

'Well, my friend Dr Love. He should get some credit.'

'So should the girl,' said Sir Robert. 'This girl Shamara we've had all the cables about. Seems quite a girl.'

'Ah. Yes. Shamara. She'll get some credit. Maybe something better than credit. She is, as you say, quite a girl.'

MacGillivray was smiling as he held out his lighter for Sir Robert's cheroot.

*   *   *

Love raised himself on his elbow and looked across the bed at Shamara.

They were in New York after a hectic few days: first, the long slow tow behind the coastguard tug into Coos Bay, Oregon; then the statements to police, the FBI; finally, the long flight east. He'd missed the vintage car rally in Mexico City, of course, but there was still the Auburn-Cord-Duesenberg meet at Macungie in Pennsylvania. He was looking forward to that. But now, he had some unfinished business, perhaps business that never would be finished.

'Penny for them,' Shamara said dreamily, watching his face. He grinned, kissed her gently.

'They're not worth that,' he said. 'Waste not, want not. I was just thinking about - us. How we met - in a cellar. How we're saying goodbye. In a bed.'

'It's not a very good place, is it?'

'Not for saying goodbye in,' Love agreed.

'Then must we?'

'Yes. You're off back to Nassau tomorrow. Then God knows where. So that only leaves today for goodbyes. Anyway, we might meet again. Who knows where? Perhaps in another cellar.'

She smiled.

'If we do, promise me one thing?' .

'Which is?'

'We won't just, say goodbye in bed. It seems such - such a waste.'

'Waste not, want not,' said Love, and moved towards her.

*   *   *

Some early editions of the Daily Express carried this news item:

FREAK WAVE KILLS ENGLISH LAWYER. Rio de Janeiro, Brazil. Tuesday.

"The body of Richard Brooks, aged about 38, a lawyer, of Basingstoke, Hants., was washed up here today.

'He is believed to have been killed in the freak wave that swept along the coast, following two undersea volcanic eruptions, and causing widespread damage to property. His passport and other personal papers were in a waterproof pouch. He will be buried in the English cemetery here tomorrow."

The following item appeared in The Financial Times.

'The death is announced, in tragic circumstances, aboard his yacht Endymion III, of Paul V. Steyr, off the coast of Oregon, USA, one of the few remaining eccentric millionaires.

'With his death, this number, always dwindling, is diminished to two or three. Mr Steyr, whose early life has remained something of a mystery to some students of commercial success, first came to prominence in the late 1940's and early 1950's when, under a variety of pseudonyms, with blocks of shares and through holding companies in which he held the majority interest, he secured control of many important chemical and industrial firms operating in West Germany and Eastern France.

'These firms which, before the war, had been predominantly Jewish-owned, played their part in the booming economy of Western Germany and France and,-without doubt, laid the foundations of Mr Steyr's enormous fortune.

'Although blind from a wartime injury, he had a full grasp of his many enterprises, including, it is believed, considerable business involvements behind the Iron Curtain, chiefly in Poland and Czechoslovakia. He controlled these through his holding company, Steyrfarben AG, which had its base in Munich. He had an estate outside Limoges, in France, but spent most of each year aboard his yacht, one of the finest in the world in private ownership, and only very slightly smaller than the royal yacht Britannia.

'His death, at the age of seventy-five, may well cause considerable disruption on many stock markets. He was unmarried. It is thought that he has no heirs.'

*   *   *

Later editions of the London Evening Standard also printed the following news item, received from AP and Reuter:

'NEW POLICE CHIEF FOR NASSAU, BAHAMAS. Chief Inspector Richard Fraser, late of Sheffield Constabulary, was appointed the new Police Chief of the Special a Department of the Police in Nassau, Bahamas, last night.

'His appointment follows the resignation of Brigadier Tam McGregor, announced from Portland, Oregon, where he is on leave, on the grounds of ill-health.'

One person who read this, after lunch, over a cup of tea in the kitchen, was the wife of the vicar of St Matthews Church, Erith, Kent. Her face was quite impassive. She tore out the paragraph and read it again. Then she lit a match, burned the paper, stubbed out the curling fragments of grey ash in an ashtray with the end of the match-box.

'Dear father,' she said gently. 'Dear, dear father. And to think I never knew...'

The front-door bell rang; she was expecting visitors, a committee meeting of the local Evangelical Young Wives' group. As she walked to welcome them, she was dabbing tears from her eyes.

*   *   *

Love climbed the stairs above the fruit wholesalers, in Covent Garden, rang the bell marked INQUIRIES, waited. There was a strong sharp smell of oranges. Miss Jenkins slid open the hatch and looked out, recognized him.

'Why, it's Dr Love,' she said. 'We thought you were in Nassau.'

'We?' Did the use of the royal or editorial plural have any special significance?

'Yes. Colonel MacGillivray and me.'

'Oh. I didn't even know you knew where I was.'

Miss Jenkins simpered. She rather liked Dr Love; it was a shame he hadn't married.

'We have our ways of finding out things, doctor,' she said archly.

'I can imagine. Anyhow, is the Colonel in? I'm on my way back to Somerset, and I've a couple of hours to wait for the train, so I thought I'd look him up.'

'I'll just inquire.'

She pulled in her head, closed the hatch, spoke into the intercom, softly so that he could not overhear her.

'Dr Love's here, sir,' she said.

'Show him in,' said MacGillivray, and pressed the button to open the electric lock on his door. He was standing, back to the window, as Love came into the room.

'And to what do we owe this visit?' he asked, as though he didn't know.

'A number of rather odd things happened on my holiday,' began Love, assuming that he didn't. 'I thought they might interest you. Might even be in your line of country. They're certainly not in mine, thank God.'

'So I believe. But from what I've heard, you've not done too badly for an amateur.'

'You mean - you know?'

'We have our ways of gathering information. And after all, one of the most wanted men among the old Nazis was flushed out.'

'He killed himself, though,' Love interrupted, seeing again Steyr's jaws moving as he chewed the cyanide capsule.

'Oh, yes. Well, that was no hardship. Saved the expense of a trial and an awful lot of muck-raking, you know. I was really referring to the character we thought was McGregor. He's given us a great deal of interesting stuff we were lacking. Hoping to cut his own sentence, of course. But that's neither here nor there.

'Very ingenious scheme, y'know. First, get a radio expert - in this case McGregor - to crack the NATO wavelength, hijack a submarine, then fit out a crowd of thugs as sailors, cross the Atlantic and use the very men half the world's been after to do your dirty work. Sort of poetic justice, don't you think?'

'In a way.'

'You don't sound sure?'

'I'm not. I think I'll be better back in Somerset. The pace isn't so fast there. One thing I regret, though - no, two.'

'What are they?'.

'Well, he beat us in the end. Sent off the radio signal that exploded the charges. He turned the tide after all.'

'But you're wrong, doctor. He didn't. He hasn't. The Gulf Stream streams on just as it always did.'

'I was there. He told me - and, dammit, the tidal waves and the explosion - that was his doing, wasn't it?'

'Surely. But he needed a chain reaction of three explosions - one in each submarine to alter the ocean currents. Only two went off. The third old submarine never left harbour. It's been found in all the debris. So he didn't win. We did. What was the other thing you regret, Dr Love?'

'Nothing serious. A trivial thing, really. Simply that I found the most marvellous graveyard for vintage cars in all the world but I hadn't time to do more than see the place. Couldn't even bring back one radiator name-plate for my collection. And I lost my luggage in Mexico.'

'And you didn't gain anything?'

MacGillivray was looking at him quizzically. Love smiled.

'Well, there are some good points in being a bachelor'

He was thinking of Shamara, wondering where she was, if they would ever see each other again. He corrected himself. For if, read when.

'Such as?' asked MacGillivray, reaching for a cheroot.

'Such as being able to bring home one very fine blue-point Siamese cat without having to find out whether a wife would mind first. Found it aboard the Endymion III. In all the commotion at the end, no one seemed to want it, so I brought it along. A loyal animal. I like loyalty - it's so rare. Especially when you're on the losing side - as this cat was. Then.'

'But not now, eh?'

'Not if what you tell me is true. As Thomas Fuller, one of the contemporaries of my old favourite, Sir Thomas Browne, used to say, "In all games, it is good to end the winner." '

'Check,' said MacGillivray, approvingly. 'And I'll add to that. In our game it's not just good. It's absolutely bloody imperative. Essential - or the game's up. Now a drink before you go? Let's toast the greatest game of all. The game of love. With a small "L", doctor, of course.'

They walked down the stairs together, and into the early evening, and they were smiling as they walked.

It was going to be fine tomorrow, Love thought. Tomorrow and tomorrow and tomorrow.

Stogumber, Somerset; Nassau, Bahamas; Mexico City, Durango and Mazatlan, Mexico.

ABOUT THE AUTHOR

James Leasor

James Leasor was one of the bestselling British authors of the second half of the 20th Century. He wrote over 50 books including a rich variety of thrillers, historical novels and biographies.
His works included the critically acclaimed The Red Fort, the story of the Indian Mutiny of 1957, The Marine from Mandalay, Boarding Party (made into the film The Sea Wolves starring Gregory Peck, David Niven and Roger Moore), The Plague and the Fire, and The One that Got Away (made into a film starring Hardy Kruger). He also wrote Passport to Oblivion (which sold over 4 million copies around the World and was filmed as Where the Spies Are, starring David Niven), the first of nine novels featuring Dr Jason Love, a Cord car owning Somerset GP called to aid Her Majesty's Secret Service in foreign countries, and another bestselling series about the Far Eastern merchant Robert Gunn in the 19th century. There were also sagas set in Africa and Asia, written under the pseudonym Andrew MacAllan, and tales narrated by an unnamed vintage car dealer in Belgravia, who drives a Jaguar SS100.

www.jamesleasor.com Follow on Twitter: @jamesleasor

BOOKS IN THIS SERIES

Dr Jason Love

Passport To Oblivion

Passport to Oblivion is the first case book of Dr. Jason Love . . . country doctor turned secret agent. Multi-million selling, published in 19 languages around the world and filmed as Where the Spies Are starring David Niven.

"Heir Apparent to the golden throne of Bond" The Sunday Times

Passport To Peril

Passport to Peril is Dr Jason Love's second brilliant case history in suspense. An adventure that sweeps from the gentle snows of Switzerland to the freezing peaks of the Himalayas, and ends in a blizzard of violence, hate, and lust on the roof of the world. Guns, girls and gadgets all play there part as the Somerset doctor, old car expert and amateur secret agent uncovers a mystery involving the Chinese intelligence service and a global blackmail ring.

'A runaway success story'
Daily Mirror

Passport For A Pilgrim

Dr Love's fourth supersonic adventure.

'Super suspense and, as usual, Love finds a way.'
Daily Express

'Bullets buzz like a beehive kicked by Bobby Charlton'
Sunday Mirror

'Action is driven along at a furious pace from the moment the doctor sets foot in Damascus.. a quite ferocious climax. Unput-downable.'
Sheffield Morning Telegraph

'Thriller rating: High'
The Sun

A Week Of Love

Seven short stories featuring Dr Jason Love, the country doctor, old car lover and sometime spy in which he solves cases in Giglio off Italy, Praia da Luz in Portugal, Amsterdam, the Highlands, Spain, England and at home in Stogumber in Somerset. Travelling in his famous supercharged Cord again and again battles a range of villains in his efforts to crack a myriad of mysteries.

Love-All

Dr Jason Love's sixth case history of suspense. Attempted political assassination in the cauldron of Beirut, sees the doctor cum secret agent in a cliff-hanging missionto the Middle Eastern drug belt.

'Fans of Dr Jason Love will take special delight in this cliff-hanger'
Daily Express

Love And The Land Beyond

On vacation in the Algarve, with his precious Cord car, the country doctor, and occasional spy, Jason Love, accepts an invitation from a rich friend of a friend. This leads to a web of double-cross, murder and mystery, connecting deaths in Oregon and Portugal, in a race to secure smuggled vital secret formulas, against East Germans and the Mob.

Frozen Assets

Dr Jason Love, a West Country physician, is regarded as one of the world's experts on the pre-World War II American Cord car. With its long, coffin-nosed bonnet with two stainless steel exhaust pipes protruding on either side, its steeply raked split windscreen, front wheel drive, retractable headlights and integral construction, it is not so much a car as a personal statement. When an insurance company is asked to insure for 10 million pounds a Cord Roadster in Pakistan, it asks Dr Love to fly out and check why the car is worth so much.

Love Down Under

Before Jason Love - the West Country doctor with a passion for the 1930s American Cord car flies out to visit Charles Robinson, a fellow Cord enthusiast, in Cairns, Australia, someone in his Wiltshire village entrusts him with a straightforward mission: to find the Before Jason Love - the West Country doctor with a passion for the 1930s American truth behind a relation's mysterious drowning accident off Cairns.

But when he arrives down under, the simple enquiry rapidly leads to other, more disturbing questions: what is the fearful secret hidden in Robinson's past that has terrified him for years, and who are the shadowy figures he dreads will find him? Who is the man with metal hands who can see as well in darkness as by day, and why should a total stranger attempt to murder Dr Love on the top of Ayers Rock?

Jason Love, in his latest and most baffling case, must battle to find the answers to these and other questions as the wheels of suspense and surprise spin as fast as the tyres on his super-charged Cord.

'A mixture of Ambler, a touch of Graham Greene, mixed well with the elixir of Bond and Walter Mitty'
Los Angeles Times

BOOKS BY THIS AUTHOR

They Don't Make Them Like That Any More

They don't make them like that any more. Cars, that is. They don't, and they never will again. Which accounts for the enormous world-wide interest in old motors of every description, and the fantastic prices that they fetch. Behind this latest manifestation of the international antique trade, lies a strange and secret world, where dealers offer for sale cars they do not own, where rich collectors willingly pay thousands for some mechanical abortion that can barely drag itself up a hill without a following wind, simply because it's rare. Usually, hazards in this old-car business - as in any other - are run by the buyer. But there are also risks for those who sell – as the proprietor of Aristo Autos discovers. He deals exclusively in motoring exotica, and when he's unexpectedly offered one of the rarest cars of all, a supercharged Mercedes two-seater 540K, he buys it immediately. There's a clear two-and-a-half thousand quid profit for him in the deal. But soon he realises there's also a clear danger of death, for someone else desperately wants this car for some very special, private reason. Someone who will kill to get it. But who, and why? The only thing to do is to find out, and he does - travelling a sinister trail, blazed by old cars and young girls, that leads from London to Spain to Switzerland.

'Number one thriller on my list ...sexy and racy'
Sunday Mirror

'Devoured at a sitting. . . racy, pungent and swift'
The Sunday Times

'A racy tale . . . the hero spends most of his time trying to get into beds and out of trouble . . . plenty of action, anecdotes, and inside dope on exotic old cars'
Sunday Express

Mandarin-Gold

It was the year of 1833 when Robert Gunn arrived on the China coast. Only the feeblest of defenses now protected the vast and proud Chinese Empire from the ravenous greed of Western traders, and their opening wedge for conquest was the sale of forbidden opium to the native masses.
This was the path that Robert Gunn chose to follow... a path that led him through a maze of violence and intrigue, lust and treachery, to a height of power beyond most men's dreams — and to the ultimate depths of personal corruption.
Here is a magnificent novel of an age of plunder — and of a fearless freebooter who raped an empire.

'Highly absorbing account of the corruption of an individual during a particularly sordid era of British imperial history,' The Sunday Times

N T R: Nothing To Report

"Superbly authentic atmosphere, taut narration. Mr Leasor would have delighted Kipling." - The Observer

"The most clinically accurate description of India and Burma about the time of the Kohima breakthrough I have yet seen." - Daily Telegraph

"Mr. Leasor brings to 'Nothing to Report' a journalist's straightforwardness, and an on-the-spot sureness about how frightened men behave, that are both refreshing and effective." - Spectator

In the early spring of 1944, when the British fortunes of war in the East were low, the Japanese invaded India.

Viewed against some other catastrophes of the war, this was only a minor invasion; an intrusion of some 20 miles or so on the North-East frontier. But, at the time, it was considered very important indeed. Political discontent was rife in India and there was constant fear that the British would withdraw as they had already done in Malaya and Burma. If this invasion were not checked and the Japs flung back there might be revolution in India.

The story concerns a draft that was sent to help repel the invasion. An odd lot, that draft, and not quite sure what it was all about. The author tells of men in adversity, some shrewd, some cynical, some loved and others lonely. In the end they sent back the message N T R—Nothing to Report. The reason behind this, illustrating all the futility of war and its consequences, is related in this moving and realistic novel.

Most books by James Leasor are now available as ebook and in paperbacks. Please visit www.jamesleasor.com for details on all these books or contact info@jamesleasor.com for more information on availability.
Follow on Twitter: @jamesleasor for details on new releases.

Jason Love novels
Passport to Oblivion (filmed, and republished in paperback, as Where the Spies Are)
Passport to Peril (Published in the U.S. as Spylight)
Passport in Suspense (Published in the U.S. as The Yang Meridian)
Passport for a Pilgrim
A Week of Love
Love-all
Love and the Land Beyond
Frozen Assets
Love Down Under

Jason Love and Aristo Autos novel
Host of Extras

Aristo Autos novels
They Don't Make Them Like That Any More
Never Had A Spanner On Her

Robert Gunn Trilogy
Mandarin-Gold
The Chinese Widow
Jade Gate

Other novels
Not Such a Bad Day

The Strong Delusion
NTR: Nothing to Report
Follow the Drum
Ship of Gold
Tank of Serpents

Non-fiction
The Monday Story
Author by Profession
Wheels to Fortune
The Serjeant-Major; a biography of R.S.M. Ronald Brittain,
M.B.E., Coldstream Guards
The Red Fort
The One That Got Away
The Millionth Chance: The Story of The R.101
War at the Top (published in the U.S. as The Clock With Four
Hands)
Conspiracy of Silence
The Plague and the Fire
Rudolf Hess: The Uninvited Envoy
Singapore: the Battle that Changed the World
Green Beach
Boarding Party (filmed, and republished in paperback, as The
Sea Wolves)
The Unknown Warrior (republished in paperback as X-Troop)
The Marine from Mandalay
Rhodes & Barnato: the Premier and the Prancer

As Andrew MacAllan (novels)
Succession
Generation
Diamond Hard
Fanfare
Speculator
Traders

As Max Halstock
Rats – The Story of a Dog Soldier

Printed in Great Britain
by Amazon